MILLS & BOON®

# New
# Voices

featuring

**Lynn Raye Harris**
**Nikki Logan**
**Molly Evans**
**Ann Lethbridge**

All the characters in this book have no existence outside the imagination of the author, and have no relation whatsoever to anyone bearing the same name or names. They are not even distantly inspired by any individual known or unknown to the author, and all the incidents are pure invention.

M&B™ and M&B™ with the Rose Device
are trademarks of the publisher.
Harlequin Mills & Boon Limited, Eton House,
18-24 Paradise Road, Richmond, Surrey TW9 1SR

MILLS & BOON NEW VOICES
© Harlequin Enterprises II B.V./S.á.r.l. 2010

*Kept for the Sheikh's Pleasure* © Lynn Raye Harris 2010
*Seven-Day Love Story* © Nikki Logan 2010
*Her No. 1 Doctor* © Molly Evans 2010
*The Governess and the Earl* © Michèle Ann Young 2010

ISBN: 978 0 263 87822 6

009-0910

tal regulations

# "What Do Mills & Boon Novels Mean To Me?"

## by
## Katie Fforde

The simple answer is, I became addicted. I started reading Mills & Boon® novels when my life was quite stressful. My husband and I were running a pair of narrow boats as a hotel, we started at Easter and we didn't have a day off until we closed for the season in October. Having a book you could pick up and put down and keep abreast of the plot, where you didn't have to read through a lot of dull stuff before you got to the "good bits" (Mills & Boon® novels are all "good bits.") was a real prop. Two or three minutes reading, away from cooking, passengers, manhandling the boat, kept me sane.

And, oh, how I related to them! I loved the thought of meeting a sexy millionaire who would "take me away from all this." I used to imagine a car stopping as I carried bags and bags of provisions back along the road to our boats, and somehow sweeping me away from my cares and responsibilities.

When we gave up our boat business and bought a house in Wales, I had babies. My time was even more limited and, with my husband away at sea a lot of the time, I was also lonely.

I found companionship in those books. If I had a little pile of them waiting to be read, I knew I could be transported in an instant, away from the nappy bucket, the coal shed and the chicken house.

Later, when my children slept better and I read with more discernment, I realised the books were not all the same. There were some writers I looked out for, Sara Craven, Penny Jordan, Sophie Weston, Betty Neels. I began to notice the different sorts of books and develop favourites. This was when I thought that I wanted to write one. I wanted to give to others the escape, the pleasure and the missing romance (my husband was a sailor!) that I had had from Mills & Boon® novels.

I also thought (in my naivety) that, as they were only half the length of most novels around at the time and they published many, many more of them each month than mainstream publishers, my chances of success must be better.

Eventually, when we got to Stroud, and after I'd had my third child, I started writing.

I loved it! I joined the Romantic Novelists' Association and found other mad, totally committed, die-hard romantic women who only wanted to write novels for Mills & Boon and I made eight attempts. And failed.

It took me eight years to find out I couldn't do it. I couldn't create characters, plot and a stonking romance and fit it all into fifty thousand words and it was a sad revelation. But I learnt so much about writing I look at those eight years of failure as my apprenticeship. All writers should try and write for Mills & Boon and when they don't make the grade they mustn't fool themselves that their writing is "too good" for genre fiction. The fact is, they are extremely hard to get right and I salute all the authors who made it. I also thank them deeply, for all the happiness, escape and pure pleasure they have given me over the years.

Consequently, I am delighted to applaud and introduce to you four writers who got their personal camels through the eye of the needle and produced fantastic stories for Mills & Boon this year. Lynn Raye Harris, Nikki Logan, Molly Evans and Ann Lethbridge have all done a brilliant job, achieving publication in the Modern™, Romance, Medical™ and Historical series. (I'm only slightly jealous!) If you love romance, you'll love *Mills & Boon New Voices* and, if you haven't read a Mills & Boon romance for a while, this collection should make you remember just how good falling for a gorgeous man can make you feel. You can travel from an Arabian principality to Queensland, Australia to New Mexico's Santa Fe and back in time to Regency England, all without moving from the safety of the sofa. There's a desert prince, a rugged Aussie, a handsome ER doctor and a Regency earl all waiting to please you – *irresistible?* I hope so. It certainly works for me!

Love and best wishes,

*Katie Fforde*

# KEPT FOR THE SHEIKH'S PLEASURE

**Lynn Raye Harris**

To LB. I miss you.
And to Mike. My everything, times two.

**Lynn Raye Harris** read her first Mills & Boon® romance when her grandmother carted home a box from a sale. She didn't know she wanted to be a writer then, but she definitely knew she wanted to marry a sheikh or a prince and live the glamorous life she read about in the pages. Instead, she married a military man and moved around the world. These days she makes her home in North Alabama with her handsome husband and two crazy cats. Writing for Mills & Boon is a dream come true. You can visit her at www.lynnrayeharris.com

**Lynn Raye Harris now writes for Mills & Boon®**
**Modern™; her latest novel, *The Devil's Heart*, was**
**available in July 2010 and she plans to**
**have a new book out in early 2011.**

Dear Reader,

I read my very first Mills & Boon® novel when I was about ten years old. I don't remember anything about it, really, except that it featured a desert sheikh, a beautiful Englishwoman and a lot of emotional scenes that made me worry whether or not everything would work out in the end.

Naturally, the romance *did* work out and the beautiful English heroine got to stay with the handsome desert sheikh who loved her so passionately. Oh, swoon. I was hooked. For the next several years, I read every Mills & Boon romance I could get my hands on. But if there was a sheikh in any of the books, that was the one I read first.

Fast-forward many years, and I am now a Mills & Boon® author writing my own stories of passion and happy-ever-after. It's truly a dream come true to follow in the footsteps of my favourite authors. I have written stories featuring an ex-bullfighter, princes and even an ex-mercenary – but until now, I've not written a sheikh.

When my editor asked me if I wanted to write a sheikh for this story, I couldn't say yes fast enough. I immediately could see the desert, the swirling sands, the heat and a gorgeous man dressed in the traditional white robes and flowing headdress. But who was his heroine? Finally, it came to me. This was a story about a second chance at love.

King Zafir bin Rashid al-Khalifa once had a passionate affair with American archaeologist Dr Geneva Gray. But the relationship didn't work out for many reasons, not the least of which was the fact they came from two different worlds and had different expectations of what a life together might be like. Ten years later, when they meet again, circumstances have changed quite a bit. The one thing that hasn't changed, however, is their need for each other.

I had so much fun writing Zafir and Genie's story and I hated letting them go in the end. I hope you'll agree that it's a passionate and beautiful love story when you've finished. So sit down, get comfortable and let yourself be swept into the desert for a few hours. Feel the heat, see the sand, smell the spices. Enjoy.

Visit me at www.lynnrayeharris.com to learn more about my forthcoming books. Or just stop by and say hello. I'd love to hear what you think about my stories!

Best wishes,

*Lynn Raye Harris*

# CHAPTER ONE

DR. GENEVA GRAY was asleep in her tent when the ruckus outside awoke her. Last night she'd fallen into bed so exhausted that she'd not undressed. Consequently she had nothing to pull on except her shoes before she stumbled outside in the pre-dawn darkness to see what the commotion was.

A group of riders in traditional desert garb whirled their mounts through the encampment, poking into bags and boxes and upending all the work the team had done in the last several days. Genie cried out as a box broke open and precious artifacts spilled onto the sand.

One of the men on horseback looked up sharply at her cry. A moment later he spurred his horse forward. Genie was riveted to the spot as the horse pounded toward her. It was like a dream, where she was being chased by a huge monster and couldn't seem to move. Her heart thudded, her brain screamed for her to run, but her feet wouldn't work.

Until he was nearly upon her.

Her feet came unglued and she spun to dash behind one of the tents. Behind her, the horse's hooves churned up the sand, coming closer and closer. She managed to duck under a tent flap, then stood and listened carefully for any movement outside. The horse circled the tent. Genie crossed to the other side and waited until she could hear the horse opposite before she made a run for it.

People were screaming and yelling in the night—male voices speaking English, Arabic and Egyptian. If she could just get to one of the Land Rovers she'd be safe. The keys were usually inside—who would steal a Land Rover in the middle of the desert?—and if she could start one up she could use it as a weapon against these intruders. At the very least she could help some of her team to escape.

She could see the cars glinting in the increasing light as she ran.

*Almost there, almost there...*

Genie had her fingers on the door handle when she was ripped backward and hauled up against a wiry body. Sharp, warm steel rested in the hollow of her throat, and a man spoke in an Arab dialect that it took her a moment to place.

When she did, the pain of bittersweet memories and regret flooded her. She barely had time to remember before everything went black.

She did not know how far they had traveled, or how long she had been unconscious, but when Genie awoke she was surrounded by sound. Soft, lilting sound that grew more excited as she opened her eyes and blinked. A face came into view, hovering over her. And then another.

Women, she realized, with a profound sense of relief.

The women urged her up, then took her to a basin filled with fragrant water. Despite her protests, they undressed and washed her, then refused to let her put her own clothes back on. Instead, they produced a sky blue robe and veil made of silk and tissue and embroidered with gold thread. Genie gave up and pulled the garments on, since hers seemed to have disappeared in the interim. She was thankful, at least in some respects, for the soft material against her skin instead of the coarse cotton of her work clothes.

"Where am I?" she asked, once she'd finished.

But the women could only shake their heads and speak in the dialect she'd earlier recognized as Bah'sharan.

Could she be in Bah'shar? That thought terrified her—and not because she was a prisoner here and had no idea when or how she would escape.

No, it terrified her because of a man. A man whose memory she'd been running from for the past ten years.

The women gave her food and water and left her. By the time they returned at least an hour had passed. They formed a phalanx around her and herded her toward a big goat-hair tent in the center of the cluster. She had no choice but to pass inside. The tent was large, with ornate carpets blanketing the floors and walls. Men in traditional desert garb reclined on the floor, lounging against tufted cushions. A servant moved between them, filling cups from a hammered copper pot.

One of the men began to speak as they walked in. Genie's attention was riveted on him, because he seemed to be talking about her. He was old, with stained teeth and graying hair, and he addressed another man who sat a little higher, and whose place seemed more ornate than the others surrounding him.

Genie followed the old man's hand gestures from her to the other man—

Her heart stopped. Time stood still. The man on the dais gazed at her indifferently, his black eyes and handsome face so cold and hard that she might not have recognized him if she hadn't known him so well.

*Used* to know him, Genie.

She hadn't seen him since college. She blinked, wondering if her eyes were fooling her—but no, it *was* Zafir.

He was still as exotic and compelling as that last day she'd seen him. The day he'd shattered her heart with the truth. She took a halting step forward. Could she possibly face him again?

She *had* to. Her freedom—maybe even her life—depended on it.

She took another step, but one of the women grabbed her robe from behind and held it fast.

Desperation drove Genie forward. Zafir was her salvation, her hope. He would not harm her—not again. He no longer had the power to hurt her the way he had years ago. For that she would need to love him. And she most definitely did not.

Genie ripped the veil from her head.

King Zafir bin Rashid al-Khalifa did not care for surprises. He especially didn't care for surprises like this. Many of the desert chieftains still clung to the old ways—he expected that, and he expected to be given gifts they deemed worthy of his station as their king. He'd even expected to be given women, though he did not desire to start a harem. And he'd always known how he would deal with it since to refuse would cause insult.

Later, he might not care whether he caused insult or not. But right now, with his reign so new, he needed these sheikhs to stop feuding and unite behind him. The future of Bah'shar depended upon it.

Yes, he'd expected women. And he'd expected he would take them back to the royal palace and give them jobs in his household. What he had *not* expected was a woman who clearly did not belong here. A woman who made the past crash down on him like an imploding building.

He blinked, but she did not fade away. She stood with her chin thrust up defiantly, her veil clutched in one hand while the other women melted away.

Genie Gray—here in the flesh. The one woman he'd thought understood him.

She hadn't, of course. He'd been taken by her beauty and

intelligence, and by the life he'd led for a brief time in an American university. He'd let himself forget that he was a prince of the desert. She had never forgotten.

His gaze slid over her. Her hair, which had always been the color of new copper, was now cropped shockingly short. A memory of him winding it around his fist while he made love to her in his apartment came to him. He shoved it away.

Surprisingly, the short hair suited her—made her seem more feminine rather than less. Heat uncoiled inside him, but he ruthlessly stamped it down. They'd said all they'd needed to say ten years ago.

Sheikh Daud Abu Bakr didn't seem to realize at first that his prize had removed her veil. When he did, however, he began to lumber to his feet.

Zafir stopped him with a word. He wanted them all gone before he confronted this particular *djinn*. "I accept your gift, Sheikh Abu Bakr."

The old man sat back down with a huff. No one said anything else. There was nothing more to say. Zafir waved them all away. They rose and made their bows before filing from the tent.

Genie stood in the same spot she'd occupied since she removed her veil, her gray eyes huge as she watched him.

Zafir leaned back against the cushion. "Well, Genie, what brings you to Bah'shar? I seem to remember you refused my invitation once."

"We were on a dig," she said, ignoring the jibe. "Across the border. Our camp was overrun and I was taken hostage. I have no idea what happened to the others."

"Ah, so it was work. Of course. I should have known."

Work. With her it was always her work. He'd offered her so much more—a life with him as a cherished companion—but she'd refused. He should have known she would do so. He could still remember the look in her eyes when he'd explained why he couldn't ever marry her.

He'd lived in America long enough to know better, but he'd been convinced she loved him. Convinced that she understood—that she would give up everything and come with him.

Her expression hardened. "Yes. Important work. I—"

"Do not worry," Zafir said, cutting her off. "I will find out what happened to your people and make sure everyone is well."

A breath huffed out of her. "Thank you." She twisted the fabric of the veil between her fingers, her eyes dropping away from his for a moment. "And how is your *wife*?"

"I'm sure you mean *wives*," he said coolly. Yes, he'd had to tell her that his father had arranged a marriage when he was a child and that he was expected to honor the agreement. It had nothing to do with love, and everything to do with duty. She hadn't understood.

*Duty.* It was a word he sometimes wished he'd never heard.

Her head snapped up. "Of course," she said, the tremble of her lips gone in an instant.

He'd wanted to hurt her and he'd succeeded. But now he felt guilty—as if he'd kicked a puppy. "My first wife died," he said evenly. "I am divorced from the second."

Genie blinked. "Oh. I'm sorry," she added.

Zafir shrugged. It was what people always said, and yet he could not accept it without feeling the usual well of loneliness—and guilt—within. He'd been alone most of his life; being married had not changed that. In some ways it had actually made it worse.

Jasmin had died because of him. And Layla? Layla had surely done what she had because of him as well.

Death, it seemed, followed him.

"These things happen," he said, because he had to say something. "And my second wife would have made a terrible queen, so divorce was not such a bad choice in that case."

Though he certainly hadn't divorced Layla for her inability to be a queen.

Genie's eyes widened. "Qu-queen? But you weren't..."

"The Crown Prince?" he finished. "No, I was not."

Once again death had played its part in forcing his life along paths he would not have chosen.

"My brother has been gone for a year now. My father died a month ago. I am now King of Bah'shar."

She looked stunned. Yes, he could well imagine. It was not what he'd ever expected to do. Not what he'd wanted or studied so hard for. He'd gone for an engineering and architecture degree so he could build things while his older brother prepared to be king. Together they would take Bah'shar into the future, make her bigger, better, more capable than she had been under the rule of their father.

Now he had to do it alone. Always, always alone.

Genie dipped her chin to her chest and swallowed. When she looked up again, her eyes were clear. "I'm sorry for your loss, Zafir. For both your father and your brother."

"Thank you."

"I've taken enough of your time," she continued. "If you could return me to my camp now, I'd be grateful."

Resentment flared to life inside him. She'd been the only woman—the only person, really—he'd ever felt close to. The only one who'd ever seemed to stem the tide of loneliness within him. But to her it had meant nothing. Like every other woman he'd ever known, she'd been with him because of what he was, not who he was inside.

She'd seemed different from the others, but the reality was that he'd been too taken with her to see the truth. She was no different than Jasmin or Layla or any of the women he'd ever dated.

He stewed with hate, regret, and, yes, even desire—and she stood there, completely unaffected. He had a sudden urge to punish her, to show her what she'd given up and could never have again. "How grateful?"

She blinked. "I'm sorry?"

He climbed to his feet. She took a step back as he moved toward her. He refused to let it bother him. Once she would have rushed into his arms. Once she would have melted beneath him.

He stopped in front of her. Her head tilted back, her gray eyes searching his. For a moment he could almost think he was somewhere else. Another time, another place.

Zafir couldn't stop himself from touching her hair. The contact was brief, but her mouth opened, her tongue darting out to moisten her lips. Need rocketed through him. Need he forced away.

"And how well do your pickaxes and pottery shards keep you warm at night, *habiba*? Is it all you thought it would be?"

She glared at him. "You know that's not the only reason why it didn't work out between us. You lied to me, Zafir."

He almost laughed. No one dared to talk to him the way she did—certainly not now that he was king. "I told you the truth, *habiba*."

"You should have told me from the beginning."

"We did not know each other well enough."

She looked outraged. "You were engaged, Zafir, and you slept with me for six months without ever letting me know that fact. I don't think knowing each other had anything to do with it! You didn't want anything to interfere with your ability to get me into bed."

He couldn't stop the smirk that crossed his face. "As if that was so difficult, Genie."

She blushed, and he knew she was remembering their first night together. Their first date. She hadn't been a virgin, but she hadn't been experienced either.

"I'd like to go back to my camp now," she said primly.

"Of course you would," he said, coming to a decision. "And yet I am afraid this is not possible."

Her head snapped up, her eyes blazing suddenly. "What do you mean, not possible?"

He almost had fun saying the next part. Almost, but not quite.

"Because I have need of you here."

# CHAPTER TWO

GENIE's heart dropped to her toes. Next came rising irritation. He was toying with her, punishing her for what happened between them ten years ago. The sex between them had been great, yes, but hers was the only heart that had been affected. She'd been in love with him, and all he'd wanted was to take her to Bah'shar and keep her as a plaything while he married someone else.

Even had he not been engaged she'd been right to break it off between them. He would have prevented her from making something of herself, from pursuing the career she'd always wanted. He would have stifled her freedom and bound her up in a perfumed prison.

She was *glad* she'd refused to go with him. He hadn't loved her and would have discarded her as soon as he'd tired of her. It'd been the hardest thing she'd ever done, walking away from him, but it had been right.

And now he was a king, and trying to use that power to prevent her from returning to her job, her life. Fury whipped through her.

"This is beneath you, Zafir," she said, as coldly as possible.

One dark eyebrow arched. My God, how could the man still be so absolutely breathtaking—especially when he was being so arrogant? And how could she want him as much as she ever had?

"Beneath me? Interesting choice of words, *habiba*."

She folded her arms over her chest. There wasn't much she could control here, but she had to insist on that which she could. "I wish you wouldn't call me that."

He laughed. "Does it bring up bad memories?"

"No," she said automatically. And then, realizing what she'd admitted, followed it with an emphatic, *"Yes."*

"Interesting. I do not remember you objecting when you screamed my name in pleasure, or afterward when I held you close and called you *habiba*."

A sliver of desire sizzled to life inside her. She'd been with a few men in the last ten years, but none had ever affected her the way Zafir had. The way he was affecting her now.

But she'd never seen him like this either. Surely that was what had her blood pumping into her veins like a runaway train? Though she'd known he was a desert prince, he'd never dressed in the tradition of his home when they were together.

He was truly magnificent in the white *dishdasha*. A gold *igal* held his headdress in place, and at his waist was a curved ceremonial dagger with a jeweled hilt.

He was exotic and forbidden in a way he never had been when he'd worn jeans and button-down shirts. When he'd simply been handsome and sexy and she hadn't been able to believe he was hers. That *she* was the one he spent time with when there were so many gorgeous women he could have chosen instead.

Except he hadn't really been hers, had he?

"That's in the past," she forced out. A past that had never really stopped haunting her.

He turned away in a swirl of robes. "I did not say, by the way, that I would *never* let you return to your dig."

Genie shook her head. "I don't understand, Zafir. What do you want from me?"

"The short answer is that my father had trouble with warring tribes in this region. I am here because I intend to put a stop to it once and for all. Since you were a gift from the chieftain of one of the tribes, I can hardly let you leave."

Genie's jaw went slack. "A gift? Like a goat or a camel or a jeweled dagger?"

"Precisely. And until I conclude this meeting I require your presence."

For the moment, she could only focus on the fact that she'd been *given* to him. "How can someone give away a human being? What kind of king are you to allow such a thing to happen?"

His jaw was firm. "I am the king of a very old and traditional nation. The ways of the desert are ancient and cannot be changed overnight."

"But you could have refused."

He crossed his arms, one eyebrow arching. "Indeed I could have. And you would now likely be back in Sheikh Abu Bakr's harem, awaiting *his* attentions."

She thought of the old man who'd been speaking earlier and shivered. "That's barbaric."

"It is the custom."

"You have a lot of customs, don't you?" she said bitterly. Like keeping mistresses while marrying another woman and having children with her.

"Indeed—which is why you will remain."

"And what if I don't want to stay?"

His dark eyes glittered. "You do not have a choice."

"You would force me to stay here against my will?"

He inclined his head. "To prove I am not such a barbarian, I will compensate you in the end. This is not a bad deal, Genie."

For who? Staying here for even a minute longer than she had to was dangerous. Because in spite of everything—all the hurt and pain and agony of the past—her heart was soaring with every minute she stood near him.

"I don't want money."

He looked skeptical. "Really? Aren't archaeological digs expensive?"

"I have funding for my projects." Not as much as she'd like, but she wasn't admitting that to him.

"Then I will give you something better than money, Genie. Something you want very much."

Genie's knees felt suddenly weak. She had a vision of him naked, of his beautiful mouth on her flesh, taking her to heaven. *No.* "How could you possibly know what I want?"

His smile was so self-assured she itched to slap him.

"I will give you permission to excavate in Al-Shahar."

Her heart nearly stopped. "The old temples?"

No one had *ever* been given permission to excavate the Temples of Al-Shahar. It would be a coup, a crowning achievement. Her career would never be the same.

And he knew it. His smile was predatory, as if he knew she would not refuse. Just as he'd believed she wouldn't refuse his proposition ten years ago because he'd been rich and handsome and she'd loved him desperately.

Did she have the strength to turn him down this time? The strength to walk away from the Temples of Al-Shahar? But how could she accept? Staying with him now, even for something so wonderful as those temples, would test her in ways she wasn't sure she was prepared to endure.

But he would keep her here regardless, wouldn't he? He had the power to do it, and the will.

"I would not refuse this, were I you," he said softly. "Don't be a fool because of your wounded pride, Genie."

She stiffened. "You are quite mistaken if you still think that affects me, Zafir. It was ten years ago."

"Then what will it be?" Again that predatory gleam. "Because turning down the jewel in the crown of your precious career would be extremely foolish. And you know it quite well."

She hated that he had her right where he wanted her. Because he was right, and she wasn't going to refuse. No matter how dangerous staying with him would be to her heart, she had to do it. It was only temporary. It would take weeks to gather what she needed to excavate in Al-Shahar, so she would have time to recover from this experience. And she need not see him when she returned. He was a king now, and she was an archaeologist who would be on a dig in his city. She had a team who would coordinate with whomever in his government handled these things.

They would not meet again. And, even if none of that were the case, she couldn't let him see that, contrary to what she said, she was still very much affected by the past.

"Very well," she said, holding out her hand. "I accept."

Zafir took her hand in his. Instead of giving a firm shake, he turned her palm up and brought it to his lips. A shiver trickled across her nerve-endings on tiny feet, bringing goosebumps to the surface.

"A wise decision," he said softly.

And then he tugged her into his arms and kissed her.

In the space of a few moments he'd decided he was going to have her again. This need buffeting him was stronger than he remembered. He'd always been enchanted with her body, but had he always felt this reckless desire to possess her no matter the cost?

Surely not. Because right now he wanted to rip the turquoise *abaya* from her body and lower her onto the furs in his tent. He wanted to lose himself in her, and he wanted to remember what it had been like between them.

The heat, the passion, the pleasure.

She'd filled that hole inside him that no one ever had, and yet he couldn't call it love. He hadn't been in love with her. But he'd needed her.

He didn't need her anymore, but he wanted her.

Her mouth parted, whether in surprise or compliance he did not know. But he took advantage of the situation, slipped his tongue against hers—and was rewarded with a sharp intake of breath. Her arms went around him, her body pressing to his so sweetly. If not for the dagger she would be able to feel the effect she still had on him.

He held her close, slanted his mouth over hers to take as much as she would give.

And she gave far more than he would have believed. Proud, beautiful Genie kissed him like a woman starved. Like a woman who'd suffered drought and deprivation and had finally stumbled into an oasis of plenty.

She still wanted him, and the knowledge fired something primal in his blood.

Zafir cupped one of her breasts beneath the soft fabric, groaned low in his throat. He wanted to bare her body and feast his eyes and senses upon her. But he could not do so here—not in the reception tent. He swept her up into his arms and strode toward his sleeping quarters.

Genie clung to him, still kissing him, her passion as hot and intense as ever. He didn't break the kiss, though he had to keep his eyes open to see where he was going. Her skin was flushed a pretty pink, and her long auburn lashes fanned across her cheeks. He wanted her to open her eyes, to look at him with those deep pools of rainwater-gray, to see the passion flaring in them as he made love to her.

A guard stood at attention as Zafir passed into the interior of his private quarters. He set Genie on her feet. She seemed suddenly wild-eyed as her gaze darted around the room—as if she'd awakened in a prison cell instead of a palace.

"Patience, little one," he murmured as he unhooked the ceremonial dagger and tossed it aside.

But when he took her in his arms again she stiffened, her hands coming up to brace against his chest. "No, Zafir," she gasped. "I can't."

Frustration and disappointment spiraled through him at once.

"Ah, so this is how it will be. I should have known." He loosened his hold and she jerked away, wrapping her arms around herself as if she were chilled.

"What's that mean?" she snapped.

"You know what it means, Genie. You tell me one thing with your body and another with your mouth."

Her chin tilted up, her eyes flashing. "I agreed to stay for the chance to excavate in Al-Shahar. I did not agree to sleep with you ever again."

His body pounded with the need for release, and she looked at him as if she'd *not* just been wrapped around him, wanting him as much as he wanted her.

She was very much the ice-cold scientist she'd always wanted to be. And that infuriated him. How dared she think *she* was the one in control here?

"Perhaps I wish to attach new conditions to the agreement."

Her eyes widened. "You wouldn't."

He took a step toward her, fury whipping him. "Do not presume that you know me any longer, *habiba*. The man I was back then is dead."

"You would blackmail me into your bed simply to get back at me? To punish me because I didn't want to be your plaything for however long you wanted me?"

Her words stung his conscience. And yet…he didn't care. He was angrier than he'd been in a very long time. Angry with fate, with her, and with the stubborn sheikhs who argued over territory and made his life difficult when all he wanted was the best for his people.

He focused on the woman before him. She tried hard to hide it, but she was flushed, her lips moist and plump from kissing, her nipples jutting through the soft fabric of the *abaya*. Not the ice-cold scientist after all.

He was tired of games, tired of lies.

"It is hardly a punishment, *habiba*. Not when we both know what we want."

# CHAPTER THREE

GENIE couldn't stop the tremor that slid along her spine. But was it the excitement of what he offered her with the temples, or the thrill of knowing that with one word she would share his bed again?

*No.* She would not do so. Could not.

"Not everything we want is good for us," she said. "Bacon double cheeseburgers with chili-cheese fries, for instance. All that fat and cholesterol." She was babbling, for God's sake, but she couldn't seem to help it.

Zafir merely shot her that sexy grin that had always been her undoing. "Do you or do you not want the exclusive right to excavate the temples?" he said silkily. "No other archaeologist has ever been allowed to do so."

Genie swallowed. With one kiss he'd stolen her breath, her sense, her will. She'd turned into a needy animal, wanting—no, *craving*—what he offered. If he'd pushed her down on the carpets there and then and lifted her abaya, she'd have been helpless to refuse.

It was only when he'd stopped kissing her, when she'd realized they were in what must be his private tent, that she'd asked herself what the blazes she was doing. She'd been about to negate ten years of her life with that single act. To propel herself back in time and into the arms of the man she'd never really stopped loving.

*Never depend on a man, Genie. Make your own career, your own life, and find a partner to share it with. But don't give up your goals for him. Because he might just leave you with nothing but broken dreams in the end.*

Genie shivered. Her mother had said those words to her so often that she could repeat them in her sleep. Zafir was exactly the kind of man her mother had warned her about.

She'd loved him, but he hadn't loved her. She'd realized it that night when he'd asked her to come to Bah'shar. She'd thought he was asking her to marry him, but she'd been confused because he hadn't said the words. He'd never said he loved her, had always pushed aside questions of his feelings with more kisses and more lovemaking. And just when she'd thought he'd asked her to share his life, her dreams had been crushed into dust by the realization that he was expected to marry another.

It had been cruel, too ironic, that she should find herself in the situation of loving a man who could never marry her.

She'd known his culture was different, that what he asked was not wrong or immoral to him and his world, but there had been no way on earth she could subject herself to the humiliation. She'd seen firsthand what loving a man who would never be yours did to a woman.

To her mother.

And she was not about to endanger her heart and her hard-earned independence by falling into bed with Zafir bin Rashid al-Khalifa ever again.

"I want the commission, Zafir. But not at the price you're asking."

"And what price is that, Genie? I am asking you to share my bed—something you've done many times before." He paused, let his gaze slide down her body. "Or have I erred? Do you have a lover? Someone to whom you wish to be faithful?"

She dropped her eyes from his and shook her head. She should lie, but she found she could not. "There is no one right now."

"Then there can be no problem, can there?"

What could she say? *Yes, there is a problem! The problem is that I still care for you and I'm afraid what will happen if I succumb to my desire instead of listening to my head!*

"The answer is still no, Zafir."

His gaze was laser-sharp. "You would really give up this commission for something so simple?"

"It's not simple in the least, and you know it."

"Why is that, I wonder?" He closed the distance between them, tilted her chin up with a finger. "It is simply sex between two adults who want each other. How can there be a problem with that?"

"I've traveled this road with you before, Zafir. I'm not prepared to do it again."

"And I thought you would sell your soul to the devil himself for the sake of your career."

"That's not fair and you know it. It wasn't my career that ruined it between us." Her breath caught at the silky stroking of his fingers along her jaw.

Apprehension whispered over her like a caress as he smiled. "No, but you *will* share my bed again. Willingly, eagerly, and without hesitation. I guarantee it."

Genie awoke in the middle of the night, shivering. For a moment she didn't know where she was. But then it all came crashing back.

The desert. Zafir. Shock. Desire. Anger. Hurt.

Loneliness.

She sat up, her eyes adjusting to the dim light from the brazier in the middle of the tent. She lay on a large feather mattress, piled high with furs, but she'd somehow managed to kick them all away in the night.

Reaching for a fur, she realized there was a large shape in the bed with her. A man.

Zafir.

He'd left her here last night, telling her to get some sleep. She'd thought she might be shown to her own tent, but he'd informed her there was no other place to go—unless she wanted to go to Sheikh Abu Bakr's harem.

She definitely did not.

So she'd climbed into this bed and fallen asleep, never realizing he'd returned. And she could clearly see what the problem was now that he was here. Zafir had always stolen the covers.

She tugged the fur away, putting as much distance between them as possible.

"What is wrong, Genie?" he asked, his voice gravelly with sleep.

"You took the covers."

"Never."

She could almost laugh if this situation weren't so surreal. Because he'd always denied stealing the covers when she'd awakened in the night in his apartment.

"It's a bad habit of yours, and you know it."

His laugh sent heat spiraling through her. "So you have always said. My wife said the same, so perhaps it is true."

Now, *why* was her heart throbbing at the thought of another woman knowing him so intimately? It wasn't a surprise, after all. A wife *would* notice those things. She didn't bother asking *which* wife.

He propped himself on an elbow. There was the gulf of the bed between them, but still it felt too intimate to be here like this. Too right and too wrong at the same time.

"Has there been anyone special in your life?" he asked,

almost as if he could see the wheels turning in her head as she thought about him with a wife.

"Yes," she said automatically, because she couldn't bear to tell him the truth. That *he* had been the only special man in her life.

"Then I am sorry it didn't work out."

"Me too." Now, why did that bring a well of tears to her eyes? And why did she have to work so hard to keep them from falling?

"Much has happened in the last ten years, has it not? Have you been as successful as you'd hoped?"

"I've done well enough," she said. But what was success, really, when she spent her days poring over old documents and maps, living in harsh conditions while she dug pottery shards from ancient dirt? It was what she'd wanted, what she'd worked for, and yet there was something empty about it too.

She'd thought, after Zafir, she might meet a man who shared her love of ancient history—a fellow archaeologist who wanted all the same things she wanted.

And yet though she'd met plenty of men who might fit those criteria, none of them had touched her heart the way Zafir had.

"You will be pleased to know, by the way, that everyone on your team is accounted for. The men who attacked your camp have been disciplined. Unfortunately you were caught between those warring factions I told you of earlier."

Her guilt at nearly forgetting about her colleagues when her senses were so overwhelmed with Zafir was somewhat allayed by the news that they were all well.

"I should be there to help them collect everything. It will need to be catalogued again, and—"

"They are aware that you are a guest of the King of Bah'shar."

The King of Bah'shar. It gave her a chill to think of Zafir as king, and yet it seemed appropriate too. He'd always been larger than life—and he'd been the only person she'd ever known who had a security detail in college. She'd never been able to forget he was someone important. Imagining a life with him had been impossible. How true that had turned out to be.

"And how much longer am I to remain your *guest*?" In her earlier excitement about the temples she'd forgotten to ask how long he intended to keep her here. *Stupid, Genie.*

"A few days, no more."

"What am I supposed to do for a few days? Stay in this tent? Isn't there another way?"

"We will not be staying. Tomorrow we return to Al-Shahar."

"But I thought you had to stay here…"

"I am the King, *habiba*. I go where I wish. Tomorrow I wish to return to Al-Shahar. My meeting with the Sheikhs will continue there."

"Why can't you just tell them to do what you want? You *are* the King, after all."

His sigh was audible. "Yes, one would think it *should* work that way. But Bah'shar is an ancient country, and things have always been done a certain way. Blood feuds often go back many generations. My father tended to ignore the violence so long as the Sheikhs paid their obeisance."

"Why can't you do the same?" Not that she thought violence should be ignored, but she wanted to know why it was important to him.

"I could, I suppose. But then things happen—like border raids, where old fools let their men kidnap Western archaeologists. It makes us look bad in the eyes of the world. I wish us to move forward as a people, not wallow in the past."

"Isn't tradition important?"

"Of course. But so is progress. And I believe we can have both—though there are those who resist."

"I remember that you were going to build skyscrapers. Do you ever get to do that?"

He sighed again. "I did, for a while. Perhaps once I've settled into this new role as king I will be able to do so again."

They'd only been together six months, but she remembered his enthusiasm for building—his sketches and grand plans. He'd been in love with the idea of creating and she'd been in love with him. God.

"I'm sorry things didn't work out the way you'd hoped," she said.

"It is as it was intended to be. I accept that." He threw back the covers and sat up. "Are you tired?"

"Not really." Too much adrenaline in one day. And too much shock.

"Then come. I wish to show you something." He hesitated a moment. "You once told me you could ride. Was that the truth?"

"Yes, but I won't be joining the Olympic equestrian team anytime soon."

His teeth flashed white in the dim light as he stood and held out his hand. "That is sufficient."

Genie stared at his outstretched fingers. Did she really want to go anywhere with him? To risk even a moment more in his company than absolutely necessary?

But what was the alternative? Refuse and have him climb back into the bed with her?

She put her hand in his. Electricity snapped along her nerve-endings, sizzling into her core.

No matter how she sliced it, she was in big trouble here. A few days might as well be an eternity.

* * *

"What do you think?" Zafir asked.

Genie could only stare at the undulating sand dunes— no, *mountains*—spreading as far as the eye could see. She'd excavated in the desert before, she knew what sand dunes looked like, but she'd never seen anything so beautiful as the pink-tinged dawn sky, the red sand that glistened with moisture which would soon be burned off by the hot rays of the sun—and she'd certainly never witnessed it from the back of a white Arabian mare.

The horse's delicately arched neck belied her strength. She'd run up this mountain of sand as fleet-footed as a gazelle. Now she stood, her nostrils flaring, her proud head held high, her bridle dripping with tassels that shook with each prancing movement.

Genie turned in the saddle. Zafir was staring at her. He sat his mount so easily, the white fabric of his *dishdasha* a sharp contrast with his stallion's bay flanks. He looked at home here, regal and otherworldly—like someone she should never have met in a million years.

"Well?" he prompted.

"It's amazing, Zafir."

He turned his head, his profile to her as he gazed over the dunes. It stunned her to realize that he very much looked like a king. How had she never noticed that royal bearing of his?

"I wanted to show you this before, but it was not possible. I am glad you are here to see it now, despite the circumstances."

Her heart throbbed. Why did he have to do this to her? Why did he have to remind her of how much she'd once loved him?

"I'm glad too," she said, though she wasn't really sure if that was the truth. Far better to be over the border, still in her encampment, digging through sand and rock and not knowing Zafir was here—so close and yet so far. In many ways, though he sat beside her now, he was farther from her than he'd ever been.

Untouchable. Unapproachable. A king.

Genie sucked in a cool breath. The desert air was frigid at night, but it was beginning to warm as the sun crept upward in the sky. Soon it would be too hot ever to believe it had been cold only hours before.

Zafir threw one leg over his horse's head and jumped to the ground. "Let us walk before we return to the camp," he said.

Genie dismounted and fell in beside him. They walked along the top of the dune without speaking. The sand made it difficult to go fast, so they took their time—almost as if it were a companionable morning stroll.

Like they'd used to do when they'd get up early and make the walk to the bakery first thing in the morning. "Should we get the donuts or the sunflower bread?" she said, and then wished she hadn't. How ridiculous to bring that up!

But he glanced over at her and smiled. "The donuts, of course."

"That was a simpler time," she said softly, not looking at him. Simpler because she hadn't known what was expected of him, because she'd believed they shared something deep and meaningful. How wrong she'd been.

"Indeed. But everyone grows up, Genie. Life does not sit still because we wish it to."

"No."

He stopped and turned toward her. His face was limned in the dawn light, the hard planes and angles both harsher and more beautiful because of it. Dark eyes gazed at her intently.

"There is no reason why we can't recapture some of that feeling," he said.

Her heart thudded in her throat, her temples. A few hours ago she'd been Dr. Geneva Gray, renowned archaeologist. Now, she was Genie Gray, the lovesick student who'd once had a passionate affair with a desert prince.

And he was tempting her with the promise of more. How could she want him again when he'd hurt her so deeply?

"I'm not sure that's wise," she said.

But he closed the distance between them, his body so close, so vibrant in the cool morning air. "Why wouldn't it be, Genie? We are adults, and we still want each other. This is not a crime."

"No, but it feels too much like digging up the past."

His smile was almost mocking. "Ah, but isn't this what you like to do? Dig up the past?"

"Not all things need to be dug up," she replied, her pulse hammering in spite of how calm she tried to sound.

His head dipped toward her in slow motion. She knew she should move away, but she closed her eyes automatically, waited for the touch of his lips against hers.

It didn't happen.

She opened her eyes again, to find he'd stopped only inches from her mouth.

"I do not believe what you say, Genie Gray. And neither, it seems, do you." He straightened and turned toward his mount. "Come, we must return to the camp before the sun is up."

# CHAPTER FOUR

GENIE had never been to Al-Shahar before. Though the city was ancient, and rife with ruins to be explored, Zafir's father had not allowed any excavation to take place. Nor had the previous kings before him. Zafir was the first to suggest it was possible, and she had to admit that the prospect excited her. She had to hope that he would still allow her to do so, regardless that he'd claimed she first had to sleep with him in order to get the commission.

He'd not mentioned it since last night, and she wondered if perhaps he'd merely been angry and acting on emotion from the past instead of truly intending to force her into his bed.

Not that it would take much to force her, she thought disgustedly. In spite of everything—the hurt and pain and anger—she still felt something in his presence. Something she'd never felt with anyone else. Was she adult enough to handle a casual affair? To know he was a king and that he could never, ever have a real relationship with her beyond the physical?

She turned her attention to the city as they passed through the ancient gates at one end. The ruins of the old temples sat on a point that was higher than the rest of the city, with the exception of the palace. She could see them clearly in the distance as she sat up straighter and pressed her face to the glass.

"You want very much to get your hands into the dirt there, don't you?"

She turned to the man sitting beside her. He was still dressed in the robes of the desert, but the ceremonial dagger was gone. And he was still as breathtaking as he had been from the first moment she'd seen him again.

"You know I do. It's a fabulous opportunity, Zafir."

She expected him to tell her that she knew what she had to do to gain the commission, but he said nothing of the sort.

"I would not have offered it to just anyone—no matter that it's past time this city's history was explored and preserved for future generations."

Warmth blossomed. "I appreciate your confidence in me."

He shrugged and turned away. "You must be very good at what you do."

"Must be?" she asked. "Shouldn't you find out before you hand over this commission to me?"

His gaze was sharp, assessing. "Should I give you this commission, there will be no need."

"I'm not sure how you can say that. It's important work, and you should get the best to do it."

And why was she saying this? Why place any doubt in his mind?

Because she wanted him to *know* she was the best, not just to give it to her because she was the only archaeologist he knew. Assuming he did so, of course.

Zafir gave her a hard look. "Your work is the most important thing in the world to you. More important than anyone or anything. No one would sacrifice so much without being determined to succeed."

A pang of hurt throbbed to life inside her. "It's not the most important thing. There's my mother, my friends—"

"But not a lover, yes?"

"I don't need a lover to prove I care about things other than work."

He merely shrugged again. "As you say, then."

"*Are* you going to give me the job?"

"That depends on you, Genie."

Genie tamped down on the irritation uncoiling within her. She wasn't about to ask him what he meant. She didn't need to.

She turned to watch the city glide by. Al-Shahar was more modern than she'd thought it would be. Cars rolled down wide streets with tall glass and steel buildings. There were sidewalks, manicured trees and plants, and designer shops lining the streets on both sides. It was still early enough that people populated the sidewalks—the men in business suits or traditional robes, the women either wearing colorful *abayas* or Western clothes.

They also passed through an older section of town, where the buildings were mud-brick and she saw more than one donkey pulling a laden cart. The air smelled of spice, exotic and fresh, and she wished she could get out and explore the old bazaars. But the Hummer continued toward the palace, finally passing through the arched gates and pulling to a halt in front of huge double doors that looked as if they were made of gold.

Zafir's door popped open. Someone had unrolled a red carpet, and he stepped out onto it, then turned and held out a hand for her. She accepted, scooting across the seat and joining him on the walkway. The car door slammed again and the vehicle moved away—everything a perfectly coordinated dance of efficiency.

Black-clad men with headsets and Uzis flanked the palace doors, while several other men fanned out behind them.

"Is it so dangerous here you need this many guards?" she asked.

Zafir frowned. "Not at all. It is simply custom."

Another thought wormed its way into her consciousness. A worrying thought. "Zafir, you said you were putting an end to an old feud in the desert. Are you in any danger from those men?"

The double doors whisked open and they passed inside while men and women bowed low. It was disconcerting to be reminded so forcefully at every turn how exalted a being Zafir now was.

And he'd wanted to renew their physical relationship? With a woman who crawled around in dirt and mud on a regular basis? She was beginning to doubt his sincerity on that score.

He stopped at another ornate door. "I am not in danger, *habiba*. Do not worry yourself."

"I wasn't worried," she lied. And she didn't believe him. He'd said there were those who clung to the old ways and didn't want change. When people felt threatened, they were capable of many things. In a volatile environment such as this, would someone go so far as to try and harm the King?

"Go with Yusuf," Zafir said. "He will show you to your quarters. I will see you for dinner tonight."

She could only stare after him as he turned to go.

But then he looked back at her. "And be sure to wear something sexy, Genie."

Zafir entered his private office and went to his desk to see what papers his secretary had left for him. But his mind was on the woman he'd left standing in the hall. It was dangerous to want Genie Gray again. He had too many things he needed to do as a new king trying to cement his rule. Distractions were unwelcome.

Most of his father's ministers had accepted him as king, though there were those who grumbled he'd spent too much time in the West, that his education in America was dangerous to tradition and custom. He was careful to pick his battles, and swift to act once he had. This issue with the blood feuds was one he intended to put a stop to as quickly as possible.

Now that he was king, he was also being pressured to marry again. A king needed heirs, and his ministers were anxious he should get started on the task. He would do so in his own time, however.

His experience with marriage thus far had not been the most pleasant. Jasmin's death had shocked him. She'd been impulsive and high-strung, and when she'd threatened to do herself harm he'd not believed her.

He still didn't believe she'd meant to kill herself.

She'd most likely meant to scare him when she'd taken the pills. She'd counted on him to find her, to call an ambulance, but he'd been delayed that day. By the time he'd found her—it had been too late. He still blamed himself for not taking her seriously, for not getting her the help she needed.

Four years after her death he'd bowed to the pressure to marry again. A mistake.

And now Genie was here, back in his life by accident when he'd never expected to see her again. Her presence brought a feeling of normalcy to the circus his life had become. She'd known him before, when he had been simply Prince Zafir, when he'd been excited about his studies and the things he would build.

Perhaps it was wrong to keep her here, but he didn't care. Because she gave him something he'd thought lost, something he hadn't realized he needed until she'd ripped off her veil in the tent.

Genie Gray gave him a sense of himself as he'd used to be. She made him feel less alone in this world, and he truly needed that right now. Oddly enough, he also felt a pang of guilt over the way they'd parted ten years ago. Perhaps he should have told her about his arranged marriage when they'd first met. Perhaps he should have given her the chance to decide for herself if she wanted to take the risk of being with a man who came from a world so different from her own.

*And what choice are you giving her now?*

He shoved the thought aside brutally. He would not force her into his bed, no matter what he'd told her. He'd been angry, and he'd said things he did not mean.

But he *would* bed her again. It was as inevitable as the sandstorms that swept across the desert.

Genie stood in the middle of the cavernous quarters she'd been shown to—the old harem, Yusuf had explained—and studied the tilework over her head. The room was vaulted, the mosaic inlaid with gold and precious gems. It was an extraordinary room.

There were marble columns, soaring arches, stained glass, and a crystal chandelier that must stand twice as tall as she if it were lowered to the floor and she could measure herself against it.

This room connected to another—a smaller room this time, with a large bed on a dais in the center. The furnishings were ornate, more modern than appropriately suited this space, and luxurious. She went through another door and found a bathroom that would more or less be considered a spa where she lived. A cutout high in the roof let natural light in, and it shafted down over a pool—yes, *pool*—from which steam arose.

A natural hot spring. Marvelous.

On a long shelf there were scented oils and cosmetics in an array of delicate blown-glass bottles. She passed into another room, and came up short. This was a dressing room, and one wall was lined with clothes. But whose clothes? His ex-wife's? A mistress's?

She plucked at the first garment. A tag was still attached to the sleeve. *Galliano*. She dropped the tag as if it burned when she saw the price. How many zeroes were possible when you were only talking about a dress?

Genie picked up the next garment, and the next. All had tags. And all had cost far more than a month's wages.

She passed back into the large reception area, to find a woman laying out a teapot along with small cakes and a selection of fruit near one of the divans.

"Please, madam," the woman said. "His Majesty sends you greetings."

She indicated an envelope on the table. Genie went over and picked it up.

"Tea?"

"Um, yes. Thank you," Genie replied. It'd been hours since breakfast, and she had no idea when, or if, lunch would be served.

Ripping open the envelope, she pulled out a piece of heavy cream paper upon which Zafir had scrawled, *'Choose a dress from the closet. They were sent over for you. Dinner is at eight.'*

He'd bought the dresses for *her*? The thought was both disconcerting and warming at the same time. Disconcerting because there were so many, and they were so expensive. Warming because he'd thought to do so.

The afternoon that followed was long and lonely. Though it frustrated her to putter around the harem when she could be working, Genie still managed to soak in the hot spring, take a long nap, and find a suitable dress. The one she chose was a soft blue-gray silk with jeweled spaghetti straps. It fell right above the knee, and though it was very nice she wasn't sure she would call it sexy.

In fact she'd worked hard to find the least sexy dress she could in the lot.

But as she looked at herself in the mirror she began to wonder if she'd succeeded. The color brought out the gray of her eyes, and her coppery hair was curlier than she would have liked due to the steam in the mineral spring. The jeweled straps winked in the light, and her bare shoulders seemed too exposed while the dress clung suggestively to her breasts.

It was too late to change, however, because Yusuf had arrived to escort her to the dining room.

Except it wasn't the dining room he showed her to. Yusuf opened a door and bade her enter, then disappeared before she could ask if there was some mistake.

This room was even more ornate than the harem. There was a living area with couches, chairs, and a flatscreen television on one wall. Off to one side she could see a bedroom, with a large canopied bed. Across the room a series of arched doorways opened onto what looked like a terrace.

She was just wondering what to do when Zafir emerged from one of the darkened entryways. Her breath stopped. He'd changed out of the traditional robes and into a dark tailored suit. He wasn't wearing a tie, however, and he'd unbuttoned the first three buttons of his snowy white shirt.

She had a sudden urge to go to him, to press her mouth into that hollow at the base of his throat, to taste him the way she'd once done. He'd always tasted exotic, spicy. She'd never forgotten the way he smelled, the way his skin felt beneath her fingers. Thinking of it now was not something she wanted to do, and yet her heart wouldn't stop throwing the memories into her head.

Zafir was staring at her, his eyes moving appreciatively over her form. "You look lovely, Genie."

She tried not to blush. When was the last time she'd been dressed up? The last time a man had complimented her for the way she looked? She couldn't honestly remember. Other than a few social functions tied to funding for her projects, she didn't get out much.

"Thank you. You look pretty good yourself," she added. "I have to admit that I'm surprised you remembered my size."

"I remember a lot of things." His voice was low, suggestive. It stroked across her sensitized nerves, set up a humming in the back of her head.

But she didn't want to know what kind of things he remembered. Her pulse was already going haywire just from being here with him. To hear the things he remembered about her...?

*No.*

Zafir saved her by holding out a hand instead. "Come, we are dining in the courtyard."

She let him lead her outside. The courtyard was enclosed on all four sides, making it very private. There was a long table in the center, one end set with candles and flowers, the glassware and delicate china sparkling in the soft light. Flickering gas lamps provided additional light around the perimeter.

Palm trees stood nearby, their fronds sighing together where the tops towered over the enclosed walls. The breeze occasionally wafted down to the floor of the courtyard, but since darkness had settled it wasn't hot or uncomfortable.

Zafir pulled her chair out for her, then lifted her hand to his lips and pressed a kiss into her palm. Tingles radiated down her arm, over her breasts, her nipples tightening in response.

And, lower, another response gathered in her feminine core. Oh, God, she ached with want for this man. How long had it been since she'd felt this kind of heat and want?

She had to force it away, had to keep her head. It was wrong to want him when he'd hurt her so badly. She had to keep her cool, had to be all business.

"This scene is set for seduction, Zafir," she said as he took the seat opposite.

His smile was wicked with intent. "Do you think so?"

*Breathe, Genie.* "You know it is."

"And is it working?"

*Be cool, unaffected.* "I suppose that depends on what's in the food."

One eyebrow arched. "Are you suggesting I would have to drug you to succeed?"

"I'm not sure what lengths you would go to," she replied. "I hardly know you anymore."

"We could rectify that tonight, *habiba*."

A team of waiters arrived then, saving her from a reply. One shook out her napkin and laid it across her lap, while another poured water and wine. A third man began to serve them, but Zafir said something in Arabic and the man set the dish down on the table. Then he moved the serving cart closer and bowed. The three men filed out, and once again she was alone with Zafir.

He stood and pulled the covers off the dishes. "Allow me to serve you, *habiba*," he said.

"It's not necessary."

"No, it's not." He dished out fragrant rice, vegetables, chicken and flat bread before filling his own plate. His movements were quick, efficient, and she thought that he must not have much freedom anymore to do these sorts of things. Indeed, the waiters had looked slightly askance at their king's request they leave, but they could do nothing except obey.

"I've never been served by a king before," Genie said, taking a sip of her water.

Zafir gave her a grin as he took his seat. "Ah, but you have, many times over. I was not exactly a king then, however."

She tore off a piece of flat bread and dipped it in the sauce over the chicken. The food was aromatic, alive with spice and flavor, and she happily ate at least half of what he'd given her before she looked up and found him watching her with an amused expression.

Heat crept into her face. "This is so much better than the camp food I've been eating for the last few weeks. No matter how you try, sand seems to get into everything."

"You have been living the life of a nomad," he replied easily. "Is this what you expected to be doing when you were in school?"

"I expected to spend time in harsh places, yes." But she'd also expected more glamour and adventure. She'd soon learned, after beginning to study archaeology as an under-graduate, that the adventurous life of Indiana Jones was more than a bit exaggerated.

He cocked his head. "It is a very odd choice for such a beautiful woman. I must admit that I never envisioned you doing such things."

"No, you envisioned me in a harem."

He sighed. "I thought we were good together. I did not wish it to end simply because I had to return to Bah'shar."

Genie fixed her gaze on her plate. She'd been so naïve back then. It was humiliating to remember how happy she'd been when he'd asked her to go with him. Before she'd understood that he was not proposing marriage and never would.

"But I should have told you about Jasmin," he said. "From the beginning."

Her head snapped up. His eyes were on her. Hot, dark, intense. Did he mean it, or was this simply another attempt at seduction, at lowering her resistance?

"Yes," she said, "you should have."

Genie's eyes flashed fire as he watched her across the table. So passionate, this woman. So vibrant and alive. She had no problem challenging him, and he found he rather liked that, even while it sometimes irritated him.

"Arranged marriages, especially between royals, are such a part of my culture that I did not consider how it might affect you. Nor did I feel it necessary to explain my life to you in the beginning, when I hardly knew you."

"And now you admit you were wrong?"

"Yes." He hadn't meant to say it tonight, because he hadn't wanted her to think he was being insincere—and yet he found he needed to do so. He wanted her to understand, wanted to explain what he'd been too young and arrogant to explain that night so long ago.

"I appreciate that, but it doesn't change anything, Zafir. Even if I'd been the sort of woman who could accept such an arrangement, I wouldn't have been able to pursue my work here."

"Bah'shar is filled with ruins that need exploring by scholars. You could have done so."

She shook her head emphatically. "No, don't go there. It was impossible. I could never have accepted the kind of arrangement you were offering me."

"I know this now," he said, shoving back from the table and drawing her up from her chair.

He was growing as tired of talking about the past as she was. It did nothing but wound, and he wanted to think of other things this evening. He had enough pain in his life.

"Let us concentrate on tonight," Zafir said, pulling her close. She didn't resist as he began to sway to imaginary music. "Do you remember this?"

"Of course," she said a touch breathlessly.

They'd often danced together when the mood had hit them, and rarely had there been any music to accompany their steps.

It amazed him how right it felt to do this, how soothing it

was to his senses. He'd been living in a pressure cooker for so long, yet the simplest touch from this woman relieved all the strain.

She was as light in his arms as she'd ever been. Her hair smelled exotic, like jasmine and spice, and he found himself cupping her head, threading his fingers into her short curls.

He simply had to have her, or he would die.

She leaned back to look up at him. Her fingers curled into his lapels. "You should let me go, Zafir. Tell the Sheikh the truth and let me go back to my dig."

A dull pain pierced his heart at the thought. "Perhaps I should," he said. "But I am not going to do so."

# CHAPTER FIVE

GENIE'S SENSES WERE on high alert as Zafir held her close, their bodies swaying together. The longer she was with him, the less she wanted to be anywhere else. And that was dangerous, so very dangerous.

His body was warm, hard, and her skin sizzled where his fingers rested against her back. The dress that had been so comfortable before now felt like the roughest cloth against her sensitive skin. She wanted out of it, and yet she did not. To take that step was to go down a path she'd never thought to travel again.

"I cannot believe you are here," Zafir said in her ear, his breath tickling her and sending a shiver down her spine. "I had never thought to see you again."

That his thoughts so eerily echoed hers only made her ache more.

"It would have been better that way," she said.

"I disagree." And then he kissed her, and she knew she wouldn't be able to say no if he kept kissing her this way. So sweetly, as if she was a treasure he'd discovered. So tenderly, as if she meant the world to him.

Yet she knew she didn't. This was physical and, yes, perhaps even a bit sentimental. She didn't fool herself that it was anything else. Could she handle that?

"Do you remember how it was between us? How amazing?" he asked, his breath soft against her mouth.

"Yes," she whispered.

"I want that feeling again, Genie."

His mouth fused to hers once more, and she melted away into a mass of nerve-endings that existed only to respond to his touch. Her body was on fire with remembered bliss, with the anticipation of more. It had been so long since she'd been with anyone—and now *he* was here, the man she'd never really stopped loving, and he wanted her.

And, God help her, she wanted him too. Just once. Just this once.

Because she didn't have the strength to fight herself anymore.

She slid her arms around his neck, arched into him. He groaned his appreciation, squeezed her closer. One broad hand spread over her buttocks, kneaded her, pulling the cradle of her hips against his erection. He found her most sensitive spot, his body putting pressure against hers in just the right location.

Genie gasped as sensation shot through her. Zafir slid the jeweled straps from her shoulders, his mouth finding the sensitive area where her shoulder joined her neck. It had always driven her crazy, and no doubt he remembered it.

Though how he remembered after so long was something she couldn't fathom at the moment. Not when desire and heat were tingling through her body like this.

"I need to know," she gasped, "if there's anyone else in your life right now."

He pulled back to look down at her very solemnly. "There is no one."

Genie closed her eyes as relief washed over her. If there had been a woman—a mistress, a fiancée—she could not go through with this no matter how much she ached for him. "Then touch me, Zafir."

If he didn't touch her she would die.

His voice was as warm and rich as melted honey. "I intend to, *habiba*. Most thoroughly."

When his fingers slid to her zipper, she felt a stab of apprehension. "What if someone sees us?"

His laugh against the skin of her shoulder vibrated through her body. "No one would dare. We will not be disturbed."

He spun her around and pulled her zipper all the way down. Then he slid the dress from her body. She stepped out of it, her heart hammering, her head telling her she was making a mistake, that this was too fast and too dangerous. That she was sinking into the quicksand of her need for this man, when she'd worked so hard to free herself from it the first time.

Behind her, Zafir groaned softly.

"You never wore this sort of underwear before," he said, his fingers sliding along the top edge of her thong.

Before she'd realized what he was doing, his hot mouth was on her back. His tongue dipped into the hollow at the base of her spine before he placed a kiss on her bare buttocks, and then the curve beneath where her leg began. He turned her with his hands, gazing up at her with such heat and need in his eyes that she shivered anew.

"I am a king on his knees for you," he said. "And I hardly know where to begin."

"You'll ruin your trousers." It was an inane reply, but she couldn't trust herself to say anything else.

"I do not care," he replied, reaching for her. He quickly unsnapped the clasp of her strapless bra, which fell away and exposed her bare breasts to his gaze.

Her nipples were hard, tight points, begging for his touch. Goosebumps rose on her bare flesh, but not because she was cold. Zafir licked first one tip and then the other, before suckling them into even more sensitive buds than they already were.

Genie's head fell back, her hands gripping his shoulders. She felt wanton, hot, restless, and so completely unsatisfied. Not that his mouth wasn't magical, not that she didn't love what he was doing, but she ached to feel him inside her again.

When he left her breasts and trailed hot kisses down her abdomen she sucked in her breath, knowing what he planned and dying for it all at once. Her panties fell away as he pushed them down her hips, and then he was cupping her buttocks, pulling her to him, his tongue sliding into her secret recesses, finding the bud of her desire.

She cried out as he circled her clitoris, sucked it between his lips, then circled and sucked again and again. Her legs were jelly, but his strong grip on her kept her upright while he drove her to completion with his lips and tongue.

When she shattered, she didn't care who heard her as she rode wave after wave of blinding sensation.

But still it wasn't enough. And Zafir knew it too. He climbed to his feet while she sagged against the table. Shrugging out of his jacket and shirt, he dropped them to the ground. A moment later he'd lifted her onto the stone table and stepped between her legs. As she leaned back on her hands he unfastened his trousers and rolled on a condom. She didn't even bother to wonder how he'd known to be prepared.

Then he was hooking his arms behind her knees and drawing her forward until the tip of his penis slid into her entrance.

Genie drew in a sharp breath. Zafir closed his eyes, swallowed. And then he plunged forward, their bodies joining so deeply and thoroughly that they both cried out.

He grew utterly still, though she could feel him throbbing in the heart of her. "Did I hurt you?"

Genie shook her head, tears building behind her eyelids. It hurt, but not the way he meant. Physically, yes, he was big, and it had been a long time, but her body accommodated him the way it always had.

No, the pain was in her heart, her soul.

"Don't stop," she said, and then he was moving, plunging into her while she wrapped her legs around him and braced herself on the table.

She hadn't known her body could be so responsive, that she could be on fire so quickly after he'd taken her over the edge. But she gripped him hard, her hips working in time with his, her body catching the wave and riding it higher and higher.

Zafir must have sensed when she was close, because he lifted her against him, angled his thrusts so they were deeper and more intense—

And that was when she exploded, when her body dissolved into a mass of fire and sound and sensation that reached into her fingertips, her toes, her scalp. Everything sizzled, and she cried out with the intensity of it, the utter bliss.

She hadn't even realized that Zafir tumbled over the edge with her until he set her carefully back down and withdrew from her body. His skin gleamed in the candlelight, his chest rising and falling more quickly than before.

He was magnificent, exotic, and her body still craved his like a drug—though she was exhausted and, at least temporarily, sated. He turned away from her, and she felt as if she'd been basking in the sun's rays only to have a black cloud block their warmth.

*What had she done?*

Genie couldn't move, though she had a sudden urge to do so. It was as if her good sense had come trickling back, but too late. She wanted to snatch up the dress and cover herself.

She felt too raw, too exposed. She'd just had amazingly hot sex with a king.

On a table. In a garden.

But that wasn't what made her want to cover up. She felt as if her heart was as exposed as her body, as if he could see that it beat only for him. That it had always beat only for him.

Because this was Zafir—her prince, her lover, the man who'd once been everything to her.

And that made her angry. Angry with him for being here, for being so unrelenting, and with herself for being unable to hold fast to her vow not to have sex with him ever again. *What in the hell was wrong with her?*

"Will you let me excavate the temples now?" she threw into the air between them. Because he'd won, hadn't he? Because she was an idiot, and because she still loved him in spite of everything, and because she was suddenly so insecure that she had to lash out to protect herself.

His shoulders stiffened, and she wished with all her heart she could take it back. But words once spoken were out there, hanging in the air, and she could no more call them back than she could undo what they'd just done together.

Zafir turned, his trousers zipped again, his gaze as hard and cold as marble. He let his eyes wander over her lazily, insultingly. She pushed herself to a sitting position and wrapped her arms around herself.

"You were good, Genie. But not that good."

# CHAPTER SIX

HE'D lied. Zafir lay in bed, staring up at the ornately carved wooden canopy, and listened to the soft breathing of the woman beside him. He'd told her she wasn't that good, but the truth was he'd been so hot for her that he'd been unable to make the trek to the bedroom the first time.

He'd wanted her so much that having her then and there, in the courtyard, had seemed the only way to assuage the heat boiling inside him.

Except that it hadn't. It had only made the need worse.

She might have had sex with him for the temples, but *he'd* done it because he could not do otherwise.

But Genie Gray had certainly not lost sight of what she wanted, and that made him angry.

He had no right to be angry with her. He was the one, after all, who'd suggested that the only way to win the commission was to sleep with him. He'd wanted to punish her, and he'd ended up punishing himself.

She'd pretended to be insulted, but she hadn't resisted when he'd carried her into the bedroom and made love to her again. No, she'd melted beneath him, her body as soft and welcoming as it had always been. Her body was paradise, and he lost himself in it.

They'd fallen asleep much later, exhausted, but now that he'd awakened again he couldn't get back to sleep.

What was it about her that made him so crazy? That made him feel as if he'd come home after a very long time away?

It had to be the connection to the past, to a simpler life. But this need was only temporary. Though he wanted Genie more than he could remember wanting any woman he'd ever been with, there was no future in it.

Soon he would have to let her go.

The light slanting through the curtains and across the bed was not the light of early morning. Genie blinked and sat up. Muscles she'd forgotten she had ached. Zafir had been intense last night, making love to her as if it was the first and last night he would ever do so.

The thought gave her a chill. She'd loved every moment of it, even if he had told her she wasn't that good. She'd been hurt at first, but she'd quickly recognized that he was lashing out at her. Just as she'd done when she'd asked if he would now give her the commission.

They'd gotten past that very quickly—at least physically. But now Zafir was gone and she wasn't certain what to do. Even if she did manage to find the dress and put it back on, she wasn't sure she would remember how to find the harem. And she definitely didn't want to run into anyone in the passageways.

"*As-saalamu 'alaykum*, madam."

Genie's head snapped up to find Yusuf patiently standing in the entry. He didn't seem at all flustered by her appearance in his king's bed, though she could feel the heat of a blush all the way to the roots of her hair. The problem with being a fair-skinned redhead was the ease with which she turned pink, she thought.

She returned the ritual greeting and waited.

"His Majesty bade me bring you clothing, madam. You will find a selection of items in His Majesty's bath chamber.

If you would care to dress, I will bring you something to eat in half an hour."

"Thank you," Genie said, and the old man bowed and disappeared again. She waited a full five minutes before she got out of bed—stark naked—and raced into the bathroom.

When she emerged again, showered and dressed in a silk pantsuit and ballet flats, she didn't expect to find Zafir waiting for her. Her heart did a little flip at the sight of him. He was once again dressed in traditional robes and headdress, and the sight of him literally took her breath away.

"You slept well?" he asked.

"Yes. And you?"

His grin was sudden. Wicked. "I was quite exhausted, I assure you. Thank you for a most pleasurable evening."

*A most pleasurable evening.*

She didn't like the way that sounded—as if she were someone who got paid to provide a service. But then, here in this place Zafir was far more formal than she remembered him ever being when they were at university.

Perhaps that was all it was.

"And how are your negotiations with the Sheikhs going?" she asked, wanting to change the subject before she mentally undressed Zafir and climbed on top of him.

"Eager to leave?" he said, his eyes growing shadowed.

"You know I want to go back to my dig, but that's not why I asked."

"Isn't it?" He shrugged and walked toward the small table that she only now noticed was set with plates and food. "Come, eat. And after this I will take you to the temples."

She joined him at the table, keeping her gaze from his while he once more dished out food for her. "I asked about the Sheikhs because I wanted to know," she said when he'd finished. "It seems a dangerous situation, and I hope you are able to end the hostility."

He sighed. His eyes, she noted, were troubled.

"I am working on it. In the old days I could have had them both executed. But times have fortunately progressed—even if I have often missed having that kind of absolute power while dealing with these two old fools. They grumble, but they will fall in line."

She had the distinct feeling there was something he wasn't telling her. "This isn't at all what you wanted to do, is it? Be a king, I mean?"

"It was not my choice to make."

"But if it had been?"

His dark gaze was sharp, assessing. "I would still be a Prince of Bah'shar, Genie. And I would still have duties to my nation."

And she would still be Geneva Gray, a girl who'd had to work hard for every opportunity she'd ever had. She speared a piece of mango with her fork. "I guess we can't ever change who we really are."

"No." He looked thoughtful. "But who are you inside, Genie? What can't you change?"

She swallowed. Who was she inside? She'd thought about it a lot lately, especially since coming here. "I suppose the greatest constant in my life was uncertainty."

Uncertainty over whether her father would come visit, whether her mother would make it to her school play or drop everything to be with the man she loved. Would Genie have to stand on the school steps long after the other kids had gone home and wait because her mother had forgotten again?

"I need control of my life. I get nervous when I'm not in control."

"Your parents were divorced," Zafir said, as if it explained everything.

Genie gritted her teeth. Why not tell him the truth? Why

not let him see how devastating his revelation about an arranged marriage had been to her?

"That was a lie," she said, lifting her chin. "A fiction I made up in order to keep from telling anyone the awful truth."

"And what was the truth?"

She glared at him. "My mother had a decade-long affair with my father, a married man. He set her up in an apartment and came to visit us whenever he could get away from his real family."

Zafir looked stunned. "You never told me this before."

"Would it have made a difference?" she tossed at him, the old anger of her childhood and the disappointment of her relationship with Zafir mingling into an acid stew inside her. "When my father tired of us he had no problem walking away. My mother was too depressed to go after him for child support. She took odd jobs to make ends meet, and there were times we went without heat or groceries because she barely had enough to pay the rent."

"I am sorry—"

"Yes, well, you can certainly understand why I wasn't prepared to put myself in the same position."

"I would have never abandoned you, *habiba*," he said fiercely.

"I imagine that's what my father said too."

Zafir came and sank onto a chair close by, tossing one end of his headdress over his shoulder with a practiced movement that was too sexy for words.

Sexy? Genie looked away, studied the food on her plate. How on earth could she find him sexy at a time like this?

"I would change the past if I could," he said, "but what I asked of you was not an insult in my world. I would not have forced you to stay with me once the marriage finally took place."

Genie tossed her fork aside. Now, why did that knowledge sting? "Very noble of you, Zafir."

She shoved to her feet before she lost her mind. She'd have never agreed to be a mistress, no matter what. *But isn't that what you were, Genie, considering he always intended to marry another?*

She pressed two fingers on either side of her forehead to stem the rising headache. "Look, can we just stop talking about this and get to the temples?"

"We will go soon. You need to finish eating."

"I'm not hungry. And I don't need your pity," she practically growled.

Zafir stood, his tall form suddenly towering over her. He was all formality once more, his robe draped over one arm, his eyes glittering dark and hot as he stared at her.

"As you wish, *habiba*."

# CHAPTER SEVEN

THE Temples of Al-Shahar were millennia old. The foundations were ancient, though the temples in their current form were only about a thousand years old. The one temple still standing bore the soaring arches and mosaic work typical of the early Islamic period. The others were in various states of ruin, but they were all an archaeologist's dream. At the very least her team would be busy here for months. In truth, they could stay for years.

Genie walked through the structure, hands in pockets, her mind not quite as engaged as it should be for something so exciting.

Zafir was somewhere behind her, his footfalls distinct in the shadowy interior. His ever-present bodyguards had fanned out to guard the perimeter while they came inside alone. It seemed to her he'd gathered more security since yesterday. She'd asked about it, but he had shrugged the question off.

They'd hardly spoken since lunch. What was there to say?

She'd told him one of the darkest, most painful secrets of her life, and now she regretted it. Because he felt sorry for her. In Bah'shar, it seemed as if a man could have more than one family and no one thought anything of it. Not the women, not the children, and certainly not the men.

But her father had mostly ignored her existence, except

for the occasional inquiry into her grades, or the awkward acceptance of a childish drawing that she'd used to believe he took home and put on the refrigerator. Now she realized he must have thrown them all out. His wife wouldn't have wanted to know anything about the woman and child he kept across town.

One day he'd finally walked out for good. She'd never known why.

Zafir passed her line of sight and she studied him from beneath the brim of her hat. She should be studying the temple, but she couldn't stop thinking about their lives together before. She replayed the kisses, the caresses, the early-morning walks, the late-night lovemaking, the look in his eyes when they'd been together—everything she could think of. How had she not realized it was only temporary?

Because it had felt like so much more. She wasn't wrong about that. She couldn't be.

But was that what her mother had thought too? Was that what had made her stay with a man who could never be hers, who'd kept her in a cage and expected her to be available whenever he wanted her?

She'd done this before, after they'd broken it off, and she was angry that she was suddenly being forced to reexamine the past after all this time. He'd accused her of needing her work more than she needed him, but it was so much more than that. Perhaps he finally realized it too.

Zafir was standing in the middle of a room, gazing down at the ruins of a mosaic on the floor. "There is much to be done here, yes?" he said, looking up and catching her staring at him.

Genie refused to look away. To do so would be to admit she'd been thinking of him and not of her work. That he'd caught her in an unguarded moment. Clearly he wasn't as tormented by thoughts of the past as she was. He'd been thinking about the temple.

"It's an extraordinary place," she said, all business. "I believe the work could take a very long time. But I also think it's a good decision to allow excavation here, even if you choose someone else to do it. This is an important site, and it should not be forgotten."

He speared her with a determined look. "I do not intend to choose someone else."

"I won't let you down if you give this to me."

"I know. It is why I made the deal in the first place."

Genie bit her lip. Whether he believed her or not, she had to say it. "I slept with you because I wanted to, not for the temples."

He waved a hand dismissively. "It matters not. The commission is yours."

She resisted the urge to stomp her foot. She'd been feeling wounded and hurt, and now he'd managed to put her on the defensive. How did he do that? "Zafir, do you believe me or not?"

He strode toward her, stopping in a swirl of robes and dust. He looked suddenly angry. "Does it matter? You have got what you want."

She swallowed as she gazed up at him, all six-foot-something of hard, arrogant male. He made her body ache just looking at him. Ridiculous the way her heart pounded. "I have never been dishonest with you, Zafir."

"Outright? No. But omission is still a form of dishonesty. You never told me what happened between your parents."

How dared he turn this around? *He* was the one at fault, not her. "What good would it have done? Besides, you were dishonest with me first."

"We were dishonest with each other."

The thought stung, and yet it wasn't the same thing at all.

"Why do we keep rehashing the past? It changes nothing. You still intended to marry a woman your father chose."

"I was obligated, Genie."

She slashed a hand through the air. "I know that, and I'm done talking about it."

He caught her close, gripping her upper arms hard. "You were important to me, whether you believe it or not. And you have no idea what it is like not getting to make your own choices in life. No one has ever told *you* that you are required to give up everything you want for the greater good of your country."

Genie jerked free from his grip. She didn't fool herself that *she* was what he'd had to give up. "Maybe not, but do you think my life was any easier? *You* were born into privilege and accustomed to having the world at your fingertips. I had to work hard for every opportunity I ever got." She took a step backward, putting distance between them, her body shaking with adrenaline and fury. "What would you know about sacrifice? You wanted me to sacrifice everything to be with you, yet you weren't prepared to sacrifice a thing!"

The words echoed through the empty temple. Zafir's gaze was hard, his nostrils flaring as they stared each other down. His voice, when he finally answered, was deadly cold. "You will never know what I've sacrificed. Do not presume to tell me I have no idea what the word means."

Genie pulled in a shaky breath. Why did she get so emotional? Why did she let him press her buttons and make her so defensive? Her life had been upside down since the minute she'd walked into that tent and seen him sitting on the dais. And she was having a hell of a time getting it right again.

Zafir glanced at his watch, dismissing her as easily as he might one of his subjects. "If you are finished here, it's time we returned to the palace."

Before she could answer, he simply turned in a sweep of robes and headed toward the entrance.

He was furious. Furious with the woman sitting so quietly beside him in the car, and furious that he was allowing her to get to him when he had far more important things to think about.

Just this morning there'd been another threat to his life. He wasn't worried. His security was tight and, besides, he knew there was always a certain level of disgruntlement to be expected when a new leader took office. The threats were vague, written on plain stationery and posted in Al-Shahar. The royal police were investigating, and Zafir had every confidence they would soon find the culprit.

At least one situation in his life required definite steps to take and had a resolution in sight. For that he was thankful.

But how did one correct a situation based on strong emotion and cultural differences? If he'd known about Genie's childhood, would it have changed his actions?

Probably. Because he would have understood how painful it was to her, and would have realized how different their worlds were. He'd asked her to give up her schooling and come to Bah'shar for what amounted to nothing more than an affair.

And he'd done it for selfish reasons, which made him furious with himself. She'd filled the emptiness inside him and he'd been reluctant to give that up. And, he admitted to himself, he'd hoped that once she reached Bah'shar, once they'd been together for a while, even his marriage to a princess wouldn't prevent Genie from staying as his lover.

He'd offered her nothing and expected her to give up everything, just like she'd said.

Worse, he wanted to do it again.

When they reached the palace, he left her in the care of

Yusuf and turned his attention to the Sheikhs. It was time to reach a solution. And, after that, time to let Genie Gray walk out of his life for the second time.

The rest of the afternoon passed quietly. Genie was shown to the palace library, where there was a vast selection of books, and did a bit of research on the history of Bah'shar. Her Arabic was tolerable, though her command of the Bah'sharan dialect left something to be desired, but she worked her way through a few texts as the hours passed.

She might have gotten through them more quickly if she'd been able to stop thinking about Zafir. He'd seemed unapproachable in the car on the way back to the palace, as if he'd closed himself off and meant to keep it that way.

Maybe she wouldn't see him again. Maybe he'd issue orders that she was to be driven back to her camp and left there. The thought left her feeling empty and bereft. And angry—because why did she want to torture herself by spending more time in his company?

Being sent away was the best thing that could happen to her.

She did not belong here. Oh, she would return to excavate the temples—she wasn't a fool—but she didn't belong in the royal palace in the bed of the King. Nothing good could ever come of a relationship with Zafir. She knew because she hadn't been able to stop herself from reading some of the Bah'sharan code. The King was duty-bound to take either a Bah'sharan wife or a royal one from a neighboring country. Genie, for all her success in her chosen field, had no place in his life—nor would she ever.

When she returned to the harem, she found the same servant from yesterday, who bore another letter with the King's seal. She reached for it, a thread of apprehension skimming through her.

Was this it? Was this her dismissal? She half prayed it was. The back of her neck tingled as she ripped it open and read it.

It was not a dismissal—or at least not an outright one. Zafir simply regretted that he could not have dinner with her, and indicated that she would be served in her room.

Genie ate dinner alone, then passed the evening with one of the books she'd taken from the library. She thought about going to bed several times, but she wasn't in the least bit tired, so she stayed up and read on one of the comfortable sofas. She was just about to close the book and go to bed anyway when the door to the harem opened and Zafir strode in.

A glance at her watch told her it was nearly midnight. She blinked at him in surprise.

"What are you doing here?"

He was still dressed in the garments he'd worn earlier. He jerked the headdress off and tossed it aside. "Disappointed to see me?"

Genie swallowed. "Not at all. But I thought you were angry with me."

He shrugged. "I was irritated."

"Where have you been all this time?" She winced at how much like a jealous girlfriend she sounded. It wasn't at all what she'd meant to convey, but if he noticed he didn't react.

"I've been trying to make a room full of grown men stop acting like spoiled children fighting over a toy sword."

"It's not going well, I take it?"

He popped two hands on his hips, his dark eyes full of fire and frustration. "It could be better."

Genie closed the book and set it on the table. "I can listen if it helps."

His gaze slid over her. "Listening is nice, but it is not what I want."

Her body felt as if he'd blazed a trail of flame over it.

"What do you want?"

His grin was sexy, sinful. "A swim in the mineral bath."

"Oh," she said, sudden disappointment swirling inside her. She shouldn't want to make love with him again, but she couldn't stop the desire coursing in her veins like thick syrup. Just as well he didn't seem affected by it.

"You may join me, if you wish." He left her sitting there, her mouth dropping open, as he headed for the spa. Genie debated with herself for a full minute before getting up and following him.

Zafir stood poolside, stripping out of his garments. Her mouth went dry as layer after layer was peeled away until he stood there bronzed, hard-muscled, and magnificently naked. He wasn't fully aroused, but he was on his way.

She should turn and walk away, should prove to herself and to him that she was capable of refusing to be drawn into another doomed relationship with him. Last night had been amazing, a reminder of all she'd missed for so long. Did she really need another when there was no future in it?

"Coming in?" he asked, before he dove cleanly into the water. He came up like a dolphin, rivulets of water rushing down his chest and arms before he flipped over and started to backstroke across the pool.

Was she? Could she really turn away and go back to her book when all this glorious male body waited for her? She stood there in indecision, until Zafir cupped his hands and splattered her with water from halfway across the pool.

Genie began to unbutton her shirt. "You're going to pay for that," she said.

Zafir swam toward her, his eyes glittering with heat and desire. "I look forward to it."

She stripped, and would have glided into the pool quietly

had he not shot up and grabbed her. He threw her over his head and she went under.

When she came up, sputtering, he was laughing. "A little slow, aren't you?"

Genie dove under and went for his feet. She jerked them out from under him and he splashed down while she powered away to the other side of the pool. But before she made it strong arms encircled her and hauled her back against his body.

The length of his erection pressed against her buttocks. Her insides liquefied.

"You give as good as you get, don't you, *habiba*?" he growled in her ear. But it was a sensual growl, not an angry one.

"I try," she replied, her pulse zipping into light speed. My God, it took nothing at all for this desire to spiral out of control. She should have known it would.

"Mmm, and I can think of so many ways to test your ability to get even with me." He turned her in his arms, his slick skin hot against hers. Part of it was the natural heat of the spring, and part was the desire between them.

Genie wrapped her arms and legs around him, feeling suddenly reckless and full of joy.

"You are welcome to try, King Zafir. I relish the opportunity."

"Do you indeed?"

In answer, she kissed him, urgently tangling her tongue with his. Zafir responded as she'd hoped, groaning and squeezing her to him. His hands wandered, his fingers sliding around her bottom, down to the vee of her legs. He stroked her center lightly and she rocked against him, trying to make him go faster.

He only laughed low in his throat, however. Genie reached

for him, wrapped her hand around his hard length and squeezed. His laugh turned to a moan.

She broke the kiss, trailed her tongue down his throat, his chest—and then she sank beneath the water and took him in her mouth. His thigh muscles tightened and she could feel the sharp intake of his breath where one of her hands rested against his abdomen.

The other stroked him while she swirled her tongue around his length. Soon, however, he grabbed her and hauled her up.

"I could have held my breath for another minute," she grumbled.

"But I'm not sure I could have held mine," he said. "I declare you the winner of this round, because I am now unwilling to wait."

He took her by the waist and lifted her from the pool. Then he leapt out beside her and hauled her over to one of the cushioned divans that lined the sides of the chamber. "This is much more comfortable," he murmured, following her down.

There were no preliminaries. There was no need. Genie wrapped her legs around him as he sank into her. Her head tilted back, her eyes closing tight as the bliss of his possession threatened to overwhelm her. "Zafir," she gasped.

His lips were on her throat, her jaw, her breasts.

"I cannot get enough of you, Genie," he said, almost brokenly. "The more I have, the more I want."

And then he was thrusting into her, hard and fast, hurtling her toward the abyss. She welcomed it, wanted it, craved it—

Suddenly she was there, crying out his name and wondering how it was possible to feel this way with only one person in the whole world. To feel as if you needed this to live, as if you would die if you didn't have it.

It was beautiful and heartbreaking all at once. She was in love with a man she could never have. Even if she gave up everything and moved to Bah'shar to be with him she would only have stolen moments of bliss like this one.

And that wasn't nearly enough.

# CHAPTER EIGHT

ZAFIR's brain had dissolved along with his sense. He rolled from her body, belatedly remembering as he came back to earth that he'd forgotten to use a condom. Icy cold fear dripped down his spine in spite of the heat in the room. How could he be so stupid?

How could he risk such a thing?

Because this was Genie, and she excited him, made him forget everything but the urge to join himself with her. She always had, though she'd been on the pill when they were at university. He prayed that was still the case.

"Are you on birth control?" he asked, his tone sharper than he'd intended.

She blinked at him, her expression confused. And then it cleared. Horror was not the emotion he'd hoped to see. She sat up and wrapped her arms around her knees, her skin still flushed from sex and dripping with water from the pool.

"I am, but I haven't had a pill in two days now. All my things were in the camp…"

Zafir swore.

"It's the wrong time of the month, though. I'm sure of it."

"If there is a baby, I want to know," he ordered. "I will provide for him, never fear, so there is no need to terminate the pregnancy."

Her lovely face clouded. When it cleared, anger was the dominant emotion. "Of course I would tell you, Zafir. What kind of person do you think I am?"

He thought of Layla, of her deception, and his jaw tightened. "You are a professional woman. Perhaps you would decide that a baby was too much of a burden for you."

"It wouldn't be easy, I grant you. But if there were a child, it would be ours. And I would want it."

She looked so fierce that he believed her. The relief winding through him was stronger than he would have believed possible. And he felt a sudden need to explain, to share with her what he'd never told anyone else.

"My second wife aborted our child. She did not tell me she was pregnant."

Genie's eyes widened. "I'm so sorry, Zafir. You must have been very upset."

"I was. Layla felt she was too young to start a family, though she failed to share this belief with me."

She had also been worried about her figure, her shopping trips abroad, and her social events, where she was determined to be the most elegant hostess anyone in Bah'shar had ever seen. When she'd gone to Europe for the abortion he'd thought she was going on another shopping trip. He'd only found out because she'd been stupid enough to use a credit card and he'd opened the bill before she could intercept it. The moment when he'd realized what the charge was for had been like a sucker punch to the gut.

Genie put her arms around him and squeezed. He fell back on the cushions with her, his heart hammering with fear, and turned his head toward her, breathed in the sweet, clean scent of her hair.

She smelled like home, felt like home. He could think of nothing better than watching her grow big with his child. Nothing better than having her in his bed every night.

"I'm sure there's nothing to worry about," she said softly, "but if I'm wrong, this is your child too. We'll figure out what comes next when we have to."

"Yes, we'll figure it out," he replied on a sigh of weariness. It had been a long, long day.

He closed his eyes. What he needed right now was sleep. And he needed to be here with this woman.

It felt right.

He was drifting off when she whispered in his ear, "Sleep, Zafir."

She said something else, but he wasn't quite certain what it was.

Right before he fell asleep, he realized what it had sounded like: *I love you.*

Sometime in the night they got chilled and moved into the bedroom, burrowing beneath the thick covers on the bed. Genie lay in the dark, listening to Zafir's deep breathing. She was in so much trouble here. In two days' time her life had been turned inside out by the past she'd tried to forget.

She still loved him, and she couldn't deny it. And, though she really didn't believe she could fall pregnant, the slight chance had her mind working overtime. What would happen if she had his baby?

He'd said he would provide for their child. But he wasn't going to offer to marry her. He was the King of Bah'shar and he could never do so.

But would he be a part of their child's life? Or would he, like her father, be absent and distant?

Genie didn't believe Zafir would ignore their child on purpose. He would not be like her father. But his royal duties and his future wife—because, yes, a king needed legitimate heirs—would most likely keep him away.

Genie shifted in the bed, trying to shove her tumultuous

thoughts away. There was nothing to worry about *yet*. She would cross that bridge when she reached it.

"Can't sleep?"

"Not well," she admitted. "You?"

"I was sleeping fine, but you kept moving."

"Sorry."

She heard him yawn. "You are worried about being pregnant?"

"I was thinking about it, yes. But I don't really believe it will happen."

"You will not have to worry, Genie."

"No, but I think I'll have to worry every day of my life if there's a child. That's just what mothers do." She turned toward him on the bed, propped herself on an elbow. "I'm sorry about what happened with your second wife, Zafir."

"It was a long time ago."

She bit her lip, decided to proceed. "What happened in your first marriage?"

Zafir did not pretend to misunderstand what she was asking him. He let out a deep sigh. "Jasmin had difficulty conceiving. When she did conceive, she couldn't carry past the first trimester."

"I'm so sorry."

"There were three miscarriages. She was depressed, though I did not realize it, and she swallowed pills. It is my fault she died. I should have forced her into treatment."

Sadness ripped through her. "How could you know she would do such a thing?"

"I should have known. She was impulsive, and she made threats. I didn't take her seriously until I came home late and found her unconscious." He sighed into the darkness. "I wasn't supposed to be late that day. I think she wanted to be found, that it was a cry for help. But I failed her."

*My God.* Genie's eyes filled with tears. How could he take

such a burden on himself? But she already knew the answer: he was a good man who took his duty seriously, be it the duty of a king or a husband. Or even a lover.

"If there's one thing I learned growing up," she said very softly, "it's that we aren't responsible for the actions of others. My mother and I both suffered because she wouldn't—or couldn't—get herself out of the situation with my father, but that wasn't my fault. It took me a long time to understand that."

"I knew Jasmin was unstable. I should have realized she would eventually go through with her threats."

Genie grasped his hand in hers. It was big, warm, and he squeezed his fingers closed around her hand. The grip was firm, reassuring, but not too hard. A wave of love and longing rocked through her.

"No one is to blame but her, Zafir. I'm sorry if that sounds harsh, but she is responsible for making that choice, not you."

"If I'd been home when expected—"

"You could have stopped her that time, but what about the next? Maybe she could have been helped with treatment, but there are no guarantees. You're wrong to blame yourself."

He pulled her hand to his lips. "You have grown wise, Dr. Gray. Thank you for your words, though I am certain I will always feel guilty about what happened."

"That's your right, Zafir." It made her sad that he would take so much on himself, and sad for his poor wife. It also made her feel badly for resenting Jasmin for so long. She'd been caught up in the marital politics of her people as much as Zafir had been. And producing an heir had no doubt been paramount to that marriage. When she hadn't been able to do so, she must have felt so desperate.

Genie burrowed in closer, wrapped her arms around him. Her heart was a lost cause and it did no good to try and keep her distance. She would take whatever time she had with him while it lasted.

He stroked the skin of her bare back, his fingers dipping farther and farther down her spine each time. Liquid heat filled her veins, but she would not act on it. This was about comfort, not sex.

Until he shifted and she realized he was fully aroused. "Wait a minute," he said, leaving the bed and then returning before she'd had a chance to miss his heat. She heard the rip of foil, and then he was on top of her, pressing inside her slick body while she moaned her pleasure to the heavens above.

They'd had a few days of bliss, but Zafir knew it would have to end. The problem was that he didn't want to let her go. That having her here seemed like the most important thing in the world. With Genie in his life, his bed, his heart, he faced each day with the determination and strength he needed to make Bah'shar better than ever.

She made this life that had been thrust upon him make sense. He'd married twice, out of duty, but he'd never felt as if he'd had a connection with either of his wives. Why did he feel this connection with a woman he could never have?

He could never ask her to give up her life for him—not now. She was a professional, successful woman. And he was still required to marry and produce heirs for the throne.

But why couldn't he marry *her*? She could still do her work, and she would come home to him each night. She'd said the temples could take years...

"Your Majesty?"

Zafir shook himself. The men gathered around the conference table were staring at him.

"Please repeat that," he said smoothly. The meeting continued, and Zafir worked to concentrate on what was being said. After nearly fifteen minutes of circular logic, his mind drifted once more.

He couldn't stop picturing Genie in a traditional Bah'sharan bridal gown.

Though Bah'sharan law did not allow for a foreign wife who was not a princess, the law was old and could be changed. It had been meant to protect the throne from overthrow, but that was not so much an issue in today's world.

It wouldn't be easy, and there would no doubt be much grumbling and arguing amongst his ministers, but changing the code *was* possible. The idea galvanized him.

Raised voices brought him sharply back to the present. Sheikh Abu Bakr had gone to stand by a window with his back to the group. Sheikh Hassan sat with his arms crossed and a militant expression on his face. Zafir's ministers looked exasperated.

Zafir had had enough for now.

"Let us take a break," he interjected. "I will return in an hour's time, and I expect you all to be here, ready to talk."

He stood. Everyone in the room shot to their feet and bowed. Zafir turned and strode out the door. There was just enough time to see Genie, maybe have a little lunch with her. He wouldn't tell her about his idea just yet. It was too new, and he was still too uncertain it was the correct path. His heart believed it was, but his head needed time to adjust.

There was a shortcut to the harem and he took it, passing down long dark corridors that were rarely used anymore. He was excited about the idea of changing the code, about talking Genie into marrying him and staying in Bah'shar, but he was torn as well. Though it felt like the best solution for him personally, was it best for his people? For his nation?

As he passed a dark alcove, a sharp pain sliced across his arm. Zafir spun as something flashed silver in the dim light. All his senses were on high alert as the assassin's knife descended again.

"Die, traitor," a voice breathed as the knife plunged home.

# CHAPTER NINE

GENIE was in the library, researching the Temples of Al-Shahar, when two men in dark clothes burst in. She recognized them as being on Zafir's security team from the Uzis slung across their chests and the microphones in their ears. She didn't even realize she'd gotten to her feet until they crashed to a halt in front of her.

"You will come with us," one of the men said.

"Where are we going?" She'd faced menacing characters before in her line of work, but these two made her heart pound a little harder than usual. Perhaps because they were part of the team that ensured Zafir's safety. If they were here, was something wrong? Was there danger?

A tremor of apprehension snaked along her spine.

"The hospital."

"But what has happened?" she said as they hustled her toward the exit.

One of the men looked down at her with a grave expression. "The King has been stabbed."

Zafir winced as the doctor probed at the wound.

"You are lucky, Your Majesty," he said. "It's only a flesh wound."

Yes, but one that hurt like hell. And one that he would

not have gotten had he not been distracted by thoughts of the woman he'd been in a hurry to see again.

"A few stitches and it will heal nicely," the doctor continued as he finished his examination.

The man went to get his supplies and Zafir turned to the guard who stood silently by.

"Is she here yet?"

"They are bringing her now, Majesty."

A moment later the door burst open and Genie rushed in. He was no longer surprised at the kick in the gut he felt when he saw her, but he pushed it down deep and put a lid on it. She was pale and her cheeks were tear-streaked. He took in her puffy eyes, her red nose, and felt a pang of guilt.

He had to let her go. For her safety. Until the moment he'd been attacked he hadn't stopped to think how his people might react to a Western woman as their queen. There were those who would never accept it. Though it made him want to howl in frustration to be forced to give up happiness just when he'd thought he might have found it, he had to do so.

For her. What he wanted didn't matter when contrasted with the risk to her life.

Because who was to say that she would not be the target of an assassination attempt at some point? She would be resented by those who didn't want change, and she might draw the wrath of extremist groups.

He could not allow that. Not ever.

"Zafir," she gasped, rushing over to him. She stopped short when she saw the bloody wound on his arm. Then her gaze lifted to his. Her voice wavered. "They said you'd been hurt."

Not as hurt as the assassin he'd disarmed. "I am fine, Genie. It's not serious."

He wanted to hold her, reassure her. But he would not.

Keeping his arms at his sides was one of the toughest things he'd ever had to do.

"Do you know who did it?" Her eyes were huge pools of rainwater gray and tears trembled on the brink of her lashes.

"Oh, yes. The conspirators will be dealt with, I assure you." Once the would-be assassin had realized he'd failed, he'd spilled his guts to the police.

Zafir said a quiet word to the bodyguard. The man went to stand outside the door.

Once he was gone, Genie reached for Zafir's hand. "I couldn't bear the thought of losing you—"

"Genie," he cut in before she could say more. He must have spoken sharply because she fell quiet instantly. He squeezed her hand before letting it go. How could he do this? How could he send away the only bit of happiness he'd ever known? He drew in a painful breath. "I am sending you back to your camp."

She bit her lip, confusion playing across her expressive face. Her guard was down and every emotion she felt was there to read in detail. It pained him to look at her, but he would not look away.

"Now? Today?"

He nodded. "You have fulfilled your end of the bargain, and I will fulfill mine. You are free to go. Yusuf will give you all you need for contacting the proper authorities for the excavation. They will be told to cooperate fully."

She looked stunned. "I... I... Why, Zafir? Why now?"

His heart was a lead ball in his chest. "It is time."

"Does this mean you've concluded your negotiations with the Sheikhs?"

"Yes," he said. "It is done." Done because one of their number had tried to kill him in order to frame the other group for murder. The leaders were so horrified they would now do anything to demonstrate their loyalty. And he meant to take advantage of it.

"That's good. Congratulations."

"There is much work yet to be done, and you have served your purpose." She winced when he said that, and he mentally kicked himself for it. "I can ask no more of you."

"Is this your revenge?" she asked. "Making me care for you again and then sending me away?"

The words pierced him. For a brief moment he thought it might be easier to let her believe that, but he couldn't do it.

"No, Genie, this is not revenge. We are two different people now, from two different worlds, and it's time we got back to them."

She took a deep breath. "Yes, I suppose you're right. I—" She swallowed "It was great to see you again."

"I enjoyed our time together." A hard lump had formed in his throat and made it difficult to speak. He ignored it. Letting her go was right. For her, for him. She didn't belong here, and he needed to get back to the business of governing his kingdom.

He thought of her swollen with his child. It nearly overwhelmed his will to release her. "I trust you, Genie. You will tell me if there is a child?"

"Of course," she said, all business. "I would never keep that information a secret from you."

"Yusuf will give you my private number. Call me when you know."

She nodded. "Absolutely. If that's all, then? The sooner I get back to camp, the sooner I can get to work again."

She stood stiffly, like a soldier. Even her hands had disappeared behind her back. He imagined her clasping them together with military precision. She was already leaving him in her mind. How easily she returned to the life she'd led before.

Perhaps his had been the only heart affected after all.

"Goodbye, Genie."

"Goodbye, Zafir." And then she was gone.

First came numbness. Then shock. Then anger. Then resignation.

When Zafir decided to get rid of her, he certainly did it in style. A helicopter waited on the pad at the palace. Genie took one last look behind her before she climbed in, her heart aching. Did she really think he would suddenly appear and ask her to stay?

She shook her head, wondering how a few days with him had so thoroughly undermined the foundations of her life. She was a respected archaeologist and researcher, and the sooner she got back to that life, the better.

As the craft lifted off, she kept her eyes on the glittering domes of the palace. It was like something out of a fairytale—from a thousand and one Arabian nights. Unlike Scheherazade, however, she'd failed to please her king for more than a few nights.

She still couldn't believe that he'd dismissed her from his life so easily. That everything that had happened between them meant nothing. Or maybe she'd let it mean more than it should.

But he'd touched her so tenderly, made love to her so fiercely. Claimed to want her desperately.

Had it all been a lie?

She watched the cloudless sky slide by and wished she'd never come to the desert.

*Another lesson learned, Genie.*

She supposed she should be thankful he'd ended it now, before she'd made a fool of herself and babbled her love. Before she'd mentally set up house with him and let her career fall by the wayside.

Her mother had been right, in her own way. A man would take your love and then set you adrift to pick up the pieces of your shattered life when he was finished with you.

She should be grateful the only pieces she had to pick up were the pieces of her heart.

When she reached the camp, she threw herself into work. Her colleagues were glad to see her, and they'd done much to repair the damage the last few days had wrought. The dig was well under control when Genie finally decided she'd had enough.

Al-Shahar was two hours away by car, and she couldn't stop looking for Zafir. She kept thinking he would arrive in a convoy of black vehicles, that he would climb out of a stretch Hummer, looking magnificent and exotic in his desert robes, and that he would tell her he'd made a mistake. That he wanted her to come back and be with him—that he loved her.

Any lingering hope she'd harbored that she might see him once more if she were with child was dashed early one morning when she got her period as usual. That was the final matter that settled it for her. She made the call to his private line, left a message—had she really expected Zafir to pick up?—and told her team she was flying home to begin preparations for their next dig.

It would be some weeks before they were ready to fly to Al-Shahar and begin work on the temples. But on the long flight across the Atlantic Genie came to another decision.

She would not be returning to Bah'shar.

# CHAPTER TEN

THE weeks that dragged by seemed to last forever, but Zafir knew she would return soon. Genie would not abandon the temples. She might have pushed him from her life easily enough once he'd sent her away, but the temples would lure her back.

And he wanted to see her. Needed to see her. She was still a fire in his blood, no matter that he'd tried to convince himself otherwise. He'd sent her away for her safety, and yet he couldn't wait until she returned.

He remembered her voice on the message she'd left him. She'd sounded so tough, so businesslike as she'd informed him there was no baby. The words had jarred him, and yet it was the outcome that was the best for them both.

He'd thrown himself into work over the past weeks. The tension in the border region remained higher than he'd like, but it was difficult to eradicate years of mistrust in only a few months. There had been no violence, no raids, and he was pleased with the two Sheikhs' commitment to peace.

He'd also been looking at the code of law, and he'd made changes there as well. He'd brought new business to the capital by offering trade incentives, and he'd met with local business leaders and politicians to determine what their needs were for growth and stability.

He'd traveled extensively over the last month, expanding

Bah'shar's ties to the world, but no amount of work had been enough to erase Genie Gray from his mind.

Soon she would be in Bah'shar again. And he would go to see her.

He knew precisely when the team of archaeologists arrived for their excavation. He'd kept out of the arrangements with the Ministry of Culture, but that date was something he'd had Yusuf find out for him. He waited two days past their arrival before he ordered a car and went to the temples.

The ruins were a hive of activity that ceased immediately upon his arrival. A plump, graying man in khaki trousers and a dirt-streaked shirt hurried over.

"Your Majesty," he said, bowing low. "We are honored by your presence."

"You are happy with the arrangements?" Zafir asked politely.

"Indeed, we couldn't be more pleased. Everyone has been marvelous."

Zafir talked with the man who introduced himself as Dr. Dan Walker for a few moments more, scanning the site for any sign of Genie. None of the women he saw could be the feisty redhead he sought.

"Excuse me," Zafir said, cutting into Dr. Walker's excited chatter about mosaics and pottery shards, "but where is Dr. Gray?"

The man blinked. "Oh, I'm sorry. Dr. Gray did not accompany us."

Zafir frowned. "She is coming later, then?"

Dan Walker's pudgy cheeks glistened with perspiration. "Dr. Gray has opted to teach at university this semester, sir. She will not be a part of this excavation."

The October air was crisp in Massachusetts, but the trees were absolutely gorgeous, their leaves turning various shades of gold and red that took her breath away. Caldwell University was a prestigious private institution with a long history and a top archaeology program, and Genie had come here as a guest lecturer for the semester. After that she wasn't certain what she planned to do. There was a dig in China coming up, and she was thinking about signing on for it.

She thought of her teammates in Bah'shar, of the temples and all they would learn. She envied them, and yet she knew she'd made the right decision. If she'd returned to Bah'shar she wouldn't have been able to give her work the full concentration it deserved.

No, she'd have kept looking toward the palace and daydreaming about a desert king in white robes, riding an Arabian stallion. As if she didn't do enough of that already. A week in Bah'shar with Zafir had ruined her for another ten years at least. She'd never stopped loving him, and she could never be with him. What would it take to forget him?

Death, probably.

The bell rang and her students slapped their books closed and dashed out. As her next class filtered into her room, she made a few notes about the text and what she'd discovered while teaching it.

A group of girls gathered by one of the windows. No doubt the latest, greatest university quarterback was strolling by outside. Tim Robbins? Tom Ribbens? Rob Timmens? She couldn't remember, and didn't really care—though a smile lifted one corner of her mouth as she remembered her own days at university.

She'd had a crush on a football player for all of three weeks before Zafir bin Rashid al-Khalifa, the new man on campus, strode into a frat party and rocked her world. Nothing had been the same since.

When it was time to begin class, the girls were still at the window, their chatter low and excited.

"Take your seats, ladies," Genie said. "We have a lot to cover today."

"There's the most amazing sight out here, Dr. Gray."

"Yes, I'm sure that's true, but please, let's get to work." Genie used her best stern teacher voice, which seemed to do the trick.

The girls sat down and Genie stood up to begin her lecture. Movement outside caught her eye, and she glided toward the window as casually as possible while beginning to explain the complexities of identifying human bones and the importance of cataloguing them properly.

A long car sat against the curb, and four men in dark suits with radio transmitters flanked it. There was a police car in front and back, and both had their flashing lights on. She could see a cop talking on the radio in the first car.

Perhaps the Governor was visiting the school. Or Senator Hall. His daughter attended Caldwell.

Genie made the trip back to the whiteboard and picked up the marker. She was just beginning to write a few notes on the board when the door swung open. A man who bore the distinct mark of a bodyguard walked into the room, and then another followed. They flanked the door and Genie turned to her students, wondering if Senator Hall's daughter was in her class and she'd somehow forgotten it.

She turned back just as a tall, dark man in an expensive suit walked in. He was handsome and regal and he fixed her with a hawk-like stare. Her heart skidded to a stop in her chest before beginning to beat double time. There was a collective intake of breath from her classroom. The girls, no doubt.

"What are you doing here?" Genie blurted.

Zafir's sensual mouth turned down in a frown. "I have come a long way to speak with you, Dr. Gray. I had hoped your welcome would be more…appropriate."

Appropriate? What on earth was he talking about? If a

Martian had walked off his spaceship and into her classroom she couldn't have been more surprised than she was right now.

She looked at her students, wondering if perhaps she was hallucinating. Surely their confused expressions would confirm she was crazy.

But the girls were staring at Zafir in open-mouthed admiration; the young men were looking at him with curiosity.

"Class," she said, trying to salvage the session and her dignity at the same time, "this is His Majesty King Zafir bin Rashid al-Khalifa of the Kingdom of Bah'shar. We are honored to have you, Your Majesty."

Zafir inclined his head, as if he'd fully expected to be welcomed like a visiting potentate. "May I speak with you privately, Dr. Gray?" he said, never missing a beat.

"As you can see, class has just begun. You'll have to come back later."

"Ah—please excuse the interruption. But if you don't mind," he said, his polite smile turning devilish, "I would like to listen."

His arrogance made her waspish. What was he doing here? How could she ever put him behind her if he kept popping up when she least expected it? "I'm afraid we don't have a throne available for you to sit on."

He shrugged. "There is a chair behind your desk. I will sit there."

Genie fumed. She didn't know why he was here and it irritated her. He'd dismissed her from his life so easily, so coldly, and now he was here, in her classroom, larger than life. Why?

No matter how she tried to ignore it, little bubbles of joy were popping in her veins like champagne fizz. She didn't trust the feeling, however.

She didn't trust him.

"By all means. Make yourself at home."

Zafir crossed to the desk and took a seat, and Genie turned back to the board. She soldiered on with the lecture for the next forty-five minutes, though she deliberately did not look at Zafir again. She could feel his eyes burning into her, and she kept hoping he would get bored and leave.

But he stayed until the class was over. Several of the girls lingered over their desks, laboriously putting their books and laptops away. Once they were gone, she turned to him.

"What is this all about?" she demanded, hands on hips, frustration and confusion zipping around inside her.

Zafir stood, his easy demeanor gone. He looked mildly angry. "The Temples of Al-Shahar. I wanted you to lead the team, but you did not come."

She looked away. "I thought better of it."

"We made a deal, Genie."

"No, *you* made a deal. As I recall, I didn't have much choice."

"I wanted you," he repeated.

"Dr. Walker is fully qualified. Hell, he's more qualified than I am, if that's what you're worried about."

Zafir took a step toward her. "I wanted you."

"We don't always get what we want, Zafir."

He closed the distance between them. "I wanted you."

He stood so close, the heat of his body reaching out to envelop her. He smelled exotic, spicy, and she remembered running her tongue along his skin. She gave herself a mental shake. "I get it, Zafir. You wanted me to lead the dig, and now you're angry because you didn't get your way."

"No," he cut in, "I wanted you. You, Genie Gray."

"Why do you keep saying that?" she cried. She whirled away from him, intending to put distance between them.

But he caught her, pulled her against his hard body. "Genie," he said in her ear, "I want you."

And then she understood. He loosened his grip and she turned in his arms, pulling away when he didn't try to keep her.

"You came all this way for sex?"

His laugh was unexpected. "I came for you. Come to Bah'shar with me, Genie."

Her heart was thundering in her ears. "Why would I want to do that?" she whispered.

"Because you love me."

She closed her eyes. Swallowed. "I do love you," she said. "But it's not enough, Zafir."

"And what if I said I loved you too?"

"I can't come with you, Zafir," she said, shaking her head. "I can never settle for being second best in your life. I can't believe you would ask me this again—"

"I want you to be my queen," he cut in.

He looked lost, uncertain, and her heart contracted with pain and love.

"You can't mean that," she said. "It's impossible."

"Why? Because of your career?"

Was he that obtuse? Did he have to make her say it? "No, because of you. It's Bah'sharan law—"

"Not any longer," he said fiercely.

Genie blinked, dumbfounded. "You changed the law?"

"It was an old law, and it made no sense. The people agreed."

"You had a vote?"

"Yes."

Her heart was beginning to believe, but her head couldn't quite accept it. "But how do you know you really love me? That it's not just attraction and—?"

Zafir groaned. "My God, woman, do you think that I couldn't find a willing female to have sex with in Bah'shar if that was my only problem? That I've flown halfway around the world to get down on my knees and beg, if that is what it takes, for you to come to Bah'shar with me simply because I have an uncontrollable erection?"

In spite of the seriousness of the situation she wanted to laugh suddenly. Somehow she managed not to. "When you put it like that…"

He looked offended. "Exactly."

"Then why did you send me away after you were stabbed?" It still hurt that he had done so, and she wanted to understand. "I was so scared for you, and you dismissed me as if it meant nothing."

"I know, and I'm sorry. But there had been threats against my life, and when I was attacked I realized that I had put you in danger too. I couldn't live with that. Your safety is the most important thing in the world to me." He blew out a breath. "But now you aren't there, and I still think of you constantly. I need you, Genie. Without you, I'm only half the king I should be."

"I'm not afraid of a little danger," she said a touch unsteadily. The conversation seemed so unreal that she was having a hard time processing all the implications. "Being an archaeologist can be dangerous at times."

"I know, but this danger was different. And though there may always be some degree of danger when one lives such a public life, I am confident the people of Bah'shar will love you as I do."

"I don't want to give up archaeology entirely," she said. "I love what I do."

"I understand this," he replied. "Just as I want to build things, you want to dig in the dirt. But there is much to excavate in Bah'shar. And if you need to go elsewhere on your digs, we will work it out."

She couldn't believe she was hearing this. The man she loved was standing here, offering her everything she'd ever wanted, and she was scared. Scared she was missing something, or that there was a catch somewhere. Could she really be Queen of Bah'shar?

"I'm not sure I'm cut out for this, Zafir."

He didn't need to ask what she meant. "I wasn't supposed to be a king," he said, "but I'm learning. You will learn too."

Genie's heart was swelling, daring to hope, daring to believe.

How could she not take the leap? She had to. *Had to*. She loved this man with all her heart and she didn't want to let him go ever again. She'd be queen of anything if that was what it took.

"You're sure you really love me?"

He put his hands on her shoulders, bent to look her in the eye. "Dr. Geneva Gray, I love you. Only you. Forever you. Come to the desert with me. Be my wife, bear my children, grow old with me."

A tremor passed through her. It was real. He was real.

"Kiss me, Zafir," she said.

"Gladly."

The kiss was everything she'd hoped. It was the kiss of a man who loved her. Happiness flooded her soul with sunshine, breaking through all the pain and emptiness of the last few weeks.

"I love you, Zafir. This time you can't get rid of me."

"Exactly as I'd hoped," he said, before kissing her again.

# EPILOGUE

*One year later...*

KING ZAFIR BIN RASHID AL-KHALIFA was in a hurry. He strode through the palace corridors at a pace that had the staff scurrying out of his way. Finally he burst into the royal apartments and kept going until he found his wife in the bathroom, removing her soiled clothing.

Genie looked up when he came in, her face creasing in a smile that did odd things to his heart. Dirt and mud streaked her fair skin. Her hair, spiked with drying sweat, stood at odd angles from her head.

Zafir thought she'd never looked more beautiful. "You are home early, *habiba*," he said.

She continued to remove clothing, dropping it in a pile at her feet. The more of her luscious body that was revealed, the more his own body responded. Oh, yes, he was definitely going to have her.

In the shower. On the bed. Perhaps even the floor if he couldn't make it to the bed first.

"I was feeling a bit tired," she said.

Zafir frowned. "But you went to bed early last night. I remember this quite well. Did you awaken?"

"No, I slept straight through." The last of her clothing fell in a *poof* of dust. She reached for the taps and turned on the shower. Zafir worked hard to make his brain function. Her gorgeous pink nipples were ripe for his touch. He needed to touch them. Needed to taste them.

Marrying Genie was the best decision he'd ever made. Not just because he needed her with a fierceness that hadn't abated in the last twelve months, but also because she made him whole. She filled his life and took away every ounce of loneliness he'd ever felt.

She was the other half to his soul.

"I have sent for the doctor," she continued, and Zafir's heart dropped to his toes. She was his greatest treasure, his reason for being. She could not be ill.

"Doctor?"

"Don't look so worried," she said, coming over and giving him a quick squeeze while trying not to soil his clothing at the same time. "It's nothing serious."

"You can't know that. You aren't a doctor—" He stopped, amended the statement when she arched an eyebrow. "Not *that* kind of doctor."

She walked into the steamy shower and stood under the spray. "I simply need him to confirm something for me."

Why would she need a doctor to confirm...?

And then it hit him. His knees felt suddenly weak, his heart thudding into his throat. He realized that Genie had opened her eyes and was watching him.

"Are you...? Do you mean...?" He couldn't find the words.

Genie smiled and opened her arms. "Why don't you join me?"

He ripped off his clothes and stepped under the spray, taking her into his arms. "No more digging in the dirt in the middle of the hot day, Genie," he ordered. "And no more crawling into dank tombs beneath the temples."

"Yes, Your Majesty," she said. "Besides, I doubt I'll be

able to get inside those narrow spaces in the next few months anyway."

"I love you," Zafir said. "More than you can ever imagine."

Her eyes sparkled. "Oh, I can imagine a lot."

"So can I, thanks to you."

And then he proceeded to show her the depths of his very creative imagination.

# SEVEN-DAY
# LOVE STORY

## Nikki Logan

**Nikki Logan** lives next to a string of protected wetlands in Western Australia, with her long-suffering partner and a menagerie of furred, feathered and scaly mates. She studied film and theatre at university and worked for years in advertising and film distribution before finally settling down in the wildlife industry. Her romance with nature goes way back and she considers her life charmed, given she works with wildlife by day and writes fiction by night – the perfect way to combine her two loves. Nikki believes that the passion and risk of falling in love are perfectly mirrored in the danger and beauty of wild places. Every romance she writes contains an element of nature and if readers catch a waft of rich earth or the spray of wild ocean between the pages, she knows her job is done.

**Nikki Logan now regularly writes for Mills & Boon. Her latest novel, *Their Newborn Gift*, was available in June 2010 and she has a new book out in November in Cherish™, *The Soldier's Untamed Heart*.**

Dear Reader,

*If you love something, set it free. If it comes back it's yours. If it doesn't…*

I was excited and honoured to be chosen as one of the *New Voices* for Mills & Boon, and I knew I wanted to write something special for this anthology. A year ago I'd had the idea of a heroine-turned-hermit recovering from emotional trauma, but I wanted Jayne and Todd's romance to bloom over a very short time-frame – feeding Todd's fears that their feelings couldn't be genuine and luring Jayne out of her emotional cocoon much more quickly than she's comfortable with.

A novella is the perfect medium to tell a *Seven-Day Love Story*.

I hope you enjoy the wonderful, fictional community of Banjo's Ridge and all the characters in it (human and otherwise). We should all have a psychological Banjo's Ridge to retreat to when the going gets tough. And a hero like Todd to come and find us there.

To anyone who has beaten fear – or is still fighting it – I dedicate this story to you.

*Nikki Logan*

## Acknowledgement

Special acknowledgement to Western Australians Dr Kingsley Dixon and Gavin Flematti, who spent years untangling the thousands of chemicals in bush-smoke to discover which one triggered seed germination. Their groundbreaking work is fictionally referenced in this story.

# CHAPTER ONE

*Friday*

'EASY now, big fella...'

It couldn't have been simple, keeping his voice level when four sets of fangs were flashing and glinting at head height, but the uniformed man standing at the bottom of Jayne Morrow's front steps did manage to keep the waver from his voice.

Just.

She stared at him, anticipating the numbness that would take over right about now—when strangers were around. She'd become used to its intrusion, even welcomed it; numbness was far better than the knee-crumbling anxiety she would have felt two years ago, back in New York.

The dogs twitched and trembled at her feet. Not one of them was a natural leader; if they were, they'd still be roaming the wilds of the Queensland hinterlands, scavenging an existence. But all four of them rewarded her for taking them in by stepping up now, in response to the presence of the stranger.

His eyes stayed glued on the largest of the dogs, Oliver. Jayne whispered her quell command and waited for four canine bottoms to lower to the floor. It took an age, but they eventually complied, sliding their lips back down over their teeth. One by one they relaxed, Oliver last.

'Thank you.' Down below her, the stranger's body sagged slightly and he stepped forward onto the first tread of the house steps. Oliver leapt straight back to guard position, issuing a guttural rumbling.

'Ollie, no,' she whispered to the brave dog.

The man slid his hands into plain view, left and right of his tense body. 'How about we just talk from here?'

*Good idea*. 'Who are you?' Her voice was steady, thank goodness.

'Todd Blackwood. I was hoping the Shire would have rung ahead to tell you I was coming.' His Australian voice was rougher than the rocky path leading to Jayne's doorway.

'No.'

'Ah. Then I've surprised you.' His eyes dropped to the hand wrapped around the largest dog's collar as if it were a lifeline. 'And frightened you. I'm sorry.'

She tossed her head back and loosened her fingers slightly to let blood leach into the whitened knuckles. 'I'm not frightened—' *such a liar!* '—just curious. I don't get many visitors.'

He glanced again at the mass of warm bodies at her feet. 'No doubt.'

'They're just doing their job.'

A gentle smile transformed his face. 'Me too. I'm here to discuss them with you. I'm the Shire Ranger.'

A ranger was as good as the police out in these parts. His face looked entirely non-threatening, his body as casual as a man being stared down by four wired dogs could be. Even so, something in her itched to run inside and lock the door. She forced herself to resist the impulse.

'Perhaps if…' He glanced up at the dogs again and lowered his considerable height to a squat. The dogs' demeanour changed immediately, and three out of four bottoms started to wiggle. Jazmine, Fergus and Dougal had no problems, moving instantly from quivering tension to comfortable acceptance. Not Oliver. He was still rigid with suspicion.

The show of trust from the stranger brought Jayne a hint of confidence. If he was here for no good he wouldn't be putting himself at risk. She wrapped her hand more firmly around Ollie's collar and then spoke softly to the others.

'Go.'

It only took one word and the three smaller dogs broke rank and leapt down the steps in an explosion of investigatory licking. The Ranger kept his chin high, away from the errant tongues, and let them rifle into his jacket and at his trouser legs with their noses. It was like the canine version of a full body frisk.

'Okay.' He chuckled, patting them individually on the shoulder, pushing back to his feet and taking all the fun a good five feet away from them. 'Now they're more like a group of kids on too much sugar.'

Jayne fought a smile. The image was very apt for the three excited dogs, but not for the little black thundercloud at her feet that hadn't had a whole lot of joy in his life. She gave Oliver's silky ears a rub. He whined his gratitude. One sharp whistle from her and all three loose dogs returned to heel and she was able to wrestle them inside. Still within reach if she needed them, but not tripping her underfoot. It gave the man at the base of her stairs some breathing space.

He looked like a ranger, but he was put together like a lumberjack. Out here maybe there wasn't much difference? 'You said you were on official business?'

He frowned at the way she still hovered, glued to her veranda. 'It's about the dogs...'

Her grip on Ollie's collar doubled. 'What about them?'

'You have four. Shire regulations only allow three per property.'

Her every instinct was to run. To protect. But she'd learned to fight that. She took a deep breath. 'I have registered them all. I'm not trying to hide them.'

'It was the registration that alerted us to the...anomaly.' He frowned up at her. 'Could we perhaps...? Could I come up?'

She'd come a long way, but the thought of having him in her house overwhelmed her, despite the uniform. 'I'll meet you round the back.'

He frowned, but nodded. Jayne pushed the eager dogs back from the front door and closed it securely behind her, then hurried through the house to the back. Fergus, Dougal and Jazmine perked up again as soon as they realised her intention. Ollie found his favourite chair and curled up on it, looking miserable.

Three would suffice.

They burst from the back door like shot from a rifle and bounded over to where the stranger stood, examining a pile of materials and an old, rickety aviary. He ignored them in exactly the way someone who knew dogs would, and that gave them the confidence to busy themselves scavenging around his feet.

Jayne cleared her throat. 'Is there some kind of paperwork I can fill out to get the fourth dog approved?'

Todd shook his head. 'State limits. Why do you have so many?'

Jayne called Jaz close to her and petted her head. 'They're all abandoned. They have no one else. And they're...security for me. I live here alone.'

*Nice one, genius! Why not tell him where you keep the spare key while you're at it?* She monitored the dogs closely.

She trusted them to let her know if his mood changed. If at any stage this became more than bureaucracy.

New habits died hard.

He nodded, and a thick, dark lock fell down over his reassuringly square brow. Stupid that a forehead should make her feel more comfortable, but it did. Maybe because the smooth, tanned flesh accentuated the deepest blue eyes she'd seen outside of a magazine advertisement. Somewhere deep inside she was sure anyone up to no good would be less... remarkable.

The eyes in question watched the hovering dogs. 'They're good protection. I can see that,' he said.

'And they're a pack now. Splitting them up is not an option.'

'You may not have a choice, Ms Morrow.'

A double shot of alarm surged through her. Of course he knew her name—he was from the Shire, and she'd included her details on the registrations. But the thought that he might be leaving here today with one of her four-legged kids chained up in his vehicle... Her chest rose and fell with tight, sudden pain.

'Please don't take them.' It galled her to beg, but the alternative was unthinkable.

'I can see that you have them well trained,' he said. 'That's a positive in your favour. And you have been very honest in declaring them.' That broad brow crinkled as his dark eyebrows lowered in concentration. He slid his glance to the materials lying piled a few feet away. 'What's all this for?'

Panic bubbled up further and disguised itself as frustration. 'Is that in breach of something, too?'

He smiled, utterly bemused. 'No. I'm just thinking...' He wandered over to the old aviary in the shade of an ancient gum tree. A giant corella blinked at him from the high perch and a possum peered suspiciously out of a nest-box in the corner.

On the ground, a bandicoot picked off the corrella's cast-off food scraps. 'You have quite a little zoo going here.'

Jayne stared at him, wondering what to say. 'More of a halfway house. The plan is for most of these guys to go back to the bush when they're rehabilitated.'

He turned back to her. 'You have a carer's licence?'

Her heart sank. 'I wasn't aware I needed one.'

That smile dissolved rapidly into a thin line. He stared at her hard, his mind ticking over visibly in his expressive blue eyes. 'If you're dabbling in wildlife rehab, yes, you'll definitely need one. But it will also solve your dog dilemma. A licence provides for more than three dogs, provided at least one of them is being rehabbed.'

The first genuine glimpse of hope burst into life deep inside her. 'Oh! But they all are. How do I apply?'

'You just fill out a form at the Shire office and pay the licence fee.'

The flicker extinguished in a gush of sudden dread. 'Is it not available online?'

His deep chuckle worked its way under her skin. 'Welcome to Banjo's Ridge. Hard copy and carbon-copy triplicate—the old-fashioned way.'

She didn't have a hope of stopping the fingers of her right hand compulsively touching her thumb. They did it of their own accord, over and over in order, bringing their odd, cell-deep comfort. The best she could do was tuck her whole hand out of view.

Those extraordinary eyes followed the brief move.

'Tell you what,' he said, his tone changing instantly to the overly loud one she'd used at her book signings when particularly frail fans queued up for her signature. 'I'll bring the form back out to you on my rounds tomorrow. We'll get you all signed up.'

It meant him coming back, but it saved her the agony of

a trip into town. Even if town consisted of only one hundred and thirty-two people. And only a third of them around at any one time. Thoughts of gift horses flitted through her mind.

'That would be kind. Thank you.' She took a breath. 'What time?'

She turned to walk towards the house. He took the not so subtle hint and followed her. 'I couldn't say. I'm rostered first thing, so it will be in the morning some time—whenever I'm out this way. That's the best I can do.'

*Oh, lovely.* A surprise visit. Nothing she liked more. Her finger-counting started over. 'Yes, that will be good. Thank you. I'll see you tomorrow.' She turned from him stiffly and retreated to the house, calling the yipping dogs with her.

Todd lifted his eyebrows as he watched her go. Not the friendliest of locals. But then she wasn't local. She'd only been in the Queensland hinterland a short time, judging by that accent. A pretty young American woman living alone had a way of standing out, but for all the townsfolk had to say about her no one seemed to know much other than her cracking impersonation of Greta Garbo. *I want to be alone.*

Yep. He got that loud and clear.

'So…guess I'll be going!' he called pointlessly at the cottage door which had closed quietly in his face, then shook his head and turned to walk around to the front of the house.

Possibly the touchiest woman he'd ever met, and certainly the most unwelcoming. It would never fly on this mountain. Neighbours needed each other. If she was being that cool to *him*—practically the law out here—he could bet there wasn't a single family this side of the ridge that would drop in to see if she needed anything in an emergency. Gorgeous or not.

And she most definitely was.

That ghost of an almost-smile stuck in his mind. Hair like spun gold. And the most unusual grey eyes, with a bit of every other colour in them. Fine pointed chin, smooth, pale skin. Soft, small lips. Everything about her seemed…refined. There was no one like her on this ridge.

Todd climbed into his truck and buckled up. He saw the tiniest shimmy in curtains that told him she was still watching. Waiting for him to go.

Nope, absolutely no one like her.

Never mind; he had bigger fish to fry than a recalcitrant licence-breacher. Old Tom Hardy had reported seeing that black panther in his far paddock again—claimed to have a footprint this time.

The fact he'd swung by Miss Prickly's refuge first said a lot about his belief in a mythical wildcat down on the Hardy farm. Still, it kept him busy. And in a town where there was barely enough cause to have even a part-time ranger, busy was a rarity. When he'd settled in Banjo's Ridge he'd been looking for a fresh start. A slow-motion kind of existence. Anything as long as it was different from his life in the city.

Mythical black panthers and enigmatic mystery women certainly qualified.

# CHAPTER TWO

*Saturday*

JAYNE's heart hammered hard enough to break a rib, but she couldn't break free of the jumbled mess of images. They no longer played out like grim movies in her mind, but the disturbing montage had a way of leaking, unwanted, into her dreams.

They saturated her with old feelings: suspicion, self-doubt, the dark, clawing fear she'd lived with for two years. No matter how hard she worked during the day to keep them at bay, they simply waited for night—and her eyelids—to fall.

The cold, wet nose of reality helped draw her back. She cracked one eye open and stared into deep black gems. Her hand slid out and curled around silken ears.

'Ollie...'

Satisfied his work was done, Oliver padded back out of Jayne's bedroom on a gentle click-clack of claws, leaving her to rise unassisted. His job was pulling her out of a nightmare. Her job was pulling herself out of bed. The place she could easily spend the entire day if she hadn't promised herself she wouldn't do that any more.

She showered and dressed in super-quick time, not prepared to take any chances. If there was going to be a stranger hanging around the place she wanted to be as prepared as possible. Her eyes flicked habitually to the small sports bag behind the front door. Spare keys, passport, cash, clean underwear. It sat gathering dust except for those bleak times she scrabbled through the contents obsessively, to make sure everything was still there for when she needed it.

*If* she needed it.

'Breakfast!' Four dogs came running as she clanked their bowls together loudly. It was the one time of the day Ollie showed he had more to his personality than cautious regard. Then she set to chopping fresh fruit and veg for her rehab critters.

Her own breakfast was a more leisurely affair. A treat to herself out on the back veranda, served on real china with tea from a teapot, amid the sweet perfume of native jasmine with the mid-morning sun to warm her. She used the ritual to force herself to slow down, to remember where she was, how anonymous she now was. How safe.

'Good morning.'

Ollie went berserk inside, but Dougal, Jaz and Fergus came galloping around the house and careened with enthusiasm into the man who'd appeared silently at the side of the veranda. Jayne's pulse leapt painfully in her throat and she lifted a shaky hand to it, clattering her teacup noisily into its saucer. She used the brief moment as he rough-housed with the dogs to recover.

Then he straightened and met her eyes. 'I've startled you again. My apologies.'

Her voice failed her the first time. She cleared her throat quietly, then tried again. 'No. It's fine. I was a thousand miles away. I didn't hear your car.'

She stared at all six feet plus of him, standing spread-footed on her land like a giant eucalypt rooting itself into the earth. Her fluttering heart took its time settling in her breast, and she forced her voice to fill the silent void. 'Would you like a cup of coffee? Tea?'

He smiled and rummaged in his jacket pockets while the smaller dogs darted around his feet like skimper-fish on a reef. 'I should get these forms back to town as soon as possible. Thank you, though.'

Jayne frowned. He wasn't supposed to say no. Not that she wanted to have coffee with him particularly, but she'd *asked*... and asking had taken some doing on her part. 'Excuse me just a moment, then.' She gathered together her dishes and then took them inside to soak in the sink. When she returned he had the forms out and ready at the base of her back porch steps. It took just a few minutes for her to detail them and sign. Male eyes rounded when she produced a roll of cash from which to peel off the modest application fee.

'Do you always carry that much cash on you this early in the morning?' he asked.

*Yes, always.* 'I wasn't sure how much the fee would be.'

He took just two notes, then bundled the paperwork up with it and shoved both into an inside pocket in his Ranger's jacket. Then he looked out at the piles of materials lying scattered around the enormous fenced yard behind the house. 'Are you going to be okay building those enclosures by yourself?'

'How did—?'

'Mesh. Timber. Wildlife. Doesn't take a genius. Can you build?' He looked as if he already knew the answer to that.

She straightened her back. 'I'll work it out.'

'You have to submit drawings with your application. So the Shire knows the animals will be adequately housed.'

Jayne groaned. *Why was everything so hard?* She was trying, wasn't she?

Blue eyes studied her and he seemed to come to a decision. He cleared his throat. 'I was wondering whether you needed any help. I'm pretty good with my...with construction.'

Turmoil ruined her tranquil morning. On one hand she did need help—desperately—especially if drawings were required. And Ranger Blackwood wasn't a *complete* stranger now.

Which didn't mean she was comfortable around him. But having his help meant he'd be back. And back. And despite all her progress she still struggled with strangers.

'I can draw up enough to keep the Shire happy and then come by after I knock off work each day—help out for a couple of hours. If you like?'

Jayne stared. It was the answer to one of her primary problems. She'd never even put together a flat-pack bookshelf. 'I'd pay you...'

He smiled indulgently and waved his hand. 'Not necessary.'

*Oh, it was very necessary.* She needed him to stop treating her like a senior citizen. Right now. Paying him would put it all back on a professional footing. She straightened her shoulders. 'Money's not a problem. I'd feel better if I paid you.'

Even the bush crickets held their breath.

He studied her closely. 'When I first got to Banjo's Ridge a few of the locals really helped me get established, and I appreciated it. I just want to pass that help on. But if you feel better paying me, we can work something out.'

He patted the side of his jacket, where her forms were tucked away. 'I'll come back as soon as my shift finishes. If we get lucky we'll have your preliminary approval ready to go.'

Five hours later Jayne hovered in the doorway, chewing her lip. Ollie looked up at her with soulful, trusting eyes.

She smiled at him. 'Okay, I'll ask.' She found the ranger

at the back of the property, pulling piles of mesh sheets into position across a gravel clearing.

'Excuse me, Mr Blackwood…'

He straightened slowly, his blue eyes steady and blessedly neutral, his rolled-up sleeves revealing strong, tanned forearms. 'Call me Todd. What can I do for you?'

'I… If you're going to be here a few days I can't leave Oliver locked up all that time. I was wondering if I could…'

He smiled, and her stomach did a clumsy somersault, but it had nothing to do with fear. His smile reached all the way to his eyes—not all smiles did that, in her experience.

Not all of them reached clear into her gut either.

'Sure—bring him out,' he said. 'He and I have to come to terms some time.'

Her chest was unnecessarily tight. Between his smile and his gentle patience for her maladjusted dog, she just couldn't get a deep breath in. 'Thank you.'

She was back in minutes, with a surly Oliver tightly restrained by the tether in her grip. Holding him gave her an anchor. Todd saw her coming and slowly stretched up to his full height, his eyes soft. 'What would you like me to do?'

Jayne laughed lightly. 'Could you maybe shrink about a foot?'

'Not much I can do about that, I'm afraid, but I'll do my best to be non-threatening.'

It had been a while since she'd not felt threatened around a stranger, but for some reason she wasn't dissolving into a trembling mess around Todd Blackwood. Although he *was* making her a whole different kind of nervous.

She brought Oliver closer, and Todd took a step back to give him some space. Jayne nudged the black dog between them. Ollie was as stiff as she was.

'Relax, Jayne. He's feeling your tension. The worst that can happen is that he'll try to bite me, and if he does he and

I will have a quick man-to-man conversation to figure out who's boss.'

She shifted until her body was slightly between them.

Todd frowned. 'I won't hurt him, Jayne. Just like people, dogs like to know where they stand with others. He might appreciate the direct approach. Let's just see how he goes.'

Human and dog ignored each other for a few moments, and then Todd took a step closer. Ollie looked up at him suspiciously.

'This could take a few minutes,' he said. 'If he sees *us* being comfortable with each other he might relax.'

*Comfortable.* Right. Jayne forced her body into a parody of a relaxed pose, triggering another one of those killer smiles. Her mouth dried, just a little bit.

The smile graduated to a deep chuckle. 'Even *I'm* not buying that. Plan B...how about just some normal conversation?'

It had been a while since she'd had any conversation that wasn't via e-mail. Todd took a tiny step closer to Ollie. The dog stayed put. It was working. She sighed. 'Okay. What would you like to talk about?'

Todd let his hand drop down to his side, close to Ollie's head so he could sniff it, but his eyes stayed locked on her. 'How about what you're doing out here all by yourself? Seems unusual.'

She stiffened immediately, and Ollie pushed up onto his feet.

Todd broke in quickly 'Or...we could talk about something else. Where did you grow up? That's not a Queensland accent I hear.'

Jayne let out a big breath, and Ollie's tail sank back towards the ground. 'Hardly. I'm from Pennsylvania originally.'

'Welcome to Australia.'

'I've been here a couple of years, but thank you.' She laughed.

Ollie looked up at her, as if surprised by the unfamiliar sound. Todd took the opportunity to slide his hand down and gently rest it on the dog's black head. Ollie forgot to flinch. 'Keep talking,' he said quietly, and then slowly closed his fingers into a rub.

Jayne drew in a breath. This was the closest Ollie had been to another person since she'd found him skulking, half-starved, down near her back dam. 'I moved here two years ago. I was looking for somewhere different to where I'm from.'

Blue eyes met hers. 'Different?'

*Safer. Further.* 'Somewhere new.'

Todd was fully squatting now, and Ollie glared at him guardedly. But he was prepared to tolerate it as long as the gentle rubbing continued. It did, and Jayne found herself transfixed by the sight of those strong fingers pushing through Ollie's black fur.

'This must be quite different to home,' he said.

'Not so much. Jim Thorpe is a small community in the valley of a mountain forest. This all feels quite familiar. The trees are different. But still beautiful.' She smiled down at Ollie and added her gentle strokes to Todd's.

'You miss it?'

She lifted her eyes back to his but couldn't hold his gaze. She glanced out at the towering forest circling her sanctuary. And then it hit her. She was making conversation. And her chest wasn't imploding. 'I miss parts of it. But everyone grows up, moves on.'

'You didn't want to stay close to your family?'

Oh, how she had—and her mother had cried and cried on hearing how far from home her only daughter was moving. But Jayne loved them too much to expose them to any further risk. Not that she'd told them about any of it.

'We stay close. We talk via the internet. We e-mail.'

Ollie shifted, and Jayne cupped his ridged silken skull and stroked him reassuringly. Then warm, strong fingers accidentally tangled with hers. A heat-burst surged up to her palm and she only just managed to suppress a yelp as she leaped back, sending Ollie scampering for cover.

Her eyes flew to Todd's. His were carefully schooled.

'Sorry.' The pointless apology tumbled off her lips.

Todd tipped his head to the side and stared at her—a burning, inscrutable regard—and shrugged. 'It's a start.'

*Ollie.* He was talking about Ollie.

'I should get back to this enclosure,' he said casually, as though the burst of static energy had been purely one-sided. Of course it had. He looked entirely unaffected.

She cleared her throat. 'Yes. I should get back to work, too.'

*Uh-huh.* As if *that* was going to happen while her heart was racing and while she had something so delightfully ornamental to look at through the window. Jayne ducked her head and turned back for the house.

Oliver trotted happily after her, oblivious to the awkward human moment he'd just caused.

# CHAPTER THREE

*Sunday*

JAYNE studied Todd through a crack in the drawn curtains of the back windows, unable to tear her gaze away from his broad shoulders and his patient, methodical construction methods. Now he was perched on a drum in her yard, oblivious to her surveillance, sharing his ham sandwich with an adoring Ollie.

Even the most mistrustful dog on the planet had a melting point, it seemed—approximately the same temperature that ham was cured at.

A man who dogs loved couldn't be all bad, right? Her four-legged friends might be easily bought, but—given their damaged backgrounds—they were even more attuned to survival than she was, and all four would have kept their distance from someone with ulterior motives, she was sure.

Or was she just looking for excuses to like him?

Todd Blackwood was not like the men she'd used to know. Every part of him screamed higher education, yet he could whack together a holding pen as if he'd been doing it all his life. His casual discussion hinted at city origins but he was hanging around a small village digging up handyman work as though he were a drifter.

It should have made her more suspicious, but it didn't.

After all, people could draw all kinds of conclusions about Jayne Morrow—J.C. Moro to her gazillions of adoring fans. A top-of-the-list novelist, living a simple life in the Australian forest; what would people make of that? She had no doubt that people back home were reading things into her absence, making up what they didn't know.

*Prima donna. Marketing gimmick.*

Only her agent and a small team of investigating officers assigned to her case knew the real story. She had a genuine excuse, maybe Todd did too? She definitely got the feeling there was a story to tell. There was one way to find out. Jayne's heart kicked up a notch. It wasn't unreasonable to ask a few questions of the man she was employing.

*Right?*

Nervous steps carried her out to the far end of her yard, where four dogs welcomed her with licks and welcome dances. Her heart hammered a protest. She silenced the frightened voice that urged her to go back inside.

This was the road to normal.

Todd looked up as she approached, then pushed himself politely to his feet. 'Back to work time?'

Jayne frowned. 'No. You've earned your breaks—take them.' She examined the beginnings of the yards that would make such a difference to her injured animals. She might not yet have a wealth of rehabilitation skills, but she could at least accommodate the animals professionally and appropriately while they healed. 'It's looking great. Thank you.'

Todd nodded and sank back onto the half-drum, leaning forward, his tanned forearms resting on his thighs and strong fingers hanging loose between relaxed legs. It was a poster image for non-threatening body language, and it immediately took the edge off Jayne's tension levels. Todd snagged up a soda can from the ground and took a long swig.

'Can I ask you a question?' No one would believe from her hesitant tone that she made her living communicating.

Todd took another swallow. 'Shoot.'

'What are you doing in Banjo's Ridge? I assume you don't live here?'

'Why do you assume that?'

'Your accent is different to the locals'. It's Australian but... different.'

'I'm from Western Australia originally.'

*Five thousand kilometres away.* 'What brings you here?'

Blue eyes blinked slowly back at her. 'The mountain life-style. The pace. It's very tranquil here.'

*And very hidden.* Even the tourists often missed it on their bush pilgrimages. 'What did you do for a living?'

His brows bunched, as if he was baffled at her sudden surge of curiosity. She sure was. 'I was a biologist.'

*Ah-ha!* 'Is that why you're so good with Ollie?'

'I specialised in flora, not canines.' He laughed. 'But I grew up with dogs. We get each other.'

Ollie showed her just how much by flopping down next to Todd's work-worn boots.

'So I see,' she said. 'I've never seen him more at ease.'

Todd used his boot tip to gently scratch Ollie's belly. 'I think he's just a dog who's had to make too many decisions. He was desperate for someone to take the responsibility from him.'

'Responsibility for what?'

'For survival. For leading the pack. For you. It's been a lot for a damaged dog to carry.'

Two years of suspicion stiffened her spine. 'Why would he feel responsible for me?'

Todd shrugged, meeting her eyes carefully. 'Perhaps he thinks you need protecting?'

'*I* protect *him*. I have since he came.' The thumping in her chest had to be audible. Surely?

'You feed him and love him. But trust me… He thinks you need him to be in charge. It's all in his body language.'

She looked at Ollie's enormous dark eyes, fixed adoringly on Todd. 'So now that you're here he's handing over responsibility for all that to you? Is that it?'

'Put simply.'

'Including me?' Wisely, Todd didn't answer. He simply stared through those deep blue eyes. The tug-of-war between anger and attraction tightened her chest and forced her up straighter. 'He's going to be sorely disappointed when you disappear at the end of the week.'

Todd reached down and rubbed a big hand over Ollie's scalp. The dog squeezed his eyes shut in bliss and Jayne understood exactly. Her skin remembered every brief moment of their fingers entangling the previous day. Gooseflesh rose in sympathy.

'A week is a long time,' he said, standing. 'Let's wait and see.'

They fell to silence. Jayne studied the shadowy angles of his face as he gathered up his tools to continue. They made a handsome combination.

Todd cleared his throat. 'So, what kind of work lets *you* live out here?'

'I'm an…' She caught herself and corrected herself. Trusting him and *trusting* him were two different things. 'I'm having a sabbatical. Of sorts.'

He nodded. 'A long one, judging by the trouble you're going to in getting these yards all set up.'

'I'm hoping to get back to it more fully soon. And also that I can continue with the animals once I do.'

'So, you'll work from home?'

She cleared her thick throat and hedged. 'My work goes with me wherever I do.'

Todd smiled, although this one didn't quite dilute the disappointment in his eyes. Why was she hesitating? She should just tell him. He was unlikely to put two and two together.

'I write.' The words practically hissed out of her.

His eyes widened. 'Really? Would I recognise your work?'

*Almost certainly.* Unless he'd been living under a rock in the middle of the desert. But her courage just didn't extend that far. She dropped her head. 'I doubt it. Just some online magazine stuff...'

Hopefully he'd have no clue how many articles or books you had to sell to make a decent living. *Let alone a great one.* He studied her hard, but didn't press the point.

'What made you decide to take some time off? To come all the way to Australia?'

'I...I told you. I just wanted something—'

'Different?' He didn't look convinced. The old fear hit her like a hammer. Her blood pulsed through suddenly constricting veins.

*He knew!* She held his gaze. Panic welled up fast. 'Unless you have a better theory?'

He was too poker-faced to look shocked, but he lifted an eyebrow at her sudden sarcasm. It only fuelled her irrational clenching. Her compulsive fingers worked double-time behind her back.

When he spoke, his voice was infuriatingly controlled. 'You don't have to discuss it if it bothers you.'

Humiliation at her outburst bled fire into her cheeks. 'Being managed bothers me.' Particularly while *he* remained as cool as a cucumber. 'Stop talking to me like I'm Ollie.'

She spun and walked away, shame tangling around her feet.

She'd just dropped her bundle in front of a virtual stranger.

Todd didn't deserve to be attacked over his lunchbreak. She'd been on edge all day, and his gentle probing had poked straight into a part of her that was sore and ultra-sensitive. Like a diver gouging open oysters in search of pearls. A vulnerable, quivering part she'd spent the better part of two years sealing up.

Her reaction didn't belong to Todd. It belonged to *him*...

The other one. Back in New York. Wrestling back power from *that* man meant trusting again—and, for all Todd's size and strength and newness, deep inside Jayne felt that she could trust him. If only her flying fingers knew that.

She forced them to still. She was kidding herself if she thought she was better. She'd convinced herself she was back to normal. Maybe with one or two quirky new habits but otherwise pretty ordinary. Compared to how she had been. She'd prided herself on the fact. But one look at the deep furrows in Todd's brow and she knew she wasn't fooling anyone.

She wasn't normal. No matter how much she convinced herself she'd reassimilated into normal life. She still did almost all her purchasing online. She still had her groceries delivered. She still saw conspiracy where there was none. But *he* was normal and, between her manic heart-thumping and uncontrollable finger-counting, some part of her crazy, messed-up body *did* recognise that Todd Blackwood was safe.

When was the last time she'd felt that on first acquaintance? It had taken her eighteen months to build up the courage just to speak a few words to Banjo Ridge's postman on his rounds.

*But you did it*, she reminded herself. Two new people in two years.

Not bad.

She moaned at the sad, sad irony.

* * *

'Todd?'

He spun around at the sound of Jayne's soft voice. Her face was pale, and she'd linked her tiny hands in front of her. The right one twitched as if it needed to be moving. Every part of him responded to the defeat in her posture. This was a woman nearly broken beneath her troubles.

And he'd thought he'd never feel compassion for a woman again.

Her eyes dropped, and then lifted resolutely to his. 'I was… That was appalling. I'm so sorry. You've been nothing but kind to me and you didn't deserve that. I just… It was nothing you did. Or said. It was me. My fault. And I'm really very sorry.'

The anguish in her voice spoke clearly and loudly. She was just like Oliver, who reacted on instinct and then tucked his tail between his legs and regretted it instantly. He guessed she'd been stewing on it the whole half-hour she'd been inside. Coming back out and owning that outburst must have been tough.

He had the feeling that graciousness was ingrained into her DNA. It had just been stretched too far. Everyone had a rupture point. Every protective part of him wanted to make this easier for her.

*'It's not you it's me?'* He let a small smile creep into his eyes. 'Did we just break up?'

Even saying the words made him wince. But right behind that was a kind of lightness—as if joking about break-ups disempowered the words, so that they no longer had quite as much effect on him.

That would be a well overdue novelty.

Jayne sucked a corner of her bottom lip between her teeth and then glanced up at him from under thick lashes, working hard not to give in to her amusement. But then a gentle smile broke free and it was like the sun rising over the treetops.

It warmed him clear through, to some cold spot deep inside he'd been ignoring.

'Seriously.' Those grey eyes turned earnest again as she spoke. 'Will you please accept my apology?'

'Readily accepted.' He stared a moment too long. 'Do you want to talk about it?'

Her laugh was bitter and instant. 'Nope. Not one bit.'

'Let me rephrase. I'm a good listener. Maybe it would be good for you to talk about it?'

She stared at him through enormous eyes and shook her golden head. 'I don't talk about it. It's better that way.'

'Maybe in the short term.'

Her brow furrowed in a dozen places and he knew he was on the right track. Jayne *wanted* to talk about it. She just didn't know how to.

'Have you talked about it to anyone?'

She lifted her head and the delicate shell halves of her lips opened to say something, then snapped closed again.

'Jayne?'

'Briefly.'

Snappy Jayne was back. Was that a good sign? Did it mean he was affecting her? He wanted to, even though with every shade paler her face bleached it hit him square in the gut.

'In New York,' she continued. 'Before I left.'

'And did it help?'

'Not particularly. I don't like being dissected.'

*Ah.* Someone had judged her. He knew all about that. He'd had more than his share of that during the compulsory counselling with Celeste. 'What if it wasn't about being dissected? What if I just listened?'

Enormous eyes rounded back on him. 'Why would you do that?'

'Because you're suffering. And because you'd do it for me if our situations were reversed.' A woman who took in traumatised animals wouldn't have species prejudice. She'd rescue a fellow human being, too. 'And because I'd like to help you.'

Jayne bristled. 'I'm not a charity case.'

'I'm not offering you charity. I'm offering you friendship. An ear.' Though it wouldn't be easy. He lowered his shield a hint further. 'I've been crippled with doubt myself. I recognise the signs.'

She stared, absorbing his words. 'I'm not crippled.'

'Maybe not. But you're limping heavily. I'm not offering to fix you. Just to listen. If you'd like someone to.'

She stared at him through haunted eyes and Todd knew she was going to refuse.

It was too hard for her.

She turned for the house, then twisted her face back a quarter and spoke softly. 'I'll think about it.'

# CHAPTER FOUR

*Monday*

'YOU have an amazing property,' Todd announced late the next afternoon, on his return from a long bush walk with the dogs. Two-thirds of her had longed to go with them. One-third won out.

'You're preaching to the choir.' Although he wasn't really. She barely saw the land she owned. Not outside of the first two acres.

'Do you know how many species of wildflower you have? It's a botanist's paradise.' Round-eyed wonderment took a decade off his face.

'You get excited by flora?'

'I *appreciate* flora. I get *excited* by orchids. You have seven species. Including the Swamp Orchid. I've never seen one growing wild.'

'That's nice. I guess.'

'They're an endangered species. You should register the croft.'

She laughed. 'I'd have to recognise what a croft is first.'

'I'll take you out tomorrow. Teach you what to look for.'

*Take you out.* Into the bush. Together. Alone. Jayne let her focus squirrel down deep into her belly to examine her body's reaction to that suggestion. 'Out' meant she wouldn't be 'in'.

And she spent most of her time in these days. But alone, with Todd…

She took a breath. 'Orchid appreciation is not the manliest of pastimes.'

There was nothing unmanly about the chuckle that rumbled from his chest. Or the slow smile that stole her breath. 'My interest is purely scientific.'

The butterflies massed together and liberated themselves into the air. How long had it been since she'd felt comfortable enough to joke with someone?

Jayne scraped around for distraction. 'Yesterday, you asked me to talk to you about…' She cleared her throat. 'To share with you…'

*Tsk.* She couldn't even start the discussion. How was she going to finish it? She took a deep breath. 'I don't think I can just leap in with it. And I know so little about you.'

He walked with her back towards her cosy cottage, his voice light. 'Would it help if I went first?'

Relief surged through her. She realised how much she *wanted* to talk to him, but how impossible it was to start the conversation. 'Yes. Please.'

Silent seconds ticked by.

'Did you ever play Three Things as a kid?'

She blinked at him.

'Okay, obviously an Aussie game. We played it in school. Each of us had to share three things that no one knew about us.'

He turned at the back steps and sank down onto one of them, stopping short of just marching inside. Thankfully. It was going to be hard enough to do it out here without taking it into her haven.

'Three things you don't know about me,' he began formally, his eyes burning into hers. 'Number one… I used to smoke.'

Jayne fought the twitching of her lips. 'I'm sure that had more impact when you were playing this at school.'

He shrugged. 'I gave up three years ago. Bloody hard, but I did it. Second… I talk in my sleep.'

Jayne fought the instant desire to find that out personally. She plastered a frown on her face. 'This seriously kept you amused at school? It's not exactly exposé material.'

His brows folded in with concentration. 'Okay. Number three… I'm a biologist—'

Jayne gasped in mock horror. 'Oh, the shame!'

He raised his hand and Jayne fell silent. 'I'm a biologist and I invented something. A propagation tool for native seeds.'

Jayne sat up straighter. 'Seriously? You invented it?'

'Discovered it, really. Nature invented it.'

'What is it?'

'It's a smoke-based germinant. For years science had been studying the effects of wildfire on germination. While everyone else was studying heat, I took a different path.'

Jayne forgot all about her anxiety. Her inner author immediately grew intrigued.

'Turns out one of the hundreds of enzymes in the smoke triggers germination of native seeds. It's now used in all forms of agriculture to boost seed growth.' He shrugged. 'The rest is history.'

'That's brilliant. It must have made your career.'

He shrugged. 'It was always there. Just needed someone to go looking for it.' He looked at her curiously. 'I think you're the first person to ask about my career instead of how much money it made me.'

She waved away the words like bush flies. 'Money's overrated. So why did you leave? How could you walk away from your career highlight?'

His eyes clouded over before flicking away to watch the dogs. When they returned they were carefully neutral. 'That's a fourth question. It will have to wait for another day.' Blue eyes settled on hers steadily. 'Your turn.'

Jayne opened her mouth, and shut it again when nothing came out. Her breath tightened.

'Start with something easy,' Todd encouraged.

Easy? None of this was easy. 'Umm…' She took a deep breath. 'Okay. Number one…'

Todd kept his body perfectly still, only speaking when she faltered again. 'Uh-huh…?'

'I'm allergic to shellfish. All kinds.'

His eyes didn't waver. 'Handy to know. What else?'

'Number two…' Swallowing could barely wet your throat at all when your saliva was like ash. 'Number two…' Her fingers started to twitch. Todd moved his leg so that his calf rested gently against hers. Just a hint. His reassuring warmth soaked into her numb flesh.

She met his eyes. 'I'm not a magazine writer. I write novels. Crime novels.'

His astonished eyebrows told her she'd scored a game point. 'You're a novelist?'

She nodded.

'Would I have heard of you?'

'Is this the third question?'

'Nope. This is question two-point-two. It's the price you pay for astounding me.'

Fair enough. Jayne took a deep breath. 'I write as J.C. Moro.'

That stubbled jaw nearly hit her deck. 'You wrote *Stealing Focus*?'

'You've heard of it?'

'I own it! And *Losing Focus*.' For the first time since she'd met him he looked genuinely nonplussed. 'Half the planet's waiting for your next book!'

She shrugged, but it didn't mean she felt casual. Her

pulse raced. 'It's out next month...' Her fingers picked up the pace. 'Could you please not look at me like I'm some kind of museum curiosity? It's just a job.'

He swung around and caught her rapid-fire fingers in his. 'Jayne, it's not just a job. I have your books on my bookshelf. Books you wrote. I'm completely...' his hand tightened '...impressed.'

The admiration shining from his eyes felt too good. The glow was uncomfortably welcome. But she'd felt like this before, and look where it had got her. She couldn't tell him now. Couldn't bear to see that admiration turn to pity.

She tugged her stiff fingers free. 'Okay, game's over. Looks like I've peaked too early. I have nothing left to top that.'

She surged to her feet and Todd rose quickly alongside her, halting her with a large hand on her shoulder. The heated touch pulled her full attention to where his skin met hers. 'There must be more, Jayne. Something's dragged you into the bush to lick your wounds, and it's not a glittering career in publishing. I'd like to hear it.'

She turned towards the house.

'Please?'

That one word was her undoing. *Please*. It meant he'd accept it if she walked away. But it also meant he was asking her to trust him.

She stared at him for an eternity. Her eyes drifted around the enormous timber sentinels lining her house clearing. 'Okay, but I can't talk about it out here. You'll have to come inside.'

Three dogs piled onto the large covered sofa with Jayne, who pulled her legs up in front of her. Her hand absently patted the nearest two warm bodies, the familiar movement comforting and reassuring. Almost as reassuring as Todd's silent presence on the single armchair opposite her. He hadn't spoken since she'd led him into the darkened interior of the place she felt the safest.

His presence there felt strangely right, and she wondered how she had not noticed before that there was something missing from her sanctuary. Someone missing. While she was coiled as tight as a spring he sat relaxed and patient in the half darkness, lit gently by one of her reading lamps.

'I moved here because it was about as far from my home town as anywhere could be.' The sound of her voice surprised her as the words fell from her lips without invitation. Todd nodded encouragement. 'I had...reason...to want to leave home. A man that—' she blew out a breath and it shuddered from her body '—someone that made it impossible to stay.'

One blue eye flickered. 'A man you knew?'

'No. A stranger.' She swallowed. 'A fan.' So much meaning in two tiny words.

'Your books?'

Jayne nodded. 'He...enjoyed them. He came to think he knew me through them.'

She lowered her eyes, but not before seeing Todd's fingers curl deep into the broad chair-arms. The tiny show of controlled anger bothered her and pleased her at the same time. It had been an age since anyone but she had worried about her well-being.

'Did he hurt you?'

Here it came. The judgement. 'No. He never touched me.' She dropped her head on a small sigh. 'We never actually met.'

The silence stretched out. Then Todd's quiet voice cut through it. 'You were stalked.'

She nodded again, relieved he'd said it, because then she didn't have to. In all this time she'd never used the word out aloud.

'Much worse,' he grunted.

Her damp eyes lifted to his. 'What?'

Todd sat forward on his seat, moving his blue eyes a world closer. 'I was just thinking that not meeting him must have been worse. Never being able to put a face to the voice. Never being able to picture him in your mind.'

She nodded, tears clogging her throat at his understanding. How many faces—sympathies—had shifted subtly when she got to this point in her story? It was why she'd stopped telling it.

But Todd understood. She gathered her courage and nodded. 'Wondering if he was passing me on the street. Or if every man I met was him, smugly watching while I slowly fell apart.' Her voice broke on those last words and she stopped to take in three deep breaths. 'I would much rather have faced him.'

'Who did you trust? Who did you tell?'

She fought the bite of tears. 'No one at first. Eventually the Police Department.'

'Did they find him?'

She nodded. 'But I'd moved by then. It got too much.'

'How long was this going on?'

'Two years. He just wore me down.' That shameful admission was more than her self-control could bear. Tears leaked over and ran uselessly down her hot cheeks.

Todd was on his feet in an instant, and nudged the dogs from their warm spots on her sofa. He slid one arm behind her and the other came across in front to pull her into his warm shoulder. Jayne's whole body sighed. He was as solid as a house and he smelled like crackling firewood.

She should have been frightened—should have been fighting—not soaking into him like rain into parched earth.

His gravelly words rumbled against her hair. 'I'm amazed you lasted as long as you did. You have nothing to be ashamed about.'

'It was my books…' The words forced their way out, peering out from the dark place she kept them captive.

He shifted her back to glare down at her. 'You were not responsible. It doesn't matter how many books you sold.'

'It's so hard to believe that. In here…' She pressed her frozen hand between her breasts. 'I kept wondering if I'd done things differently…'

His arm tightened around her.

She shuddered. 'He confessed. When the police interviewed him, he confessed to everything. He said he hoped going to jail for me would finally prove his devotion.'

She felt the shift in his body as he shook his head. 'How long was his sentence?'

'Twenty-eight months. But he was released six months early.' She laughed weakly. 'Good behaviour.'

Todd's whole body tensed. His words vibrated against her skin. 'He's out?'

Jayne nodded and twisted deeper into his hold. Hideously inappropriate, she was sure, but she hadn't felt this safe in a very long time. Or this warm—inside as well as out. As if nothing could touch her while these steel bands of flesh were around her. She straightened up and looked up at him. 'He doesn't know where I am. No one does. Only my agent and my parents.'

Todd smiled encouragingly and did his best to look convinced. A talented stalker would have had her location within hours. No matter where she went. Not exactly on the ranger training syllabus, but Celeste's brother was a cop and he'd heard all Danny's stories.

'You never heard from him again?'

The pause stretched interminably. 'My agent got an apology letter. I told her to burn it. I'm not interested in forgiving him. I don't want to think about him at all.' She sagged back against his arm. 'Is that wrong?'

Todd clenched his teeth on a curse. The stalker was still controlling her, even with his protestation of remorse. The best thing the jerk could do would be to move to another planet and never touch Jayne's life in any way ever again. But Todd couldn't say that. It wouldn't help her. Instead, he said, 'You do whatever you need to.'

J.C. Moro might have the world at her feet, but Jayne Morrow was a shattered woman who surrounded herself with canine protection and put ten thousand kilometres and a whole heap of forest between herself and her entire support network. Who jumped two feet off the floor if a door creaked. A woman holed up in the forest, licking some serious wounds.

The signs were everywhere now that he cared to look. The nerves. The suspicion. The way she scanned her surroundings before entering them. The dogs. The isolation. Someone else might have sought anonymity in a city crowded with witnesses. Jayne had chosen mute, blind forest. His grip tightened.

'It feels good to have told someone. Thank you for listening.' She looked up at him with a bright, blazing intensity that radiated warmth straight to his core. It dawned on him suddenly that this woman who trusted no one, trusted *him*. A vortex opened up low in his belly.

He settled her more comfortably in the silence and lifted his hand to stroke her hair. But at the last moment he hesitated and let his hand drop away. Without the heavy, horrible words saturating the air, a few other things finally penetrated his consciousness. Her closeness. Her smell. The way she felt in his arms. And the static charge that crackled around their melded bodies. He knew it immediately, although it had been some time since he'd last recognised it.

Awareness.

He locked up instantly. Those kind of feelings only went

one way, and the last time he'd indulged them he'd ended up married to a woman who didn't love him. She didn't even need him. Their blazing affair had led to a bleak, one-sided marriage that had only ended when he'd struck it rich professionally.

Jayne's small hand slid up to rest softly on his chest, directly over his heart. It was an unconscious move, he was sure, but there was no way she'd miss the wildly thumping muscle beneath. He forced himself to wait a moment before straightening slightly and shifting away. Her hand fell back to her lap and she let a bolt of her blonde hair slide down in front of her face, obscuring it from his view.

He cursed himself for his tactlessness. Just as they'd been beginning to make a connection. Now she was embarrassed. Her flaming cheeks burned with it.

She pushed up brightly. Too brightly. 'Cup of tea?'

'Jayne…'

She ignored him and marched into the small kitchen across the room.

He clenched his jaw. His fault for joining her on the sofa, but his heart had just bled for the pain and self-recrimination he'd seen in her whole body. That she could seriously hold herself responsible…

'Have you thought about going home?' He followed her into the kitchen, but took care to keep the little timber island safely between them. 'Back to your family?'

Her hair swung like strands spun from pure light. 'Not until I know it's safe.'

'For who?'

Saucer eyes lifted to his. 'For them. I couldn't live with myself if something happened to my family.'

'How would they feel if they knew you were going through all of this alone?'

She shrugged too casually. 'Who says they don't know?'

'If they knew they'd be here with you. You're protecting them.' It wasn't a question.

'Maybe I'm protecting me? One less way for him to get at me.'

'That wasn't a criticism, Jayne. Protecting is part of who you are. But the more people you tell, the more support for you.'

She spun around to face him, the half-filled kettle in her hand. 'I couldn't *tell* people!'

'You say that like you're talking about contracting a nasty disease. This is a crime. You're the victim, not an accomplice. Do you understand that?'

Her nod was too slow in coming, and he realised she didn't believe it. Not really.

His mind immediately started working on ways he could help her. Building shelters was one thing: neighbourly, in a small town. But the kind of help Jayne needed was in a whole other league. What did *he* know about what she was going through? He'd taken one psych unit at uni and had two months of pointless counselling with Celeste. That was the limit of his experience.

He took a deep breath. No, he couldn't fix her, but he could support her. Help her help herself. She put on a great show, but ultimately she didn't even convince herself. Her stalker had stolen more than just her career, her family. Her liberty. He'd damaged her self-confidence and her self-worth.

He'd broken *Jayne*. That was the thing Todd was ready to kill the guy over.

And feeling that way about a woman he'd known for four days bothered the hell out of him.

# CHAPTER FIVE

*Tuesday*

'I RAN into a young bloke out front, bringing you this. Where do you want it?'

Bright morning sunshine streamed into Jayne's kitchen, but it was the presence of Todd that really brightened things up. He carried two boxes of groceries as if they weighed no more than tissue paper. That immediately impressed her.

'Good morning.' She stood back and made a space on the bench.

'You get everything delivered?' he asked, sliding the second box down. 'When was the last time you went into the village?'

The more moments like this that they had, the more self-conscious she became about some of the choices she'd made in the past two years. It might have felt normal to get everything delivered, to buy everything online, to do all her communicating by e-mail, but it wasn't. Somehow she'd convinced herself that technology was wasted if you didn't make the most out of it. But the truth was she was just avoiding going into the township. She hadn't been in more than a year, and it was only eight kilometres away.

She hedged, frowning at herself. 'A while?'

'Mmm...'

Less than a week and she could read him already. His body language. His mannerisms. That disapproving little *mmm* sound she got *a lot*. She eyeballed him and tackled the criticism head-on. 'You think I should go in? Why?'

He looked up at her, at the end of unloading the first box of groceries. 'Just so you know you can.'

'If I wanted to, I could.'

'Uh-huh...'

'I could. Let's go right now.' She had to force her casual shrug.

Todd stared at her, his sparkling eyes particularly keen. 'How about dinner?'

Even the anxiety nibbling at her gut stopped and looked up. 'What? It's nearly lunchtime.'

'Tonight. You and me, in town. Dinner. You *do* remember dining?' His blue eyes smouldered.

Her stomach rebelled at the thought of going anywhere new at the same time as it clenched at the thought of going on a date. With Todd. 'Why?'

'Because you can. And because this way I'll be with you. Just in case.'

'In case of what?'

Todd leaned on the kitchen island. 'Come on, Jayne. It's going to be hard. I'd like to be there.'

'You want to hold my hand?'

Blue steel eyes flicked down to where her hand rested on the bench, then they slowly dragged back up. Jayne's breath caught at the whisper of unmasked expression. 'If you'd truly prefer to fly solo, I'll respect that. But everyone needs a little hand-holding now and again.' He waggled his eyebrows. It was alarmingly cute. 'Whaddaya say?'

She'd swaggered herself square into a corner. She swallowed. 'Okay. Dinner. But not too long. I've never left the dogs home alone.' *I haven't left the house in months!*

Todd smiled. 'Understood.'

Jayne worked herself up into quite a state in the short time Todd was away. It wasn't that getting dressed up—as dressed up as she came—wasn't a thrill. But the novelty simply didn't last long enough to excise the nerves she could feel, even now.

All the dogs regarded her suspiciously, grudgingly, even though they couldn't possibly recognise the signs of her getting ready to leave the property—they'd never seen them.

Jayne rested her hands on her hips and sucked in several deep, slow breaths. It helped a little. She rubbed clammy fingers together to warm them, terrified that Todd might have been serious about the hand-holding and that sliding hers into his big, warm, dry ones would be like slapping a cold wet fish into his palm.

Ridiculous. There would be no hand-holding. He just wanted to help her get out. To make it easier. And it would. Him just being there would be a bonus.

Being distractingly rugged didn't hurt either. In the past twenty-four hours Jayne had caught herself appreciating the way his overgrown hair fell across his forehead into his eyes when he was concentrating on measuring something. The way his lips were a last bastion before giving way to his heart-stopping smile. The crinkles in the corners of his blue, blue eyes that said he knew how to laugh.

Suddenly she wanted to know who he'd been laughing with and how she could get him to do it with her.

*Ridiculous!* It had been a long time since she'd been around a man, and even longer since she'd been attracted to one. She'd been progressively more isolated since she'd first hit the big time with her books.

She frowned. But that meant she'd started closing herself off *before* the stalking...

A loud rapping at the door followed immediately by an explosion of dog barking yanked her roughly from her thoughts, and her heart flipped instantly from anxiety to anticipation. Beating just as hard but for a very different reason.

She smoothed down her simple dress and pulled the front door open.

Todd raised his eyebrows pointedly. 'Who is it?' he mocked, since she hadn't thought to ask. Possibly a first.

Jayne smiled slowly. 'If it wasn't you the dogs' tails wouldn't have been wagging.'

'Fair enough.' His shoulder-shrug drew her eye immediately to the light jacket he wore, the white open-necked shirt beneath it and the deep tan beneath that. The man sure did a blazer justice. She'd have felt bad for ogling if not for the fact that his eyes were measuring her up the same way, his smile slow and lazy.

'For a woman who doesn't like to attract attention, you certainly know how to dress.'

Something about the combination of Todd's delicious accent, the suit and the stare made his casual reference to her past two years almost like flirting. It forced her fears into context. Much more than if he'd been carefully tiptoeing around the subject.

'Thank you. I think.' She laughed again. How easily it came when he was around.

He looked down at her. 'Ready to go?'

The question meant so much more than whether she had her handbag and keys. She looked past him to where his sedan sat at her gate. Her sweet, familiar, safe little gate.

Her heart started to thump.

Was she ready? She wanted to be. Desperately. She longed to be normal again. To live a full life instead of her sheltered existence. But wanting and doing weren't always the same thing.

*Thump…thump…thump…*

She followed Todd's broad back down her front steps towards his car, and the sound of her rushing blood expanded to fill her ears.

*You can do this, Jayne.*

She kept walking, her eyes glued firmly to the breadth of Todd's shoulders. Remembering how his arms felt around her. How he smelled.

*It's only town.* She remembered Banjo's Ridge from her ride as she'd first passed through on arrival in Australia. A pretty, friendly little hamlet. Barely peopled. Todd stopped at the passenger side of his car and opened the door, watching her closely. Her breath came heavily now, not quite steady. She went to step forward.

'I can't…'

The admission broke out of her and she turned and hurried stiffly back to the house, tears springing into her eyes. Sensation rushed back in with the adrenaline. Disappointment at herself. Fury at the anonymous creep who'd started all of this. Anger at Todd for witnessing her humiliation in Technicolor surroundsound.

'Why couldn't you just leave well enough alone?' she ground out as he followed her up the steps. 'I was doing fine. *We* were doing fine.' She shoved through the front door, ignoring the delighted welcome of her dogs and rejecting Todd's gentle aid. She didn't want gentle right now. She wanted to be mad.

Being mad helped.

She sank down on the sofa and let her hands cover her face. Todd sank down next to her and waited. Silently.

'I hate this,' she finally said, muffled behind her hands, then lifted her face and stared at him. 'I hate being so weak.

It's not *me*. I used to walk out onto live television stages with nothing more than damp palms. I've met the President!'

'What makes going into town different?'

She stared at him, at a loss to explain.

He took her hand. 'He's not in Banjo's Ridge. He's not even in Australia. So what is it you're scared of?' His thumbs stroked circles on her flesh.

She ground her teeth and stared at him through stinging eyes. Deep down, she *did* know that. 'I'm afraid of how it feels. Of what it does to me. Of what it means.' She leaned into Todd as he moved his hand to stroke her damp hair away from her face. Then she looked up at him. 'I'm afraid of being like this for ever.'

The only sound in the room was six sets of lungs breathing heavily.

'Do you trust me, Jayne?'

She did, God help her. She only had to look at him for her whole body to relax.

He smiled. 'I have a Plan B. How do you feel about fish and chips by the river? Just you and me. And the dogs. No shellfish.'

Jayne shook her head, not understanding. 'The dogs?'

'Sure. They've earned an outing. We all have.'

Jayne let her eyes drift to the four anxious sets of eyes lined up across the living room. They were mortified by her outburst. Ollie trembled violently.

'Oh...' She opened her arms and all four ran in. That triggered another rush of tears. She lifted her eyes back to Todd's as soon as they'd all settled. 'The dogs will be there?'

'Yep.'

'And you'll be there?'

There was the slightest pause before he answered. 'Yep.'

She stared around her house, then out to the car, then back

at the patient man beside her, who was being so very gentle. Her heart thumped again—but nothing like earlier. 'Okay.'

It felt as if something significant had shifted in her universe. She reached out to steady herself on the sofa top. Then she smiled. It was watery, and not very big, but it was genuine. 'Okay. But I should change if we're going to the river.'

'Don't change,' Todd said quietly, his eyes blazing. 'I'd like it if you'd wear that dress.' Their gazes locked together and all thoughts of anxiety fled at the intensity in his eyes. 'Please, Jayne.'

A deep fluttering bloomed in her chest. Her belly. Heat soaked through her.

And in that moment, despite what had just happened, she truly felt normal.

Sharing a car with four excited, gassy dogs had a way of taking your mind off your troubles. Jayne laughed herself to tears as Todd exclaimed loudly after every infraction and wound his window down, sputtering dramatically. Having them along was a priceless kindness. Not only for the moral support as she trudged so definitely out of her comfort zone, but also for the first-class distraction from what would otherwise have felt very much like an awkward first date.

Both made her equally nervous.

'For crying out loud, it's like a symphony back there!' he admonished the unrepentant and oblivious dogs. They wagged delighted tails, which only served to fan the problem forward.

Jayne added her protests to Todd's loud ones.

'Saved by the bell!' Todd dropped his speed and swung his car left as they passed into the town limits and pulled up in front of a harmless-looking café with a gaudy fish on its roof. The neon blinked in almost perfect synch with Jayne's slow-pounding heart. She took a deep, controlling breath.

*I am stronger than 'it'…*

Todd killed the engine. 'Okay…' He turned to her and handed her the keys. She stared at them wordlessly. 'If anything happens that makes you feel frightened or uncomfortable, start the car and drive yourself home.'

'I can't abandon you on the side of the road, Todd!' She laughed half-heartedly, although deep down she feared she would do exactly that if push came to shove.

'I'll follow on afterwards if I have to. Besides, my house is just around the corner.'

That was a thoroughly distracting thought. She'd not let herself imagine what kind of house he lived in. Or who with. Suddenly the question loomed large in her mind. It shouldered some of the anxiety out of the limelight. Here she was, having all kinds of thoughts—feelings—about Banjo's Ridge's Ranger, and he might have a wife and kids at home. Not all men wore a ring. What if she was the only one thinking this was a quasi-date?

*Trust…trust…*

'Nothing's going to happen…' She faked bravado.

'That's what I'm counting on. But I want you to feel like you can drive away if you need to.'

Her voice clogged up with emotion. 'Thank you. That's very kind.'

'Trust me, there's nothing kind about leaving a woman locked in a sealed car with the Banjo's Ridge Symphonic Quartet for company.' He glanced at the happy dogs in the back seat. 'I'll be five minutes. I ordered ahead, so I only need to pick up and pay.'

She scrabbled for her purse. 'I should pay! You've done so much.'

'No. This one's on me. You can buy the next one. Lock the doors.' With that he was off, briskly walking towards the fish and chip shop. She activated the central locking and tried very hard not to ogle the denim-clad rear walking away from her. It set a bad example for the dogs.

'Never do this,' she told them, not taking her eyes off Todd until he turned into the doorway of the shop.

*You can buy the next one.* It sounded so comfortable on his lips. As if he really thought there would be a next time. Contemplating both those things took her mind off her worries for about twenty-five seconds. Twenty-five blissful seconds before she remembered where she was and how exposed she was.

Another deep breath...

Four doggie heads swung to the left at once, as someone passed by the car closely on that side on the footpath. Jayne's heart cramped. The pedestrian continued past and turned into the same shop Todd had gone into, entirely unaware of the tumult his presence had caused. Jayne waited just a second before deciding. She scrambled over the centre console and settled into the driver's seat. It smelled and felt like Todd. Her tension instantly eased back.

Then two little octopus hands slapped onto the glass of the window, immediately over her right shoulder, and all four dogs decamped their positions and leapt around, pressing their noses to the small child's that squished against the window from outside.

'Doggie!' the urchin exclaimed, muffled against the glass.

Only the fact that the dogs were *excited* by the arrival of the mystery child kept Jayne from shrieking aloud. But she gasped, and slipped the keys into the ignition for good measure. Which freed her right fingers to start doing their counting thing.

*Oh, dear...*

A woman about Jayne's age peeled her child off the car with a half-smile, half-grimace and a mouthed apology. Jayne forced herself to smile back and wave trembling fingers at the disappearing pair, as though the incident hadn't nearly suspended the function of her heart. The woman with the child looked friendly. She had an overly large smile designed for long, lazy chats with lots of laughter. The squeeze in Jayne's chest turned to a pang.

How she missed long, lazy chats with girlfriends…

Todd appeared at the door to the café and moved towards the car, carrying a steaming paper parcel. Halfway back his eyes found her, perched stiffly in the driver's seat. He altered his trajectory effortlessly.

Jayne popped the locks.

'Looks like you're driving, then!' He slid into the front passenger seat.

It was all he said—the only reference to her horribly dysfunctional behaviour. Jayne blinked at him for seconds, and then interrupted the nervous twitching of her fingers to start the car when he did nothing more than settle himself in and pull his seatbelt on.

She'd just survived her first trip to Banjo's Ridge.

'I'm in town.'

He smiled. 'I know.'

Hers widened to rival that of the lady with the child. 'I mean, *I'm in town.*'

Todd laughed. 'Yes, I know. Are you planning on staying here all night?'

She matched his laugh and pulled away from the kerb. She couldn't help looking at him several times as they drove off into the evening light. He looked entirely unconcerned by the turn of events. Not quite the same as thinking her behaviour was *normal*, but Todd clearly didn't think it was disturbingly *abnormal*. Knowing he accepted it went a long way to helping her accept it.

'Can we go past your house?' It was his turn to look at her. Jayne faltered. 'I'd like to see where you live.'

*I'd like to see if there are children's toys on the front lawn, or a second car in the drive.*

She realised how little she actually knew about him. Other than what he'd told her. 'Sorry. Is that creepy?' It did smack just the tiniest bit of her psychotic follower.

Todd laughed. 'Only marginally. Let's go.'

Not only were there no extra cars and no well-used swings or battered toy firetrucks on the lawn at Number 3 Wollemi Road, there really wasn't much about the whole house that told her anyone lived there. It reeked of rural rental. And of bachelor.

Why his marital status should be of such cosmic importance all of a sudden was a mystery. It wasn't as if tonight was a *date*-date or anything. It wasn't as if it was going to lead to anything.

Jayne frowned silently. But her expression caught his attention.

'You don't like it?'

'I...' *Oh, what to say...?* 'It doesn't seem very you.'

He considered that, and shifted the hot food parcel on his lap. 'It's not. It's just a place I put my head at night.'

'How long have you lived there?'

'About a year. Since I arrived from Western Australia.'

'You haven't wanted to spruce it up a bit? Make it more comfortable?'

He shrugged. 'I don't need a lot. I'm enjoying a more simple existence these days. The next house I live in will be one I've built myself. Or at least improved myself. There's something very rewarding about working with your hands. Constructing things.'

He turned to her as the car idled. 'For me, building my own place would be really therapeutic—kind of healing.'

She opened her mouth to ask him what he needed to heal from, but he held up the fragrant food parcel in his lap.

'We'd better get moving—unless you're partial to cold, soggy, fish and chips?'

She put the car into gear and slowly pulled away from his sterile, soulless rental as he directed her towards the river.

It took a good twenty minutes before Jayne felt the stiffness in her body start to ease. Her eyes scanned the roadway approaching the riverside for a last time, before finally skidding to a halt on Todd's steady blue ones.

'There you are.' His smile was as soft and calm as his voice. 'Welcome back.'

Jayne knew she'd been absent since they got out of the car. Todd had kept up a steady stream of non-challenging conversation—a monologue, really, because her distracted responses didn't really qualify as discussion—along with a steady supply of potato wedges from the brown paper parcel that was their supper.

She'd tasted the delectable saltiness, the lemony lightness of the beer batter and, somewhere down deep, had delighted in it. But until this moment her priority had been scanning up and down the riverbank, across the river, out on the road.

Survival beat pleasure in the game of psychological rock-paper-scissors.

But now something had shifted. Something to do with the steady reliability of Todd's eyes. The closeness of his body. His sheer presence. The steady vigilance with which he watched her and everything around her.

Her relief rushed out on a single breathy word. 'Hi.'

'Food's pretty cold, I'm afraid.'

She couldn't rip her eyes from his if she tried. It would be like surrendering a lifebuoy at sea. 'I don't care. It's amazing.'

He seemed in no hurry to break the contact. The corner of each eye crinkled. 'Fish and chips is amazing?'

Jayne smiled. 'The food. The river. Being here. Being *out*.'

*Being with you.* Her laugh bounced off the glassy river and ricocheted off the other bank. Her eyes fell to his lips as he popped another chip in and spoke.

'You could have come here any time.'

Her shaggy blonde hair blew lightly in the breeze as she shook her head. 'No. I really couldn't have. Thank you for helping me.'

'It was our pleasure.'

*The dogs!* That sent her gaze searching for her four-legged family, although it meant leaving Todd's warm regard behind. She twisted until she found them, stretched out on the grass nearby, communally tethered to a small sapling tree.

She flopped back onto the earth next to Todd and stared at the sky that would soon change from electric blue to mauve with the sunset. 'It's so beautiful from here.'

'Same sky at your house,' he murmured, lying next to her and following her gaze upward. 'And in Pennsylvania.'

She tipped her head sideways to look at him. 'Actually, I'm not sure that's technically true, but I get your point. Somehow from my house it doesn't seem so vast. It makes my own problems seem insignificant.'

Todd looked at her. 'They're not insignificant, Jayne. But you've been handling them. He hasn't beaten you.'

Jayne scoffed. 'You've done more to help me in five days than I've managed to achieve in two years.'

He frowned. 'I've done nothing but intrude on your privacy and then pester you into coming out with me. Hardly sterling work.'

She sat up and stared earnestly at him. 'I'm outdoors, Todd.

I'm not sure you understand how monumental that is. The last time I was on this side of my property line I was moving in.'

'That's my point. *You've* done it. You drove yourself here today, Jayne. I'm merely keeping you company. Give yourself some credit.'

Jayne frowned. He was determined to play down his role. She swung around to face him, determined he should recognise the significance of what he'd done for her. 'I'm here because of you, Todd. I went to the village because of *you*. A complete stranger peered into the car and I didn't freak out because of *you*.'

Gratitude washed through her, a warm and tingly force. '*You* are the reason I did all of those things. Thank you.'

Before she thought about what a risk she was taking, she leaned forward and pressed her lips to his still salty ones. It was an awkward, bumpy kind of kiss, and it caught him enough by surprise that her weight pushed him easily back onto his elbows, sending her tumbling half across him. She slowed the crash with two hands on his broad, warm chest.

His heart thundered beneath her palms. His blue eyes flared wide. Jayne froze, waiting for him to make the next move. Three painful, silent seconds went by, then five, and finally she realised Todd was not going to pull her passionately into his arms and roll her into the dirt like a scene from a film. Her gut twisted.

Had she really expected it?

Her pride screamed at her to scramble off, to run off into the trees and hide from the awful reality she could see in his carefully vacant expression. But, despite everything she'd done in the past two years, she'd never been an *emotional* coward. Running from him would solve nothing. And he deserved better.

Todd's eyes changed as he watched the thoughts play out on her face, until they finally settled on an expression of abject, unadulterated pity. The twist in her gut became an inner cramp. She pushed away clumsily.

His hand shot out to snare one of her wrists and keep her close. 'Jayne—'

She tugged harder, but he held on. She should have been panicking, but all she could feel was embarrassment. How ironic that the first *normal* reaction she had to another person was unreciprocated. She tried harder to straighten up. To get off him.

He grabbed her other wrist and pulled them together against his chest. He drew her face back to his and moved them both up to sit. 'Jayne, look at me.'

His rough fingers stroked her jaw—a slight analgesic against the pain of having got it all so horribly, horribly wrong. She lifted her gaze to his.

'I could kiss you now,' he said, eyes shining. 'I could have kissed you a dozen times over the last forty-eight hours if my own needs were all I was worrying about.'

Those blue eyes pierced her skin and burrowed down to soul level. 'I just wanted to thank you...'

His laugh wasn't amused. 'If you kiss me, I want it to be because you can't help yourself. Not because you're grateful.'

The tiniest flash of hurt decorated his high cheekbones. Jayne pressed her lips together and sagged back onto her haunches. Put like that, it wasn't really unreasonable. 'I'm sorry. This is all so... I feel like I'm fifteen again—all these different feelings running amok in my body. I don't know why.'

He laughed. 'It's called attraction, Jayne...'

She stared at him, shocked at his honesty. Then she smiled. 'Just my luck. A second crack at puberty.'

He kept his eyes locked firmly on hers. 'Trust me with what you're feeling.'

She weighed that up for a bit. 'Euphoric. Alarmed. Excited. Confused. Delighted.'

*Aroused*. But she wasn't going there. 'Like being in a wild-running river and I'm just tumbling along, trying to keep my head above the surface.'

Acknowledging this forced her attention to the way a thousand thoughts and images coursed like transfused blood through her body. Distracting. Confusing. Some good, some bad. Most of them featuring Todd.

'Is it possible to feel crowded and exposed at the same time?'

Apparently it was.

Her right thumb touched her pinkie finger and then skipped straight on to the next three fingers in sequence before starting over. The ritual forced some space between the clamouring feelings. Todd slipped his hand out, down her arm, and closed it around hers. His fingers threaded through her busy ones. Heat soaked into her hand and he ran gentle circles across her skin. Stopping her fingers in full flight wasn't easy. For her.

For him it seemed it was just a question of a squeeze.

'I don't like being such a novelty to you,' she whispered.

'Everything you do is novel to me—and not because of this...' His long fingers closed more securely around hers. She felt instantly rooted to the ground. 'Because you are unique. I've never met anyone quite like you.'

She laughed—a short, sharp bark. Jazmine echoed it, then settled back down in the grass again. 'I bet you haven't,' she snorted.

'Don't do that.'

She knew what he meant. And she knew exactly what she was doing. Still, her face must have asked the question.

'Don't put yourself down,' he clarified.

She stared at him and sighed. 'After the first few people

thought I was making too much of my stalking I learned to get in first—to have a crack at myself. It seemed to get them more on side.'

'Inviting them to ridicule you?'

She stared at him, heat rising. But she had to be honest. 'Excusing it.'

He let that one sink in, and Jayne realised what a terrible thing it was she'd done. 'I just wanted to protect myself.'

'I understand the urge.' Again, no judgement.

Todd lifted her fingers to his lips and kissed them briefly, then pulled on them, dragging her to her feet. 'Come on. Let's make the most of this outing. The dogs could use a run.'

'Dougal, keep up.'

The small terrier kept dashing off into the bush after rabbits, but emerged moments later to rejoin his pack as they strolled along the riverbank. All four dogs revelled in discovering their new environment, but stayed close to Jayne—and she called them back if they strayed too far. Todd chatted quietly about his smoke discovery, about how it had revolutionised agricultural propagation. Jayne found every word fascinating. She'd grown so out of touch with the outside world.

'So you're rich, then?'

He looked at her through narrow eyes. 'Planning a takeover?'

Jayne joined his laugh, and it felt fabulous. She tossed her head back and met his eyes brazenly. 'Guarantee you I'm richer.'

His scoff was as good as a caress. 'Do you know what the Australian agriculture industry is worth? This economy has grown to one be of the strongest in the world on sheep and crops.'

She countered. 'Do you have any idea how many books

you have to sell to top the *New York Times* bestseller list for eighteen weeks?'

Todd glared, then smiled. 'I'll show you mine if you show me yours...'

As teasing went, it was sexy as all heck. Jayne burst out a laugh and glanced behind her to call Dougal back from his most recent sojourn into the bush that lined the river. 'I can't believe we're arguing over who has the most money when both of us live like paupers.'

'I'd happily give it all back...'

Jayne caught the shadow that came into his eyes. The awkwardness that had flared between them earlier faded in the presence of his pain. She put her arm on his and stopped him. 'Tell me.'

Todd looked away into the deep forest. 'It's nothing...'

*Nothing compared to your troubles.* It practically flashed in neon with the force of his not saying it. She squeezed his arm. 'Someone once did me the favour of just listening while I shared my toughest feelings. I'd like to return the favour.'

He stared at her hard, then took her hands in his. 'I have a wife, Jayne.'

The bottom of her stomach—her world—dropped clean away, taking her breath with it. But then her mind flashed back to that very lonely driveway, the curtainless windows, and her fear retreated. She forced herself to remain calm. She believed in Todd...

'Where is she?' she whispered.

'This month? Who knows? We separated thirteen months ago.'

*Tell me about it.* She hoped her patient gaze spoke for her.

Todd groaned, and then started them walking again. 'Celeste and I married young. "Hasty and ill-advised" was the final opinion of the counsellor the courts made us see. You'd think nine years would be enough to get us past that.'

'What happened?'

He was silent for a moment, as if ordering his thoughts. 'I like to blame the money.' He called Dougal back from the trees and bent to pat him when he came. 'But the truth is we were doomed from the start. Celeste was...celestial...' He laughed, but not with humour. 'She lit up any room and I was entranced. Trapping her in the suburbs was like trying to keep a comet in a jar.'

'Nine years is a long time to let yourself be trapped.'

'Celeste was easily distracted. I tried to let her have her head. Let her go to the parties. Let her go travelling. Fed that need.'

'*Let* her?'

Todd looked at her. 'I didn't challenge her. She may not have had personal strength, but she was stubborn and easily influenced by those around her.'

Jayne allowed her hand to tangle its way into his. It felt right to touch him. They walked like that in silence for a few moments.

'When the money came in she had expectations. A bigger house. A jet-setting lifestyle. She didn't take...disappointment well.'

'You didn't want any of that?'

'I never did. Still don't. I like the life I'm living now. Simple. Honest. A reasonable dollar for an honest day's work.'

Jayne recognised the feeling. The absurd amount building up in her bank account still overwhelmed her. Although it *had* saved her when she'd needed saving. 'What finally happened?'

Todd stared at her hard. 'She left. I didn't stop her. The end.'

There was more to that story. 'She left all that money? Hard to imagine.'

His eyes dropped, then lifted back to hers with more humour than she'd thought she'd see at that moment. 'She's suing me for it as we speak. And spending it already. Barbados. Spain. Paris. New York.'

'She must be confident.'

He shrugged. 'She knows me well.'

Jayne bristled at the thought that someone other than her should get to share Todd's thoughts, his space, his secrets. Ridiculous… She'd only known him five days. She sighed. 'Why do bad things happen to good people?'

Todd looked at her—hard. 'Maybe because we're equipped to deal with it? Look at us. We've both survived.'

For the first time Jayne saw the past few years from the outside. She *had* survived. Sure, it had been a dark, lonely and painful journey, and she'd grown accustomed to the feeling of being a stranger in her own body, but she'd come further than some stalking survivors she'd read about. People who still sheltered deep inside themselves, paralysed by fear. She'd built a new life, just as Todd had. Different from the one she'd had before, but just as good. Possibly better in some ways.

If you discounted the isolation.

'Dougal.' She called the smallest dog to her again, then twisted when he didn't appear. 'Dougal—come!' All three of the other dogs stopped and looked back to where he'd last been. Ollie's hackles rose as he sensed Jayne's sudden anxiety.

'Dougal!' Todd called, adding his booming voice to Jayne's.

*Nothing.* She looked at him urgently.

'Don't panic. He's probably just on the trail of something— not paying attention. Give him a minute.'

*Don't panic.* As if she had any control over that. She clenched her twitching fist.

They continued to call, and then backtracked to the spot

they'd last seen him. A minute passed, several minutes, and the little terrier was still a no-show.

'Can he swim, Jayne?'

*The river...* But wait. 'Yes...I've seen him swim in the dam.' But he was hopeless in so many other ways when it came to the bush.

'So he's in the trees. I'll go after him.' Todd glanced at the sinking sun, and then at Jayne's strappy sandals and bare legs. 'Wait here. Search the banks. Keep calling.' He turned towards the bush. 'Ollie, come.'

And then he was gone, taking the big black dog with him.

Jayne stood rooted to the spot, alone and in a strange place. Her heart pounded painfully, like in the bad old days. She concentrated on forcing the fear back down.

*Dougal needs you.*

She called Jazmine and Fergus to her side. Why hadn't she thrown vanity aside and just worn jeans? Then she could be with Todd instead of out here alone. *Because you wanted to look pretty for him.*

'Dougal! Come on, pup!' She turned and started walking up the riverbank, calling as she went, steadfastly ignoring how cool it was suddenly getting.

'Todd will find him. Todd will find him.'

The verbal mantra helped as much as the repetitive movements of her fingers. She clenched her hand shut and willed the fingers to be still, dragging the memory of Todd's hand closing over hers for extra ammunition. It worked.

If she let them start, they'd never stop. And she couldn't lose it out here alone.

She just couldn't.

She must have searched five kilometres up the river and back again over the next hour. Her blistered feet felt every step.

But her steps faltered as she came back around the bend and found a dozen people gathered near Todd's car. In the middle of the throng Todd stood, giving instructions. Ollie spied her and sprinted towards her.

*No Dougal.*

One of the gathered throng nudged Todd, and he looked her way then spoke quietly to the group and turned to walk towards her.

Between thumping heartbeats, Jayne vaguely recognised a few faces. The man who had been bringing her post every day for two years but whose name she still didn't know. The lady whose child had pressed her nose to their car earlier this evening. Ten others she didn't know.

'I've called in the cavalry.' Todd's serious eyes said that he knew this would be hard for her.

Jayne swallowed. What could she say? Then she cast her eyes for the hundredth time into the shadowy threat of the trees. Dougal was the youngest. The smallest. The least experienced.

'He'll be down a wombat burrow,' a red-cheeked man declared with confidence.

'It's the panther,' another announced with utter certainty.

Todd glared at that man meaningfully. 'It's not the panther, Tom. Don't start with the conspiracy theories.'

*Panther?* Her heart-rate spiked. 'There's a wild cat loose?'

Todd turned to her. 'No, there's not, Jayne. There's no evidence of that at all.'

Tom muttered under his breath. 'You weren't singing that tune when you were measuring that paw-print in my lower paddock, lad.'

'Maybe it was a pelican?' a woman with a well-worn face helpfully volunteered. 'I saw one on the coast pick up a Chihuahua once...'

Jayne didn't know what to say to that.

Todd swept in and spoke for her. 'Thanks for giving us a couple of hours, folks. We're looking for a Fox Terrier cross, about the size and colour of this one.' He indicated Jazmine, who tucked her tail between her legs at suddenly being the centre of attention. Jayne sympathised entirely, and tightened her hold on her collar. She looked around, amazed. A group this size would only turn out for a lost child, surely? Not a dog belonging to a total stranger.

'My primary concern is 1080,' Todd went on. 'If he's wandered out of the river valley into the National Park.'

'1080?' *Was that ranger code for something?*

'It's a poison, Jayne. The Park is baited with it to control the foxes.' He frowned. 'It would be deadly to a dog Dougal's size.'

Her eyes instantly watered. Todd scooped her forward. Twenty-four eyes locked firmly on her. 'This gives me an opportunity to introduce you all to Jayne Morrow, who lives out on the south ridge. Jayne, this is…half of Banjo's Ridge.'

The mob chuckled. Even Jayne wasn't convinced by the pathetic smile she drummed up. If she'd had a tail it would be between her legs, like Jaz's.

Todd leaned over and whispered in her ear. 'Say something.'

*What?* 'I can't,' she whispered back furiously.

'Just something to rally the troops. They've all come to help you.'

'They've all come to stare at the freak,' she hissed back. And they were certainly staring hard enough. But if they helped her find Dougal…

She felt Todd's reassuring strength pressing against her from behind. Jaz anchored her to the earth, too. She lifted her voice. 'Um…Thank you for coming out. Dougal is one quarter of my Australian family. He's been with me since I first arrived in Banjo's Ridge and I…' She lost her confidence, but then Todd's hands slid down her arms and captured the cold fingers of her free hand where it hid behind her back. She held on for dear life. 'He's not much of a working dog, so he probably wouldn't have value to anyone else, I know. But he's an important part of my family and I really would like to make sure he's safe.'

That was more words than she'd spoken to strangers in her whole time in Australia. They all looked a bit shocked she could speak at all—maybe in the town legends she was a mute?—but her simple words seemed to galvanise them. They immediately shifted into action, splitting into pairs, swapping mobile phone numbers. Todd drew a hasty map in the dirt and split the land around them into quadrants.

'We'll lose light in ninety minutes. Just do what you can in that time. Dougal's a bit gun-shy, but he's a good sort and he'll come to you if you're gentle enough.'

Todd's eyes strayed to Jayne just then, and she had the sudden suspicion he was talking about more than just the dog. His voice dropped. 'Jayne? Shannon is going to stay with you and recheck the banks. Will that be okay? I should do one of the quadrants.'

Jayne glanced at the friendly face from earlier in the evening. What choice did she have? She could hardly go crashing into the bush in a loose dress and strappy sandals, and she could hardly expect everyone else to be looking while she and Todd took a leisurely stroll down the riverfront.

She folded her fingers painfully into a fist and smiled to reassure Shannon. 'Sure. Good luck.'

Todd stepped towards her briefly. His left hand wrapped around her white-knuckled grip on Jazmine's collar and pried her icy fingers loose. His right hand slipped behind her head. His lips pressed briefly, hotly, against her clammy forehead.

'Good girl,' he murmured, before jogging off, Ollie in hot pursuit. And then he was gone.

Jayne turned to an expectant Shannon and smiled tightly, entirely at a loss as to what to say. She must have looked as lost as she felt, because Shannon went straight into mother-mode. '*Tsk*. Look at your feet—they're bled raw.'

Jayne glanced down and grimaced. Shannon's description was very apt. Several of her blisters had burst and were bleeding all over her strappy sandals.

Minutes later Jayne found herself sitting up on the bonnet of Todd's car while Shannon used a full packet of Band-Aids to turn her feet into something from a museum sarcophagus.

'That should hold you,' she pronounced, satisfied, and then snapped the first aid kit shut. She looked around at their canine company. 'I should have brought Emily. She would have loved walking with the dogs.'

They turned together and headed up-river, back the way Jayne had come, and Shannon stuck firmly to the one thing that Jayne could actually talk about without difficulty. Her dogs. Shannon was easy company, undemanding and entertaining, and Jayne felt herself relaxing far more than she would ever have expected given her anxiety about Dougal.

Her anxiety about everything.

So much so that when Shannon indulged her secret passion for Hollywood gossip, Jayne didn't hesitate to tell her where she hailed from.

For the first time in two years she found herself talking about the outside world. For the first time she found herself talking about New York.

# CHAPTER SIX

*Wednesday*

'What do we do now?'

The last of the searchers reversed out of the car park, head-lights slashing brightly through the darkness and throwing a moment of light onto Todd's pensive face. 'I guess we go home.'

'We can't leave. What if he comes back?'

'It's already past midnight, we can't stay here all night, Jayne.'

'Why not? We can wait in the car. In case he comes back.' She grabbed Todd's arm urgently. 'I couldn't stand the thought that he might find his way back and we're not here. I may never see him again.'

Jazmine and Fergus were already in the car, curled up asleep on the front and passenger seats.

Todd glanced at her and clutched at his coat. 'Okay, we'll stay for a bit. But not all night. Let's play it by ear. Even in the car I think we'll get cold.'

Moments later they were all loaded again in Todd's four-by-four. Jayne followed Todd into the vacant back seat and closed out the cold with a click of the door behind them. Ollie took up position high in the rear window.

'Oh, this is so much better,' she said, rubbing her icy skin.

Todd slid off his jacket and leaned forward to drape it across her. Its latent warmth soaked into her. Its smell seduced her. Then they fell to silence. It should have been awkward, but it wasn't. Jayne shifted in her seat, twisted her sandals off and let herself sink more comfortably into the fabric.

Todd glanced down at her feet, then caught one up and dragged it gently onto his lap, twisting her towards him. His touch warmed her far more than his jacket as he began to rub between the swathe of Band-Aids.

'Some advanced civilisation is going to find your perfectly preserved toes in two thousand years,' he said, pressing his large thumb up the arch of her aching feet, 'and think that twenty-first-century man honoured his dead by mummifying their feet.'

She was too cold and too tired and too worried about Dougal not to accept the gift of laughter. It tumbled out as a half-laugh, half-sigh in response to the heavenly pressure of his hands on her sore flesh. 'Do you think the blisters will still be there then?'

He smiled and rubbed harder. Higher. Deep into the curve of her Achilles. She sighed and let herself relax fully back into the door of the car. It probably wasn't appropriate— but then neither was spending the night squished into a car with someone she'd known less than a week. That thought made her open her eyes. 'Why would they help me? All those people? They don't know me.'

He shrugged. He rubbed. 'Country people help each other out in difficult times.'

'I wouldn't have thought a lost dog counted as difficult times around here.'

'Well...I asked them.'

*Ah*, now they were getting to the truth of it. 'And they just came? They must think highly of you.'

'I've done as much for most of them. It's what we do around here.'

She stared at him for long moments. 'Thank you. Even though I think half of them were here to get a look at the town hermit, and even though we didn't find Dougal, I appreciate that you tried. That they tried.'

Todd gestured for her other foot. 'You're welcome.'

His hard strokes gradually grew softer, higher, taking in her ankle, part of her calf. Slow, steady, heavenly strokes. The silence between them was pure gold. Jayne realised how long it had been since someone had touched her. Emotionally *and* physically.

'You did well tonight,' he murmured slowly, his heavy eyes lifting to her and then dropping back down to his handiwork.

The praise wheedled its way deep inside her, touching a part of her that she'd long forgotten. The part that had used to want to do well for her parents. Her publisher. The part that cared what someone else thought and whether they were proud of her. When had she stopped caring what others thought? The day she'd started *fearing* what others thought?

Todd's gaze earlier had brimmed over with certainty that she could handle being with so many strangers. He'd believed in *her*, damn him. And in that split-second she realised exactly how much she wanted to earn that bright, blazing confidence.

And why.

Some time in the past few days her feelings for her gallant knight had swollen from gratitude to something more. A whole lot more.

Her heart began to thump—heavy and hard.

'My third book releases next month.' she blabbed in urgent diversion. 'They want me to do a promo tour.'

His surprised glance reminded her of the ludicrousness of that concept. The woman who could barely face the postman? Except that she *had* just faced him. Even *met* him. And she was no worse for it.

'Great.' He went on, 'When do you leave?'

'Ha ha.' She gave him an arch stare, then sighed. 'Publicity is a condition of my contract. I signed it before the—' She sucked in a huge breath. 'If I don't go, I'm in breach.'

'Then what happens?'

'No more books. That's what happens.'

His magic hands started kneading the tight muscles of her calf. 'Your publisher doesn't know about your stalker?'

She shook her head. That could hardly surprise him. She hadn't even told her family.

'How long can you live on your earnings?'

'If I'm frugal?' She shrugged. 'For ever.'

His hands stilled, then he turned them and let the broad backs slide smoothly over her skin. They left an invisible trail of tingles in their wake. 'There you go, then. Break the contract. Live on your savings for the rest of your life.'

She looked at him. 'I thought you'd tell me that was a cop out.'

He shrugged. 'You don't need the money...'

'I like to write.'

'You can write. You just won't get published.'

'I like people to read my books.'

'Then publish on the internet.'

Jayne frowned. Dropped her eyes.

'You like the celebrity?' he murmured.

Her eyes shot back up to his on a stabbing pain in her midsection. 'I do not.'

'It's not a crime to enjoy a bit of fame, Jayne. You worked

hard on your books. You should take pleasure in people reading them.'

Her frown doubled. Her eyes darted away. Her fingers started to tap on the edge of the seat.

'Talk to me. Why won't you let yourself enjoy it?'

She could hardly bear to *have* her thoughts, let alone utter them. Her fingers hit their familiar rhythm. Silent moments passed.

'What if I caused it?'

He leaned in, the better to hear her whisper. 'What?'

She turned to him, eyes enormous with grief. 'I liked it too much. The touring. I liked meeting people. I liked them telling me how fantastic my books are.' She shuddered. 'I got so much validation out of that. I never would have been stalked if I hadn't put myself out there like that.'

Heat flushed red where his shirt collar parted enticingly. 'You think you *deserve* to be hunted?'

'I *created* him, Todd. He wouldn't exist if I hadn't put myself out there.'

'Sure he would. He just would have been targeting someone else.' Jayne pressed her lips together. 'He could have gone after someone weaker. Someone he might have hurt. Or, worse, controlled for years the way he's tried to control you.'

'He hasn't tried. He's succeeded.'

'You don't really believe that. Look at you. You're out in the community. You met people tonight. You're hunkered down in a car with me. He's not controlling you tonight.'

The realisation that he was right sent a stunning surge through her whole body, waking it from where it had slept for so long.

'Drawing his eye did *not* mean you deserved one bit of what happened to you,' he said, sitting up more fully and pulling her into an upright position, bringing an end to the heavenly foot-rub. 'And it doesn't mean it wouldn't have happened if you hadn't had your face in the paper. He could have seen you on a bus or in a checkout queue. It just means he was captivated.'

She snorted. 'By what?'

'By every part of you. Your beauty, inside and out. Your creativity. Your books. Your brilliance. And, believe it or not, your courage. Your strength. I bet that drew him like a moth to a flame.'

She sat perfectly still, the world trembling on the point of a major shift. 'You think I'm beautiful?'

A battle broke out in his deep blue eyes. But he didn't hide it from her. 'Every part of you is beautiful, Jayne. I'd have to be blind not to notice that.'

She swallowed past a lump. 'I've felt ugly for so long.'

He winced at the crack in her voice. His hand snaked out to curl around her cheek. 'Trust me on this one.'

His thumb stroked her cheek. Her heart hammered hard. She stared at him. Took a breath. 'When you look at me...I don't feel ugly.'

He closed his hands into tight fists and clenched his jaw so hard she could see it.

Jayne had never felt closer to anyone. She burned to express that. 'Can I kiss you now, Todd? If it's not impulsive and I'm not in crisis? Just a woman kissing a man? Because she wants to?'

He paled. 'I promised myself I wouldn't take advantage of you.'

'You wouldn't be.'

'I would feel like I was.'

Earlier, she'd taken his reluctance personally—as a sign he wasn't interested. But something had shifted between them in the hours since Dougal had disappeared. She'd grown a new fearlessness. 'One kiss. You don't even need to participate. I'll do all the work.'

He shifted immediately and put some space between them. Squashed into the back seat of his car, it wasn't much. Newly freed hormones dashed, celebrating, through her reawakened body. She shifted forward onto her knees. 'You can't sanction me one minute for not controlling my life and then rebuke me when I take charge. I'm asking for what I want.'

Todd watched her warily, frowning as though he was in physical pain. She curled her fingers around his, her hand small in his large one. Then she smiled at him, knowing he had nowhere else to go.

He groaned. 'One kiss?'

Jayne held his eyes as she pushed forward onto his side of the seat, heart thumping. 'Just one.'

'Uh-huh. Good luck with—'

When her lips met his, every thought in her head fled to make room for the rush of sensation that followed. Warm, soft, masculine lips. The earthy, eucalypt fragrance of his hair. The tentative warmth of his breath as he hissed against her lips. The butterfly touch of his lashes fluttering closed. Her blood raced. Her skin prickled.

But he held his ground, didn't kiss her back. As though he wasn't feeling every second of what she was doing to him.

She frowned and doubled her efforts, determined to break him, desperate to see him capitulate. Just this once. Her kiss became surer, bolder. She lay more fully across him, opened her mouth and slanted her head to fit more comfortably against his. Todd shuddered in a breath and clenched his teeth. She nipped and nibbled, working the kiss as best she could.

His hands started to tremble from the force of not reciprocating.

'Todd…' she breathed against his lips. 'Please…'

The moment the 'L' of her plea brushed against his lips Todd's control gave way. Both his hands slid around her body and up her back, pulling her closer and higher against him.

And he kissed her back.

He was hard everywhere she was soft. He fitted her wherever her body changed shape. She met his surrender and let her lips fall open at the first touch of his tongue. Somewhere right at the back of her mind a desperate, drowning warning clanged. She ignored it. She didn't want to think about the fact she'd stolen this kiss. That breaking him wasn't much of a triumph.

She just wanted to feel. And taste. And smell. And *live*.

It had been so long since she'd felt alive.

Jayne stretched to keep them firmly locked together and he twisted her more comfortably into the seat, drawing her more fully along his length and fusing their bodies together. His hands were in her hair, her dress.

Everywhere.

She tugged his shirt from his jeans so that her fingers could knead the flesh of his back. They were unusually co-operative, she noticed. Clearly happy to be engaged in this kind of movement rather than in their obsessive counting.

The whole time they kissed. Hot. Hard. Urgent.

Todd pushed himself up onto one fist, giving her a moment of air and increasing his access. The shift of his body meant he could slide one giant hand up between them. She lurched in his arms at that first electric touch, and then pressed her body harder into his, desperate to re-establish contact. He lowered his head again for another kiss.

But as she stretched up to eagerly meet his lips an explosion of barking suddenly tore through the car. They lurched apart, to their knees, and Jayne flung the door open and was out before she'd taken more than a sufficient gasping breath to shout, 'Dougal!'

The little dog galloped along the riverbank towards them, every bit the springing terrier. Jayne fell to her knees and braced herself for the slam of his little body into hers, and her arms went soundly around him when it came. The other dogs leaped out behind her, and for a few moments it was a joyful tongue-fest of reunion kisses. She pushed Dougal back to check him for injuries. His white bits were as brown as his brown bits. Filthy from head to toe.

'Johnno was right,' Todd's thick voice said from behind her. 'Wombat burrow. They can go for a hundred metres underground. If he got deep into one he never would have heard us calling. He probably fell asleep.'

She took Dougal's muzzle in her hand and made him look at her. 'You and I are going to have a long talk about bush etiquette, young man.' Then she pushed herself to her feet and picked Dougal up, holding him close. Happiness flooded through her as she followed Todd back to the car, even though just moments ago it had been *him* pressed so close to her breast.

Everyone she cared about was safe and together. Her dogs. Todd.

Herself.

For the first time she felt no hint of anxiety or fear at being out of control in a strange place. The stunning realisation was like a glorious sunrise, warming her from the inside out.

She had a safe home, a good career, and a man she was well on her way to loving. She was overdue for some happiness.

Maybe, finally, things were going to go her way.

Todd hovered by his vehicle.

The dogs had galloped ahead into the house to share stories of their adventures. They'd stolen centre stage on the ten-minute journey home, forcing some space into the pulsing gap between him and Jayne which had minutes ago been full of simmering heat.

*What was he thinking?* Was he really that hungry for punishment? To risk hurting Jayne as well as himself. Not 'risk'… because that implied only a chance. Whereas she was most definitely going to be hurt. And soon.

And by him.

'Are you coming in?' Her eyes were bright with nerves.

He guessed her heart would be hammering as hard as his. He'd been in her house a dozen times over the past few days, but suddenly those simple words took on a whole new meaning. He set his jaw and followed her inside like a dead man walking.

She opened the doors, threw her purse onto the side table, turned on a few lights, topped up the dogs' water bowls, straightened a few cushions and then—finally—turned to face him. Brave. Beautiful. She stepped towards him with nervous promise in her eyes, but—much as it killed him to do it—he lifted two hands in front of her and stopped her with her name.

Her whole body lurched to a halt as she caught his tone. That part of her that trusted no one immediately shot up protective shutters. She stumbled backwards, self-loathing masking her gentle features, her voice strained, her laugh bitter. 'Fool me once, shame on you. Fool me twice…'

'Jayne, I'm not…This is not…' *Goddammit!* He moved carefully back from her, but didn't let the eye-contact go. If he did that, she was likely to run off into the trees and disappear for ever. 'Can we talk about this?'

Her back stiffened impossibly further. 'You're in the mood for conversation?'

*Nope, not one little bit.* What he wanted to do he needed a bigger back seat for.

She shuddered in a deep breath. 'Do you have any idea how hard it was for me to reach out to you? To take this risk?'

Every part of him burned to go to her. To wrap her in his arms and never let her out. 'Yes. I do. Which is why I'm doing *this* instead of throwing off my clothes right now.' He turned away. Took three deep breaths. Turned back. 'I need to ask you something.'

Her cold silence wasn't exactly *go ahead, Todd,* but it wasn't no either. He took her shoulders and directed her to the sofa, then lowered himself down onto a footstool, spreading a leg either side of her to keep her close. Contained.

'Can you be one hundred percent certain that what you're feeling now is genuine?' he asked.

She started shaking her head even before he'd finished. 'I want you, Todd.'

'Is this…' he waved his hands at his still dishevelled hair, his partially pulled out clothing '…about me or about what I represent for you?'

Her eyes widened. 'You think I can't tell the difference?'

'I think we've spent a lot of time together and been through some pretty intense experiences. I think it would be easy to blur the lines.'

Fine blonde eyebrows shot up. 'Are your lines blurred?'

*One hundred percent.* 'We're not talking about me. We're talking about you.'

'Oh. Sorry. Is this therapy? I didn't realise that's what the couch was for.'

Her fingers started flying and his stomach lurched. He wrapped his hand around hers and brought it to his mouth, pressing the cold, frantic fingers to his lips. 'It kills me that I'm causing this,' he mumbled against them. 'That I'm upsetting you enough for—'

'Why can't I just care for you, Todd?' Jayne's brow

crumpled with pain and she extracted her hand from his and forced her fist closed. 'Why is that so inconceivable?'

'It would be natural for you to rely on me...'

'You think I only want to be with you because you make me feel safe?'

'*Do* I make you feel safe?'

'Of course you do. But I'm thirty years old. I think I can tell the difference between love and—'

Abject horror spread across her face and she clamped a hand to her mouth. Todd's heart sank clear into his boots. The only sound he heard for nearly thirty seconds was his own pulse battering his body.

Finally he spoke, though it killed him to say it. 'You don't love me, Jayne. We haven't known each other long enough.'

Her face had drained of blood and it made her grey eyes look like enormous, round fissures in an ice shelf. 'Stranger things have happened.'

*No.* He shook his head. 'It never happens. It never lasts.'

'In your experience.' Her voice shook. 'You expect me to trust you, but you can't trust me.' She took his hand and pressed it hard to her breast. Her thumping heart. 'Trust this.'

He'd give his whole fortune to be able to close his fingers. But, no... This was exactly how it had happened with Celeste. Fast. Infatuated. He gently pulled his hand away, though it hurt him to know it might be the last time he touched her. 'You weren't going to tell me because you knew I'd question it—make you question it—and rightly so.'

Tears soaked into the twin ice-pools.

A desperate part of him wondered if maybe some loves *could* happen this fast? Walking away from Jayne was certainly going to be the hardest thing he'd ever done. But it was what he had to do. 'I need more than just attraction between us before I risk myself again. It's a promise I made myself.'

Jayne dropped her eyes and frowned. Then she forced them upwards again. 'You don't feel more than physical attraction?'

He did, but he couldn't tell her that. Not when he'd just managed to force some distance between them. Distance he desperately needed. 'Let's get to know each other better. Spend more time together...'

'We don't have more time, Todd.'

Unbearable tension leaked out of him on a harsh laugh. 'Why? It's not like you're going somewhere...'

Her shocked expression drove a spike straight through his heart. But maybe it was time Jayne faced some realities. Things worked differently out in the real world. Even if it made him feel like a jerk.

'Actually, I am.' She straightened. 'I have a contract to honour.'

The room sucked the oxygen right out of his blood cells. He stared at her, a fatefully familiar sensation washing over him. 'You're going back to New York?'

She nodded. 'I think I need to. I have some demons to put to rest.'

'A week ago you were settling in for the long haul.'

'A week ago I was a different person.'

A week ago they hadn't met. It seemed like another lifetime. Tension surged through him. For himself. For Jayne. This was Celeste all over again. 'Meeting twelve people is a good start, but it's a long way from fronting back up to an entire city. To who might be *in* that city.'

Jayne threw her arms in the air. 'I'm confused, Todd. I thought you'd be supportive of me taking control back.'

Some of the pressure leached out in his raised voice. 'I'm worried you're doing this to make a point. I don't want you to get hurt.'

*I want you to come back.*

She smiled thinly. 'Too late.'

His stomach dropped. He knew she was right. He felt dismal for stacking up hurdles instead of helping her to do what she must, but fear was shoving at his back. 'What about the dogs? Your rehab animals?'

She stared at him. 'I'll hire someone to be caretaker.'

'They're not chattels, Jayne, they're family. You can't just throw money and a stranger at them and the problem goes away. They love you.'

*Desperate times...*

Jayne surged to her feet and looked down at him angrily. 'I can't be everything, Todd. I need to be there for myself first in order to be there for them.' Confusion roiled in her belly. 'I'm no good to them if I'm broken.'

He stood and took her arctic hands in his. 'You are not broken, Jayne. You've been mending.'

'Not fast enough.'

'Says who?'

She stared at him. How could she answer? How to explain the pressure she put herself under to be normal again? She was sure she looked as bleak as she felt.

Todd dropped his head on a sigh, then lifted his eyes. 'I could stay here for you. The dogs already know me—they trust me.'

She frowned and blinked her surprise. 'Why would you?'

'Because it's something I can do. To help.'

Her heart pounded. 'Does that mean you want me to go?'

Todd's eyes fell shut. 'I want you to heal, Jayne. I'll do whatever I can to make that happen. But, no, that doesn't mean I'll be happy to see you go.'

'But...you don't want *me*?'

His gaze blazed. 'Not wanting to rush and not wanting

are different things. I raced in and screwed things up once before. I don't want to do it again.'

She stared at him. 'Your wife?'

He took her hands. 'Understand that letting you go will be hard for me, Jayne, even after only a week. I gave Celeste a long leash trying to give her happiness. She ended up choking me with it.'

'What do you mean?'

'She came home from her most recent flit around the planet with the man she'd prefer to be married to. Her divorce lawyer. So you'll have to forgive me if I don't see you off at the airport. Partings don't hold good memories for me.'

Jayne's gasp brought at least one dog into the room to check on them. 'Oh, no, Todd. That's awful. I'm sorry.'

'I dodged a bullet with Celeste, but those lessons are burned into my soul.'

She stared at him long and hard, aware of the impact her leaving would have on his still wounded heart. But knowing what staying would do to hers. 'I have to try.'

He took her hands in his again. 'I know. But I won't be celebrating.'

What more was there to say? He was too good a man to ask her to stay, even if it *was* hurting him. Her heart squeezed hard enough to pulp. 'I would love it if you would stay at the cottage. There's no one I would trust more with my family. Thank you.'

They stood like that for moments, hand in hand. Then he pulled her carefully towards him. 'How long will you be gone?'

'Maybe a few weeks?'

She felt his nod in the slight shift of his body. 'Not so long.'

Ten times as long as she'd needed to fall in love. 'Can I call you?'

His voice was thick. 'No. Don't call me. Don't e-mail.' He pulled her head into his shoulder. 'Just come back to me.'

# CHAPTER SEVEN

*Five months later, Thursday*

TODD shoved a spreading Ollie with his hip, to steal back some room on Jayne's battered sofa. The black dog snorted in half-sleep and adjusted around the inconvenience of Todd's presence. Todd flicked the remote and the television glowed into life.

The late-night US variety programme was a day old by the time it aired in Australia, but he'd take what he could get. The internet was good for general news and the occasional media photograph, but it did nothing to give him his Jayne fix in more tangible terms.

Not that it was healthy to be craving fixes at all. Enough time had passed that he should be able to go a week—heck, *a day*—without thinking about her. Wondering how she was doing. Wondering *what* she was doing and who with. Wondering why she hadn't come back.

His heart ached. He'd been so sure she would.

Ollie gave a shuddering snore before dropping back into deep sleep. It echoed Todd's mood exactly. He didn't like staying up late to catch a glimpse of her. He didn't like searching through magazines in the news agency for any hint of her name, and Mark the newsagent didn't much like it either. He didn't like trawling the internet for anything that would give him a clue to how she was going. He was as bad as her stalker—sifting through the world's information for hints about her.

She'd looked ethereally pale in most of the photographs he'd seen of her initially. Hard to know whether that was her Queensland tan bleaching off in a north-east winter, or a sign that she was finding it tough. Or possibly both.

He just didn't know.

*Don't call. Don't e-mail.*

He'd made her promise and she'd been as good as her word. He'd known she would be, no matter how tough for her. Or him. She wasn't one to shy away from tough things. Just like she'd been on the day she'd climbed in Thommo's taxi to head to Brisbane to catch her flight, the day she'd left her house and her dogs. The day she'd left him. She'd been completely terrified. But done it anyway.

Her courage inspired his.

Letting Jayne walk away had been the hardest thing he'd ever done, even after only a week. Infinitely harder than ending his nine-year marriage. Buying off Celeste had been perversely empowering; her smug expression had told him she thought *she* was the big winner, but Todd had walked out of that conference room feeling richer than he'd felt in a decade. Even Celeste's own solicitor—a new one since Mr Divorce Lawyer had moved on to greener pastures—had quietly asked him if he was certain when he signed over everything to her. Hopefully all those zeroes would attract exactly the sort of person to his ex-wife that she'd turned out to be.

He'd given Karma a million-dollar sweetener.

The promo for the programme finished and the American host, John Tidwell, came bouncing out onto stage and started his formulaic bantering with the audience. Then he chatted to a couple of members of the show's band, and they exchanged on-screen anecdotes about their weekends.

Todd was nearly at breaking point by the time Tidwell finally ran through the line-up for the evening.

'And right after the break: "When Life Imitates Art": America's reigning Queen of Chill talks about her latest thriller, and her lost years at the hands of a stalker. Coming up next on *Tidwell Tonight*.'

Todd's stomach lurched and collided with his hard-thumping heart.

And then there she was. A backstage camera cut to Jayne in the Green Room, a glass of water in her left hand. She smiled as the camera turned on her, and raised the glass of water in a shy salute to the viewing audience.

His first thought was that she looked fantastic. New York haircut. Knockout blouse and skirt. Every bit the successful author. Calm. Confident. Courageous. But in the dying seconds before they broke to a commercial Todd absorbed all the things he wasn't supposed to see.

The pale skin and shadows beneath the heavy television make-up.

The overly-bright television smile.

The tightly clenched right fist.

Pride surged through him. Terrified, but doing it anyway. He speared his fingers anxiously into Ollie's short fur. The dog grumbled. She'd seemed alone in that waiting room. Was someone with her, or was she facing this by herself? How could she when there was nothing more public than prime-time television beamed right around the world?

It hit him then. Her stalker was bound to be watching. From wherever.

*She'd have to know that.*

His lip curled in a snarl and his fingers tightened. Ollie leapt to the floor in protest. Todd mangled a sofa cushion instead, and slid right onto the edge of the seat. Commercials for a bank, fast-food and a reality television programme played out while he went slowly insane.

*Come on...come on...*

Finally the host's face reappeared, and the cameras pulled back to reveal Jayne sitting demurely in the guest's seat, her hands neatly folded together in her lap. Every part of Todd bled for her. What she was doing was unthinkable. Exposing herself to this degree. He felt the thousands of kilometres between them more keenly now than at any time in the last awful months.

Thousands of kilometres and a day.

No matter what he saw tonight, or how fast he acted, Jayne had already been dealing with the fall-out of this programme on her own for twenty-four hours. That thought sickened him.

He prayed to God she had her family with her. Someone. Anyone.

Even if it meant another man.

Her pale face glanced at the live audience, at the camera linking her to millions more around the planet. This was not what he had imagined when she'd said she wanted to go back to America and fight to take her life back. He had thought she might start frequenting her favourite restaurants. Visit the theatre. Get empowered.

Not strip naked on international television.

'Welcome to the show, J.C.,' Tidwell started. 'We'll talk about *your new book* shortly, but first let's talk about the past couple of years of your life. "Lost years", you call them. Tell me about that.'

Todd held his breath.

Jayne started to speak, her voice soft but steady, recounting the circumstances leading to her stalking and acknowledging the Police Department for their dogged assistance and eventual success. The presenter chimed in with prompting questions to keep her talking, and she shared her fear, her confusion, and her loathing of her own weakness. The camera cut several times to audience members blinking back tears as she communicated her crippling pain in such a dignified and restrained manner.

Todd swallowed hard. He'd thought he'd known what strength was...

'You know your stalker's identity, yes?' Tidwell asked, his eyes full of compassion.

Jayne nodded. 'But some people never know theirs.'

'Would you like to name him here? Perhaps warn anyone he's currently involved with?'

Jayne paled impossibly further. She dropped her head in that trademark face-shield. But then she lifted it again and stared resolutely at her host. 'No. Thank you.'

The presenter frowned. 'You're protecting him?'

'No. I'm protecting the people who love him. Who have done nothing wrong. They don't deserve to suffer for his sickness any more than I did.'

Todd's heart nearly exploded with admiration. His eyes stung, but he ignored it.

Tidwell pushed back in his chair and puffed out his cheeks. 'After everything you've just told us, you think he's worthy of being loved?'

Jayne smiled sadly at him. Her mouth said, 'Everyone deserves to be loved. No matter what.' Her eyes said, *even me.*

Todd felt a pained, guttural sound break from his chest and fill the little room. She'd said it with such conviction. Like the new woman she clearly was. Or perhaps the woman she'd been before her stalker. The strong, confident woman.

Would that woman even need him any more? Let alone love him.

Tidwell went on to discuss the release of the third in the

*Focus* series, and commented that it was already topping the major bestseller lists. Jayne smiled graciously and thanked him for his praise.

'Are you working on number four yet?'

'I'm halfway through.' She smiled.

'Have you incorporated your experiences at the hands of your stalker? To send him a message?'

Her eyes clouded over. 'I'm eager to replace the bad experiences with new, happy ones—not to relive them in print.'

'So you have nothing to say to your persecutor?'

'Not verbally. But…' She glanced at the camera. 'May I?'

Tidwell nodded his eager consent. He could smell a ratings earner.

Jayne turned to the camera and slowly lifted her fists out in front of her. Like opening lotus flowers. She let her slender fingers straighten. They were not entirely steady, but the tiny tremors spoke only of nerves, nothing more. Her tortured right hand sat entirely at rest. Not so much as a twitch. Todd held his breath.

While Tidwell frowned his confusion in the background, Jayne lifted her lashes and stared defiantly down the barrel of the camera, the tiniest of smiles teasing around her lips.

Todd's heart thundered. It was a message, all right. To her stalker. Letting him know he had no more power.

And to Todd. Letting him know as well.

He dropped his head into his hands and broke down.

Lifting her suitcases from the truck that doubled as Banjo's Ridge's sole taxi service was like a crazy kind of déjà vu. This exact same vehicle had brought her here two and a half years ago. Dropped her in this exact same spot to start a new life.

Feeling every bit as anxious, but for very different reasons, she turned to the driver who'd helped search for Dougal all those months ago. Turned out he was Shannon's husband.

'Thank you, Thommo.'

'Will you need anything else, Jayne?' the burly bearded man asked.

'Not if everything goes to plan—nope.'

'Give Shannon and me a hoi when you're ready to come round for tea, then, eh?' He gave her an enthusiastic thumbs-up and forced the truck into low gear.

Jayne halted nervously at the base of the front stairs. Two alert barks sounded somewhere in the distance, and a moment later two matching bookends with fur came sprinting around the house, yipping wildly. Jayne dropped to her knees and wrapped her arms around them as Fergus and Jazmine crashed into her. Seconds later Dougal and Oliver caught up.

It was a wet-nose-and-tongue-fest, and Jayne twisted her face high and away so that neither ended up smeared all over her. She'd gone to some trouble to try and look fresh for this moment. But it was hard not to just bury herself in their familiar, effervescent furriness.

They smelled and felt like home.

'Need a hand?'

Her eyes found him instantly, standing at the top of the steps. All pale and serious. Her heart squeezed. She gave the quell command and all four dogs dropped instantly back.

*Impressive.* 'You kept their training up?'

'I didn't want you coming home to an unruly pack.'

She stared at him, drinking in every feature. Rediscovering all the things she'd wondered if she'd imagined. The creases in his face, the line of his jaw, the blue of his eyes. They were all completely real. And they still gave her goosebumps. 'You were so sure I would be back?'

He studied her a moment. 'I knew you wouldn't leave them for good.'

*Them.*

The dogs scampered ahead of her up the stairs and in through the door Todd had left open, eager to show her around her own house. She lifted her suitcases and followed them. Todd reached for both suitcases as she neared the top. Jayne surrendered one, then nearly leapt as his warm, strong fingers brushed hers.

Inside, everything was just as she'd left it. As though that cab had picked her up yesterday, not five months ago. Todd had thrown open all the windows she'd used to keep behind thick curtains, and glorious bush light saturated the room's furnishings with a rich golden light.

Or was it just that everything looked richer to her these days?

Todd took the second suitcase from her and placed it next to the first. Waiting. Watching. Oliver nudged her wrist with his wet nose. Instinctively her hand curled around his soft ears. Familiar warmth rushed through her.

'Welcome home, Jayne.'

That was what it was, the warmth. Liquid home.

Todd's jaw was rigid and his eyes were shuttered. Jayne did a mental recount of dogs, and then moved to the window that faced south onto the wildlife-holding yards. Her corella was still there, plus a few new residents. Everything seemed okay on that front. So what was with the trepidation?

Wasn't that *her* job?

'I was worried about you,' he said quietly. His eyes should have been brighter, given the way the light made the rest of the room glow.

'I know… I…' Her right hand burned to start moving, but she let part of her mind go through the exercise her specialist had taught her—sectioning off that bit of her brain so it could do one thing while the rest of her did another. Her hand remained still. She took a breath. 'You asked me not to contact you. I knew you'd find me if anything happened to the dogs.'

*But not if something happened to you.* Worrying if he was okay took up large parts of every day. Whenever she wasn't overtaken with a signing or an appearance or meetings with her publisher, Todd Blackwood would sneak his way back into her thoughts.

Almost as if she'd traded her obsession with her stalker for one about Todd. Except this one wasn't sickening. Thinking about him had become almost a ritual, so frightened was she that she'd forget what he looked like. That he'd disappear from her heart for ever. So frightened was she that maybe he'd been right about her feelings for him. That they weren't real.

They felt very real now, as she stood before him with a wildly thumping heart.

'You must have gone to the airport straight from the Tidwell studios to have made it home so fast,' he said.

Jayne swallowed. 'You watched the show?'

'Last night. You were amazing. Congratulations.'

She smiled. So easy to do these days. Even easier now she was back where she belonged. 'I was terrified.'

'You masked it well. You had the audience spellbound.'

'I hope someone watching found it helpful. I really wanted my situation to help someone else.'

Such polite conversation—almost as if he was interviewing her. When all she wanted to do was throw herself into his arms and never crawl out. She'd worked so hard these past months, healing herself.

Making sure she was ready.

Yet the granite under his flesh wasn't giving away any secrets. If anything, he looked...angry. She took a breath.

'Thank you for looking after everything here while I was gone. I know it was…longer than you agreed to.'

'How are you feeling?'

*A million bucks, thanks. Top of the world.* She'd practised this on the plane, over and over on the long nineteen-hour flight. But all she could think to say was *better now that I'm with you again.*

The last thing she could ever say. He'd only read that as a sign that she was still relying on him. Not that she loved him. She'd have to find another way of convincing him of that.

'It was hard, but I had professional help and joined a programme. It was such a relief to know others had shared my experiences.'

Todd frowned, and it felt as if he shrank a bit further away from her in that moment. But his words were neutral enough. Almost stilted. 'I'm glad you found them.'

What was this? The two of them had never had trouble talking before. He was the one person she *could* talk to easily. The awkwardness congealed as agony, deep in her chest.

'Look, I'm sorry.' Confusion bubbled into the vacuum where happiness should be. 'This is all wrong. It's not how I imagined coming home would go.'

Icy blue eyes watched her. 'How did you imagine it?'

She took a steadying breath. Took a risk. Just one of many she'd realised she had to take in life to get back on track. 'In my head, you opened the front door and then opened your arms. I walked into them. The end.'

'Short book.'

She tightened her mouth. 'You're punishing me. I took too long to come back.'

'No, I'm not punishing you.' He tipped his head to meet her downcast eyes. 'You don't think I'm happy to see you?'

'You don't look very happy.'

'What if I'm just afraid?'

She squinted. 'You don't *do* afraid.'

'I'm afraid now.'

'Why?'

'Because you've come back and everything's different,' he said. 'You're so different.'

*He feels it.* The change. Her throat thickened. The panic that welled up had nothing to do with the past. 'I thought you'd be happy for me.'

He reached for her hand, snagged her fingers into his. 'I am happy that you're recovering. It's what I wanted for you more than anything.'

She was so tired of hearing what she needed or wanted. So tired of being the centre of her own world. 'What did you want for *you*?'

He stared at her a long time, his face shadowed. His admission, when it came, was quiet. 'I liked it when you needed me.'

She sucked in a breath. 'I went halfway around the world to stand on my own and you prefer me needy?'

He didn't answer for the longest time. 'I spent nine years with a woman who needed what I could give her but didn't need *me*.'

'You gave me no reason to stay, Todd. What if I'd never come back? Would you have let me go for ever?'

'It was a gamble. But you came back.'

'Barely! I'd almost convinced myself that you would never accept my feelings for you. You gambled with so much more than your own heart.'

Brilliant blue eyes blazed down on her. He swore and turned away, then spun back with a frustrated glare. When he finally spoke it was the last thing she would ever have expected.

'This isn't working. *Out.*'

Pain lanced through her. 'What?'

'I said, *out!*' He grabbed her by the hand and dragged her through the lounge. The old Jayne would have freaked out at being so man-handled. The new Jayne protested by putting her entire weight behind her and resisting. It made no difference whatsoever. Todd's superior strength wasn't even tested. He opened the front door and, with no further ceremony, thrust her out onto her own front porch.

The door slammed shut behind her.

Shock held her frozen for a moment. Then she turned and pounded on the front door, five months' worth of hurt and resentment surging back to the surface. 'Don't you dare throw me out of my own house!'

Never mind that it had been *his* house for the past five months.

She pounded again.

A deep muffled voice. 'Who is it?'

The ludicrousness of that question robbed her of speech. Jayne took three deep breaths and ran through another of Dr Steele's emergency exercises before answering through clenched teeth. 'It's Jayne. Open the door.'

He opened the front door wide and stared at her.

And then he opened his arms.

In an air-sucking rush she realised what he was doing. And what it meant. The blood thundered around her body, alerting her every sense and exciting her cells. Her heart pounded heavy and fast and she gazed at him, disbelieving, as he stood like an idiot with his empty arms outstretched.

Idiocy had never suited anyone more. She took a deep breath...

...and stepped forward.

Two tree limbs wrapped around her firmly, and she interlocked her fingers against his broad, hard back, letting her skin absorb the natural heat of the man she loved. The man she had a lifetime to really get to know. One large hand forked up into the hair at her nape and the other anchored her firmly against him. She settled her body against his—into his—and let her eyes flutter shut on a huge sigh.

She'd waited five months for this moment. She wasn't about to relinquish it in a hurry.

'I missed you,' Todd whispered against her hair, the warmth of his breath teasing her scalp and his lips following.

The magic words made her smile. 'I thought about you every day.' Admitting it didn't feel weak. It made her feel stronger. 'It nearly killed me not to call you.'

'Why didn't you just ignore me?'

She'd practised this speech on the plane, too, but it wouldn't come easily. 'I gave you my word, and I knew if we spoke I'd want to come home. Before I was ready.'

*Home.* The cottage. The man. The dogs. It was all part of the complicated blend that was Banjo's Ridge.

She pulled back enough to look up into his beautifully familiar face. 'You were right. I was using you as a crutch. And it was easier for me to let you help me than to help myself. If you'd been with me I never would have taken the risk.'

'I didn't need you whole, Jayne, just *here*.'

She shook her head. 'I needed to put it all behind me. To start with a completely clean slate.'

He pulled her back into his arms and dragged his mouth back and forth over her hair. She burned to tilt her face up to his, but settled for pressing into his throat and inhaling the gorgeousness of soap, eucalyptus and Todd.

'I would have liked to be the one to help you recover,' he murmured into her hair. 'Not some anonymous support group.'

'You did help me. You were my motivation every day to go to those meetings, to risk opening myself up with my doctor. You kick-started my final recovery the day you turned up on my doorstep.'

She felt his deep swallow, the lurch of his Adam's apple against her face as she buried herself into his neck.

His voice was pure gravel. 'Then we saved each other.'

Something about those thick, quiet words brought her head up. She stared up at him.

'Just for the record, I do love you, Todd Blackwood.' His eyes fell shut. 'And not because I need you—although I do. And not because my mind is clouded…' She smiled up at him from under thick lashes and ran her hands lower down his back. 'Although right now it is. I love you because after the fear finally went I was totally empty, and the only thing that could fill that emptiness was thoughts of you. And of our furry family. And of us being together for ever.'

She swallowed sudden nerves. But she'd been through too much and given up too much to waste this new opportunity. 'You were my path out of the trees, Todd. I'll wait for you to be free, but then I don't ever want us to be apart again.'

He frowned. 'I'm free now. My divorce was finalised three months ago.' He took her face between his hands and tilted it up to his. 'But I don't know that I can promise you a wedding ring just yet. I still have a heap of healing of my own to do.'

She leaned her cheek into one of his hands and smiled. 'I don't care about a ring. Only you. And I'd like to help you heal. Let me give you that back, Todd.'

His smile down on her was one hundred percent indulgence. 'You think you can make me better? How?'

'Like this…' She turned her face into that hand and pressed her lips against the work-roughened flesh.

'And this…' She pushed herself up on tiptoes and narrowed the gap in their heights. Todd closed the rest of the distance. His lips were warm and soft where she touched them with her own. He let her kiss him, then, as she went to pull away, he pressed her harder to him and extended the kiss, moving his mouth lazily over hers, a hint of tongue to excite the gentle caress.

'I feel the wounds scabbing over already,' he murmured.

Jayne smiled against his mouth, her heart thumping steadily and noisily.

He pulled back and stared at her seriously. 'I've loved you since that evening when you sat so pale and frightened in a car filled with farting dogs, trusting me implicitly to come back to you.'

They kissed then, long and hard. Todd spread his fingers to support her head that tipped backwards against the heavenly pressure of his mouth. Her chest throbbed.

'Todd…' She struggled to get the word out between kisses. Between rapidly stolen breaths. 'Todd!'

He lifted his lips and stared at her with dark smoky eyes.

'Can I *please* come in now?'

He lifted her easily off the porch timbers and swung her into his arms, turned around and crossed the threshold of their new life together.

And kicked the door shut behind them.

# HER NO. 1 DOCTOR

**Molly Evans**

**Molly Evans** has worked as a nurse from the age of nineteen. She's worked in small rural hospitals, Indian Health Service and large research facilities all over the United States. After spending eight years as a Travelling Nurse, she settled down to write in her favourite place, Albuquerque, NM. In days she met her husband and has been there ever since. With twenty-two years of nursing experience, she's got a lot of material to use in her writing. She lives in Albuquerque, NM in the high desert, with her family, three chameleons, two dogs and a passion for quilting in whatever spare time she has. Visit Molly at: www. mollyevans.com

**Molly Evans now writes for Mills & Boon® Medical™; her novel, *Children's Doctor, Shy Nurse*, was available in June 2010.**

Dear Reader,

Thanks so much for picking up this volume. I'm thrilled to have my story, *Her No.1 Doctor,* included with stories by three other new authors. What an opportunity for all of us to reach out to new readers everywhere.

*Her No.1 Doctor* is set in Santa Fe, New Mexico, USA, which is one of my favourite cities to visit. Fortunately, I live not too far from there and can visit several times per year. The food and atmosphere are excellent, and I've tried to infuse the story with some of it, so I hope you can almost smell the green chilli roasting when you open the pages of this book. I hope to set many books in the future in this area of the country. It is, after all, one of my favourite places to be. The country, the people and the culture are very diverse and there is no lack for entertainment here. If you visit the USA, consider New Mexico as a stop on your agenda.

Pursuing any dream is never easy and becoming a writer is no different. Becoming a published author has been a dream of mine that at first was just something I wanted to do "some day." Then I quickly realised that "some day" would never arrive if I didn't put pen to paper. It's been a long journey filled with many roller-coaster rides. I never knew the meaning of frustration until I began to write! But now, I'm ready to jump back on that roller coaster, throw my hands in the air and take another turn around the track.

Happy reading,

*Molly Evans*

Pam, Becky, Beth, and Dawn: you will be missed
more than you will ever know.

# CHAPTER ONE

*Santa Fe, New Mexico, USA, September*

TRAVEL nurse Carla Lopez pulled her car into the parking lot of the first farmers' market she found. She approached the vendor, who stood at a roasting station a little apart from the rest of the building. Breathing in the exotic rich tang of the flame-roasted green chili made her mouth water. Nothing said Santa Fe or New Mexico the way green chili did. It was the sacred symbol of the southwest and *ristras*, and bundles of drying chili hung from nearly every doorway. When strung, the chiles were green, but as they dried, they turned a vibrant, exotic red. Decorative, and useful to spice up recipes as well.

"You look like you need some of this," said the man who supervised the roasting station. Round metal cages, about three feet wide and nearly two feet high, rotated over gas flames, and roasted the chili, with the popping and snapping of the pod skins adding to the whole sensory experience.

"Yes. I could eat the whole bag. I haven't had fresh green chili in three years." She planned to make up for it right now—even before she checked into her new apartment or called her sister.

"Oh, no." He shook his head at her and clucked his tongue. "That's terrible. No one should go so long without chili. That's almost a crime." He reached into one of the already prepared sacks of steaming chiles and pulled out two steamed pods, put them on a paper plate and handed them to her. "Here you go. Enjoy."

"Oh, thank you," Carla said, and reached for the plate. "I am in heaven."

"You know it." The man gave a laugh, watching her.

Carla picked up one of the roasted pods in her fingers and took a bite. "Mmm. Oh, this is so much better than I remember." There was a little heat, a small bite on her tongue, and the flavor was pure bliss. This pungent vegetable influenced the cooking and the culture here like nothing else.

"Next time you think you're getting sick, you roll one in a tortilla and add shredded cheese, or make some stew with it, and it will cure anything." He snapped his fingers. "Just like that."

"That's what my mom said when I was growing up." The Lopez family was traditional New Mexican, right down to the food.

"You live here?" He hefted a large burlap sack full of fresh chiles and dumped them into one of the roasters. The sizzle and snap were instant.

"I grew up here. Just back for a visit." A two-month long visit, to be precise—just long enough to fulfill the terms of her latest contract, and then she'd be off again. Although she missed pieces and parts of home, travel nursing was her life now. One she'd never expected and one she wasn't going to give up easily.

"Well, welcome home." As the man roasted another twenty-pound sack of fresh chiles she stood by and watched the process, remembering how she'd taken this for granted when she'd lived here. She wasn't doing that anymore. She was going to have to learn to grow chiles in a container if she didn't have access to the fresh stuff from now on. There were certain things in life she was not willing to give up, and this was one of them. Coffee and chocolate were two of the others. Shoes came a close fourth.

Life was good if she got to eat green chili her first day back in her home town. The capital city of New Mexico was a mix of cultures, and it boasted the finest cuisine and the most glorious old architecture, which still influenced building structures today. When she'd lived here she'd barely noticed how lovely the city was, its the pueblo-style buildings reminiscent of ancient native dwellings. Now, her eyes couldn't get enough of it, as if her mind were thirsty just for the sight of the desert.

"Let them steam for a few hours before freezing them." The stallholder advised as he carried the heavy plastic bag to her car, already overloaded with her worldly belongings. Somehow she made room for it.

"I will. Thank you." She got into her car and drove to her sister's home.

Just before seven a.m. the next day, Carla entered the ER of the hospital she'd used to work in. Since she had left three years before many things were different, but many remained the same.

"Are you Carla?" The charge nurse, Elaine, asked her as she approached the nurses' station.

"Yes, I am. Carla Lopez—your new travel nurse." Although Carla had worked in this hospital before, she was under different rules as a travel nurse, and was essentially a new employee starting from scratch.

"Welcome to Santa Fe." The trim blond smiled.

She hadn't been at the hospital when Carla had worked there. Of course the staff in the ER changed frequently. It was just the nature of the job, and part of the reason that travel nursing kept her fresh.

Elaine checked the clipboard in her hands. "I've got you hooked up with Kenny for orientation this morning. He'll be able to show you around and introduce you to the other staff as you go."

"Sounds good." She probably knew some of the staff, but it would be easier having the introductions when it wasn't so hectic.

"You can put your backpack in the lounge. We'll get you a locker before the end of the day."

Carla nodded and headed to the staff lounge, but before she could push the door all the way open the intercom rang out.

"Trauma incoming. All available staff to Trauma Room One."

Carla dashed into the lounge, threw her backpack beneath the table and raced back to the trauma room. When an all-staff page was called, it was going to be bad.

"Elaine, give me a job to do," she urged, her heart racing in anticipation of the approaching emergency.

"It's your first minute here," Elaine said, her eyes wide with surprise. "Are you sure you're ready for this? You haven't been properly oriented yet." Elaine focused her concerned eyes on Carla.

The doors burst open, admitting two stretchers and two ambulance crews. "I'm sure," Carla said, knowing there was no choice if lives were to be saved.

"Then go to Room One with Kenny and Dr. Kelton. I'll take the second one."

"Max Kelton?" The adrenaline already surging through her shot to a higher level.

"Yes. Go." Elaine rushed after the second patient.

"Oh, boy." At hearing Dr. Kelton's name, she felt the nerves that had been calm now surface.

Hands trembling, Carla arrived at Room One at the same

time the stretcher did. On it was an unconscious woman who was in an advanced state of pregnancy, and Carla's nerves tightened. Nothing was more fragile than a pregnant woman and an unborn child. The female patient was approximately twenty-five years old, and though covered in scratches and glass particles she appeared in good health.

"I'm Carla—travel nurse. Ready to help out." She grabbed a set of gloves from the box on a wall rack and the entire thing fell off with a clatter to the floor. "Oh! Sorry, sorry, sorry!" She tried not to turn beet-red as she scooted the boxes and rack to the side with her foot, wishing she could crawl under the stretcher.

"Don't worry. It happens all the time," the male nurse with 'Kenny' on his nametag reassured her.

"It's such an embarrassing impression to make." One that no one in the room was likely to forget—including herself.

"Here's your trial by fire," Kenny said.

"Not the first time," she said, and hooked the woman up to the heart monitor, then an automatic blood pressure cuff. "Vital signs look okay now. Should we call for fetal monitoring?"

"Yes," Dr. Kelton said, and frowned at Carla through his protective goggles.

Carla held her breath. Would he remember her? But it seemed she'd failed to make the same impression on him as he'd made on her all those years ago as he quickly began his assessment of their patient.

He shone a small light into the patient's eyes, looking for pupilary response. The bump on her forehead was indicative of some sort of head trauma. With a nod, he clicked the light off and returned it to his pocket. "Keep the fluids going."

"Yes, Doctor. Do you think we'll need another line for blood?" she asked.

His intense focus on the patient made her wonder whether

he heard her or not, but then he lifted his head and looked at her. "Not sure yet, but might as well put one in just in case."

He gave her the instructions, and for a second their eyes met over the patient. Even with the goggles on, she couldn't help noticing his bright blue eyes and her stomach curled again. She looked away before her hands started to tremble so she couldn't get the IV in on the first try.

"Will do." Carla recorded the patient's vital signs and took a calming breath as a nurse from Obstetrics arrived to monitor the fetal heart tones. Carla moved to the counter and retrieved the IV start supplies.

"I'll get it. You do the fetal stuff," Kenny said, and took the IV supplies from her with a shiver. "Not my forte."

"I'll help you get the monitor on her," Carla said, and uncovered the patient's abdomen to reveal some light rubbing from an over-the-shoulder seatbelt. "Looks like she's about seven months, right?"

Just about the same as her sister.

"Hard to say for sure. We'll call for her records from her OB's office." Jeannine, the obstetric nurse, was managing the monitor. "Women carry their pregnancies differently."

"Though she's got lots of superficial lacerations, I'm more concerned about her head," Carla said with a frown, and looked at Dr. Kelton for confirmation.

"You're right. The abrasions are minimal, but the bump on her head is the biggest issue," Dr. Kelton said, and listened to the patient's lungs for a few seconds. "I just hope she was wearing a seatbelt."

"Oh, she was. There's a light mark on her chest and across her abdomen, though she should have had the belt *beneath* her abdomen." Carla frowned, trying to remember her obstetrics rotation from nursing school. "Right, Jeannine?"

"Yes. Some people just don't know to tuck the belt under the baby, rather than over it," Jeannine said, and shook her head.

"Oxygen saturation is okay—ninety-six percent on two litres, Doctor." Carla observed the fetal monitor, but it looked like a bunch of squiggly lines to her. Totally unlike the heart monitor's squiggly lines, which she could read without interpretation from someone else. "Should we get her to Radiology now?" she asked.

"After I finish my assessment." Dr. Kelton's serious blue eyes flashed to Carla for a second.

She swallowed, nodded, and looked away at the subtle reprimand. The statement was clear in very few words. He was in charge here, and he wasn't going to let her hurry him. She turned away and recorded vital signs on the nursing assessment form. It busied her hands and hid her flush of further embarrassment from the others. Dr. Kelton had verbally spanked her in front of the others. It was horribly reminiscent of their working relationship in the past, and she didn't like it.

"Okay, I think we can call Radiology now. We need to see if there's anything going on in her head."

"Everything cool in the belly, Jeannine?" If it weren't, they'd be rushing to the Operating Room for an emergency Cesarean section instead of Radiology for a CAT scan.

The older nurse nodded as she watched the monitor. "Looks like it. No decelerations observed, good rate. She's having a few mild contractions, but that's not uncommon. There's some specific lab work we ought to order, as well, but I think we're good to go for now."

"Get Radiology on the phone, please," Dr. Kelton said, and slung his stethoscope around his neck. The tension in the room eased a bit at his confident manner. If the doctor in charge was calm, then everyone else was as well. Carla had learned that a long time ago.

"I got it," Kenny said, and grabbed the phone near where the rack of gloves had been hooked to the wall.

Carla busied herself trying to keep her nerves calm as she prepared the patient and equipment for transport. This wasn't quite the start to her assignment that she'd anticipated, but she'd learned to roll with the ever-changing nature of working in an ER setting. Then she noticed something that reassured her and sent a warm pulse through her chest.

"She's moving," Carla said, and smiled. Any lingering embarrassment fled. This was a good sign. She watched as the patient's hands gravitated toward her abdomen. Though she didn't open her eyes or speak, her first thought was for her unborn child. Mothering instincts ran deep in some women. Carla was more hopeful now that the patient and her baby would be fine.

Leaning over, Carla spoke in a soothing tone into the patient's ear and stroked her hair back from her face. "You're in the hospital. There's been a car accident, but you and the baby are doing okay now. Your husband's on his way to see you, and we're going to take you to have your head checked out."

When she stood upright she caught Dr. Kelton watching her, and she stiffened, her heart racing, anticipating a smart remark from him.

His bright blue eyes roved over her face, then he removed his goggles and tucked them into his lab coat pocket. "Nice touch, Carla."

A blush warmed her face. She hadn't expected to hear kind words right away, and it caught her off guard to hear them from Dr. Kelton, whom she didn't remember as being forthcoming with compliments in the past. Maybe this was a good sign that this could be a good assignment. "Thanks, Dr. Kelton."

For a second or two she was transported back to a time when she had been very new on the job and just out of nursing school. She'd disagreed with him over a patient and he'd corrected her misinterpretation rather sharply, in front of several of their colleagues. Though they'd been quick to remind her of Dr. Kelton's sometimes abrasive ways, she'd never forgotten that moment, and had never misinterpreted the same lab work ever again thanks to him. Some lessons in a medical career were harsh. Although she'd never forgotten the incident, he probably didn't even remember it happening.

"Since you're going to be working with us for a while, call me Max, please."

He peered at her, and gave a sideways smile that made her stomach drop. The man was as devastating to her senses now as he'd been back then. He still made her nervous and edgy, but at least she could now hold her own when working on a patient with him.

"Yes, Doctor. Max." The corner of her mouth curved upward at the memory. "I'll try."

"Good." Although he smiled, the expression didn't reach his eyes. He was so serious, so focused. She hoped she'd learn to relax a little more around him, or she'd be knocking more things off the walls in the future. The maintenance department would not like that.

After unscrewing the transport IV pump, she prepared to heft it onto the siderail. Max reached for it and easily handled its awkward weight. "I'll put that over here," he said, and clamped the small but weighty machine onto the metal side rail for the trip to Radiology.

"Thank you," Carla said, and meant it. She looked up at Max who held her gaze for a few seconds, then nodded.

Something passed between them, but Carla wasn't sure what. A shiver rolled over her.

"They're ready in Radiology," Kenny said, and removed the blood pressure cuff from the patient's left arm. "Let's roll."

# CHAPTER TWO

AFTER delivering the patient to the ICU, for critical care and continued fetal monitoring, Carla was ready for a break. She entered the staff lounge to the fragrance of an exotic coffee blend fresh in the air. Max sat on the couch with his feet up on a chair. Casual, yet commanding, ready to go at a moment's notice. Her pulse jumped at his unexpected presence. The plain and simple truth was that he made her nervous. She had been around plenty of handsome doctors in the last three years, but none of them made her pulses flutter the way that Max did.

Forcing down the impulse to withdraw from the room the way she would have in the past, she walked straight in and did her best to appear as confident as he did. On the outside she looked the part, but on the inside she was a jumble of nerves.

He smiled and indicated the coffee pot. "Just made some fresh, so help yourself."

"Ooh, I love it when a man knows how to do things." She reached for a mug, filled it, but left room for sweetener and milk. A change of pace would be good right about now.

Max snorted, amusement evident in his brilliant eyes. "Oh, yeah? Like what? Changing tires and fixing car engines? Manly stuff like that?"

Carla turned with the mug in her hands and held up one

finger. "Make *good* coffee—that's essential." She held up a second finger. "Do his own laundry without turning everything pink." The third finger went up. "And change the toilet paper roll."

At that last one, Max laughed. "Grew up with boys?" he asked.

"No. Just my sister and me. But my dad was the worst about not doing things for himself. With three women in the house he had too many things done for him." She shook her head, then sipped her coffee, but there was a warm feeling of affection for her father. He always got the important things done.

"So what made you chose an assignment in Santa Fe?" Max asked.

She hesitated a second before answering. Having a chat with Max in the lounge wasn't something she'd ever thought would happen. "Actually, I'm from here. My family all still live here. In fact my sister is seven months pregnant and has been placed on bedrest for the remainder of her pregnancy. So I'm here to help her, before heading off again to another assignment when she's settled."

No doubt about it. It would be good to visit home for a few weeks, but good to be gone, too. Returning here permanently was not an option. It hadn't been since she had left. When she'd decided to be a travel nurse she'd changed her life. She wasn't about to change it back now.

Max huffed out a sigh and frowned. "Every time travel nurses come through here I always wonder what they're running away from." He shook his head.

Carla's brows shot up at that insult to the livelihood she'd worked hard for. "Running away? I can't speak for all travelers, but the majority that I know certainly aren't running away from anything. They're running *to* things." As if he knew anything about it anyway.

"Like what?" He sat up and focused on her, the intensity of him more than a little unnerving, but she continued, determined not to allow him the upper hand in this conversation.

"Like adventure, new experiences, travel." There was so much out there to see and do. Staying in one place had little appeal. She swallowed another sip of coffee and ignored the pang in her stomach that she felt at his words. There was no truth to that supposition whatsoever.

"So what are *you* running from?" he asked.

"Excuse me?" She couldn't believe he'd just asked that, after what she'd told him.

"I'm not certain I believe your theory." He leaned back again. "Seems to me that people who take such temporary jobs are afraid of facing something in their life and use the travel as an excuse not to deal with things. And here you are back in your home town, but only for a short time. What's with that?" The gleam in his eyes turned cool.

"I'd say it's none of your business, but as I already told you I'm here to help care for my sister, who is in the middle of a high-risk pregnancy."

Her heart wanted to smash against her ribs at the insinuation. How dared he? Although he was incredibly handsome, he was supremely arrogant. She'd known this in the past, and she couldn't believe she'd forgotten it so easily.

"There are huge nursing shortages all over the country and someone has to fill in. Why not me?"

That was one major benefit to picking where she wanted to go at any time. This assignment happened to be perfect—to visit home at the right time. She controlled her destiny; it didn't control her.

"If nurses didn't travel around the country there wouldn't be such a shortage. Why don't you stay in one place? I simply don't get the appeal of uprooting a life every few months. There's no stability in that."

"It's my job to move around." And she liked that. "And that way I also don't have to put up with arrogant, overly opinionated doctors for more than three months at a time."

This time Max laughed, and raised his coffee cup to her in salute. "Touché. You're right, it's really none of my business, but I hope your sister does well with her pregnancy. Is it her first?"

"Yes." She took a breath and tried to release the irritation his words had caused her. So what? Maybe she *was* running away from a few things in life? But he was right in that it wasn't any of his concern. He knew nothing about what her life had been like before and had no right to make judgments about it. This was her life to live, and she'd clung to that belief for three years. She wasn't about to let go of it now.

"Pregnancy can be a real physiological disturbance for some women, even though it's a natural state. Still, if your sister can keep her blood pressure under control she'll do fine. How compliant is she?"

Carla gave a snort as she thought of her sister. "Tabi? She likes to do things her way, but she'll behave herself for the baby. Mostly." She frowned. "I think. Which is part of the reason I'm here. To make her behave."

"You do like a challenge, don't you?" He raised his dark brows at that.

"What do you mean?"

"In my experience, it's not very easy to tell a pregnant woman what to do." He grinned, and some of the tension in her eased.

"Well, that's the truth. And with Tabi I'm not sure how successful I'll really be." She looked down at her nearly empty cup and considered refilling it. That *was* good coffee he had made, but filling it again meant lingering in here with him.

She dumped the dregs. "But it is going to be good to visit family and friends again."

"Isn't being a travel nurse rather complicated? Having to learn new things all the time? Learning new systems at each hospital you go to?"

"Sure, it can be. But it doesn't have to be overwhelming or insurmountable. That's one thing I've learned by travel nursing. We choose to make our lives too complicated sometimes. There are already enough complications in life without choosing to add more to it, don't you think?"

She knew that for a fact. In all of the places she'd been there had never been any shortage of people in messes of their own making, which was why ERs were bursting at the seams.

"Is your life without complications?" It was her turn to grill him.

"Hardly." His brows returned to their normal position. He had sandy blond hair that had a tendency to flow over his forehead if he wasn't scraping it back from his face. His brows were darker than his hair, and his blue eyes were very bright and inquisitive. With a heavy sigh, he looked down at the cup in his hands. "For me, it's more that I'm going in one direction in my work life and another in my personal life."

"What do you mean?" she asked, surprised at the revelation. She moved to sit on the couch beside him. After the last few hours on her feet she needed to sit.

"I shouldn't really be telling you this, but I've been offered the position of Medical Director, starting in a few months. Beatrice is retiring."

"Well, that's good, isn't it? What have you told her?"

Max seemed to struggle to find an answer. His confidence was one of the things that made him so attractive, and this was a side of him she hadn't seen. His arrogance overshadowed the rest of him at times.

"I want the promotion. No doubt." Another sigh left him. "It's been on my career agenda since I left med school. There are so many things in the world of medicine that can be fixed or changed. I can start with my small part of the world."

Although his words said one thing, his demeanor said quite another, and that made her wonder what *he* was running from. That thought quite surprised her, as from the interactions she'd had with him now and in the past she wouldn't have thought he'd run from anything. But who knew what secrets people kept to themselves?

"Sounds like a big job. Not something everyone would want to tackle." Certainly not for her.

Max rubbed his chin, which showed a day or two of stubble, and seemed to consider her words. "Yeah. I know. But I'm up for it."

"Wouldn't work for me."

"No? Afraid of commitment?" There was the gleam in his eyes again, but this time a spark of humor shone through and she responded to that.

"No. Too many complications. In the three years I've been traveling I haven't regretted it. I've learned to live my life and to leave the expectations of others behind. That's all you'll have—high expectations—when you take the job." She'd had enough of that in her life. Especially those of her family. It had taken some effort to loosen the hold they'd had on her, and if she stayed around too long she was afraid they'd resurrect those same expectations. Okay, so maybe she *was* running. A little. She wasn't about to admit that to him, though.

"Really? You don't mind moving around so much?" he asked, seeming genuinely surprised.

"Nope. There's always another assignment over the next hill and another one after that." She paused. "It's the best way I know of to be on permanent vacation and have a full-time job at the same time."

"That is such a strange concept to me." He leaned back against the couch.

"Well, it's certainly been good for me." Like nothing else in her life. She could see that he didn't understand that, but that was okay. He didn't have to, and it wasn't her job to convince him.

The door opened and Kenny popped his head in. "Carla, how about some very exciting paperwork? We need to do your skills checklists and stuff like that for the orientation requirements."

Carla stood. "Sure." She looked down at Max and hoped that working with him wasn't going to be so intense for her entire assignment. "Thanks for the coffee."

"Any time," he said, and she felt his gaze follow her as she walked out the door.

*Intriguing.* That was the word that kept coming to Max's mind the next day as he raced down the wooded trail on his mountain bike. He ought to add the word *distracting* to that, because if he didn't pay attention to the path in front of him, instead of thinking about Carla Lopez and her unusual life philosophy, he was going to pay for it by kissing a tree the hard way.

Putting her out of his mind would be the best, but for some reason her exotically shaped eyes kept appearing in his mind, and her words resonated unexpectedly somewhere inside of him, drawing out things that had been filed neatly away over the years. He knew who he was and where he was going. Unfulfilled dreams didn't fit into his plans.

After negotiating a serious part of the trail that got a little too close to the edge of a severe drop-off, he focused on the scenery around him, putting Carla and her words to the back of his mind for a while.

The rest of his ride was uneventful and burned off some

stress. Hot and depleted of energy at the end of the trail, Max secured his bike on the roof of his SUV and drove to his favorite restaurant. The Cow Town Café was a place often frequented by hospital staff, just a block or two away from the hospital. The atmosphere there was casual, the food excellent, and it was open twenty-four hours a day. What more could starving and overworked hospital staff ask for?

Squeaky wooden floors and décor that spoke to the history of Santa Fe only added to the dining experience. Right now, though, he was depleted, and he didn't care what the place looked like. He wanted food that didn't come out of a can. He opened the heavy wooden door to find the place packed and his mood deflated a bit. Deciding to place his order to go instead of waiting for a table, he approached the hostess.

"Max! Hey, Dr. Kelton," came a voice from the back of the restaurant, and he looked around, smiled and waved.

"I'll wait at the table over there." He bypassed the hostess and wound his way through many tables, stopping where several of his co-workers sat. It seemed as if half the ER department was there. They had pushed several small tables together to create one large one. People squished closer together, and someone grabbed a chair and shoved it in the middle of the group across from Taylor.

"Hey, good to see you out and about, Max. Have a seat," Taylor said. He was a fellow physician at the ER, a friend, and another adrenaline junkie. Taylor wore his passions out in the open for everyone to see. Max hadn't ever been able to do that.

"Thanks," Max said, and sat.

He was not quite as comfortable in social situations with staff outside of work as Taylor. Though Max knew these people on the inside of the hospital, getting to know them outside of work had never been easy for him. He did better with the boundary of medicine between them. Once he took the director job, evenings like this would be a thing of the past. Boundaries would be too strong to overcome.

He looked around and nodded or waved to the others around the table. Curiously enough, at his left side sat Carla Lopez. "What's the party for, and why didn't anyone invite me?" With raised brows he looked down at Carla, whose face turned a light shade of pink beneath her tanned complexion.

"It was my fault," she said, and dropped her gaze. "I'm sorry."

"She didn't think you'd come," Taylor said with a laugh, and shoved a basket of tortilla chips closer to him.

Reaching out, Max absently took a chip and considered whether he would have accepted the invitation had it been offered. With another sideways glance at Carla, he guessed she was probably right. Looking around at the people here, the camaraderie so obvious among them, he wondered if those personal boundaries he held in such high regard were holding him back. They certainly protected him—but from what? He'd always separated work from play, but now a small pang hit him as he felt the friendship around him. What had he been missing because of it? Had holding people who were supposed to be friends at arm's length not been as beneficial as he'd thought? Taylor had recently become engaged to a woman who had been a travel nurse, and was now happier than Max had ever seen him.

The waiter brought a glass of water and Max reached for it, wanting to guzzle the thing down, but sipped instead. Dehydration was no man's friend.

"No party," Taylor said, and handed him a menu. "More like spontaneous revelry." He looked down at Piper, his fiancée, and curved his arm behind her back and pulled her closer.

"It was Carla's suggestion," Piper said. "She's full of fun ideas."

Max looked to his left. "Why am I not surprised?"

"Spontaneity is good for a body, don't you think, Max?" Carla asked, and raised her brows right back at him. There was challenge in that look, and it was the one thing he never backed down from. Challenge always got his attention and Carla certainly had it now.

"I do indeed." The waiter returned, and Max ordered his food to go.

Carla spoke to him, but her words were lost in the conversations around them. He leaned closer. "Sorry? I didn't hear."

Carla leaned closer and spoke into his ear. "I just asked what you had been up to today." The second her breath touched his skin he nearly shivered, but somehow controlled the response. Though the contact was innocent, his reaction to it was not. The attraction that had been brewing melded into a surprising hum of desire.

Turning in his chair to face her more fully, he looked at her, down into the depths of those gorgeous, snapping brown eyes of hers. Beyond the beauty and the nerves was a woman with a brain. That was a very interesting package.

"Mountain biking," he said, and pulled back slightly. "It's great for stress relief after the long days we put in." It was his second great passion—the thing that kept him sane when his first passion wore him out. When he took the directorship he might not have the time for riding that he normally did, and that would be a profound loss for him. Still, meetings came before mountains.

"Where did you go?" she asked.

Meeting his gaze, she held it for a moment, and surprise surfaced. Watching her lips curve upward slightly made him wonder if they were as soft as they looked. Before he became mesmerized by the sight of her, he moved back a little to his safe zone.

"Today I went to Pacheco Canyon. It's one of my favorites." There were several places he preferred to go for various physical challenges, but Pacheco was rapidly becoming his top pick due to the varying terrain. "Do you bike?"

Her eyes widened at his question. "Oh, no. I'm not like you, Dr. Adrenaline." She shook her head and sipped her wine to hide a smirk.

"What's that supposed to mean?" he asked. It was his turn to be surprised. She was just full of it tonight, and he responded as if she'd waved a red flag in front of him.

Carla nodded at Taylor, who still observed them. "You two. You're like the adrenaline-junkie twins. Out for the greatest thrill you can possibly find. ER medicine isn't enough, so you thrill-seek wherever you can find it." She shook her head and gave a laugh. "Just driving across town is enough for me."

That got him where he lived, and he fully turned to her.

"So you have no interest in de-stressing after work?"

"Of course I do. I just choose things like yoga and meditation, rather than seeing if my hair will catch on fire racing down the side of a mountain." She reached for her water glass this time and took a sip, again trying to hide that smirk of a smile.

"I see. So, you're scared." It was a statement designed to challenge her. It worked.

Carla nearly choked on her water. She put the glass down and wiped her mouth. "Excuse me?" Her eyes were wide in disbelief.

"The only reason you can possibly want to diss mountain biking is because you're afraid you're not up to it physically. It's very obvious, Carla." He couldn't resist goading Carla, he loved the way her eyes flashed with annoyance. It made her look even more vibrant and beautiful. "You don't have to hide it any longer. We understand."

"That's so not true."

"No? Then why don't you do it?"

"I simply prefer other methods of stress release. Not pounding my backside down the mountain on a flimsy piece of machinery."

"Back to being afraid. Am I right or what, Taylor?" He sighed and reached for his glass again, thoroughly enjoying this little repartee with Carla.

Taylor laughed instead of answering, and continued to observe the interaction at the table.

"When's the last time you took a yoga class, Doctor?" Carla asked, her shoulders and back stiff. "Got in touch with your mind and spirit instead of just your muscles?"

"Uh, never." He didn't even have to think about it. "I don't bend that way."

"I'll bet you can't even touch your toes, can you?"

He glared at her in answer, afraid that she was right. "No idea. Don't need to touch my toes."

"So you're afraid you can't handle it? Afraid you'll look bad if you tried it?" she said, her gaze brimming with challenge. "Big, bad Dr. Adrenaline can't sit still for an hour."

Taylor laughed and slapped the table. "She's got you there, buddy." He looked at Piper. "This is way better than late-night television."

"She. Does. Not." Max spoke to Taylor, but kept his gaze on Carla, not sure he was enjoying this anymore.

"I have the perfect suggestion, you guys," Piper said. "Carla, go biking with Max. Max, take a yoga class with Carla."

"No," they said in unison, and looked at Piper as if she'd lost her mind.

"Why not? It's the perfect solution to see who's right and who gets their panties in a wad."

Taylor laughed again and kissed Piper's cheek. "You're right. Wish I could follow them and watch."

"I'm not getting on a mountain bike," Carla said, and dropped her gaze.

"So you're admitting you're afraid right now?" Max asked, not certain what was making him pursue this further, but he just couldn't drop it. It wasn't just being teased by friends—something about it wouldn't allow him to let up. Carla Lopez was not going to get the better of him.

"I'm admitting nothing." Glaring at him, she raised her face and narrowed her eyes at him.

"Then I'll pick you up tomorrow afternoon at three." It was settled for him. He'd bike her into the ground and make her admit that he was right. Again.

"What? No. I didn't agree to this." She shook her head, setting her short bob swaying.

"It's the only way out. I have a spare bike and a helmet you can use." Although she didn't agree, her lips pressed together so firmly, he knew she was waffling and a glow began in his chest. Her pride was on the line. Hell, so was his.

After a long-suffering sigh, she said, "All right. I'll go."

"Good." Oh, he loved being right.

"And you can plan a yoga class with me next Wednesday evening at six. Loose clothing, bare feet. And an anti-inflammatory for the pain you'll be in."

There was that damned smirk again. He was going to enjoy seeing that disappear on the mountain tomorrow. Unable to say no, he simply nodded, knowing that he'd likely regret it.

The waiter arrived with Max's order and he paid, thankful to have an end to this outrageous conversation. "Guess I'll head out now."

Carla stifled a yawn. "I think I'm going to go, too. I drove three days to get here, followed by two of twelve-hour shifts, and now half a glass of wine. I've had it." She moved her plate away and rested her arms on the wooden table. "Earlier I was full of energy and wanted to go out, but now, I think I should go before I fall asleep in the basket of *sopapillas.*"

Quickly she covered her mouth as another yawn overtook her, and Max immediately knew how she would look all sleepy and rumpled in bed. He looked away, determined to put an end to those stray thoughts of his. "I think we've all been there at one time or another."

She stood. "G'night, everyone. See you in a few days." There was a chorus of goodbyes and waves as Max also stood and picked up his food.

"I'll walk you out. Can't be too safe around here."

They walked from the nearly overwhelming volume of the restaurant to the sudden quiet of the parking lot. Darkness had eased in on the day, and only a hint of pale orange hugged the edge of the mountains.

"So, the time works for you tomorrow? I've got a few meetings that I have to be at, then I'm free the rest of the day."

She gave a stiff nod. "Yes. I'll be helping my sister most of the day, so the afternoon works fine." She shook her head slightly.

"Something wrong?" he asked as they walked to her car.

"Not really. I just wanted to say that I didn't call to invite you tonight because I honestly didn't think you'd come."

He thought about that for a second, uncertain if he'd have accepted the invitation. "Not a problem." He paused a second, looking down at her in the twilight. "Not going to back out at the last minute, are you?" Something made him want to make sure that she'd follow through with it.

"I won't back out. I keep my word." Light from the street-lamps glittered in her eyes. "I hope you do, too."

"I do. See you at three."

"See you at three." She got into her car and drove off.

Ignoring the pinch of guilt wanting to surface, Max got into his SUV and went home, anticipation developing inside of him.

# CHAPTER THREE

"So, how's life in the ER?" Tabitha asked Carla. She was a petite brunette, and looked a lot like her sister except for the large belly, and was propped up against the headboard of her bed. "Is it weird being back there again?"

"Kinda strange. Busy, as usual, but there are a few friendly faces, so that's good." Carla told Tabi about some of the patients that she'd cared for, and some of the staff that she'd renewed acquaintance with. "It was fun seeing them again. Some people never change."

"There is a bit of comfort in the sameness of things, isn't there? To know you can depend on certain people to always be there," Tabi said.

Tabi had always been a creature of habit, needing repetition and uniformity to be happy with her life. It was Carla who in the end had become the non-conformist—the one with stars in her eyes, and dreams that reached far from Santa Fe.

"Sometimes. For me, though, I can only handle the sameness for two or three months before needing a change." That was one reason travel nursing worked so well for her. It was a perfect outlet for the restless nature of her soul.

Tabi paused a second, watching Carla. "Have you considered returning here permanently? I mean, now that you're back could you stay a while, think about settling down?"

A wave of shock raced through Carla. "Oh, no. Although

this will always be home, it's not where I want to live the rest of my life." Tabi dropped her gaze. "I'm sorry that disappoints you, but this is who I am." And she needed to be who she was now, not return to the shrinking violet she'd been. She'd worked hard over the past three years, pushing herself to put her own needs first. She wasn't the meek and mild Carla anymore, terrified to rock the boat. But the closer she'd gotten to home, the stronger that fear had grown inside of her. Maybe that was why her conversation with Max had hit her so strongly.

"I'm not disappointed in you—just disappointed I can't see you more." Tabi stretched her hand out to Carla and squeezed a second. "I miss you, that's all."

"I've missed you, too. I hope that I can visit and see this baby now and then."

"If you took a permanent job here you could."

Carla laughed. Her sister was nothing if not persistent. "Who knows? Maybe I can just extend my time here if all goes well." She shook her head. "Uh, did you know that Mom and Dad wanted me to stay at the house with them for this assignment?"

"Oh, no. I didn't know that." Tabi shivered and made a face. "After the life you've led the last three years and then moving back in with Mom and Dad? Not an option."

"That's what I thought, too. But I did promise them I'd have dinner with them soon." Carla sighed. She could make that concession without compromising her lifestyle. Boundaries that she'd been unable to keep up while living here were now easier to manage. The conversation she'd had with Max the other day came back to her. If she weren't running away from home, why *couldn't* she stay a while?

"That's good. You won't have to cook, either. Mom will make all your favorite foods."

"Good point." The memory of who she'd been intruded,

and a pang of insecurity surged in her chest. She took a deep breath and reminded herself that she wasn't ever going to return to being that person again. "Sometimes I feel like another person. The life I lived here is totally different than the one I have on the road." Somehow similar to Max's comparison of his life.

"Well, in a way you *are* a different person. You've grown, you've changed."

"I guess so." She paused. "I like who I am now, and I don't want to give that up." She thought of Max again for a second, wondering if he'd ever know how much she'd changed. Wondered if it mattered.

"No reason to, but I would like to see you more. Three years is a long time to go between visits."

"I've missed you, too. E-mail and calls just aren't enough. I know that. But I was so afraid of coming back at first." So afraid that she'd stayed away for three years. She admitted it to herself and to Tabi, but she wasn't going to admit it out loud to Max.

"Afraid? Of what?" Tabi's eyebrows raised, genuine surprise showing on her face.

Tears pricked Carla's eyes, but she held them back. Tabi knew her secrets, her dreams. "Of returning to the person I was back then, of not being strong enough to keep my new life."

"Oh, Carla."

"Now I know that I am. I can visit home, and I can leave here, too." She wasn't strong enough to stay. She knew that.

"You're strong enough to do anything you want to. I'm so glad you're my sister," Tabi said, and reached out for Carla's hand again. "Now, help me up. I gotta pee."

With a laugh, Carla felt the tension in her ease for the moment, and she helped Tabi to the bathroom.

\* \* \*

After returning to her apartment and getting ready for her outing with Max, Carla tied her athletic shoes, filled a water bottle, applied sunscreen and waited. This wasn't a date. This was about salvaging what was left of her pride. Dates usually involved dinner and a movie, or something in the evening hours. This was two people out trying to win a challenge against each other. But when the doorbell rang the butterflies in her stomach knew otherwise.

Max stood in her doorway wearing much the same attire he had had on yesterday: loose shirt, shorts, athletic shoes and a hat. He looked yummy.

"Ready to go?" he asked.

Nodding, she grabbed her water bottle and locked the door behind them. "So, where are we going?"

"Pacheco Canyon—where I went yesterday. Have you ever been there?"

Carla followed Max to his vehicle. She could have identified it because it was the only one in the parking lot with two bicycles attached to the roof rack.

"Only once or twice. Been a while, obviously. I think the last time I was here part of the trail had been washed out by a big storm."

She watched as the terrain changed from high desert to a more alpine landscape and her palms began to sweat. Up into the trees they drove, to the trailhead not far from town.

"I remember that. This is one of my favorite trails, so I know it well."

Anticipation hummed through her. Maybe today wouldn't turn out to be too bad after all. Pride had gotten her through some tough times in the past. It would see her through today as well.

Max parked the SUV beside several other cars and hefted the bikes off the rack. As the muscles in his arms flexed and bunched with the activity Carla watched, trying not to pay too much attention to the way his strong arms easily carried out the task. But it didn't work. She'd always been curiously attracted to Max and had harbored a secret crush on him years ago. Back then there was no way she'd ever have had the confidence to think about dating Max. Now? She'd changed. Being alone in the wilderness with him was intoxicating to her senses even though she knew he was going to mop the floor with her. She was no match for him physically. Still, if some of the other nurses knew she was on an outing with him they'd be extremely jealous.

In minutes they were off up the trail, with Max leading the way. "There are a few changes since you were here. I'll point them out so you won't get lost."

She hid a grin. Maybe he had a sense of humor after all, but it was buried beneath his stern doctor persona. "I'm certain I won't get lost." Not that she minded being behind him, though. The scenery there was fine as well.

Every few minutes he looked behind him, checking on Carla to see if she was keeping up. She was athletic, but unaccustomed to the strain of altitude exercise after being gone for three years. Her body had lost its acclimation and it would take a few weeks before she got it back.

Not. Giving. Up. She concentrated on pushing first one foot, then the other. Left. Right. Left. Right. Up. The. Damned. Hill. Sweat poured off her and she was certain that her face was an unattractive shade of red. She wasn't giving up. She wasn't going to let Max or the mountain beat her, though her lungs were about to burst. With a glance ahead she noticed that the trail leveled out flat and Max was waiting by the side of his bike, grinning.

That did it. She couldn't give up. Maybe in the past she'd have stopped, but not now. Taking on Max and the mountain didn't make her afraid. Giving up did.

"Hey, Carla. Looks like you need a—"

She blew right by him and didn't even say a word. The level terrain made it easier for her to gain some speed. With a laugh and a look over her shoulder, she saw that Max had jumped on his bike and raced after her. A sudden burst of energy filled her, and now she knew what Max was talking about. Adrenaline junkie indeed. Maybe she was turning into one with a single trip up the mountain.

Max caught up to her quickly, though, and whizzed past her, shifting the bike into higher gear for more power. Now it was his turn to look back at her, but this time there was a grin of pleasure on his face instead of the gloating one he'd worn earlier.

Finally her surge ended, and she had to stop or her heart was going to collapse. Coasting to a stop at the side of the trail, she straddled the bike and waited for Max to turn around and come back for her. At least she had the satisfaction of seeing him breathe nearly as hard as she was.

"So how do you like it?" he asked, and pulled his water bottle from its holder.

"So far…so good… But I gotta wait…to breathe…again." She grabbed her water for a much needed drink, too.

"I have to admit I'm a little surprised." His blue eyes were hidden behind his reflective sunglasses, but she knew he stared at her. "You hung in there very well for your first time out." He laughed out loud. "I didn't think you'd make it past the first turn." He shook his head, his doubt somehow turning into admiration—and that was something she hadn't expected.

"My last few assignments were at sea level, so you have an advantage over me." Finally her heart slowed its frantic pace.

"Going from sea level to eight thousand feet is quite a challenge in just a few days. I didn't even think about that."

"It's okay. I'd nearly forgotten about adjusting to the

elevation." She relaxed a little as her breath returned to a more normal flow. "In a week or two I should be fine." She wiped her forearm across her forehead. "We can try it again then."

"Sure," Max said, and put away his water bottle. "No worries."

"So I surprised you, huh?" she asked, and watched him.

"Yeah. You sure did. It's not often that happens."

"Maybe it's time someone shook you up, Max." Hearing his admission warmed her. Maybe he really wasn't so bad. She might not admit to having fun yet, but so far things were not as bad as she'd expected.

"Indeed." He removed his sunglasses and tucked them in the front of his shirt. He looked more closely at her. "And you think you're the one to do that? Think you'd be up to having dinner with me after this?"

Swallowing the lump in her throat, Carla stared back at him, liking the look of him standing in the sunshine, hot and energized from the workout. She might not have what it took to really shake him up, but it would be interesting to give it a try. She'd never had a fling while on assignment. Certainly could add some spice. She looked him up and down, considering.

"Uh, no."

"No?" Genuine surprise shone in his eyes. "Why not?"

"I gotta see what you can do in yoga class first."

Max had opened his mouth to reply to that when someone coming down the trail called out. "Coming through!"

Carla watched as a group of six bikers filed past. The group consisted entirely of women with gray hair. They wore matching shirts that bore the words "Wicked Widows" on the backs.

Carla laughed and waved as they swooshed by. "Wow. I hope I'm that fit when I'm their age."

Max cast a glance up and down her body—similar to the one she'd given him. "You look like—"

A scream screeched up the trail, startling Carla and Max. Cries for help soon followed.

"Uh-oh," Carla said, and stowed her water.

With barely a glance between them, Max and Carla mounted their bikes and quickly followed after the group of women. They found them hovering at the edge of the trail, looking down the side. Carla swallowed and looked at Max.

There were only five of them.

"What happened?" Max said, and shoved his bike off the path, and dropped his pack, in charge of the situation without having to say so.

"Jane went off the edge," one of the distressed ladies said.

Carla moved closer and looked down at the rocks and jagged-looking outcroppings that made up the embankment. A sick feeling of dread as to what she was going to see squirmed inside her. She and Max were alone, with little or no equipment. It certainly wasn't like an ER setting, where they had help and state-of-the-art medical machinery at their fingertips. If they were to help this woman they had only each other to depend on.

After scouring the hillside a few seconds, she pointed. "There's her bike."

"Jane? Can you hear me?" one of the women called to their friend.

"Yes, I hear you." Her voice was strong. That was a good sign.

Carla knelt by the edge and Max grabbed her by the back of the shirt, holding onto her. "Careful of the loose rock. That's probably why she went over."

That sick feeling of dread curled in her stomach. She

backed up a little, grateful that Max still held onto her, and moved closer to his reassuring presence.

"Are you okay down there? I'm a nurse and my friend is a doctor. Are you injured?" Carla called down. She still couldn't see the woman, but if she was calling for help that was a good sign.

"I'm okay, I think. Scraped up. But my foot is stuck," Jane said. "I can't get loose."

Max squatted beside Carla while still holding onto her shirt. His senses were on high alert and the adrenaline surging through his system wasn't just from the physical exertion. Everything around him looked brighter, more intense than it had a few moments ago.

"Can you pull your foot out of your shoe?" he asked.

"No. It's wedged between these damned rocks."

Carla turned to Max. "Do you have any equipment in your SUV that could help? Don't you climb, too?"

The look of trust in her eyes floored him. They really didn't know each other, but there it was. She'd put her trust in him.

"Yeah. I leave all of my climbing gear in it." He nodded and squeezed her arm. They were on the same wavelength. "I'll go get it and be back as soon as I can."

"And bring any first aid supplies you have, too."

Carla looked at him—so close, so concerned. On impulse, he leaned forward and pressed a kiss to her cheek. "Stay back from the edge in case it crumbles again." He jumped onto his bike and raced back down the mountain, determined to return with whatever he could carry.

# CHAPTER FOUR

"IF ANYONE has a cell phone, call the emergency services and tell them what's going on." Carla kept her eyes on Max until he disappeared around a bend in the trail. What was that kiss about? Still, there was no time to wonder about Max's intentions now—the emergency demanded all of her attention.

"I've got one. My son insists I carry mine when I'm out. Especially after that awful search and rescue accident last year." One of the women dug the phone out of her pack and made the call.

Carla didn't know about the incident she referred to, but knew that first responders sometimes faced greater difficulties than anticipated. Carla thought ahead to the possible scenarios they faced with the injured woman. She hoped that the circulation was adequate to Jane's foot, or she could lose it. She remembered hearing about a hiker in Colorado who had cut off his own arm after it had been crushed beneath a boulder. She shivered. Didn't pay to hike alone or without a means of communication.

Minutes later Max returned with the gear. He breathed heavily, but was much more accustomed to the elevation than Carla. Working quickly together, they pulled the gear out of his duffel bag.

"Tell me what to do." Carla took in a breath as adrenaline

and anxiety pulsed through her. "Climbing is out of my skill set," she said with a tight smile.

The attempt at a joke fell flat to her ears. Working in the ER in a relatively controlled setting was one thing. Being out in the near wilderness with little equipment and no support staff fried her nerves. Wilderness medicine was out of her comfort zone. But Max looked as if he were completely in his element, totally in charge and at the height of his game, and she had to admire him for it.

Max tied one of the ropes to a sturdy tree across the trail, and Carla assisted him with his harness, then handed him his gloves and helmet. "I know you're going to need these," she said, and spontaneously reached out to hug him. She pulled back. "Be careful. Don't take any chances."

The look in her eyes made him pause before going over the edge. The worry surprised him. He knew his skills as a physician and a climber. This was one of the reasons he had become a doctor in the first place and had dedicated his life to it. He simply loved it. Retrieving people off the side of a mountain gave him a bigger thrill than working in the ER did, and it wasn't something he wanted to give up. But right now he couldn't think of anything except the situation in front of him.

Reaching out to her, he stroked a gloved finger down her cheek. "I will, and I won't. Don't worry." Max gave her a look of confidence and the thumbs-up signal, then began the descent over the edge of the embankment.

Anxiety filled Carla as she watched him disappear. She hoped he was going to be okay. Thinking of his confidence and his skills as a physician calmed her a little. He wouldn't risk himself if he couldn't get to the woman. Everything in him was focused on putting one foot after the other.

"Max! How is everything?" Carla called down to him as

sweat poured off her. Her heart was racing nearly as fast as when she had been puffing up the hill not long ago.

"I'm nearly to her."

Tense minutes passed as Carla waited at the top. She wanted to call out to Max, to encourage him, but she held her silence, not wanting to be a distraction.

"Okay, Carla, get ready. She's coming up first."

"Okay!"

The calm tones of his voice reassured her. A cheer of excitement erupted from the other Wicked Widows, and warmth spread through Carla's chest. Carla listened to Max's instructions and held tight to the rope, putting tension on it to keep Jane steady. Every few feet the woman had to pause, but she made it to the top.

With Max climbing right beside her!

Several things happened at once. The sirens of the arriving rescue team cut the silence, the Wicked Widows gathered around Jane, easing her the rest of the way onto the trail, and Carla helped Max over the edge.

"Max! You should have waited." Carla's heart raced as she realized that Max was climbing without his safety harness or the gloves that he'd given to Jane. Fussing over him, she brushed off bits of dirt and plant matter that clung to him, checking for injuries, then picked a few cactus thorns from his shirt.

"Relax. It was okay, really. This is what I live for." He caught her hand and squeezed. Energy and adrenaline rushed through him. He felt more alive in this moment than he had in a long time. This *was* what he lived for in his career—these moments when he made a difference to one person, when his actions made the difference between life and death.

"What's wrong? Are you hurt?" she asked, and ran her hands over his arms, looking for injuries.

"No. I didn't mean to worry you. Jane needed the harness

more than I did. Coming up is easier than going down. Really." He patted her hand. "Let's see how she is now."

"Okay. Okay." Nodding, she held onto his hand and they moved to Jane. The Wicked Widows made room for Max and he knelt beside her.

"Carla, could you get the inflatable cast out of the first aid pack for me?"

"Sure." Glad to have a second to herself while she dug in the pack, Carla took a few cleansing breaths. After finding the splint, she returned to Max and Jane.

With gentle hands, Max removed Jane's shoe.

Jane sucked in her breath and winced as Max eased the shoe from her swollen foot, which was beginning to discolor. "That smarts!"

"I'll bet it does." He examined the foot and ankle. "That shoe probably saved your foot from a more serious injury. It's a good one. Sorry I had to cut it up some."

"No matter. Small sacrifice to save my foot."

"True." He looked up at Carla, who still frowned. He hadn't meant to frighten her. He'd make it up to her somehow.

"Here comes rescue," Carla said, relief evident on her face, and waved at the team of people coming their way, led by one of the Wicked Widows.

"Good. They can take you to the ER and have you really checked over." Max applied the inflatable splint.

"Oh, but the girls can take me in," she protested, and removed Max's helmet and gave it back to him. "I don't need a circus parade."

"Jane, these people came all the way up here to help you. Why don't you let them?" Max said, and patted her leg.

"Oh, okay. You're the doctor," she said with a frown, obviously not liking being fussed over.

When the rescuers arrived Max briefed them on the woman's condition. "I'm afraid the bike's not as lucky as Jane."

"I've been looking for an excuse to get a new one, so here it is," Jane said, and squealed, then giggled like a girl, as two of the men lifted her onto a hard plastic litter to be carried down to the ambulance. "Wow! You guys know how to give a girl a pick-up."

"You're just a little bit of nothing, ma'am," one of them said, and gave her a very big smile.

"Now, does your mother know you're flirting with older women?" she countered with a grin as they strapped her in.

"I won't tell her if you won't," he said.

Jane just laughed. "Carry me away, boys."

"Take care," Carla said, and gave Jane a reassuring smile and a pat on the arm.

"I will. I want the two of you to come in to my restaurant, the Roadrunner Café, and I'll treat you to Sunday dinner on me." She gave a wave as the men carried her off.

"Jane, that's not—" Carla started.

"We'd love to, Jane. Thank you for the generous offer," Max interrupted her and squeezed Carla's arm, neatly roping Carla into going there with him. She looked up at him with a curious light in her eyes, as if she knew exactly what he had done. He hadn't forgotten her refusal to have dinner with him. He did like to win.

The other ladies walked with their bikes down the rest of the way, following Jane on the litter.

"I think she's going to be fine," Max said and released Carla's arm.

Carla nearly snorted at his assessment. "Yeah. It helps to be carried around like Cleopatra and treated like a queen."

A laugh barked unexpectedly out of Max. "That's one way to look at it."

Carla laughed and watched the entourage disappear around a bend in the trail. "I wish I could be in the ER to see that whole group arrive. You know the bunch of them will take over and probably be serving coffee and cookies to the staff before Jane's out of X-ray."

Max chuckled. "I think you're right." He looked down the trail after the group, a good feeling lingering in him. "Light's fading, though. Why don't we gather up the equipment and call it a day?"

Half an hour later they drove away from the trailhead and back to town.

"Sorry we didn't get to finish our ride," Carla said. "I know you live for adrenaline."

"It's okay. We can try it again another time."

"Okay."

"Unless, of course, you're willing to admit it now." Max kept his eyes on the road, but watched her with his peripheral vision.

"Admit what?"

"That you enjoyed yourself and mountain biking isn't bad for stress relief."

"I can't admit that. Halfway through our excursion someone fell off a mountain and distracted me from making a full assessment! That was not stress-*relieving* in any way." She paused for a second. "Guess that means we have to do this again sometime, doesn't it?"

He grinned and looked directly at her for a second. In so many ways she was quite a surprise, and not at all what he'd expected. She was much stronger than he'd anticipated, both physically and emotionally. He'd expected someone who gave in easily, but instead he'd discovered someone who challenged him. "I'll count on it."

"Next time no rescue, okay?" But it just wasn't in her to abandon anyone who needed help. Max wouldn't either. That much she knew about him. He was solid in his convictions and his duty to medicine.

"I'll do my best. So, dinner's on me tonight. Where do you

want to go?" They were stopped on the side of the road that led back to town.

Hesitation paired with a burst of excitement bubbled up inside of her. She hadn't expected this. Somehow Max, Dr. Adrenaline, was turning into someone very different than she'd suspected he was. She'd heard all the gossip, of course. Who could work in a hospital setting and *not* hear it? Half the staff, it seemed, had a crush on Max. At least the female half anyway. But most were too intimidated by him to even consider asking him out. It seemed as if his reputation was pretty much as it had been when she'd briefly worked with him in the past. He put up a barrier and she had seen it in action, so it made her wonder a bit about dinner.

"Did you have some place in mind?"

"Your choice."

"Oh, you're leaving yourself wide open for this one." She paused a second as she thought.

"Go ahead. I can take it."

"There used to be this little bistro on the Santa Fe Plaza that served the best food. I wonder if it's still there," Carla mused aloud.

"Are you talking about Tito's?"

"Yes! Do you know it?" Pulses of pleasure and fond memories shot through her chest.

"Sure. It's one of the hallmarks of the city."

"Take me there, please." Her mouth was already watering in anticipation.

"Yes, my queen."

Carla grinned. Okay, so if he took her to her favorite restaurant he couldn't be all bad, right? She could admit that without losing anything.

A short while later they were seated at Tito's, *al fresco* on the patio, in the evening air that was just perfect. No humidity. No bugs. Just a perfect night all around them. The lights from other businesses on the plaza lent a festive glow to the entire area. In Santa Fe beautiful food was nearly as important as beautiful art. In some restaurants it was the edible equivalent.

The waiter arrived and attempted to hand them menus. "Don't need one," Carla said as her appetite exploded. She rattled off her order and grabbed a tortilla chip from the basket on the table.

"I'll just have what she's having—except for the Margarita. I'm driving." Max handed his menu over and leaned back in his chair to engage in what was rapidly turning into a fascination: watching Carla.

# CHAPTER FIVE

"Oh, THESE are so good," Carla said, and dunked a chip in Tito's house salsa. "This is definitely one of the things I missed."

"Looks like you're making up for it now." He was enjoying the glow of pleasure on her face. She was seriously enjoying herself—which made him realize how different his life was from hers. She took off at the drop of a hat, while he hadn't been on vacation in two years, and had kept the same job for years until now.

"Oh, I am so sorry," she said, and sat back with a horrified look on her face.

"What's wrong?"

"I'm sitting here making a pig of myself and not sharing." She pushed the items away from her and across the table, closer to him.

"Oh, no. That's not right." He returned the items to be directly in front of her, stood, then moved his chair around the corner of the table to her right, and sat beside her instead of across the table from her. "There. Now we're both closer to the food." Being physically closer to her was enticing—more than he'd counted on.

"Thanks."

She placed a hand on his arm, and he liked the feel of her skin against his. Placing his hand over hers, he squeezed.

Surprise showed in her eyes, but she didn't withdraw from his touch.

There was definitely heat going on between them, and it wasn't from the salsa. Green chili was nowhere near as hot as Carla Lopez.

"So, why don't you tell me about some of your travels?" he asked, trying to keep the conversation neutral between them.

"Aren't you tired of hearing me talk?"

"Not yet."

"That's sweet."

She leaned closer and kissed him on the cheek, then hesitated, with her face very close to his.

It would only take a fraction of a movement for their lips to touch. A hunger for her stirred in his belly. She was the one who was sweet. Her eyes were wide and assessing, holding his gaze. Curiosity stirred there, and her lips were parted slightly. With everything he had in him, everything that he called male, he wanted to reach out to her—wanted to put his arms around her and see if she were as soft as she looked, if her mouth were as tempting as the rest of her.

"I want to kiss you, Carla Lopez." Reaching toward her, he cupped his right hand behind her neck and drew her closer, watching as her eyelids fluttered closed.

"Oh! So sorry to interrupt." The waiter arrived with her drink and set it in front of her. "Sorry!" He hurried away.

Carla laughed at the interruption and blushed. Max took in a deep breath, pulling her fragrance into his mind. She was sweet and spicy—an interesting mix of woman.

With a mental sigh, he leaned back and reached for another chip as Carla reached for her drink and sipped.

"Oh, this is *so* good. Let me tell you, the best Margaritas are made right here in New Mexico. I've missed them."

"So, why don't you stay and enjoy them more?" he asked,

and reached for the water jug to cool his libido, which wanted him to go galloping away with Carla. He wanted to guzzle the whole thing down, but refrained. The other option was to dump it onto his lap, and he wasn't about to do that either.

"My life is on the road now." She dropped her gaze and twiddled with the edge of the chip basket.

"But why not settle here for a while? It's a wonderful place to live."

"I know. I grew up here, remember? That makes it home. But you know the saying: you can never go home again."

"Oh, that's a bunch of garbage. You have to live somewhere, and why not in a place that is filled with family and friends?" He watched her closely.

"It's not that I don't want those things." She huffed out a sigh. "I'm sure my life is boring and dull compared to what *you* do every day."

"Go on—tell me. I want to hear." He did, and was surprising himself at how much. "Just how many assignments have you taken?"

"In the last three years I've worked in twelve states. I've made friends in every place I've gone to."

"But?"

"It's all temporary. The friends seem to last only as long as the assignment, and then we all part company, off on our separate journeys."

"Doesn't that get old? I mean, I'm all for adventuring, but to uproot your life every few months must get tiring." He couldn't imagine doing it. The lifestyle of a travel nurse was something that he had never understood, despite so many of them coming through his ER.

"Oh, sure. There are loads of things that get old. Packing and unpacking is one of them. Missing so many holidays with family."

"That's got to be a big one. And what about your sister?

After the birth, you're going to miss so much of your niece or nephew's growing up." His family was here, and he could see them any time he wanted. Not that he saw them a lot, but the opportunity was always there.

"I know. I know. But this is what I do now. I can't live my life in the past and be afraid all the time anymore."

"So you *are* running away from something after all? What are you so afraid of?" This spontaneous conversation was getting somewhere.

She flashed him a quizzical look. "I was such an introvert growing up. I was afraid of my shadow. I let other people make decisions for me—boyfriends, my parents, even my friends—because I was too afraid to make them myself. It wasn't until I realized that my last boyfriend had been basically using me, taking advantage of my insecurities, that I knew I had to leave—if only to find myself. I decided to focus on the one thing I felt I could be good at: my nursing. Away from here, I was finally able to make a new start."

She snorted. "You know, we *have* met before. But I'm sure you don't remember me."

"We have? When?" That was a newsflash.

"When I was just out of nursing school, doing my practicum in the ER. I was helping out with a code and misinterpreted arterial blood gas results."

"They can be tricky."

"Well, you corrected me in no uncertain terms, and I have never forgotten since." She sipped from her glass.

"Sorry. I don't remember." He held her gaze. "You certainly aren't that person now."

"No. No, I'm not. But I'm afraid that if I stay I'll go back to being her again." She dropped her gaze again, making him wonder about the hidden Carla.

Their dinners arrived and Max pulled back from her.

At unsuspecting moments during their meal her leg

brushed against his. The contact kept him constantly aware of her presence, so close to him.

"Oh, my, that was good," she said, and pushed her plate back. There were only a few crumbs left, so he knew she had enjoyed it. It was good to see a woman with a healthy appetite.

"I'm glad." He pushed his plate back, too. "I think I've about had it too."

Carla finished the rest of her drink. "Can't let my first really good Margarita in three years go to waste." After she'd slurped down the last bit she looked at him, but her fingers toyed with the glass. "You know, you were really good back there."

"Back where?"

"With the rescue. I've never been first on the scene with a wilderness rescue, but you were great." She nodded. "It's only fair that I tell you that—even though I'm reserving judgment on the cycling as stress relief issue."

That made him grin. "Thanks. It is something that I enjoy. I worked as a paramedic through medical school, so I have more familiarity with rescue than you probably do."

"You'll be wasted in administration. And I mean that."

The statement made him pause. "What do you mean? Administration certainly isn't all glamour, but there are certainly needs to be fulfilled in it."

"Agreed. But can't it be done by fuddy-duddy old men who have had their careers already?" She grabbed onto his wrist. "Young, talented people like you need to be on the front line, where you are needed most. If you hadn't been in the right place at the right time, hadn't had the skills you do in climbing and in medicine, Jane could have been more seriously injured or been stuck in that rock for a lot longer than she was." She released her grip. "That was all because of *you*, Max. Are you sure you want to give up what you are so good at?"

Max swallowed down the lump of uncertainty in his throat. This promotion was what he wanted. This was what he needed to do. He'd been groomed for it for years now, and it was the next obvious step in his career. "There's so much I can contribute at that level."

"I know. But the next time you're in the ER, up to your elbows in a complicated patient, just ask yourself if you are prepared to give it up." She shrugged. "But who am I to be telling you what to do? I barely have my own act together."

"That's not true, Carla. You're an excellent nurse and have a very good rapport with patients. You put them at ease and get the job done very well." He'd seen it firsthand more than once. She'd be an excellent asset to any ER, and once he took the directorship he wouldn't hesitate to offer her a permanent position.

"Well, thanks." She curved her hair behind her ear.

"How long do you plan on travel nursing? Haven't you even considered settling down?" The more he found out about her, the more curious he became.

"Not sure." She shrugged. "Initially I was going to take just a few assignments, check out a few places and see where I wanted to land. But the enticement of the next assignment and the one after that has so far been too much to resist." She shook her head. "Sometimes I just don't know. I know I can't travel forever, but there just hasn't been the right situation for me to stay." She shrugged and gave a sideways smile. "With the skills I have now, I could go anywhere."

"Or *stay* anywhere." The implication was clear. "With the nursing shortage, as you pointed out, there are certainly permanent positions."

"True. I just have to figure it out on my own."

That was what everyone had to do. Figure it out on their

own. Listening to others was all fine and well, but ultimately a person had to make his own decision. He'd wanted to save the world, one sick person at a time. Countless times over the years he'd been advised to give up on his dreams, and he'd begun to. Until now. Until Carla had reminded him of them again.

Those voices from countless advisors rang in his head. Resisting them had become a way of life, but now that they mingled with Carla's words he was sure he would have to fight harder to ignore them.

The waiter delivered their check, and some of the lights around them started to go dim. "Looks like they're closing up for the night. Are you ready to go?"

"I think so. This was a very nice dinner. Thanks."

She reached out to touch his arm and left her hand there. The touch was soothing and arousing at the same time. The hairs on his arm stood up at that simple contact. Denying the attraction between them wasn't going to be as easy as he'd thought.

"You're welcome," he said, and reached for the bill on the table. He placed some cash with it, and stood.

After a short drive they arrived at her apartment complex and he parked the SUV, but let the motor run.

"Thanks for a very interesting day."

She reached to the floor between her feet to retrieve her purse. When she turned to face him he reached for her. With his hands cupped around her face he brought her closer to him, savoring, anticipating the sweet touch of her mouth against his.

The first touch of her lips on his sent shards of desire racing through him. She tipped her head back and parted her lips. Wanting more, Max touched his tongue to hers, searching for her response. The silken glide of her tongue against his stirred him. Teasing, tasting, testing, she responded as he had hoped and a flush of desire raced through him. She tasted like tequila and salt and something else. Heart racing, Max plundered her mouth, her eager response urging him on. The electricity that had been between them flared.

Surprise had filled Carla when she'd turned and found Max so close. But there had been no thought of resisting his touch. She'd wanted him to kiss her for a long time. Parting her mouth to his, she allowed him access to her. He was powerful, masculine, and brought out the feminine side of her. She groaned, letting him take it as far as he wanted. Sometimes control was totally useless.

Everything male in him came to life and arousal flashed in his belly. With a groan, he tried to bring her closer to him. He wanted to feel her against his body, touch her curves and press them against him.

Unfortunately bucket seats were an insurmountable barrier to intimacy in a vehicle.

Carla pulled back with a shaky laugh. "Wow."

"Wow is right." Much more of a wow-factor than he'd imagined as he caught his breath.

"I knew there were going to be sparks if you ever kissed me." With a quick look, she glanced at him, then dropped her gaze.

"Were there?"

"Oh, yeah. Plenty of sparks going on here."

Max pressed a soft kiss to her mouth, then withdrew. "I'll walk you up." If he didn't have some physical space between them his body was going to override his good sense.

He reached for her hand and held it on the short walk to her door. He liked the feel of her small hand in his. Though she was anything but fragile, her hand seemed so delicate, and a protective male instinct surged in him. He wanted this woman.

Carla unlocked the door and turned to face him. "Goodnight, Max."

"Goodnight. See you Sunday."

"Sunday? What's on Sunday?" Surprise showed on her face.

"Jane's restaurant. She invited us, remember?"

"You were serious?"

Max twitched his brows high and gave her a narrow-eyed stare. "A bachelor never, *ever* turns down a free Sunday dinner." He grinned and squeezed her hand. "I'll pick you up at eleven a.m."

# CHAPTER SIX

"ARE you sure there's only one baby in there?" Carla asked Tabi. "You seem to have got bigger overnight!"

Tabi laughed and patted her stomach. "So far all we know about is one. Mom says that babies come when they're ready, so who knows when this one will be ready?" Then she grimaced and motioned Carla closer.

"Ooh, is it moving?" Carla sat on the edge of the bed and placed one hand either side of Tabi's belly. Waiting for movement didn't take long, and Carla felt the shifting of the baby. "Oh, there it is. That's so exciting."

She was very happy for her sister. This was what she seemed to be made for—having a family. Unlike Carla, whose ideas had changed over the last few years of being away from the hub of her family and its influence. Maybe she just wasn't cut out for family life. Though there were things she knew she'd missed out on.

"Yeah, it's exciting until she stands on your bladder." Tabi held a hand out. "Time to go to the bathroom again."

"She? Do you know it's a girl?" Carla asked, and placed a hand around Tabi's waist. "I thought you didn't want to find out."

"Oh, we don't know for sure, but I have had a sense of a girl the last few days." Tears pricked her eyes, but she flung them away. "I've been more emotional too. I don't know if that's hormones or what."

"Just being pregnant is my guess," Carla said, as she waited outside the bathroom for her sister.

When Tabi was settled again, she asked, "Can you come to lunch tomorrow? Mom and Dad will be here." She laughed. "They're going to *allow* me to stay on the couch, and they'll eat at the table."

"That sounds tempting. But I have a lunch date tomorrow at the Roadrunner Café." Carla filled Tabi in about the mountain biking adventure.

"Oh, dear. I hope the woman is going to be okay." Absently, Tabi stroked her hands over her abdomen, just as Carla had seen many pregnant women do.

"I'm certain she's going to be fine. Might have a broken foot. You should have seen Max, though." Carla slapped a hand on her thigh, still amazed at what he had done. "He free-climbed up the side. He gave Jane his safety equipment and climbed up beside her."

"That must have been something," Tabi said, her eyes watchful. "He sounds like quite a guy."

"He is. He's being promoted to medical director, too. But he's very smart and skilled as an ER doctor. I think it will be such a waste to take a doctor like him away from the front line." Carla thought of their conversation last evening, and of what it had felt like to be in his arms. "He's also very attractive."

"Now, *that* adds a little spice to your assignment, doesn't it? Tell me more."

"There's not much to tell." She curved her hair behind one ear and looked away from Tabi, who knew her better than anyone. "Didn't you say you had laundry for me to do?"

"There has to be more. You work together, you went on

a mountain bike adventure, he took you to dinner, and he's taking you out again tomorrow. Spill it, sister."

Unable to contain the blush that flashed across her face, she had to admit to herself and to Tabi that there *was* something going on. "Okay, okay. I like him. He's arrogant and opinionated, but there's something there." Especially the way she felt with him. That sense of femininity had been long absent in the last few years. It was nearly as intoxicating as her Margarita and had way fewer calories.

"And does he like you?"

"Judging by the way he kissed me last night, I'd say that's a possibility." Her lips had tingled for an hour afterward.

"You didn't think a kiss was an important detail?" Tabi asked, her eyes wide and watchful.

"Well, I don't like to kiss and tell."

"Ha! You're off the hook for lunch tomorrow, since Max is taking you out, but I expect a full report later." Tabi covered a yawn. "For now, though, I think me and the babe need a nap."

"Sounds good. I'll talk to you tomorrow some time."

"Just enjoy yourself. Don't worry about anything and relax. I'll have enough help with everyone else fussing over me."

"I'll try." Carla didn't know if that was possible, because when she was around Max there was always tension of some sort between them.

She entered her apartment to a ringing phone. "Hello?"

"Carla, this is Elaine at the hospital. I know it's short notice, but we're desperate. Can you come in for a few hours?"

"Sure. I'll be there as soon as I can." She changed and went to work.

What was supposed to have been a few hours turned into a full twelve-hour night shift. By the time Carla reported off, drove home and showered, she was exhausted. Her head hurt, her back hurt, her feet hurt, and she was too tired to eat.

Sleeping for a few hours was what she needed before going with Max to Jane's restaurant—but she didn't have that long! She set her alarm clock to give herself half an hour before he arrived.

And the doorbell woke her. Damn. She'd slept right through the annoying screech of the clock. Without checking the security window she opened the door, knowing the only possible person on the other side of it was going to be Max.

"Hi." The smile on Max's face melted off. "Are you okay?" He cleared his throat. "Sorry. That didn't come out right."

"It's okay. I do look like hell. Come in. I had a rough night. I got called in for a few hours, then got home about twelve later."

"Are you still up for going out?" Concern filled his voice. He knew what it was like to be up all night and then be woken up out of a comatose state. But she didn't want to disappoint him.

"If you'll give me a few minutes to get ready, I'd love to go. I'm starved."

In short order, Carla had brushed her hair, applied make-up, put on jeans, sandals, and a red silk blouse, then returned to the living room.

"Wow. You look great."

"Why, thank you. So do you." Did he ever. She was so accustomed to seeing coworkers in their scrubs that when she saw them in civilian clothing the sight was somewhat startling. Max filled out a pair of jeans nicely, and a knit shirt and loafers completed his casual attire. With his damp hair combed back, he looked as if he'd stepped straight from the shower, and he smelled like a dream.

They got into his SUV and drove to the restaurant. "You know, I'm only going with you to follow up on our patient's condition," she said.

Max gave her the questioning look that she was coming

to associate with him. He questioned everything. "Really? That's it?"

"Yes."

"Why don't I believe you?"

"Your mistrustful nature?"

At that he made a rude noise in his throat. "I don't think so."

When they arrived the parking lot was already jammed, but they found a spot to park and entered the restaurant.

"This is a popular place," Carla said.

"Another hallmark of Santa Fe. Are you sure you haven't missed it here?"

"There are things that I've missed, sure." There was challenge in his question, but she wasn't going to fall for it. She was on to his sneaky ways now.

Just as Max opened his mouth to reply a familiar face arrived at their table.

"There you two are! I was hoping you'd come today." Jane, seated in a wheelchair, eased closer to their table. She reached out and took a hand from each of them. "I want you to know how grateful I am for what you've done for me." She leaned toward Max and reached out for a hug. "Without your efforts I probably would have lost my foot." Pulling back, she wiped a few tears away. "Don't think I don't know how you risked your life to save me. I won't forget it either." Leaning back to Carla, she gave her a hug, too. "I won't forget either of you."

"Oh, Jane, we were just glad we were there when we were. Some things are just meant to be." Carla pulled back and patted Jane's scratched hand. "We're just glad you're okay."

"It's what we do, Jane. As Carla said, we're just happy to have been there," added Max.

"Well, you two are a great team. Keep up the good work."

Carla motioned Jane closer. "You have to tell me—did the Widows take over the ER while you were there?"

Jane barked out a hearty laugh. "You bet they did. I think they scared that doctor who was taking care of me."

"I don't doubt it. You are all a force to be reckoned with, Jane. Don't let up, either," Max said. "Your attitude is keeping you active and healthy."

"That's what I tell the Widows when one of them wants to quit or give up on something. We're not going to live forever, so we have to make the most of every second of every day—don't we?"

"We sure do," Max said, and looked at Carla as those words sank in.

Ellen, one of the Wicked Widows, arrived by their table, too. "Jane, you've been in the chair for two hours now. Time to get in the booth and put that foot up for thirty minutes."

"Okay, okay." Jane leaned forward. "She's my self-appointed nurse," Jane said in a conspiratorial whisper, then looked at Ellen. "Just wanted to talk to these two for a minute."

"You go get that foot up. We'll be fine, Jane. It's good to see you up and about." Carla smiled, glad to see the woman doing well.

"Four more weeks of this. I'm not sure I'll live through it." She tossed a glare up at Ellen.

"Oh, you'll be fine," Max said with a glance at Ellen. "Just do what the nice nurse says and no one will get hurt."

"I like you," Ellen said, and pointed to Max. "Let's go."

They moved away, and Carla laughed. "It must be good to have such long-standing friends."

"They look like they've been at it a long time, don't they?"

"Only sisters and people who know each other well can

talk to each other like that." Carla yawned, then stretched. The night was catching up with her again. "Oh, I'm sorry."

"Why don't I take you home and you can get back to sleep?" Max asked.

"Again, not the day I had planned, but sometimes sleep wins out over everything else."

She gave him a soft, sleepy smile and his gut cramped. Waking up with her that soft and sweet-looking would bring any man to his knees.

Carla walked ahead of him. As they were about to leave the restaurant the sound of a croupy cough caught his attention, and he paused. He turned back and looked for the person who was coughing. Instincts were something he'd learned not to ignore.

"Max?" Carla said.

"Can you hang on a minute? I want to see that kid." It was nearly always a kid making such a sound. Kids and airway infections went hand in hand. Max approached a table with a child who looked about four years of age and his mother. Both looked as if life had treated them harshly.

"I noticed your son's cough," he said, addressing the mother.

"Sorry he disturbed you. He's sick." The look she gave him said she was at the end of her tether. There was little hope in her eyes, and her child was desperately ill. After so many years in the ER he knew sick when he saw it.

"He didn't disturb me. I was concerned about it. I'm a physician and I want to help, if I can. If you'll let me." He squatted beside the table rather than looking down on the woman. The abject poverty in them made his heart cramp. Years ago he had wanted to help people like this, but the longer he'd gone in his career the farther away he'd gone from those ideals.

"I don't have money to see a doctor." She dropped her gaze from him and picked up her fork.

"I don't want any money." She'd probably spent the last money they had on the skimpy meal in front of them. "But your son needs medication and I can help you."

Nervous, the woman looked at Max, and mistrust shone clearly in her eyes. "Why would you wanna do anything for us?"

Why indeed? "Because it makes me feel good to help people. That's why I became a doctor." Wasn't that the bottom line for him? He felt good when he helped others. Sure, there were headaches associated with any job, but how many people in the world helped others in concrete ways?

"There's loads of doctors who don't care about people." Her face hardened, and he knew she'd likely been a victim of being treated on her appearance rather than her needs, and that maddened him. Those who needed help the most often received the least.

"I know. But for the sake of your son won't you accept a little help from someone who's willing to offer it?" Pride and pure stubbornness had probably gotten this woman through many tough times, but now it was getting in the way of her son's care.

After a few more minutes of discussion, she nodded, and then sniffed. "Okay. For David. He needs the help. What do I have to do?"

Max asked a few pertinent medical questions, which she answered. "I'll call in a prescription for him. You go pick it up and you won't be charged for it. Tomorrow I want you to take him to the free clinic and ask for Dr. Renee Lynch. She's my friend, and I'll let her know you're coming. She'll take it from there if he needs anything more."

Tears filled the woman's eyes and she placed a hand on Max's. "Thank you. Thank you, Doctor. I can't ever repay you."

"Getting David better is all the thanks I need." He rose, but her hand on his shirt stopped him.

"What's your name?"

"Max."

He turned to find Carla watching him intently. He'd been so intent on his conversation that he'd nearly forgotten she was waiting for him.

"I'm sorry to make you wait."

"That woman and her son definitely needed your help. That croup sounds awful." She cast a glance back at the table where they sat. "I hope she follows through with it."

"I hope so, too."

# CHAPTER SEVEN

"MAN, what a long day," Carla said, and shouldered her purse. She'd just given her report to the night nurse, Kenny, and was taking a few moments to catch her breath in the lounge.

Her pulse went on alert as Max entered the room. They hadn't seen each other much during the last week or so. Since their abandoned Sunday lunch at the Roadrunner Café Carla had been too busy with work and Tabi to see Max except in passing at work. She'd had to postpone their yoga class until next week.

Carla turned her attention back to Kenny and blinked at him. He had asked her something, but she couldn't remember what. "I'm sorry. What did you ask?" How embarrassing. Max walked into the room and she lost her brain!

Kenny shot a quick glance at Max, leaning against the counter, and then winked at Carla. "It's not important. Have a good night, and get out of here before they keep you over. Feels like a busy night coming on." He patted her on the shoulder and left the room to go see his patients.

Without looking, Carla knew that Max was watching her. Electricity raced through her neural network and set her body on fire. Then she looked at Max, and the way he watched her made her mouth water for him. There was something different about him—something stronger, sexier, than she'd noticed before. Maybe it was just her perception of him, but, man, he looked good.

Retrieving her empty coffee mug from the table as an excuse to hide the trembling of her hands, she rose to wash it in the sink beside Max. The trembling in her limbs didn't go away with the task, and she had to reach behind him to put her mug in the drying rack.

"You know, you could move over," she said, and looked into his eyes. The intensity pouring off him was almost enough to make her take a step back, but she didn't.

"I could. But then I wouldn't be able to do this." With one hand he reached for her and pulled her face closer to his. Eyelids drifting downward, he pressed his lips against hers.

That fire that had begun in her limbs now raced to other parts of her body and began a slow burn. The kiss was soft and gentle, but by no means without effect. Pulling away, she looked up at him, knowing what he wanted. She could see it in his eyes, and that want certainly had to be reflected in her own face.

"Are you working tomorrow morning?" he asked, his voice a bit gruff.

"No. Are you?"

"No. Interested in having something to eat or a glass of wine with me tonight?"

His glance dropped to her mouth and she parted her lips, wanting to feel the heat of him against her. At the end of a long, hard day that would be the best pick-me-up she could think of. To share long, slow kisses with a man like Max… Pure sin. She hadn't been interested in a man in a long time, and hadn't found one as interesting as Max in forever. Maybe now was the time to reach out, to connect again, to open up and let herself experience life to the fullest again. Protecting herself had become a way of life that she no longer needed.

"I'd like that. A glass of wine would be lovely." Some

small part of her resisted, warning her not to get involved with someone—especially in a place she wasn't going to stay. But now was not the time for the voice of reason. It had overtaken her life for too many years. Now was the time for feeling, for yearning, and for satisfying needs long untended. "I'd like to run home to shower and change first. Feels like I'm wearing my day on my shirt. Can you wait that long?"

"I'll wait." He drew one finger down the curve of her cheek. "Meet me at Tito's in an hour—or should I pick you up?"

"I'll meet you there," she said, and the sweet tendril of anticipation curled low in her belly. With a nod, she left him still leaning against the sink in the lounge and tried not to race out of the ER to her car.

Elaine was on the phone at the nurses' station and Carla waved to her. "Goodnight."

"Carla, hold on a second."

Elaine motioned for her to wait. She must have forgotten something. She moved closer to the desk and waited until Elaine put the call on hold.

"What's up?"

"We've got a patient coming in."

Rats. Kenny had been right. She was going to get held up leaving. "Are we short-staffed?" That popped the bubble of anticipation she'd been living in for a few moments.

"No, that was your brother-in-law on the phone. Tabitha's coming in by ambulance." Elaine's eyes filled with compassion as the full import of her words hit Carla and her jaw dropped.

"What? Tabi?" Anxiety filled Carla and sent her heart racing. "Is it the baby?"

"Sounds like it." Elaine eased Carla into a chair. "Sit for a second or two. They'll be here in a minute, and you can help out with her if you think you can."

Carla hopped up. "Yes, yes, *yes*. I've got to be with her."

"Got to be with whom?" Max asked, his sharp and assessing gaze moving between Elaine and Carla.

"Something's happened to my sister," she said, and almost reached out to Max, but hesitated. "I don't know the details, but she's coming in by ambulance, so it must be bad." Tremors filled her and she sat down again. Closing her eyes against the shock of adrenaline coursing through her system, she took a few deep breaths and tried to calm down.

"You can't be a nurse for your own sister, Carla," Max said, his gaze serious. "That's a bad idea all around. You can see her, but only after we get her assessed and figure out what's going on." He turned to Elaine and tossed his backpack beneath the desk. "Call Obstetrics and Neonatal ICU. Get both doctors on-call down here with their teams in case we have to move fast."

"Yes, Doctor." Elaine grabbed the phone.

Max knelt beside Carla. "Look at me." He placed his hands on her hands, which were clenched in her lap. "You can only do so much. Your family is going to need you to be strong. Do you think you can do that?"

She nodded, clenched his hands. "I can. Max, I have to be in there with her. If anything happens to her—"

"Shh." Max squeezed her hands back. "Trust me."

Tears filled her eyes and her lower lip trembled. "I do."

The sound of raised voices and the whoosh of the ambulance bay doors spurred both of them to action. Tabi lay on a stretcher, unconscious. One of the crew held an oxygen mask on her face, so that meant that she was breathing.

Staff from all directions followed the group to the first trauma room. It was large, and set up for an abundance of emergencies.

"Carla!"

A male voice raised above the din caught her attention

and she looked around. Tabi's husband Mike waved at her. He was as pale as the shirt he wore. She reached him and hugged him.

"I'm going in there with her, but quickly tell me what happened." A history of events was vital for treating Tabi.

"I helped her to the bathroom after dinner. She said she was seeing golden rings or something around all the lights, then she collapsed."

"Halos. Had she been having visual disturbances for a long time or was it recent?" That was a sign that preeclampsia was worsening.

"Recent. At least that's all she told me about." Mike ran a hand through his hair and turned away from Carla. "I don't know— I don't know if I can do this, Carla. You've got to help us."

"I will. Dr. Kelton is staying to help, too, so she's in good hands. I'd trust him with my life." Carla backed away. "I'll find out what's going on as soon as I can."

She hurried into the trauma room and found it stuffed with people. Both the NICU and OB teams had arrived in case of an emergency C-section. In a worst-case scenario they'd take the baby out right there.

Max stood at Tabi's head and assessed her eyes with a flashlight.

"BP is one-sixty over ninety," Kenny said, and adjusted the blood pressure machine to automatically check the blood pressure every five minutes.

Jeannine, the OB nurse that Carla had worked with before, was putting a fetal monitoring belt onto Tabi. "Nice seeing you again," Jeannine said.

"Yeah. I wish it were under different circumstances. This is my sister," Carla said.

"Oh, dear. We'll take good care of her," Jeannine said, and began to watch the monitor. "Looks okay here."

That was one small relief. Carla watched Max as he assessed Tabi's neuro signs.

"Get a magnesium drip going," Dr. Patsy Haskins said.

She was the OB in charge at the moment. Obstetrical emergencies were complicated, because there were two patients to care for at the same time: the mother and the fetus. That was why there were two teams, because each patient was a specialty unto themselves.

"I'm concerned about an AVM," Max said to Dr. Haskins. "Has she had headaches during the pregnancy?" He looked at Carla to answer.

"Nothing out of the ordinary. At least not that she said to me—and she would have. She knows what to watch for."

"Pregnancy stirs up all kinds of unknown issues. But she must have been preeclamptic for a few weeks, so that's my first guess. Let's get some stat labs." Max rattled off some orders and Kenny drew blood immediately. "I think she's stable enough to take to Radiology now, so we can see if she's had a bleed in the brain."

Max looked at Carla, who nodded. She'd told him that she trusted him, and she did. Not only with her sister's life, but with the life of her sister's baby.

"I'll get consents signed." That was the least she could do. Right now she felt so ineffective, so helpless, but at least she could get some paperwork signed that would expedite the process. Anything to help her sister pull through this.

"I'll call Radiology." Kenny handed the blood tubes to a technician for transport to the lab and grabbed the phone on the wall. He spoke for a few seconds, then hung up. "They can take her now."

"I'll be right back." With hands that trembled, Carla took the consent forms for treatment and possible surgery to Mike, who signed them with a hand that also shook.

"Tell me I'm doing the right thing, Carla," he said, and moisture filled his eyes as he looked at her.

She'd seen that look a thousand times, in the countless faces of patients and families she'd cared for over the years, but her heart had never raced the way it was now. It was something she'd hoped to never see in a family member.

"It's the only way we can save them. If they have to take the baby out to save Tabi, they will."

Tears filled Carla's eyes, but she brushed them away. Now wasn't the time to break down. Now was the time for her years of nursing experience to kick in and for her to be strong for her family—just the way Max had said. She couldn't be afraid or weak now. Not in front of them. Years ago she might have broken down, but not now.

She embraced her parents, who wore that haggard, tense expression she'd seen on others. They would be counting on her to bring information and interpret the medical jargon into language they could understand. "I'll be back as soon as I can."

"We'll pray for her, *mija*," Carla's mother said.

"That would be good." Hearing the Spanish term of endearment that her mother had always used renewed the tension behind her eyes. It was a simple word for daughter, but her mother said it with such affection that it held special meaning for Carla.

Mike stood as she started to walk away. "When can we see her?"

"I'll let you know."

She returned to Tabi's bedside with the consents.

Two hours later, Max found Carla staggering to the coffeepot in the staff lounge. She was exhausted, but wouldn't leave her sister's bedside except when forced to.

"Hey. How are you holding up?" Max asked. He slid a

hand over Carla's shoulders and gave an affectionate rub. At first she jumped, then she settled back and looked up at him.

"Thank you, Max. Thank you for everything." She clutched Max around the neck and his arms automatically went around her. Tremors shot through her, and he felt them in her back and her arms. He hoped that he could help calm her.

"Is someone with Tabitha?" he asked, and pulled back from her, pretty sure someone would be.

"Yeah. Mike is with her for the night, I think. Thankfully they're allowing him in the ICU." Carla allowed her hand to rest on Max's chest, and she rested lightly in his arms.

"He's what she needs right now. I'm glad she's started to improve. The magnesium seemed to do the trick, and has bought some time for the baby. If she keeps going the way she is she might not have to have the baby early." Stroking one hand down Carla's back, he tried to soothe nerves he knew were fried from a long day and extreme emotion on top of it. Being right here with Carla, holding her, supporting her, stirred feelings in him that he hadn't known were possible.

She brushed her fingertips across her eyes and nodded. "That is a good thing, but I know she's not out of danger yet. I'm just thankful she didn't have to have brain surgery. An AVM... I never would have thought that pregnancy could cause such vascular change in the brain." She shook her head and looked at him, but then dropped her gaze to her hand on his chest. "I can't imagine waking up after something like this having had brain surgery *and* a C-section at the same time."

Tabi and the baby were still at risk, but for the moment they were stable, and everything that could be done was being done. Mother Nature would take it from here. Max eased his hand up to the back of Carla's neck. There were knots there beneath the skin, indicating that her tension coiled in that spot.

"You should go home now. Get some rest. Nothing's going to happen overnight, and if it does Mike can call you. If you're not up to the drive I can take you. I'm about ready to go, too."

"I had planned to leave, but I stopped for a cup of coffee and couldn't bring myself to get out of the chair."

"You're a mess, Carla Lopez." He moved his fingers up her neck and into her hair, finding more knots of tension. He clicked his tongue.

"Thanks. You're a real pal, Max Kelton."

"Why don't you let someone take care of you for once?" He knew she hardly ever did that. Probably not since she'd left town three years ago. She took being strong a little far. He could see it now.

"Me?" Her surprised gaze flashed to his. "I don't need to be taken care of. It's my sister that does—though I appreciate the offer."

"Then why are there so many knots right here?" he asked, and put a little pressure with his thumb onto her trapezius muscle between her neck and shoulder.

Carla winced and sucked in a breath. "Ow. Ow. *Ow*. Okay. Okay. I've had a tense night."

Max eased the light pressure. "Okay. Let's go to my house and chill." After the day they'd had, he could use some downtime, too.

"Are you kidding? After this I won't sleep the rest of the night. Even though my body is exhausted, my brain won't shut off."

"Then come home with me and let me work out some of those kinks in your neck. You'll sleep if you can let your body relax."

"Okay." She pulled her cell phone out of her scrubs pocket. "I'll let Mike know I'll be back in the morning."

Max nodded, and waited while she made the short phone call.

# CHAPTER EIGHT

CARLA took a shower at Max's house, and put on a spare set of his scrubs. Steam billowed in white fluffy clouds from the bathroom as she entered the hallway to find Max in the kitchen.

"That was lovely, thank you." Barefoot, she staggered to the coffeepot that spewed out something sinfully good-smelling. "I need some of whatever you have going there." Although midnight approached, she didn't care—as long as that coffee tasted as good as it smelled.

"I thought you might." He poured her a cup, and she fixed it to her liking. After the first sip, she closed her eyes. "This is heavenly. It's that local roaster, isn't it?"

"Yes." Max took her hand and led her to the kitchen table, turned a chair around backward, then pulled another directly behind it. "Sit, and I'll work some of those knots out of your neck."

"It's okay, Max. You don't have to. It's late. I'm sure you're tired, too." Though she could certainly use the therapy, he had to be as tired as she was. But the thought of having his hands on her in such a way made her want to melt.

"Did I say this was a hardship?" he asked, and nudged her closer to the chair.

She sat and placed her mug on the table. "Then, if it's no hardship, go to work, Doctor."

"Happy to."

The smell of cocoa butter filled the small kitchen as Max greased his palms with lotion. The very second he touched the muscles in her neck the tension began to ease there, but another sort of tension filled her. The kind that occurred every time she was around Max and one that had become harder and harder to resist. It was a tension that she found herself no longer wanting to resist, either. After today, she was too tired to fight anything—including herself.

A moan of pure ecstasy came out of her throat.

"Feel good?" His voice was a husky whisper in her ears.

"Oh, yeah. Better than I ever thought."

Applying more lotion to his hands, Max lifted the hem of her scrub shirt and placed his hands on her lower back, pressing his thumbs into the muscles there. "How about down here? That's another spot where tension likes to hide."

Without a word Carla leaned forward and gave him greater access to her back. Chills coursed across her skin at the firm and masterful touch of his hands. Oh, the man knew what he was doing. Any resistance she might have thought of having melted away at the sound of his sigh.

"You are just gorgeous," he whispered, stroking his hands up and down the length of her back. Being clean and fresh, she hadn't put her bra and panties back on after the shower. And now no barrier was offered between his hands and her skin.

Leaning back, she placed her head against his right shoulder and looked up at him. Electricity crackled in the air between them, and Max adjusted her in his arms. He was going to kiss her and she wanted it, needed it—needed him.

She reached for him as he groaned, and his glance bounced off her mouth. Automatically her lips parted. As he took her mouth with his he devoured her with a kiss that sent shock waves to her toes. Her arms clasped around his shoulders and his hands adjusted her position so that she straddled his lap. Hands on her hips, he pulled her tight against him.

His arousal was obvious in the thin scrubs he wore, and the feel of his hardness against her core sent surges of desire through her. Then he eased his hands beneath the scrub top and moved them upward. His thumbs stroked the tight buds of her nipples, stirring her further.

His breathing tightened and his heart pulsed wildly in his chest. The feel of Carla in his arms, so soft and pliant, made him want to make love to her the rest of the night. Her skin, with the fragrance of his soap on it, branded her as his. Groaning, he clutched her tight. After tonight, he wasn't sure he would be able to let go of her.

No man had touched Carla in years. She'd trusted no one the way she trusted Max. Being with him now deepened that trust.

Briefly, she moved back from him. Pulling the hem of the shirt up, she tore it off and dropped it onto the floor. Now there would be no barriers, no hidden blocks between them. She wanted him, and she knew that he wanted her as well. The desire in his eyes made her respond in kind and she licked her lips, anticipating his kiss, his touch. With her hands she urged his shirt off, and ran her hands, over the smooth expanse of skin now bared for her.

"You're just beautiful, Carla." He eased his hands up her back, seeming to take pleasure in just touching her. When his gaze met hers, a glimpse of hesitation showed. "Are you sure you want this? You're tired, and you've been through a lot today."

"This is a moment we've been heading toward long before today." She leaned closer and let the tips of her nipples brush his chest. "Today has only taught me to reach out, not to wait for things, because they could be gone in an instant." She prayed that it wouldn't be gone for her sister, but the scare had opened her eyes to the possibility. "I want to make love to you, Max." Her breath came on a tremble. "I need it. I need *you.*"

"Carla. I want you." His intensity, his focus on her, only fanned the flames of desire higher.

With her lips grazing his, she whispered her deep desire into his mouth. "Show me."

That was all the assurance Max needed. She was right. They had been headed here long before today. He clasped one hand around her waist and one behind her neck to keep her mouth pressed against his. With her lips parted, he explored the sweetness of her mouth. The silken glide of her tongue against his made his heart race as fast as when they'd been on the mountain. Drawing in the clean fragrance of her only heightened his desire. Breathing in was like breathing a part of her inside him, and he didn't want it to leave.

He clasped her firmly around the waist and stood. Automatically her legs held him tight. As quickly as he could, he moved to his bedroom and placed her on her back on the bed, then eased down on top of her, wanting to feel every inch of her beneath him.

Being in her arms was what he had wanted for so long. Now that he was here he wanted to savor every second with her. Her olive skin was smooth and silky beneath his fingers, and he wanted to touch her everywhere at once. The cocoa butter fragrance only heightened his senses, made him want to make love to her on a beach somewhere. Any beach. Anywhere.

Breaking free of her sweet lips, he kissed his way down her neck and drew one nipple into his mouth. Teasing it to a tight peak with his tongue, he held onto her as she arched her back and little moans of pleasure escaped her.

When Max moved to her other breast, she shoved her fingers into his hair and held onto him. He was so hot, and the weight of him was perfect on her. She didn't want to let go of him and wrapped one leg around his, bringing their cores closer together. This was what she needed. Kisses became deeper and more urgent as her heart fluttered away. With a strong movement of his hand and arm he seemed to sweep away the rest of her clothing, and she lay naked and vulnerable before him. In seconds he had removed the remainder of his clothing as well, and lay beside her, their legs in a tangle.

Max pulled back slightly and stroked her hair from her face. "Are you on birth control?" he asked, and moved his trembling hand over her face.

"No. It's been years since I've needed it," she said, with a slight flash of heat to her cheeks. "I hope you've got a condom. Or two." She bit her lip. If he stopped now, she'd die.

The expression of need on his face made her catch her breath. Lord, she must be falling for him. He only had to look at her like that and she was more than ready to make love with him.

For a few seconds he pulled away, and she heard him unwrapping a cellophane packet. Eager to touch him, she reached for his hands, helped him apply the condom to his arousal, wanting to touch him intimately, wanting to please him.

Then he drew her forward, on top of him, and guided her knees to either side of his hips. "Why don't you take the lead? I don't want to hurt you."

As she leaned forward and kissed him his hands were everywhere. Tugging, stroking, teasing, torturing her with his touch. When the tension building in her could be contained no more, she eased up and he guided her hips to him. "You won't hurt me."

"Show me," he whispered against her mouth, and eased her body down over his erection.

As he slid home, she gasped at the pressure inside her, and stilled. Ripples of pleasure pulsed through her as she adjusted to the fit of him, and she gripped his shoulders until the sensation passed.

"Are you okay?" he asked, his voice tight, his hands clutching her hips.

"I'm way past okay." Leaning forward again, she captured his lips and slid her tongue against his. She moved her hips, slowly at first, then built to a steady rhythm, rocking him back and forth, the feel of him so right inside of her.

She sat upright and leaned back, bracing her hands on his knees. She'd never felt more feminine power than she did at this moment. The tender feel of Max's thumb against her feminine pearl took her over the edge. As he stroked her, her body broke free and spasms of pleasure flashed through her. Using her legs, she continued to rock her hips, drawing out the pleasure for both of them. Then Max dug his fingers into her hips and pulled her hard and tight against him. His cries soon joined hers as he claimed his release, and she collapsed on top of him. She held tight to him until the tremors between them ceased.

Long moments passed before either of them could draw a steady breath.

A wave of emotions flooded through Carla as Max stroked her back and hips with his hands. She'd never known the touch of a man to be so perfect, or to fit so perfectly with her. Easing down, she adjusted her position so that her head lay cushioned in the crook of his shoulder.

"How are those knots in your neck?" Max asked, and kissed her forehead.

She smiled. "What knots?"

"Good." He sighed and flipped the covers over them with one hand. "Can you sleep now?"

"Yes."

Without a doubt this was the closest place to heaven she'd ever been. Here was something that she didn't want to let go of. Not simply sex, but true intimacy with Max. Was that something she could walk away from?

Max roused Carla in the early pre-dawn and they made love again, each touch between them yearning and bittersweet, as if they both felt the press of time on them. The discovery of each other was a wonderful thing, and not something he was going to let go of easily. What had started out as flirtation and attraction had melded into something deep and true. He'd touched Carla as well. He'd seen it in her eyes, felt it in her touch and the way she held him. He'd also seen panic follow soon after.

After that he took her to her apartment to change clothes, then back to the hospital to meet with her family. Max sat in his car in the parking lot and watched the staff file in for the morning shift. He'd been doing that for years, following the same routine, the same job, working with the same people, reveling in the continuity of life. Dammit, this was what he did. This was who he was. He wasn't a man who pushed paperwork around.

A different sort of adrenaline shot through him. He needed to stay at the bedside, not fill his days with the tedium of administration. Maybe Carla was right. It was a job for someone else, not him.

The scare with Tabitha had shaken her up. He knew that. And she was right. It was enough to make you realize what you could lose in an instant. He was certain that Mike had been on his knees for half the night, praying to keep his family together.

He shot out of the car and raced into the hospital, then took the stairs to the ICU, determined to find Carla. She was the key that had brought him to where was right now, and he needed to find her, to hold her again. He found her. Stone-cold asleep in the chair beside Tabi's bed. Her lips parted slightly with her breathing. Something in him stirred. Not just desire, but protectiveness surfaced in him. Unable to stop himself, he moved forward and knelt beside her.

Without even being aware of it, he'd fallen in love with her. Now, watching her sleep, he knew he wanted to be with her in any way possible.

A movement on the bed caught his attention and he looked at Tabi. She blinked several times, then opened her eyes and focused on him.

Grinning, he slid his hands up Carla's thighs. "Carla? Sweetheart?" He squeezed her slightly. "Wake up."

Slowly her eyes opened, and he *knew* he loved her. Now wasn't the time for declarations—but he did have good news for her.

"What are you doing here?" she asked, and reached out for him.

"Tabi's waking up."

"Oh!" Carla bolted upright and twisted in the chair to see for herself. Max moved back a little, but kept one hand on her leg. "Tabi? Can you talk?"

She nodded, her hands reaching for her abdomen. Like the woman in the car wreck, her first thought was of her child. The only cure for the pregnancy-associated illness of pre-eclampsia was the birth of the baby, but the doctors wanted to give every chance they could to the baby. Slowly wakening from the sedation, and the effects of the preeclampsia, Tabi licked her lips.

Carla reached for a mouth sponge and the glass of ice water on the bedside table. She held it to Tabi's mouth and she

sucked the water out of it. Stroking Tabi's hair back from her
face, Carla let out a trembling sigh, and she squeezed Max's
hand as tears fell. "We were very worried about you. How
do you feel now?"

"Tired. Better. Headache's gone." Tabi's gaze darted
around the room, then she frowned. "Mike?"

"I'll call him right now. He was so tired I kicked him out
for a while, but he was here all night with you." She smiled
at her sister.

Tabi's gaze landed on Max, and her brows twitched
upward.

Carla had to laugh. Tabi was definitely back if she wanted
to know what this man was doing with his hand on her sister's
thigh. "This is Max. Dr. Max Kelton. I told you a little about
him."

"I remember."

"I'm glad you're doing better," Max said, and rose.

Carla made a quick call to Mike. "He'll be here in ten
minutes." She patted Tabi on the arm. "I'm just so glad you're
doing better."

"Thank you." Tabi reached through the siderail and took
Carla's hand. "I'm so glad you're my sister."

"Me too." Tears filled Carla's eyes, but she turned away
from Tabi.

Max saw them. He knew how hard she worked to control
her emotions. Without a word, he pulled her into his arms
and simply held her. Any declarations he had to make could
wait until later.

# CHAPTER NINE

OCTOBER neared, and at Santa Fe's elevation of over seven thousand feet, the weather got interesting. Days were clear and warm; the chilly nights required a light blanket or a friend.

Carla had to content herself with the blanket for the moment. Memories of the night she had spent with Max crept into her mind at the oddest moments. He'd been so good to her. It wasn't just about sex. She'd been safe with him. She'd trusted him with her vulnerability and he hadn't disappointed her. The man was a gem, and one she could hold onto for a long time.

At the end of another long day, Carla put her aching feet up onto a chair in the lounge, leaned her head back, and groaned.

"I thought I'd find you here," Max said. He leaned over and planted a kiss on her upturned nose. "I made fresh coffee."

"That's why I'm here." She lifted her head and smiled, watching him move around the lounge. "I could smell it a mile away."

"How's Tabi today?" he asked, and leaned against the sink. "I haven't had a chance to go up to see her today."

"Me, either. But Mike said she's doing much better." Just the sight of Max made her forget some of the miles she'd put on her shoes today. He was something she wasn't going to be able to leave easily. The smile slid from her face at that thought.

"What's wrong?" he asked.

"Oh, nothing. It's okay." It wasn't, but she couldn't face the thought.

With two cups of coffee in his hand, he approached her and sat. "No, it's not. I know that face, and something is wrong. Spill it, or no coffee for you."

The playful tone in his voice made her want to respond in kind, but this was too serious for that. The thought of leaving him in a few weeks hurt almost more than she could bear. She loved him. It was as simple as that.

"I didn't know this was going to happen when I came here." Oh, she must be tired if tears came that easily to her. She flung them off her cheeks. "I'm sorry, Max."

"I didn't mean to make you cry. You can have the coffee if you stop." Distress showed on Max's face, and he eased the cup closer to her.

That did make her smile, and her mood lifted a little. "It's not the coffee." She placed her hand on his cheek. "It's you."

"I'm making you cry?" That blue gaze held hers.

"No. Thoughts of leaving you do." There. She'd said it aloud, and Max hadn't run screaming from the room. She cared for him more than he knew. He made her want to stay.

Max swallowed hard, and all playfulness left him. His eyes, so dark, so serious, held her gaze and she couldn't look away. "I don't want you to go, Carla. There's something going on between us that's very special, and I don't want to let go of it." He took her hands and squeezed them. "Would you stay in Santa Fe? Stay to find out what's really going on between us?" He squeezed her hands. "I didn't expect to care so much so quickly, but the thought of you leaving just about kills me."

"I don't want to leave you either. But I can't stay here. I don't want to return to being who I was in the past. I can't do that." She'd worked too hard to find out who she was.

"You won't. I know it." He cupped her cheek and made her look directly at him. "You are one of the strongest people I know. That won't just go away." He leaned closer and let his lips hover close to hers. "We have a good thing, Carla, and… and I've fallen in love with you. I don't want you to go."

His words shocked her. She'd never expected to hear them from him. "Oh, Max. You'll be so busy with your new job you won't have time for me."

"I'm not taking the job. I've already told Beatrice."

"What?" The look in his eyes surprised her. He was serious.

"Being with you has made me realize what I really want out of life, and it's not board meetings and budget reviews." He kissed her. "I want *you* in my life. If you want to be there."

"I want to be there—more than you know."

As his arms wrapped around her, she knew there was no better place in the world for her to be. Max clasped her face in his hands and kissed her. Desperation and urgency filled the air between them. Max pulled back, kissed her forehead, then sat in a chair.

"We can do all the adventuring you want. Nothing will be dull and boring as long as we're together."

"These last few days have made me realize how important good friends and family really are."

She looked up at him, and in the clarity of the moment all her worries and self-doubts fell away. Nothing could hold her back. She was strong, and she could handle anything that life threw at her. Her time here had proved it to her as much as the last three years had. She just hadn't seen it until now.

"I have missed it more than I realized. Until I came back, until the last few days, I hadn't realized how very much I'd missed it." She moved forward and knelt between his knees. "I don't want to leave Santa Fe, Max. And I don't want to leave you."

"Then don't. Stay. We have something between us that will never go away."

"I love you," Carla whispered, then pulled him down to kiss her.

"Will you come home with me tonight?" he asked, his breath hot against her cheek.

"Yes." Happier than she could have imagined, she felt the glow of love warm her chest. Max had shown her how not to run away from anything. With him by her side she wouldn't have to ever again.

He helped her to her feet and tucked her against his side. "Let's get out of here."

Nodding, Carla clung to his side. As they left the ER she looked up at him. "About that yoga class…"

# THE GOVERNESS AND THE EARL

## Ann Lethbridge

**Ann Lethbridge** has been reading Regency novels for as long as she can remember. She always imagined herself as Lizzie Bennet or one of Georgette Heyer's heroines, and would often recreate the stories in her head with different outcomes or scenes. When she sat down to write her own novel, it was no wonder that she returned to her first love: the Regency.

Ann grew up roaming England with her military father. Her family lived in many towns and villages across the country, from the Outer Hebrides to Hampshire. She spent many memorable family holidays in the West Country and in Dover, where her father was born. She now lives in Canada, with her husband, two beautiful daughters and a Maltese terrier named Teaser, who spends his days on a chair beside the computer, making sure she doesn't slack off.

Ann visits Britain every year, to undertake research and also to visit family members, who are very understanding about her need to poke around old buildings and visit every antiquity within a hundred miles. If you would like to know more about Ann and her research, or to contact her, visit her website at www.annlethbridge.com. She loves to hear from readers.

**Ann Lethbridge now writes for Mills & Boon®
Historical and her new novel, *The Gamekeeper's Lady*,
will be available in December 2010.**

Dear Reader,

I am so lucky that my imagination is allowed to wander wherever it will. I get to visit all kinds of different places with my characters, and I hope you enjoy visiting them with me. This time Sarah and Brand took me to Yorkshire, where the moors stretch as far as the eye can see. I had so much fun exploring the house and the local countryside, but I had to find very special people to inhabit my world.

As a single father raising a child in the Regency period, Brand required a very particular sort of lady to help him out. A governess. Although he definitely wasn't looking for one as tempting as Sarah. And of course she would be the first to deny any kind of attraction to her employer. I do hope Sarah and Brand's story takes you on a pleasant journey, too.

If you want to learn more about me and where flight of fancy might take me next, please visit me at www.annlethbridge. com or write me a note at ann@annlethbridge.com. I would love to hear from you.

Best wishes,

*Ann Lethbridge*

# CHAPTER ONE

*Yorkshire 1813*

THIS HARSH AND FORBIDDING place was her last chance. Sarah Drake peered through the carriage window at stone crenulated towers stabbing the purple velvet of dusk. Fail this time and her family's gleefully dire prediction of a bad end for her would likely come true. From here Merrivale Hall didn't look the slightest bit merry. Not even the ivy hanging over the doorway in the slate-grey wall between the two towers softened its fortress-like appearance. Definitely *gloomy*. No other word would do.

In that respect it matched her mood, since this position might well be her biggest mistake yet. Governess to the son of a murderer. Was she really so desperate?

The silent answer came back a ringing yes.

The carriage slowed and Sarah reached for the door handle. A jolt flung her back against the plush squabs of the Ralston carriage's interior as it turned into the courtyard at the back of the house. A hot flush scalded her face. *Stupid.* Only guests and family entered by the front door. Governesses used the back door, like the rest of the servants.

When the horses halted outside low-slung stable buildings she picked up her valise, opened the door and jumped down. The coachman might let down the steps, but if he did not it would be far too embarrassing. And besides, she proved herself quite capable of leaping a foot or so to the ground.

The coachman, Miles, touched his forelock from the box. 'If you'd care to go inside, Mrs Drake, I'll see your trunks are brought up.' He gestured to a low arched doorway. 'You are expected.'

'Thank you, Mr Miles.' Sarah stepped smartly across the cobbles. The heavy iron-studded door swung back as she raised a hand to the black iron knocker, and a large male figure blocked the light from the passage behind him. 'You are late.'

How rude. She gave him a glare. 'The stagecoach was held up at—'

He waved an impatient hand. 'Well, you are here now.' He had a deep timbred voice with a cultured drawl.

The man stepped back into the light, revealing the face of a fallen angel beneath tousled black hair. He wore no coats. Reddish-brown stains that looked suspiciously like blood splattered his open-necked shirt and a day's worth of stubble shadowed his jaw. His expression was as dark and forbidding as the house, his features starkly beautiful.

Dissolution personified.

This must be Brandon Talbot, Earl of Ralston, her employer. It felt as if a flock of pigeons were looping over and around in her stomach. Parts of her she'd thought were long dormant warmed and stirred at the sight of his cold male beauty. A frisson of awareness rippled across her shoulders.

Attraction of the worst sort. Great heavens, what was the matter with her? This man was rumoured to have killed his wife and, according to Iris, in his youth he'd been a well-known rake!

A man to be wary of at all cost.

But why on earth was he answering the door?

Putting a hand to her throat, she swallowed. An urge to

run tensed her shoulders, but she couldn't. She had nowhere to go. She endured his sweeping gaze in silent indignation.

'I was expecting someone older,' he said in disgruntled tones.

Then they were both disappointed. She'd been hoping for something more welcoming. She mustered a calm voice. 'I can assure you—'

'Come in.' He pointed down the passage. 'Up the stairs on the right.'

Rude, and autocratic to boot.

It didn't matter, she told herself, hefting her valise. She'd long become accustomed to her place in the world. She could endure this disreputable man and his offspring for two months. She didn't have a choice.

She swept past him without a word.

As she marched along the stone passageway, his presence behind her had the hairs on her nape standing on end. The skin across her shoulders felt tight and her ears strained to hear his footsteps. Was he drawing closer?

*Stupid.* He wasn't going to harm her! He needed her to educate his son, and for that she had to be living and breathing. She took a deep steadying breath and stopped at the foot of a stone stairway that wound upwards. From an open door further along the passageway pots clattered in an oddly cheerful manner. That must be the kitchen. She glanced back for instructions.

The broad-shouldered Earl manoeuvred around her with a whiff of lemon soap and something fruity—an odd, if pleasant, combination.

'Follow me,' he said. 'Watch your footing and keep to the right, where the steps are widest.'

Good Lord, the place was as medieval inside as it was outside. Fortunately, sconces placed at intervals on the high stone wall lit the uneven stone steps. After one flight her calves burned with fatigue. She pitied the poor maids and footmen who ran up and down these stairs.

On the second landing he ducked beneath an arch and strode down the corridor leading off it.

Expecting to be shown her room, she followed him into a chamber halfway along. She blinked at the sudden dazzle of candles, staring at the four-poster bed where a small blond child was propped up on its pillows. The boy stared back with large blue eyes.

A liveried footman, aged about sixteen and nigh as tall as the Earl, stood stiff and straight just inside the door.

'Wait outside, please, Peter,' Ralston said.

The young man slipped out silently.

The Earl crossed the room and dropped to his knees beside the bed. He clasped the boy's small pink hand with a worried frown. For the first time since she'd met him Ralston looked approachable, and the concern in his gaze caused a softening in her chest.

She stiffened against such foolish female sentiment. Her weakness, Iris called it.

'Jonathon,' Ralston murmured, patting the boy's hand, 'here is Mrs Drake, your governess. She doesn't look so very bad, does she?'

Both Earl and child regarded her gravely.

Candlelight glinted gold in the Earl's brown eyes and shone onto a sticky substance amid his hair's dark waves. Blood on his shirt and something nasty in his hair. What had he been doing when she arrived?

Inwardly Sarah shuddered. She didn't dare imagine!

Dash it, she was a governess. Here to teach a small boy his letters. The Earl was her employer and what he did with his time was none of her business.

She smiled at the little boy, who looked like an absolute angel—the kind one found painted on church ceilings.

'Good evening, Jonathon. I have been looking forward to our meeting.'

The little boy's gaze swivelled to his father. 'I don't want a governess. I want Maddy.'

The crease between Ralston's jet brows deepened. He shook his head wearily. 'You are too old for a nurse.'

The little boy stuck out his bottom lip and dragged his hand free of his father's. 'Want Maddy. Want Maddy. *Want Maddy!*' He kicked his feet in time to his chant.

Ralston slammed his fist into the mattress. 'Enough.'

Sarah jumped and the little boy burst into tears.

Ralston leapt to his feet and strode to the window. He gripped the curtain as if he'd like to tear it to shreds. He looked like a man pushed to the edge of his patience, a man trying to regain control. Well, she knew what that was like; children could be absolute monsters when they wished.

After a moment or two, the Earl drew a deep breath and turned back to his son, his face stern, his eyes dark with regret. 'Enough, Jonathon. Nurse Maddy is gone. Be a gentleman and shake Mrs Drake's hand.'

Gone where? Sarah wondered. And why, if the child loved her so much?

Tears running down his cheeks, Jonathon crossed his arms tight over his chest and tucked his hands beneath his armpits. 'Don't want to.'

'I'll take you up on my horse tomorrow,' Ralston coaxed.

Oh, dear. No wonder the child threw tantrums. Sarah pressed her lips together: criticism of an employer only led to dismissal.

'Promise?' Jonathon said, looking a touch triumphant. At his father's nod, he untangled his hands.

Ralston beamed. A ray of light shafting down between

storm clouds could not have been a more awe-inspiring sight. 'Good boy.'

Sarah couldn't prevent a shiver of feminine appreciation as she took the boy's outstretched hand.

'I'm pleased to meet you, Mrs Drake,' the lad said in a small high voice.

'Excellent.' Ralston said. 'Now that's done, I will show Mrs Drake to her room.' He leaned down and gave his son a brief kiss on the forehead. It was a mere brush of lips against delicate blue-veined skin, but it made her heart ache. Whatever his reputation, this man loved his son.

Ralston headed for the door. 'This way, Mrs Drake.'

What an odd household, to be sure. In the absence of a wife, normally the housekeeper looked after these duties. At the very least a footman should have answered the door.

Sarah smiled at her new pupil. 'I will see you in the morning, Lord Jonathon. We have lots to learn.'

The boy hunched his shoulder and turned on his side. Clearly the effect of the bribe hadn't lasted more than a moment.

She followed Ralston out.

'The candles should be extinguished before the child goes to sleep,' Sarah said to the footman.

'Yes, miss. I'll see to it.' He stepped inside and closed the door.

It was strange for so young a child not to have a nurse, but a footman would do just as well, she supposed.

An impatient-looking Ralston waited further down the hallway beside an open door. 'This is your room,' he said, gesturing her in.

Quelling her continuing astonishment, she squeezed past his large form. Once more the stains on his shirt caught her eye. They really did look like blood. Had he been hunting and not yet changed? Or did his wild appearance have something to do with the nurse's disappearance? Had the woman sparked the simmering anger she'd just witnessed?

Her heart beat a little faster.

Use your head, Sarah. Only a murderer in one of Mrs Radcliffe's novels left the evidence of his crime all over his shirtfront. And the nurse must have left weeks ago, when Ralston had contacted Iris about employing a governess.

And yet her stomach felt as if those pigeons were swooping around in there again.

Ralston made a sound in his throat.

She jumped with an audible gasp and stared at him.

'Does it not meet with your approval?' he asked, his voice chilly.

Oh! Busy with her runaway thoughts, she'd scarcely noticed her surroundings. He must have taken her silence as disgruntlement.

Her eyes widened. Cream and pink furnishings gave the spacious chamber an elegant look. It was far better than anything she'd been offered in years.

Her trunk sat beneath the window, and she dropped her valise next to it. 'It is perfect. Thank you.'

'Good. I'll see you in my study in one hour to discuss your duties.'

She whirled around.

He'd already closed the door.

Sarah sank onto the edge of the bed. Discounting rumour as vicious gossip had been easy in London, but now, face to face with this brooding man, she wasn't so sure.

A shudder ran down her spine.

Desperation had put her in an impossible position. And whose fault was that? Her own, mostly.

Well, she was here and she would do her best. After all, this really was her last chance.

\* \* \*

Damn!

Brand stripped off his shirt and he splashed cold water on his face.

Why had he hired her sight unseen?

Just because his aunt had said Mrs Chivers's school produced the best governesses, it didn't mean he had to take the first one she'd offered. Except he couldn't spend all his time keeping his son happy, and no one else had applied. He was lucky she had such an impeccable reference, but why someone of her calibre would want to work for him was certainly suspicious.

He dried his face and stared into the glass. The letter from Iris Chivers hadn't said a word about her being more than passably handsome. He glared at his reflection. Oh, she looked modest enough, in her drab grey pelisse and brown skirts, but with her sapphire eyes and wheat-blonde hair she was far too young and attractive for a man sworn to celibacy.

Hell.

Wister, his ancient valet, barged in. He picked up the shirt and gazed at the stains with raised eyebrows.

'Plum jam,' Brand said.

Wister cocked his head and tugged at his thinning forelock with a pointed nod. 'Ye've something…'

Brand put a hand to his head. It came away sticky. He touched it to his tongue. 'Blancmange.'

No wonder Mrs Drake had looked at him with pursed lips. She must have thought him a veritable pig at the trough. He caught the wet towel tossed by Wister and rubbed at his hair.

'Master Jonathon still not eating?' Wister asked.

Brand let go a sigh. 'No. He misses Maddy, damn her.' The recollection of the nurse's betrayal sent a surge of red-hot fury to his brain. Maddy was lucky he hadn't strangled her on the spot.

He didn't need another death added to his list of crimes. He pulled on a clean shirt and shrugged into his waistcoat.

'Miles says she's pretty,' Wister said, brushing lint from Brand's coat.

Brand looked up from the buttons.

'The governess,' Wister added.

'Hmph.' He'd expected a woman of experience, one with a gimlet eye and a large bosom who would make Jonathon listen. Not that Mrs Drake was lacking in bosom endowment. It wasn't large, but it swelled above her small waist in a very... He squeezed his eyes shut and willed his body under control. 'Miles needs to concentrate on his work.'

Wister grinned. 'He said she seems like a nice lass.'

God, yes. A nice, calm, practical woman. Deliciously soft in all the right places. The kind of female who would be happy in the country teaching a child. The kind of woman he should have married. Would have, if he'd known.

'He needs a mother,' Wister added.

Bile rose in Brand's throat. 'One more word and you'll find yourself following Maddy down the road.'

The craggy old Yorkshireman grinned. 'Temper, temper, lad.'

Somehow Brand stopped himself from throwing his hairbrush at his valet's head and used it on his hair. 'She's a governess. She will occupy Jonathon's mind until his tutor arrives in two months' time and then she will leave. In the meantime, perhaps she can teach him some blasted table manners.' He snatched his coat and resisted Wister's efforts to help him into it.

'Cook wants to know if Mrs Drake is to take supper in her room?' Wister said.

Lord, he should have remembered she'd had a long journey from York and would need feeding. 'She can dine with me.'

The words were out of his mouth before he thought. To

change his mind now would give Wister more grist for his mill, so he merely glowered.

'Will there be anything else then, my lord?'

'No, thank you.'

Not unless the valet could find a way to put things back the way they were, make life feel normal again.

Unfortunately Brand had destroyed any hope of that.

A stone-cold silence weighed heavily in the air as Sarah descended the winding stone steps. The thick walls absorbed all sound except for her footsteps and her breathing. Peter, standing outside her charge's door, had directed her to the Earl's study on the first floor by way of the tower at the other end of the hallway. There she found a wider set of steps, true, but just as circular.

A gothic arch led off the landing; this must be it. She stepped into a gallery-like corridor. Doorways ran along its length on one side and windows on the other. Second door on the left, Peter had said.

Feeling breathless, as if she'd climbed up those twisting stairs instead of descending, she knocked.

'Come.'

A quick breath, a smoothing of her hair and she breezed in, the perfectly confident governess. Not too confident, though. Not arrogant or proud; competent.

A fire blazed cheerfully at one end of the comfortable and very male room. The upholstery on the heavy chairs each side of the hearth showed signs of wear. The linenfold oak wainscoting shone with the quiet pride of antiquity.

Ralston sat at a polished mahogany desk. He'd exchanged his mired clothes for a pristine shirt, a cravat and a navy coat over an ivory waistcoat. With his chiselled jaw freshly shaved and his hair neat he looked every inch a proud nobleman. And darkly handsome, if somewhat jaded by life.

Indeed, his air of world-weariness made him far too attractive for Sarah's peace of mind. She tried not to see the bleakness in his gaze, or the lines of worry bracketing his mouth, which tempted her to offer help.

'Please,' he said. 'Take a seat.' He indicated the chair in front of the desk, straight-backed, wooden and businesslike.

She sat. Or rather she perched on its edge and folded her hands in her lap, hoping she gave no sign of her fast-beating heart. To show weakness with this man might well be her undoing.

Leaning back, he regarded her intently, making a long, slow perusal with dark unreadable eyes. Prickles ran across her shoulders. She had the feeling he could see right through her skin to the blood pulsing in her veins. His gaze said he knew her secrets, her desires.

He couldn't. No one could.

'You have instructions for me, my lord?'

His gaze dropped to the sheet of paper in front of him. 'Ah, yes. Your reference from Mrs Chivers is glowing. Your last position was with a family by the name of Blackstone in Gloucestershire, I understand?'

'Yes, my lord.'

'The ages of the children?'

'Eight, six and five, my lord.'

He looked at the letter and nodded, clearly matching her answers with the information provided by Iris. For a man, he was being far more careful than she'd expected. After all, Iris had said he was desperate.

Worry that he might turn her away shivered down her spine, but somehow she managed to keep her expression politely attentive.

'You attended Mrs Chivers's Academy for Young Ladies for several years?' he continued.

'Yes. I also helped as an assistant teacher during those

years.' To help pay the fees that her relatives had found such a burden. She forced calmness into her voice. 'I assume you want Lord Jonathon to learn all the usual subjects? Arithmetic, reading, writing?'

He huffed out a breath. 'Manners, also. His nurse indulged him too much.'

'A nurse can't replace the guidance of a mother.'

A bleak expression flashed in his eyes, quickly hidden by cool remoteness. 'Nor can a governess.'

Her cheeks stung. How awkward—and what ridiculous comments—hers and his. 'No, my lord.'

He glanced down at the letter. 'I am not sure you have enough experience.'

Her stomach gave a horrid twist. Dismissed after one hour. How mortifying—and devastating. She clenched her hands in her lap so hard she felt the bite of nails in her palms. A trickle of cold sweat ran down between her shoulderblades. 'I am as well trained in the social niceties a young gentleman must learn as I am in academic subjects.'

His dark gaze rested on her face. A slight tightening of his mouth hinted at a lack of confidence in her assurances.

Because she was young, or because her thoughtless words belied her mental capacity? If he would just come out and say what was on his mind she might have a chance to argue her case.

She returned his gaze silently.

He sighed. 'I suppose I don't have much choice in the matter, since yours was the only application I received.'

A huge sigh of relief gathered in her chest. She kept it contained, along with her smile. He didn't need to know how much she needed this position.

'You have one week to prove you are up to snuff.' His dark glance held a challenge.

Only a week. She winced inwardly, but didn't dare ask for

longer in case he changed his mind altogether. 'Thank you, my lord,' she said as meekly as she could manage. She rose to her feet.

'I have additional instructions, Mrs Drake.'

She sat down again.

'Lord Jonathon is to remain within doors at all times.'

She felt her jaw drop. 'Young children need fresh air and exercise. Your son should learn about the natural world around him. Any governess worth her salt would say the same.'

His jaw flexed. The hand at rest on the table clenched and the sinews in his neck corded. At any moment he would strike the desk the way he had struck his son's bed. Apparently the man really did have a dangerous temper.

He slowly uncurled his fingers—strong, long fingers. He stared down at his hands for a very long moment, his broad chest rising and falling with each slow breath. Finally, he looked up. 'Very well, but my son must be accompanied by a footman outside the house. He is not to go beyond Merrivale's boundary or converse with strangers. Do I make myself clear?'

What made him so protective of his son? His stern command prevented her from asking. 'Perfectly clear.'

He rose to his feet, looming above her. The coldness of his face chilled her like a north wind in winter. She resisted the urge to shrink into her chair.

'There is one final thing I require,' he said softly, with a bitter twist to his lips. 'You have no doubt heard rumours about my wife's death.' The words reverberated around the room like thunderclaps.

Her gasp of shock refused to be suppressed. She stared up at him, her heart pounding against her ribs.

He nodded grimly. 'I can see you have. They are not to be repeated in my son's hearing. Do I have your word?' An unspoken threat of dismissal hung in the air.

'You do,' she whispered from a throat too tight to swallow, though she very much felt the need.

'Then you have a position, Mrs Drake.'

'May I address something with you, my lord?' For pity's sake, did she really want to do this now? But she already had his attention.

His dark cold eyes observed her from beneath lowered brows as he sat down. 'Well?'

No help for it but to speak her mind. She kept her gaze deliberately steady. 'I do not believe in rewarding children for bad behaviour...bribing them.'

He stiffened, his glower deeper and fiercer. 'I'll not tolerate corporal punishment, Mrs Drake.' His voice was a deep growl.

She flushed hot. 'Oh, no, certainly not. I believe it is better to explain things to children than buy their obedience or indeed use force to gain compliance. They learn bad habits as quickly as they learn good ones.'

A dark eyebrow shot up and his fierce expression turned quizzical. 'I will watch your methods with interest, then.' Amber lights flickered in his eyes.

Was he laughing at her? Did he think she could not manage a small boy? Though she'd regretfully given up thoughts of a family of her own, she loved the idea of helping other people's children through the pitfalls of growing up. She'd made enough stumbles of her own to give her an understanding of the pangs of youth.

Fine, let him laugh. She'd make him eat his opinion, and she'd do it in a week. 'Thank you, my lord.' She rose.

'You will dine with me,' he said.

The command jolted every nerve in her body. Attraction or fear? If she had any sense, it was fear. Men of the Earl of Ralston's ilk did not dine with governesses—not unless they had ignoble intentions.

Had he somehow guessed the unruly flutters excited in her body? If he had, she'd need to be on her guard. Against him. And more importantly against her own inclinations.

'A tray in my room will suffice.'

He curled his lip. 'Don't the servants have enough to do without running trays upstairs as well as attending me in the dining room?'

'Oh.' She sounded quite as stupid as she felt, and the heat rushing to her cheeks didn't help. Here she was thinking he had wicked designs, and he was thinking about his staff. Surely the dip in her stomach was not disappointment? 'Thank you, then, my lord.'

He rose and held out his arm.

Wordless for once, she rested her fingers on his sleeve. Lightly. The knowledge of muscle and bone beneath the fine cloth of his coat scorched the tips of her fingers. Fires sparked in her blood. Breathing seemed out of the question with her heart hammering so hard against her ribs. Inside, far below her skin, her body shook, fear battling with joy.

She tried not to feel his heat or notice the faint scent of brandy and lemon-oil soap teasing her senses. Five years ago, walking into dinner with a man like Ralston would have been the pinnacle of her hopes. A foolish young girl's dream, long dead. Until this man crossed her path with his fallen-angel looks and aura of sorrow.

How would she ever keep her distance?

# CHAPTER TWO

HER stiff demeanour reproved him. Perhaps greeting her half-dressed had been a bad idea, but he'd been in the middle of convincing Jonathon to eat.

The real puzzle was why, when she'd walked into his study, had he experienced a rampant surge of desire?

Hair the colour of wheat in late summer and eyes of celestial blue were common enough. Nor was she exceptionally pretty. Her sharp little nose gave her face an inquisitive bent. A you-can't-hide-anything-from-me face.

Yet all the time she talked he couldn't stop looking at her full lower lip. A mouth that spouted practical governess things had no right to make a man think of kisses. The tilt of her head when she pronounced her opinion—a very decided opinion for a woman who could not yet have reached her thirtieth birthday—made her oddly fascinating.

But it was her eyes that drew his gaze over and over again. Intelligent, far-seeing eyes. When untroubled, they deepened to the blue of a calm sea. Disturb the surface and they glittered like sapphires in sunlight.

She intrigued him. Such interest hadn't been fired by any woman for years. It was not a good thing. He should give her a month's wages and let her go. Women had caused nothing but trouble in his life…misery.

He gave her a sidelong glance as they walked side by side to the dining room. She looked impassive, but her inner disquiet washed up against him like gentle surf on a shallow beach: eddies of unquiet water beneath a calm steady rhythm.

She hid her nervousness, but not well enough to fool him.

He made her afraid. And why would he care? As long as she managed Jonathon satisfactorily he had no need to see her at all. Indeed, having sworn off all female company since Maria's death, why did he now find himself leading this one to his dinner table?

Because there was more to her than met the eye. He needed to uncover her secrets before entrusting her with his son.

They entered the dining room, where they found Trenton waiting. As instructed, the butler had set two places opposite each other at one end of the long formal table. The butler had suggested the breakfast room, a smaller, less intimidating space. Coward that he was, Brand had discarded it as too intimate, too cosy. He did not want physical closeness with this woman. He merely wanted his curiosity satisfied.

His body responded instantly to the thought of another kind of satisfaction this woman.

He really should have had a tray sent to her room.

He helped her into her seat. She accomplished the manoeuvre with grace and an ingrained pride one didn't expect in a governess. He'd always thought them meek little things, all fluttering handkerchiefs and apologies.

When Brand was seated, Trenton poured them each a glass of wine, set the first course on the table and withdrew.

Brand raised his glass. 'To my son's success.'

She acknowledged the toast with an inclination of her head. 'To Jonathon.' She sipped the wine. The ruby liquid stained her delectable lips, making him want to lick them clean.

Years of deprivation were taking their toll, he supposed,

though he had never been bothered much before. He shifted in his seat, seeking a more comfortable position.

Her lashes lifted, and he found those blue eyes studying him warily.

'What did you want to ask me, Mrs Drake?'

Shadows clouded her gaze while she apparently considered the risk. His anticipation was heightened as she inhaled a breath, her high breasts lifting deliciously beneath the drab brown gown. His body tightened.

'I couldn't help but notice your son is so very fair.'

'While I am as dark as a gipsy.' A harsh laugh broke free at her clumsy attempt to pry. 'He has his mother's looks. A constant reminder, you might say.'

'I am sorry.'

'Don't be. I'm not.'

Shock flittered across her face, as he'd intended. She wouldn't go there again.

He placed slices of roast beef on her plate, then added some buttered parsnips and aspic.

He passed her the gravy boat. 'You didn't stay with the Blackstones very long, I notice?'

A slight hesitation stilled her hand, then she poured gravy on her meat. 'We had a difference of opinion.' She cut the meat into small pieces. 'About my responsibilities.'

He cocked his head on one side. 'Is it not for the employer to choose?'

A delicate colour washed her cheekbones. She shifted slightly. 'Not if the employer is wrong.'

'You have strong opinions on this matter?'

'I do.'

'It does you credit.' Her quick glance suggested she didn't believe him, nor did she offer further explanation. No matter. Eventually she would be an open book.

She popped a small piece of meat in her mouth. A look

of enjoyment crossed her face. No meat at Mrs Blackstone's table? The thought of her being provided with inadequate sustenance brought forth unexpected anger. He kept his expression mild while she chewed and swallowed. He found himself watching the movement of her elegant throat, noticing the pulse-beat in its hollow—a strong beat he could almost hear.

'I hope will find something of interest at Merrivale to occupy your free hours, Mrs Drake. The nearest town is four miles away.'

'I have heard much about the beauty of the moors. I shall enjoy exploring them.'

'If you value your safety, you will stay close to the house.'

'I will consider your advice.'

'I do not say it merely as advice.'

She bridled. 'A command?'

'A warning.'

Blast her, she looked unconvinced. Women like her—independent, free-thinking women—required explanations. 'Our weather is unpredictable. When storms arise on the moors there is very little shelter. You will heed me in this. I have no wish to comb the countryside for a woman without the sense of even a peahen.'

She glared at him.

'Nor,' he continued, 'will I endanger the men of my estate in undertaking a search.'

Eyes wide, she absorbed this statement. 'As you wish.'

Was this the sort of difference of opinion she'd had with her previous employer? If so, the Blackstones had missed the fact that Mrs Drake hated to inconvenience others. A necessary attribute in a governess, he assumed.

'I presume there is a village nearby?' she asked.

'Hutton-Le-Hole. It boasts an inn and a haberdasher.'

'And a hostelry with a carriage for hire? In case I should need to visit York?'

It was wrong to expect a young woman to live in complete isolation. Maria had hated it. But the thought of Mrs Drake coming and going at will clenched his gut.

'If needed, you may request use of my carriage.' A way to keep her under his eye.

Trenton removed the covers, then returned with dessert.

'I hope you don't mind if we have what I call a country dinner, Mrs Drake?' Brand asked. 'I don't find the need for several courses.'

'I have eaten my fill,' she said, her plate clean, her expression contented. Her look was of the sated kind, and very sensual.

He'd like to see her expression after lovemaking if she looked this tempting after a good meal. His body hardened as his mind's eye filled with luscious images of pale limbs and long blonde hair.

He gritted his teeth. What he had intended as pleasant conversation with an intelligent woman, and perhaps the seduction of information, was turning into a test of his control. And she had told him very little. He'd allowed her to sidestep his questions for the enjoyment of watching her eat.

'You will try dessert or risk disappointing Cook,' he said.

'I shouldn't,' she said.

He helped her to some blancmange. 'Why on earth not?' He poured himself another glass of wine.

'Will you not join me?' She delicately swallowed a spoonful of the sweet pudding.

'I helped Jonathon eat his earlier,' he admitted, dragging his gaze from her throat to her watchful face. 'He likes it with plum jam, and got more on me than he did in his mouth.'

An odd expression crossed her face. Surprise? More disapproval?

'You think it wrong for a father to feed his child?'

'I admire your devotion.'

Her demeanour, her uncomfortable expression, said otherwise. 'He hasn't been eating well since his nurse left.' Hell. Why explain? He answered to no one.

She put her spoon down in her empty bowl. 'Might it have been wise to keep her until he was comfortable with a replacement?'

The dry fear rising to choke him had his fingers clenching around his glass. 'Not at all.' The words rasped in his throat.

'I see.'

She saw only what rumour had painted on his canvass. Let her believe what she liked. He took a deep draught of his wine and set down his glass. 'If you are finished, we will adjourn to the drawing room.'

A crease formed between her brows. An urge to soothe it away had him reeling.

'I thank you for dinner,' she said, 'but I fear I am tired from the journey. And besides...'

What new blade would her tongue wield? Fascinated, he waited.

Her gaze slid to a point over his shoulder, then came back to rest on his face. 'In future I will either take my meals in the schoolroom, with Lord Jonathon, or in my chamber.'

A slow burn rose up his neck. A set-down, by God. 'Then I will bid you goodnight.'

She rose and headed for the door. He leaned his head against the chair-back and watched the sway of her skirts. Sensual, enticing—and out of bounds.

He swallowed a groan of frustration.

At the door, she turned. 'I notice a footman stands in

the corridor outside Jonathon's room. Does he stay there all night?'

The hair on the back of his neck rose. 'Yes.'

'Why?'

He straightened. Gazed at her. She looked innocent enough. 'A simple precaution, Mrs Drake. Goodnight.'

She bobbed a curtsey. 'Goodnight, my lord.'

She went out and closed the door.

Brand heaved a sigh. The time had passed quickly in her company. Too quickly. The rest of the night loomed long and empty.

He got up and headed for his study. Hopefully his accounts would keep his mind off the lovely but untouchable Mrs Drake.

Two rooms formed Sarah's new domain as governess. The schoolroom, containing desks and shelves of books, and, adjacent to it, a small parlour where meals were served to student and teacher in the day. That room was also assigned as her private sitting room at lessons' end. A typical arrangement in most noble households.

When Sarah entered the parlour at seven the next morning, she discovered not only her charge, sitting on a pile of books at the breakfast table, but also his father with a blob of porridge on his cheek and a harried look on his face.

An elderly gentleman hovered beside the sideboard.

'Good morning,' Sarah said. 'Am I late?'

Lord Ralston glanced up like a drowning man hoping for rescue. 'Not at all. Jonathon is an early riser.' He tousled the boy's hair. 'Isn't he, Wister?'

The elderly gentleman rolled his eyes. 'Up with the lark, my lord.'

With love for his child shining on his face, Ralston certainly didn't look like a man who could commit a heinous crime this morning. Her heart smiled at the thought.

Eyes on his father, Jonathon lifted his spoon to his closed lips.

Ralston opened his own mouth in encouragement.

The little boy opened his.

'Quick,' Ralston said. 'Before Mrs Drake decides she is hungry for porridge.'

Jonathon's gaze flicked up to her. She raised her brows. 'Mmm. I love porridge.'

He put the spoon in his mouth and swallowed. 'Gone.'

'Then I suppose I will have to make do with toast.' She sat and took a piece from the rack in the middle of the table.

'Try the plum jam,' Ralston said. 'A woman in the village makes the best in the county.'

'Mine,' Jonathon said.

'No,' his father said. 'It is for all of us to share.'

Sarah buttered a piece of toast and added a small dollop of jam. A bite provided a delicious burst of flavour and the same scent she'd smelled on Lord Ralston the previous evening. Blood, indeed—talk about a wild imagination!

Wister set down a pot of tea and one cup. 'Will there be anything else, Mrs Drake? Eggs?'

She tried not to look surprised or thrilled at the courtesy. 'No, thank you.'

Wister bowed. 'I'll tell Trenton to come for the tray in half an hour.'

Lord Ralston nodded his agreement and the servant left.

She poured herself a cup of tea.

Jonathon spun his spoon on the tablecloth.

'If you have finished your porridge, Jonathon,' Sarah said with a smile, 'please put your spoon in the bowl so Trenton can take the dishes away when he returns.'

The little boy looked at her in surprise, then darted a glance at his father.

'Mrs Drake is in charge, remember?' he said gently.

Jonathon put down his spoon and folded his hands in his lap. Mischief glinted in the azure depths of his eyes.

This child was not cowed, or treated badly, as she had feared when Iris had talked of the father's reclusiveness. He looked like any other five-year-old boy ready for naughtiness.

'After breakfast I'm going riding,' Jonathon announced.

Oh, yes, last night's bribe. 'After you complete your lessons,' she said firmly.

Ralston's jaw tightened. 'I made a promise.'

'You can keep your promise after luncheon. Lessons go better in the morning.' She frowned. 'Unless you have other more important duties this afternoon?'

He hesitated, looking from her to the pouting Jonathon, clearly torn between pleasing his son and enforcing his earlier statement that she was in charge. 'After lunch,' he said finally.

The little boy glared and kicked the table leg.

Sarah ignored the way tea slopped into her saucer. One fight at a time was quite enough.

'No arguments, son,' Ralston warned. 'Those are the rules.' He rose to his feet and once more ruffled his son's guinea-bright curls. 'I will send for you after lunch.' He strode out of the door.

Jonathon bit his lip and his chin bobbled. He looked at her, no doubt awaiting a reaction.

Sarah dabbed at her mouth with her napkin. 'We have a busy day ahead of us.'

Jonathon scrambled off his pile of books.

Oh, dear. She'd have to teach him to ask permission to leave the table. But not today; too much at once and he'd balk. She needed his trust.

Jonathon ran to the corner of the room and opened a chest. Toy soldiers were soon scattered all around him, as he began lining them up in rows.

Sarah went through to the schoolroom, where she turned the smallest desk to face hers, ready for lessons. It seemed odd to have only one pupil. At Mrs Chivers's Academy she'd been in charge of fifteen girls. Mrs Blackstone had had three progeny in the schoolroom: two girls and their second son. The oldest boy had been away at university. She'd become fond of the children during her six months there. Did they like their new governess? She hoped so.

It didn't do to become too attached to one's charges. She was an outsider. One small step up from a servant. She'd never again make the mistake of thinking of herself as part of the family.

Satisfied everything was ready for her pupil, she went to find him. 'I think we will try counting this morning.'

'I'm playing soldiers,' he said, not looking up.

'Bring them along. Or some of them.' He had enough to make an army. 'A good general needs to know how many troops he has if he is going to win his war. Counting is important.'

Looking puzzled, but interested, Jonathon picked up two handfuls of soldiers and brought them through. Perched on his chair, he proceeded to line them up on his desk: cavalry to the front, infantry in the rear.

'How many soldiers do you have altogether?' she asked.

He pointed at them. 'One, two, five, six, three.'

She smiled. 'Almost. Let us try again, slowly.'

The morning passed swiftly. From counting they moved to letters. Jonathon, with his tongue thrust between rosebud lips and a crease between his fair brows, was copying the last in several rows of the letter A when the door opened.

Looking up, Sarah half expected to see Lord Ralston. A

prick of disappointment at the sight of Trenton with the lunch tray came as an unwelcome surprise.

Of course he wouldn't come—not after she'd bade him stay away.

Jonathon stuck his quill in the inkwell. 'Goody, lunch!' He had rather more ink on his fingers than he did on his paper.

She hid her smile. 'Finish your letters, Lord Jonathon. We never leave a job half done.'

With a pained sigh, he swirled the nib in the ink and applied himself to the task. The quill scratched and stuttered across the page. 'All finished.'

She left her desk to see. There were a couple of blots, and some of the letters fell below the lines she'd drawn, but for a first attempt it was a good one.

'Excellent,' she said.

He beamed. 'Now I'm going riding.'

'Luncheon, then riding.'

At first he seemed inclined to argue. Then he sighed. 'I'm hungry.'

'Me too.' Whatever the cook had prepared, it had a wonderful aroma. 'Off you go.'

Jonathon made a run for the other chamber.

In spite of her initial fears, the child had proved to be a delight, with a bright mind and a happy disposition. He seemed much calmer when his father wasn't present.

A worrisome thought.

Aware of the sharp bite of hunger, she followed her charge at a leisurely pace, though she quite felt like running too. It had been months since she'd eaten as well as she was doing in this house.

Jonathon was already washing his hands in one of the bowls provided, and she proceeded to do the same.

A steaming tureen of chicken soup sat in the middle of the table, with two bowls and a basket of bread. Once they were seated she served Jonathon, and then herself, after which they said Grace.

She tasted the broth. Delicious!

Trenton popped his head in the door. 'His lordship's compliments, Mrs Drake. I'm to take Lord Jonathon down to the stables as soon as he's eaten. There will be no more lessons for today.'

'Thank you, Trenton.'

Sarah considered the words of the master of the house. She felt a kindness behind them, as if he'd guessed her first day might be tiring. Pure imagination, of course. Or, worse, wishful thinking. Whatever it was, it must stop.

Her new employer was neither kind nor thoughtful, if even only half of what was rumoured was true.

The boy manfully worked his way through the soup, and even ate all of his bread. She smiled her approval. 'Now you can leave the table.'

Sarah was sorely tempted to offer to take Jonathon to the stables herself. She had a nonsensical longing to see Ralston on horseback. But it was a longing she must fight. There was a line that must not be crossed: a governess could not be friends with her employer or her charges. A lesson she'd learned the hard way.

Jonathon hopped down from his chair and shot out of the room.

Sarah followed. 'Make sure he wears his coat,' she called out to the butler.

'Aye, ma'am,' Trenton said.

Sarah wandered back into the schoolroom. It had been a good day—well, half-day really. But there was still a great deal to be done before she could count herself finished. A list of supplies, for one thing. And a plan for the rest of the week's lessons.

She sat down at her desk.

\* \* \*

Brand watched the youngest of his grooms, Algie, ready Sir Galahad for his afternoon ride. Anything to stop him thinking about the blonde woman on the third floor of his house. If he'd thought her enticing last night by candlelight, he'd found her just as tempting this morning at breakfast. What would it be like, breakfasting with a woman like her each day for the rest of his life? Her hair, pulled back tight from her face beneath her cap, had glinted like sovereigns in the morning sunlight. Her smile when it rested on his son had lifted his heart.

Most surprising of all, he'd felt comfortable leaving Jonathon for the first time since Maddy had left.

Hades! He'd even given her permission to take Jonathon outside and promised her the use of his carriage. It seemed this woman already had him wrapped around her small finger. And why? For the pleasure of seeing her smile? Or was he hoping for more? Damn it. He would avoid her the way he avoided the rest of the world, or be counted a fool.

He backed Gally out of the stall and led him into the courtyard. He did wish he hadn't written to Mrs Blackstone the previous evening. To his chagrin, he'd even thought about riding to the Hole and retrieving his letter from the post office. Then he really would be thinking with the wrong part of his anatomy.

'Papa!'

Jonathon ran full tilt across the cobbles, his face full of excitement. Trenton trailed him with a big grin.

'Lead Gally to the mounting block, please, Algie,' Brand said to the groom.

Jonathon's face shone with excitement. How like his mother he looked with that expression. He had that same *joie de vivre* everyone had loved in Maria.

She'd sparkled under the adoration.

A light had gone out of the world when she'd died. A bright flickering flame that had wavered and bent to the wind.

A stab of guilt twisted in his chest.

His was the gale that had snuffed her light out.

'Up you go, my child,' he said, and lifted him up on Gally's back.

Jonathon laughed, just like Maria.

The knife in Brand's belly twisted.

# CHAPTER THREE

SARAH ran a finger down the list of supplies, beginning with Cumberland lead pencils and ending with an atlas.

A knock sounded at the door. 'Come,' Sarah said.

Trenton entered. 'A note from his lordship.' He held out a silver tray.

Why would his lordship send her a note? Her stomach slid away. Had he already found her work unsatisfactory? She took the note with a smile of thanks.

After Trenton left, she stared at the note as if it had teeth. She took a deep breath. She might as well discover the worst.

She unfolded the paper.

Please bring Jonathon to the drawing room after dinner tonight.

The R which followed was black and bold, and finished with elegant curlicues. The note didn't ask; it required.

Her heart gave a dangerous lurch of joy.

She quelled it with a frown. A governess routinely presented her charges to their parents after dinner. On this occasion she wished she had a reason to refuse—an excuse not to spend another evening in Ralston's company. She loved the way he cared for his son, but she hated the effect he had on her pulse. Not to mention other parts of her traitorous body.

Unfortunately, even if his allure did cause unwanted desires to spring to life, she had no choice but to obey his summons.

Brand sat in grand and lonely state in the dining room. He stared into his wine glass. Had he completely lost his mind? He should be working on the breeding programme for his flocks, not dallying over tea in the drawing room.

And yet something other than irritation coursed through his veins: a warmth, a rush of vigour, anticipation.

Because in a few moments he'd be seeing Mrs Drake— *Sarah*. He savoured the sound of her name in his mind.

While the wariness in her gaze offered no encouragement, her rare smiles heated his blood in ways he hadn't experienced in years. Just the act of conversation with her made him forget the past, made him feel part of the world.

That was not necessarily a good thing, in light of the world's condemnation.

The clock on the mantel struck seven. He'd asked her to bring Jonathon down, and he'd damned well abide by his impulsive decision or look as mad as he felt.

He pushed his chair back from the table and wandered down the hallway to the drawing room.

His son and Mrs Drake were already there, sitting primly on gilt-legged chairs. He felt the urge to grin.

Jonathon hopped out of his seat. 'Papa.'

Brand fielded the child and tossed him in the air. Each time he thought about losing his son a cold fist seized his heart and stopped his breath. Brand whirled the fragile body upside down to squeals of delight, then set the boy on his feet.

'Again,' Jonathon demanded, arms raised.

'Once more,' Brand agreed, with a feeling of relief. Already

Jonathon seemed happier, less distressed about Maddy. This time he grabbed an arm and a leg and spun him.

'Whee,' Jonathon cried. 'Look at me! I'm flying.'

Mrs Drake's face flashed past as they whirled around. She was smiling. Slowly he lowered Jonathon to earth in a giggling heap on the carpet.

Mrs Drake laughed outright. 'Are you dizzy?'

'Yes,' Brand said. He staggered theatrically in a circle.

'Not you,' Jonathon said. 'She means me.'

'*She* is the cat's mother,' Brand corrected.

'She is?' Jonathon's little forehead creased.

He turned serious eyes on the governess, whose soft blue eyes twinkled.

'A little too subtle, I think,' she said, in her low musical voice.

With her face wreathed in smiles, she looked lovely. Warm, gentle and kind. Brand became aware of her widening eyes and parted lips. The air hummed with tension of a most pleasurable kind. She felt it too. Her blush gave her away. His body roused.

No! He would not succumb to lust. He would not be attracted to this woman. She was here to teach his son and nothing else. Only Jonathon was important.

He directed his attention to the little boy at his feet.

'How should I have explained?'

'Unambiguously.' Mrs Drake replied. 'Jonathon, when you speak of a lady you must use her name when she is present, instead of *her* or *she*.'

His small brow looked no clearer. 'Oh…'

'You aren't listening,' Brand said.

Mrs Drake glanced up at him with a gentle expression. 'New ideas always take time to understand, and he learns quickly.'

To his surprise, Brand felt a rush of pleasure at her praise.

His smile broadened. 'You are correct to fault my impatience, Mrs Drake.'

'He is still very young,' she said calmly, with a fond smile at his boy. *If only someone would look at* him *that way, perhaps life wouldn't seem so empty.*

He clenched his jaw. He was becoming far too maudlin—something he would not tolerate.

Trenton arrived with the tea tray, and Mrs Drake dispensed cups and polite conversation. To Brand's amusement, try as he might, Jonathon could not stay awake. He leaned against the cushion in the corner of the sofa and his eyes drifted closed.

Sarah stroked his cheek with one finger. 'He has had a busy day. I am not surprised he is sleepy.'

Brand felt the urge to capture her small caressing hand and taste it with his lips. He got up and paced the circumference of the room in hopes of dispelling some of the energy surging in his blood.

He felt caged, unlike himself.

Because he wanted her.

That was not his purpose in inviting her here this evening.

She watched him circle the room. Her expression grew warier with each passing moment. 'I think it is time Lord Jonathon and I retired,' she said. 'With your permission, my lord, I will ring for Peter to carry him upstairs.'

'I will do it.'

He strode to the hearth and tugged at the rope. Peter arrived within seconds. He grinned at the figure sprawled on the couch. 'I'll take him up, my lord. Wister is waiting to put him to bed.'

Mrs Drake rose to follow.

'A word, Mrs Drake,' Brand said silkily.

Her eyes widened. She sank back into her chair with a worried look.

And once more the hairs on his scalp prickled a warning.

# CHAPTER FOUR

HE'D sworn no harm would come to Jonathon as long as he had breath in his body, and while this woman appealed to Brand's baser senses, he'd been betrayed too many times for lust to prevent him from assuring himself she presented no danger.

He sat down beside her on the sofa. She shrank away—an imperceptible movement of fear. The thought that women, and this woman in particular, feared him was a kick to the gut.

He pretended not to notice and stretched out his legs. 'I know all of my employees at Merrivale very well except for you, Mrs Drake. You will forgive my questions, but I like to know whom I harbour under my roof. Who is your family? What made you decide to become a governess?'

Her expression became carefully bland. Every suspicious bone in his body went on alert.

'My parents died when I was very young,' she said quietly. 'A distant cousin kindly arranged my schooling. It was always understood I would eventually earn my own living and, since I enjoy teaching children, work as a governess seemed the ideal choice.'

Not an uncommon story for an indigent female relative of good birth. 'Yet you married?'

An odd expression crossed her face—rueful, he thought. 'Much to everyone's surprise. Including mine.'

'It was what is known as a love-match, then?' Was that a note of envy he heard in his voice? Hardly. Romantic notions were as false as notions of chivalry and honour, but it didn't surprise him that some young buck had been smitten by her attractions.

He was feeling a little smitten himself as the sweet curve of her cheek tempted his touch. Smitten with lust—it could be nothing else.

She gazed off into the distance. 'My husband left England three months after our wedding. He died on the retreat to Corunna.'

A soldier. A man who'd died for his country. A good man. He felt more than a little envious. 'I'm sorry.'

She raised her gaze from hands demurely folded in her lap. 'Did you grow up here at Merrivale Hall, my lord? It is a very odd-looking house.' She coloured, as if she had spoken for once without weighing her words and feared his response.

Glad to move on, he allowed himself a brief smile. 'Talbots have always lived in this house. Did no one explain its origins?'

She shook her head. 'I have not as yet had a chance to converse with any of the servants.'

Nor did she seem the kind to gossip. 'It is an interesting tale. At least to me.' He'd been fascinated by it as a lad. Proud of it too.

'I should like to hear it.'

The shadows in the room dissipated with her smile. She seemed genuinely interested. The old pleasure in his home, for his family history, washed over him more strongly than it had for a very long time. As a young man he'd been very aware of his heritage. He still was, even if future generations would curse him for tarnishing the lustre of a once great name.

Including his son, once he learned of his father's deeds.

He forced a smile. 'I can do better than mere stories. Come with me.' He ushered her out of the room, not giving her a chance to refuse. 'We will go to the gallery. This way, Mrs Drake.' For some reason it seemed imperative she knew who he was and where he had come from.

In the great entrance hall he waved an encompassing arm. 'Can you tell its original purpose?'

She gazed at the walls and the floor. She gave a shrug.

He took her hand and brought her closer to the door. He felt the pulse of her blood in her palm. Her fragrance, lavender and woman, drifted around him, more dizzying than a bottle of brandy finished in one sitting.

His body sprang to life.

Damn. He dropped her hand and stepped away. 'Up there.' He pointed up to the ceiling, to the black jagged points of protruding metal.

A smile curved her lips. Her full bottom lip drew a perfect bow. She didn't often smile so openly and generously. The joy of it lightened the weight on his shoulders.

'Should I believe it?' she asked, her head tilted back, her throat exposed in a delicate vulnerability he longed to taste. 'Is that really a portcullis?'

Quick-witted, this woman. He'd played this little trick many times over the years, with many visitors, but few had caught on as swiftly as she.

He smiled down at her. 'Yes, a portcullis.'

'Then this must have been built as a gatehouse.' Her voice rang with the thrill of discovery. 'No wonder it looks so peculiar.' She clapped a hand to her mouth, her eyes twinkling with mischief and horrified apology.

He laughed, the sound echoing around the high chamber. A flash of the past—during his mother's time, when the house had rung with laughter—gave him a feeling of comfort he hadn't experienced since before her death. He had the strong urge to lift the strait-laced governess off her feet and whirl her around in a circle, the way he had spun Jonathon. His foolishness made him smile, and she looked more than a little startled.

'It is Merrivale's claim to fame,' he explained, unable to keep the pride from his voice. 'I would not have it otherwise.'

She twirled around, seeking other evidence. 'The carriages must have come through there.' She pointed at the wide arch over the front door. 'Those steps must have led to a murder hole.'

The steps' outline were mere shadows on the grey stone wall. 'Blocked up now,' he said. 'So our guests have nothing to fear. And you can see the shape of bricked-up arrow loops on either side of the arch.'

She turned to face him, her face full of curiosity. 'How did a gatehouse change into a manor?'

'The original house lay further back. It was destroyed by fire. The family moved into the gatehouse and over time my ancestors adapted it to suit their needs.'

'The outside looks forbidding,' she said. 'Inside it is surprisingly cosy.'

He basked in her praise for his home. Maria had hated the place, always wanting to leave for London and excitement. 'There are drawings in the gallery showing the full story. Come. I'll show you.'

She hesitated. For a moment he thought she would refuse. He didn't like the sudden sense of something hollowing his chest. It felt too much like disappointment. When she walked towards him the sensation left as swiftly as it had arrived, and he turned and led the way. Behind him, her footsteps tapped on the flagstones. He liked that about her. No languid graces, no mincing, just quick, decisive steps.

The gallery ran the length of the east wing—an early addition in the history of the house—and its gothic ceiling arched high above their heads.

'It was originally open to the elements,' he said. 'No doubt used for exercise in inclement weather. Now we use it to display the family portraits.'

He pointed out the oldest document the family owned. 'This is the licence to fortify, granted by King Edward the second.'

She peered at the Latin script. 'Extraordinary that you still have it.' She sounded pleased.

A glow sprang to life beneath his skin. He felt like a boy again—eager, unsullied, with something precious to share. He swallowed. Coming here with her was a mistake. Too many emotions swirled in the air, some of which felt very foreign. He moved on, suddenly anxious to be done. 'With each new drawing you can see how the property changes.'

Head tipped to the side, she inspected the drawings, lingering over each one in turn. Standing slightly behind her, he allowed his gaze to wander the delicate slope of her shoulders, the hint of a curvaceous figure beneath her straight skirts. He let desire drift him along on a sweet current of longing that must not be fulfilled.

Viewing the earliest drawing of all, she furrowed her brow. 'I can see the original house in the background.' She leaned closer, her nose wrinkled in concentration. 'It was smaller than the gate.'

'And much less comfortable, I am sure.'

'Fascinating.'

He moved to her side, taking in her profile. Stray wisps of hair floated around her temple. His hand twitched with the urge to touch them, to feel their texture. Instead he rubbed at his chin. Touching was not allowed. Nor should he be looking. 'You enjoy history?'

'I love the history of families.' Her voice had a yearning quality he hadn't heard before.

'Including your own family?'

She stilled. 'Too dull, I'm afraid.'

Another avoidance. There seemed to be shadows veiling her past. He wanted to break through her reserves, he wanted her trust.

For the first time in a long time he desired something for himself. An irresistible force was rising up from his soul to take something he wanted.

'There must be family stories you loved as a child,' he encouraged softly, close to her delicate ear.

She shivered deliciously, arousing him more. She was not quite as unaware of him as she tried to pretend. But then he'd known it from the first.

'There are some noble connections,' she admitted, rather unwillingly. 'Distant ones now.'

*Now.* An interesting choice.

As if she feared she'd said more than she should, she turned around. He gazed into her eyes. Desire danced like a flame in their blue depths, a delightful betrayal.

Entranced, he dared tip her chin with one finger. Her eyelids lowered a fraction. Her chest rose and fell. The whisper of her rapid breaths stirred the air. The ribbon at her neckline trembled. Oh, yes, she was aware.

Lovely. His body tightened. He dipped his head. 'You are a beautiful woman,' he murmured.

The silence was full of beating blood and heat and short sips of air. Her lips parted on a sigh, inviting his kiss.

He grazed her soft mouth with gentle brushes.

Her eyes fluttered closed and a tiny sound of pleasure escaped her throat. The sensual sound spoke of fulfilment and longing, impatience and acceptance.

Her mouth was pliant beneath his lips, welcoming,

seductively responsive to his gentle pressure. He nibbled the full bottom lip, demanding entrance to more erotic delights.

She gasped with pleasure and surprise. Or surprise at the pleasure. His blood beat heavily in his veins.

He swept her mouth with his tongue, tasted the flavour of tea and a sweetness all her own. A sultriness that drove him to want more.

Much more.

One hand flattened on her back, and he gently shaped the indent of her waist with the other, followed the arc of her ribs, brushed the underside of her breast.

Another gasp. It sent shudders of pleasure racing through his bones. He drew her imperceptibly closer, heady with the taste of her mouth and the sensation of her body touching his chest.

Not close enough.

A tremor shook her frame. She drew back, her face flushed, her eyes hazy. 'Oh, no. We can't.' Her voice pleaded for understanding.

He let his gaze drift over her face and saw the horns of her dilemma: desire warring with fear.

She was right to fear. God, he sometimes feared himself. What the hell had made him kiss her? He stepped away, felt the chill of loss. 'I beg your pardon. My enjoyment of your company led me one step too far.'

She bit her lower lip. 'I should beg *your* pardon. I made it seem as if...' She turned away, obviously distressed.

He wanted to hit something. Or take her in his arms and persuade her into his bed. Make her his mistress. That was what he would have done in the old days, when he'd been a rake on the town. He had a son now. Responsibilities, duty. Perhaps even a shred of honour.

He drew himself up straight. 'I apologise. It will not happen again. I bid you goodnight, Mrs Drake. I assume you can find your way back to your chamber?'

He strode down the gallery and headed for his lair, as Maria had used to call it. His sanctuary. The place where he hid from the world.

Sarah watched his lithe, confident strides carry him away, a lonely man with sensual appetites she found hard to resist. She touched a fingertip to her mouth that had been branded by his kiss. Her body tingled and little pulses fired low in her centre. Primal urges made her long to call him back, to hold him in her arms and feel his strength against her body.

It had been so long since anyone had brought those urges alive—and never like this.

The deep loneliness in his gaze made him impossible for her to resist.

Was that what it was? Sympathy for a lonely man? Or was her own loneliness leading her astray?

A mistake with this man would lead her to a place from which she would never recover. Iris would never forgive such a transgression, the breaking of a cardinal rule: a Chivers governess was never importuned by the males of the household. She'd already had one brush with disaster. Fortunately Iris had believed her story. It could not happen again. She straightened her shoulders. Her whole future depended on her maintaining a decorous distance from her employer.

At least this time no one had seen them.

Her heart beating loudly in her ears, she strolled along the gallery, giving the heat in her cheeks time to subside.

Casually, she inspected the row of family portraits— paintings arranged in chronological order, each successive Earl with his family around him. The last and most recent one caught her attention: two adults in powdered wigs and a child. The young countess wore a patch at the corner of her mouth and a come-hither smile as she gazed on her husband.

He smiled back wolfishly. Sarah had never seen anything like it. They actually looked as if they loved each other.

The boy, aged about ten, was smiling too. At his parents. His dark eyes with their golden flecks gave him away. Brandon Talbot, now Earl of Ralston. He looked joyous.

Nothing like the stern, cold man he was today. Although occasional glimpses of the boy in the portrait peered out from those deep brown eyes when he looked on his son. They'd been there when he'd laughed in the entranceway, and in the moment before they'd kissed.

Once more her fingers touched her lips, as if assuring herself it was not a dream. Perhaps she would be safer if she pretended nothing had occurred.

She frowned at the line of portraits. There was no picture of Brandon with his wife and son. How sad.

She pressed her palms to her cheeks. Finally cool. Time to scurry back to her chamber.


The next day threatened rain. Sarah frowned at the clouds of white and grey racing each other to the horizon, vaguely irritated by the incessant sound of ivy tapping on the schoolroom windowpanes.

Lord Ralston had not appeared at breakfast or lunch today. An enquiry by Jonathon when Trenton had collected the dishes revealed his lordship had ridden out.

Seeing Jonathon's dismal expression as he laboured over his sums, Sarah couldn't help feeling a twinge of guilt that she'd demanded his father stay away.

'Why don't we go for a walk?' she suggested. 'You can show me the rose garden.'

'All right,' he said, looking up, his blue eyes alight. She adored his sunny temperament, his trusting smile.

She dressed him in his coat, hat and gloves, picked up her own outer raiment from her room and off they set.

'It would be best if we went out through the kitchen,' Jonathon said, tugging her hand as they walked downstairs. 'It is quicker.'

Unlikely. But she let him lead the way down the narrow passageway through which she'd entered on her first evening and into the kitchen. A fierce-looking man in a starched apron and a tall chef's hat looked up from a pot over a blazing fire.

Trenton, seated on a settle on the other side of the hearth, struggled to his feet. 'Mrs Drake.' He sounded startled.

'Jonathon and I are going for a walk,' she said. 'He is leading the way.'

'Aye,' the cook said. 'Maddy always brought him this way.'

'This is Farkey, Mrs Drake—our cook,' Mr Trenton said.

'I'm pleased to meet you, Farkey,' Sarah said, smiling at the gimlet-eyed man.

The cook waved his spoon. 'I won't shake hands—too sticky. But there are biscuits in the barrel, as always, young master.'

The reason for Jonathon's circuitous route, judging from the beam on his face as he brought forth a triangle of short-bread from a china jar on a low shelf.

'Are we having treacle pudding today, Cook?' he asked, spraying crumbs in all directions as he gazed at the basin wrapped in cloth on the long kitchen table.

'We are.' The cook grinned.

'Oh, goody.'

Sarah brushed off the front of his jacket.

Jonathon grabbed her hand. 'Come along, Mrs Drake. We mustn't be late back for dinner.'

The two men chuckled. 'Like your pa, you are,' Farkey said. 'He always had a sweet tooth.'

Sarah remembered his lordship's instructions. 'I'm in need of a footman to accompany us, please, Mr Trenton.'

The butler frowned. 'Peter is still sleeping, and I just sent the other lad to the village on an errand.'

'Is there no one else?'

'His lordship prefers to keep a small staff,' Trenton said, a little defensively. 'There is Wister, but he's busy in his lord-ship's dressing room.'

'Come *on*, Mrs Drake,' Jonathon urged.

Oh, dear. After her promising him an outing, he was going to be terribly disappointed—and just when he was beginning to give her his trust.

Jonathon gave her hand another tug.

What harm could it do? They were only going to the rose garden, for goodness' sake. Sarah let him drag her out of the kitchen into the stableyard.

'This way,' the boy said, letting go. He darted through a gate beside the stables. On the other side of the wall she entered the formal gardens spread across the side of the house.

Despite the late season, pink, red and yellow roses enclosed in neat box hedges tossed their heads. Their perfume swirled around Sarah with every gust. Jonathon raced along one of several gravelled paths to the stone bench in the centre. He jumped up on the seat. 'I won.'

'So you did.' She held fast to the brim of her bonnet as a gust tried to dislodge it.

'Can we go up there?' He pointed to a hill some little distance from the house. 'Peter says you can see the whole of Yorkshire from up there—and Hutton-Le-Hole.'

The child had far too much energy for a gentle stroll in a flower garden. He needed to run and jump. If only a footman had been available.

'Please.' His blue eyes begged her to say yes.

Faced with such an appeal, she didn't have the heart to say no, despite a twinge of guilt. 'As long as we stay within sight of the house.'

He raced through another gate and into the grounds, only stopping to make sure she followed.

After watching him try so hard at his letters and numbers this morning, it was good to see the boy running free. He needed this. She should have remembered about the footman, though, arranged it ahead of time. His lordship was not going to be pleased.

Dash it, they were only going for a walk. If Lord Ralston wanted them accompanied by a footman, he needed to assign one to the task.

The crest of the rock-strewn hill was far further than she'd realised. Leaving behind the manicured lawns, they climbed steadily up the rough terrain, and Merrivale Hall began to dwindle to doll's-house size.

'Eew,' Jonathon said, stopping short.

'What is it?'

'Sheep.' He wrinkled his nose and picked up his foot. 'Stinky.'

He had stepped in the animals' droppings. Pellets were everywhere, though there was no sign of the creatures who had left them behind.

'Wipe your shoe off on the grass and we'll clean it properly when we get back. From now on please watch where you are stepping.'

Jonathon dragged his foot over the short grass a few times, checked the sole of his shoe, and for the next little while leapt like a demented frog from one clean patch of grass to another. Until he forgot and raced ahead.

He scrambled up the tumble of rocks on the peak. 'I'm the king of the castle,' he taunted.

'Get down, you naughty rascal,' she replied, catching him up with a laugh.

Up here, the wind stole her breath. As did the view. The countryside seemed to go on for ever. Devoid of trees, and harsh, it rolled right up to the distant grey clouds. Stone walls sharpened the ridges and disappeared into gullies. The roofs of a village were clearly visible in the distance. Boulders and sheep dotted the green and brown landscape in every direction, except for the formal lawns around Merrivale.

Jonathon disappeared over the top of the rocks.

Her heart gave a lurch of fear. 'Jonathon?'

His head popped up. 'Come down here. There's no wind.'

She found him sitting cross-legged on a flat rock below the crest of the hill. She sat beside him, glad of a respite.

'Maddy said my mama used to bring me up here when I was a baby,' he said. Then his little face crumpled. 'She died.'

'I know.' She gave the boy's shoulders a squeeze.

The sound of approaching hooves brought her to her feet. Could it be Ralston, looking for them? She spotted the rider further down the hill, in the opposite direction from the house. It wasn't the Earl. This man had light brown hair and rode a chestnut mare. He turned his mount, cleared a wall, and headed straight for them.

Sarah pulled Jonathon to his feet and kept a tight hold on his hand.

The man's fair cheeks were wind-reddened. He offered a pleasant smile and a bow. 'Good day, ma'am.' He spoke with the accent of a gentleman. His gaze swept over Jonathon and returned to her. 'David Langford, from yonder, at your service. He pointed to a red-tiled roof not far from the village. 'My land abuts Ralston's. You must be the new nurse.'

It didn't surprise her that a neighbour would know of her

arrival. Gossip abounded in the country, just as it did in Town. 'I am the governess—Mrs Drake. How do you do, sir?'

He leaned down and shook her hand with a considering expression. 'I'm surprised to see you out here with the child.' He looked at the boy. 'He has the look of his mother. Too bad she didn't live long enough to see him grow up.'

The anger in his voice sent prickles down her spine. 'Jonathon, go up on the rocks and see if your papa is coming.'

Langford watched the boy climb with a deep frown.

'Well, if you will excuse me, sir,' Sarah said. 'I must stay with my pupil.'

He glanced down at her. 'Merrivale is not a good place for a gently bred woman. If you find yourself in trouble, Mrs Drake, you know where I live.'

Was he trying to scare her? 'I can't imagine what sort of trouble you might be thinking of, Mr Langford.'

'There's a saying in these parts, Mrs Drake. There's no smoke without a fire.'

'And there's no fire without fuel,' she snapped, feeling unaccountably defensive because she knew he spoke of Ralston.

His brows shot up. His face turned a deeper shade of red. 'You are welcome to your beliefs.' He bowed stiffly. 'Good day, Mrs Drake.' He brought his mount's head round and trotted downhill.

Feeling as exhausted as if she'd just fought a battle, but unsure if she'd won or lost, Sarah picked up her skirts and hurried after Jonathon. It seemed she could not allow others to voice her own fears about her employer. She inhaled an impatient breath. No doubt she was being her usual soft-hearted self.

She caught Jonathon up at the top of the hill.

'Look,' Jonathon said, pointing off to the right. 'There's

Papa.' He waved both hands in the air. Ralston turned to meet them.

Caught! Her stomach knotted. As she followed Jonathon down the hill, she braced herself for the coming storm.

The large black gelding plunged to a halt in front of the boy. Ralston doffed his hat. 'Mrs Drake. Jonathon.'

He glanced around, clearly looking for a footman. She winced. 'We walked to the top of the hill and back.'

'Can I ride Gally, Papa?' Jonathon jumped up and down beside his father's stirrup. The horse pranced.

'Take care,' Ralston said. With graceful ease, his coat swirling around him, he dismounted. He swept his son up and plopped him into the saddle. 'There you go.'

Jonathon beamed and clutched the horse's glossy mane. They turned their steps for the house.

'I'm sorry we didn't take a footman,' Sarah said, annoyed at how breathless she sounded. Guilt had a way of tightening one's chest and shortening's one's breathing—much like fear. She did not fear this man. She didn't. 'No one was available.'

Ralston shot her a glance. 'It is a good day for a walk.'

Now she felt worse than ever. If he'd given her a dressing down she might have had anger to push guilt aside. And there was still more to own to. 'We met a Mr Langford on the other side of the hill.'

Ralston stopped. He stared down at her, his eyes unfathomable. 'What did he say?'

'Nothing of any consequence. He pointed out his house, bade us good day.'

Ralston lowered his voice. 'Did he speak to Jonathon?'

'Not really. He spoke to me.' Her heart thudded hard against her ribs. 'I'm sorry.'

A bleak look passed over Ralston's face. 'Strange that on the first day you walk out with Jonathon you meet my neighbour.' He could just as easily been saying his enemy, the way he spat the word.

'He was riding on the other side of the hill when he saw us among the rocks.'

Ralston gazed off into the distance for a moment. 'I'll send him a reminder that he is not welcome on my land. Next time you *will* take one of the footmen.'

The ice in his voice froze her to the bone. It could have been worse. He could have dismissed her. 'Yes, my lord.'

'Papa, I can count to ten,' Jonathon said vying for his father's attention. 'One, two, three...'

Ralston smiled. He looked calm, icily calm, but the storm she'd expected roiled beneath the cold surface. Oh, how she wished she'd not set a single foot out of the house.

She trudged along beside the horse, listening to father and son talk without hearing a word. Her thoughts kept returning to Langford's ill-disguised warning

# CHAPTER FIVE

THREE days had passed since the walk on the hill, and Ralston had not been near the schoolroom. Nor had he asked to see Jonathon in the drawing room after dinner, though he always visited the child at bedtime.

Already Sarah had grown so fond of Jonathon she knew she would miss him terribly when she left. She'd tried her best not to get too close. For his sake as well as hers. But she just couldn't seem to help it.

With supper over, and Jonathon in bed for the night, Sarah trotted downstairs with the list she'd not yet had the courage to bring to the Earl's attention. What was she afraid of? That he'd kiss her again? Or that he'd present her with the stony glare of their last encounter?

She inhaled a deep breath. It was her duty to make sure the schoolroom was fully equipped, and according to Trenton she'd find his lordship in his study at this time of day.

She paused outside the door. The thump of her heart sounded loud enough to be heard on the other side. She knocked.

A long silence ensued.

Should she knock again? Perhaps Trenton had made a mistake and Ralston had gone elsewhere.

The door jerked open just as she started to turn away. Dressed only in his shirtsleeves, and looking disreputably rumpled, Ralston gazed at her in astonishment. 'Mrs Drake?'

Heat scalded her face. She was clearly intruding. Her wits had gone begging if they'd allowed her to trouble him with trivialities at this time of night. Or had it been her desire to see him again, overcoming reason?

She stepped back. 'I am sorry to disturb you, my lord. My errand can wait.'

He hesitated, looked torn, then gestured for her to enter. 'Please. Come in.'

Having knocked, she could scarcely refuse his invitation. She stepped inside a room lit only by the fire. He'd been sitting alone in a dark room.

How sad. A lump formed in her throat. For him. For herself. But it was a sympathy she must not give in to. She held out her list. 'I am in need of some supplies.'

He walked to a chair by the hearth. On a low table beside it was a decanter and a half-empty glass of brandy. His dark blue coat lay over the back. He shrugged into it with an apologetic smile. 'I was not expecting company.'

'I should have waited until morning.'

As he lit the candelabra on the table, she couldn't seem to drag her gaze from the triangle of dark hair at the base of his throat.

Her limbs felt weak, her stomach chaotic. A yearning for something that must not be.

If he noticed her confusion he kindly ignored it. He held out a hand. 'Show me your list.' He took it from her nerveless fingers. 'Please, sit down.'

'I don't wish to keep you from…' She waved at the chair and the brandy. 'I'll leave the list with you. We can discuss it tomorrow.'

He glanced down at the paper and raised a brow. 'Pencils?'

Of course he'd want an explanation. It was his money she wanted to spend. 'Jonathon will find them easier to use until he masters his letters.'

'He did have a lot of ink on his fingers this evening,' he said. 'Wister had quite a time scrubbing it off.'

He smiled, a sweet smile that had golden lights dancing in his eyes. Her heart gave a jolt. She clenched her hands, as if by doing so she could somehow keep a grip on reality.

'He worked hard today.' Her voice didn't shake at all, though trembles shivered through her body.

'Are you pleased with his progress?' He once more gestured to the chair.

Defeated by the weakness in her limbs, she sat. 'I am pleased. But he worries too much about his mistakes—hence the pencils.'

He sat opposite her, his expression worried. 'Explain.'

'Pencil mistakes are easily corrected.'

'I see.' He cast her a quizzical look. 'It would be wonderful if all errors were as easily removed.'

There was a world of regret in his voice, despite the twinkle in his eyes.

'It would indeed.' Her own mistakes would require a cart full of erasers.

'I will send one of the grooms to York tomorrow,' he said. 'I doubt the village shop will have an abacus.'

'We can count soldiers in the meantime.'

He laughed. A deep rich sound in the shadowy room. '"Necessity, who is the mother of invention", I gather?'

She smiled at the quote. 'Plato had a way of getting to the point.'

'Hence the need for sharp pencils.'

Her chuckle escaped before she could catch it.

'This last item…' he said.

'The atlas? Perhaps it is too expensive?'

'Certainly not. But I am certain I have an *Atlas Maior* somewhere. No need to buy another.'

'I wasn't thinking of anything so costly.'

'He might as well have the best. Why don't I find it for you?'

'If you would.'

'Come along, then.' He unfolded his long lean body and looked at her expectantly.

'Now? Tomorrow will be quite soon enough.'

'Never put off what you can do today,' he said with a cheerful smile. He crossed the room and held open the door.

She sighed and rose to her feet. There really wasn't any way to refuse and not insult him.

In the corridor, she carefully kept her distance, trying to walk a little behind. But no matter how much she slowed, he matched his steps to hers. So she walked at his side, too aware of his maleness, his power to make her heart beat faster, to utter a sensible word. And so she remained silent. They arrived at a set of double doors at the end of the hallway.

'This is it.' He flung the doors wide and ushered her in.

Eyes wide, she gazed around. Shelves covered every inch of wallspace from floor to ceiling. The two tall windows on the south wall would provide plenty of natural light during the day and, unlike the study, all the sconces and candelabra were lit. A rolling ladder rested against a bank of shelves and a large polished table in the middle held piles of books.

'I had no idea you housed such an extensive library.'

'Merrivale Hall has many secrets.'

She wished his words didn't sound quite so ominous. Something cold slid down her back. Fear again. What did she fear? Was it his reputation? Or his power to stir her secret desires? She wished she didn't have the strong feeling it was more of the latter.

He crossed to the shelves between the shuttered windows. 'The atlas should be here.'

She went to help him search, squinting at the gold lettering on the spines. 'I don't see it.'

He dragged the ladder round and climbed up, scanning the shelves as he went. 'I must have left it upstairs.' He jumped down. 'This way.'

At the far end of the room he ran his fingers over the ornate carving on the side of a shelf.

She frowned. What on earth…? A portion of the shelf swung back. 'Oh, my word!' she muttered. 'Is this another Merrivale secret?'

His smile turned wolfish. 'Everyone who lives here knows about it, but not everyone gets an invitation to visit my lair.'

The deep low voice with its hint of amusement touched a nerve low in her abdomen. A lair sounded dark and mysterious—and terrifyingly intimate. She should not take one step further.

His expression turned self-mocking. 'Afraid, Mrs Drake?' Beneath the wry humour in his gaze she saw the shadows of pain, and then acceptance. 'Wait for me here, then.'

She'd hurt his feelings with her distrust, when it was really herself she feared. 'What? And miss seeing more of this amazing house?' she said lightly. 'Lead on.'

A smile broke—the smile of the boy in the picture in the gallery, a smile without a hint of his usual bitterness, and, oh, so charming. Her heart gave a little skip. She closed her eyes briefly. This was yet another mistake.

Too late to change her mind. He was already through the opening. She stepped over the raised threshold and found herself at the foot of another set of interminable winding stairs. One of the smaller towers at the back of the house, no doubt.

What if no one else really did know about this staircase?

What if searching for the atlas was simply a ruse? A wife had died and a nurse had disappeared. Her mouth dried, but she continued to follow. He hadn't, after all, closed the secret door behind them.

Up they wound, one floor, then another, past the stone arch leading to the second floor.

'Not much further.' His voice echoed off the stone walls. 'I promise.'

With a theatrical groan she continued the climb.

He chuckled softly. A warm, intimate sound that made her insides flutter wildly. Clearly she was far too attracted to this man—dangerously so. She took a deep breath. It must stop.

At the next landing, the stairs ended. In front of them was an iron banded door. Wind whistled through an arrow-loop. He pulled a key from his fob pocket and turned it in the lock.

A locked door. A private place.

His lair, he had called it. Her heart picked up speed, slamming against her chest. Her body trembled with something far more elemental than she dared examine.

When he turned to usher her in he must have seen something in her face, because he huffed out a breath. 'Trenton also has a key.'

Right. Everyone knew about these stairs. He'd said so. The door creaked as she pushed it back against the wall.

The circular chamber startled a gasp from her throat. Tapestries lined the stone walls on each side of an enormous medieval hearth, complete with blazing fire. On the opposite wall was an oriole window, its seat filled with cushions. A jewel-toned oriental rug littered with cushions and blankets covered the floor. It looked like her idea of a harem.

'You sleep here?'

He laughed a little self-consciously. 'No. Not usually. My

chamber is on the second floor in the west wing. I come here for the view.'

He toed off his shoes. 'For the sake of the carpets,' he said at her look of surprise. 'They are very old.'

Shrugging, she followed suit, then picked her way among cushions and pillows of every hue to the window, which was the only thing that came close to providing proper seating.

'Would you like some wine?' He opened a cupboard tucked beside the fireplace.

'No, thank you. We came to find the atlas.'

'So we did.' He rummaged around inside the cupboard. The flames from the fire dancing across his face deepened the hollows and sharpened the planes of his features. He was sinfully dark, an unholy male beauty, and so wickedly attractive she could scarcely draw breath.

'What do you do up here?' Her voice sounded scratchy.

Her body flashed hot and then cold as she gazed at the cushions. What *would* a man do with such an array of pillows? The image of him among a tangle of female arms and legs flashed into her mind. Heat stirred low in her abdomen, sparking little fires along her veins. Breathlessness made her head dizzy, her limbs languid.

This constant burning for her employer was driving her to distraction. She had to control this see-saw of emotions or lose her sanity.

'Did you find the atlas?' There—that sounded more like the kind of thing a governess would ask. Much more sensible.

'Not yet. The sky is wonderfully clear tonight,' he said, closing one cupboard door and opening another. 'Lots of stars.'

She glanced at the window, and then back at the door through which they had entered. 'Is there a balcony?'

'Not exactly.' He set a green leatherbound book on the seat beside her. 'Here is the atlas.'

She picked it up and turned the pages as he went back to the hearth. Colourful maps artistically drawn, with detailed Latin inscriptions and text, met her wondering gaze. 'This is beautiful—and very old. Are you sure you want Jonathon to use it?'

'Very sure.' He picked up a long pole topped by a hook resting against the chimney breast. He raised it above his head, and she looked up to see a trapdoor in the ceiling. With some deft manipulation he unhooked a latch and carefully lowered the wooden door to reveal a large patch of dark open sky.

Cool air flowed around them, bending the flames in the fireplace.

'Come and look.'

She picked her way through the cushions and looked up. 'I see stars.' Off balance from staring up, she staggered. A strong hand steadied her elbow, a large warm body forming a sturdy brace.

She felt safe, protected, for the first time in many years. The urge to lean into his solid form, to let him take the weight of her body and her burdens, left her swaying. She must not. She'd made her own bed and, lumpy though it was, she must lie on it.

He released her arm. 'Relax back on the cushions. It really is easier.' He went back to rummaging in his cupboards.

She darted a glance at him. Was he serious? Lying down on a cushion-strewn floor at the command of a man who made her body tremble every time he smiled seemed more than a little foolish, if not downright dangerous.

Her heart gave a happy little skip. No matter how desperately she wanted to be calm and sensible, he ripped good sense away with one look from those dark seductive eyes.

Around him, she had no defences.

A troubling thought, when she'd already let him kiss her and longed to have him do it again. The pull he exerted on her senses was like nothing she'd ever felt before. It was sweeter than honey on the tongue, and it hurt like knives in her chest to remember she'd soon be leaving.

'I really should go now.'

'Must you?' He sounded ridiculously disappointed, and awfully like Jonathon. He handed her a cylindrical object—a telescope. 'You can see the stars quite clearly through this, but it is much easier if you are supine.'

Sly man. Clever man. She'd never held a telescope before, never looked at the stars with anything but her own eyes. Did he have any idea how much he tempted her curiosity? From the small smile playing about his mouth it seemed he did.

She shouldn't.

If she didn't, he'd never ask her again. A proud man would not easily accept a second rejection.

And she did so want to look.

Dash it, why shouldn't she? It was her duty to expand her knowledge for the sake of future pupils. She dropped to her knees, carefully ordering her skirts around her legs, before sinking back against the cushions.

He handed her the telescope. The metal was cool against her palms. She raised it to her eye.

Everything looked blurry. 'Oh,' she said, dismayed.

He fell to his knees beside her, pinning her skirt, tugging the fabric across sensitive female flesh. A bolt of something hot flashed up from her belly, tightening her breasts. She swallowed hard and quelled the urge to feel his hard body pressed along the length of hers. She squeezed her thighs together and managed to set off a little burst of pleasure in her core.

She almost moaned aloud.

'Let me help you,' he said.

Yes, please. No. 'I—'

His hand brushed hers as he fiddled with the telescope. Tingles shot up her arm.

He meant to help her with the telescope, not her bad case of desire. She flushed hotly.

With his face inches from hers, she could see the small lines at the corners of his eyes, the fan of his dark lashes, the swoop and curve of his lovely lips. The male scent of him filled her nostrils and scrambled her thoughts.

'There,' he said.

Dragging her gaze away from his beautiful face, she stared through the eyepiece. Nothing but black. Then a small circle of sky burst into clarity.

'Oh! Now I see.'

He chuckled, deep and low. Warm strong fingers, slightly rough, tangled with hers. Bare skin on bare skin, when they ought to be gloved.

'Slide the cylinder in or out for clarity,' he was saying.

Ah, yes, the sky. They were looking at the sky. Nothing more. Yet when his hand left hers she felt bereft.

Contrary woman. She'd told him no and that was an end to it.

She let the glass wander across the small area of sky above their heads. Stars leaped towards her.

'The moon is quite a sight when seen through a telescope too. Of course you get a better view outdoors, because you can observe more. But it is warmer up here this time of year.'

Arms aching, she let the telescope rest on her chest and gazed up at the stars overhead. 'Is that why you built this room? For observation?'

He lay alongside her and put his hands behind his head. 'No. My father had it built for my mother. She died when

I was eight, but she loved the night sky and said watching the stars made her troubles on earth seem small. She spent most of her time up here during the last few months of her life. We all did.' The loneliness in his voice made her chest squeeze.

'Your mother was right,' she said, looking into the heavens. 'The vastness makes one feel insignificant.'

'My father never came up here again. I did for a while...I imagined something of her still lingered.' He shrugged as if embarrassed. 'Childish nonsense, of course.'

'Do you study the stars?'

He laughed a little wryly. 'A gentleman's pastime. Maria resented the time I spent on it, so I gave it up.'

'What were you looking for?'

'Anything. A comet, perhaps, or a new planet, or an undiscovered star. Did you know Miss Caroline Herschel discovered eight new comets and more than five hundred stars? I heard her give a paper at the Royal Society.'

She shifted to look at his face. With only the muted glow from the fire providing light, she could make out little of his expression—a grimness about his mouth, perhaps, a haunted look in his eyes. 'She is an extraordinary woman.'

He rolled over and faced her, now no more than a dark shape blotting out the fire, and she was aware of the scent of brandy, lemon soap, and man in the dark.

'I should have guessed you'd know about Miss Herschel.'

'Because I'm a bluestocking?' She smiled. 'I know her father invented the largest telescope in the world, and the Prince paid for her astronomy work.'

'I have one of her father's telescopes. I could set it up, if you are interested?'

'I'd like that.' The words fell out of her mouth before her mind had a chance to consider their import. A scarcely veiled admission of interest that left her vulnerable. She wanted to call them back the moment they left her mouth, but words could not be erased any more than kisses could be rubbed from memories.

# CHAPTER SIX

SHE glanced up at stars that had shone down on earth for countless millennia. In five years' time only two people would remember this night, and she could have a memory of something wonderful, or recall what might have been.

What did she have to fear? She wasn't an innocent miss. She knew the joys of the body and had thought never to experience them again. Who would it hurt besides herself? If indeed it caused anyone harm? She felt that in some way she could bring him comfort.

But he was too much the gentleman to act without her permission—not after she'd already told him no.

Tentatively, trembling, she reached out her hand and placed it flat against his jaw.

He sucked in a breath, as if surprised by her boldness.

What if she had misread his interest? If he really had brought her up here only to look at the stars? The remembrance of the power of their kiss gave her a burst of courage.

Her heart drummed harder against her ribs. Risking all, she leaned forward. In the dark, she caught the corner of his mouth. It was a stumbling, awkward affair of a kiss—a touch of softness, the graze of stubble. She inwardly winced. Clumsy, so clumsy.

His hand, warm and strong, caught her nape, stilling her

inclination to withdraw. His head turned a fraction, angled, and their lips melded.

A blissful union of mouths and tongues.

*Mine.* Her pulse beat time to the word pounding through her brain. For a while, at least, the other side of her mind cautioned—the sensible side. She didn't care—or didn't want to care.

Desire clawed its way up from her belly to settle aching and heavy in her breasts. Lust pooled hot between her thighs. It had been a long time since a man had aroused such inner heat.

Too long.

In a month or two she would be gone from here and they would never meet again.

He pulled back, and she felt his gaze on her face like a touch.

She used her fingertips to trace the strong bones of his lean cheeks and hard jaw. He was lovely. He suffered her touch for a while, then pulled her close for another mind-drugging kiss.

She ran her fingers through his hair, felt the silky softness against her palms and brushing the back of her hand. She inhaled his scent: lemon and earthy male, with hints of sweet wine and cigars. A banquet for the senses.

His hand cupped her breast, deepening the ache of need. Tendrils of desire licked out from her centre in sharp little pulses. Pleasure, not forgotten but suppressed.

Her hands sketched his form, imprinting the contour of his shoulders and the breadth of his back on her mind, the feel of his strength beneath the finest of wool on her fingertips. His warmth surrounded her. She plunged her tongue in his mouth, heard the hiss of his breath, and again felt the arrow of pleasure deep in her core.

She too had the power to arouse. His lust simmered beneath

the surface, still banked, but she sensed that once he allowed it to flare his heat would leave her in ashes.

Fear stilled her and her heart raced in panic. Stop! Now— before it was too late.

Surely he would let her go if she begged? Cried mercy?

He must have felt her withdrawal, because he raised his head. He gazed down into her face, his expression a dark mystery. 'What is it?' he murmured.

If she wanted this to end, it would have to be now. No doubt he'd think her a terrible tease. Why was it so hard to do the right thing? She shivered.

'Are you cold?' he asked softly. He reached behind her and pulled a blanket across them, enclosing the heat of their bodies within its protection. The back of his hand stroked her temple. 'Better?'

Such caring, such tenderness filled his voice, she wanted to weep. She had no strength when it came to this man, no will. Just a heart full of lost dreams and the feeling he could make them come true.

'Yes,' she whispered. 'Much better.' She twined her arms around his neck. Tonight she'd forget honour and duty. Tonight she would choose what *she* wanted for once.

She offered her lips up for his kiss. He groaned, a deep low sound in his throat, a primitive growl. He ravaged her mouth.

Blood flowed hot through her veins and her senses swam. The world seemed very far away from their dark warm cave at the top of a tower.

She wanted him so badly.

She arched her back, pressing close to his long lean length. A large hand cupped her bottom, gently massaged, then gripped firmly and pulled her tight against him. His arousal pressed against her hip, delicious, hard.

The tingles low in her core rushed outward, tantalising

her with the prospect of pleasure. A physical manifestation of her desires.

So close, yet so far away…

So seductive.

He eased her onto her back. One long hard-muscled thigh pressed against the juncture of her thighs, while his lips and tongue plundered her mouth, licking and sucking and nipping until she thought she might go mad with wanting him inside her.

His hand covered her breast, exploring, shaping, teasing the nipple with little flicks of his thumb. Delicious, tormenting. She moaned her approval into his mouth, tilting her hips in encouragement, wanting all he could give.

His mouth left hers and trailed little kisses across her cheek. He blew in her ear and her skin danced and tingled.

She nipped his earlobe in punishment. And reward. He muffled a laugh against her neck and continued kissing and nuzzling, down her throat, across her collarbone to the rise of her breast. Clever fingers traced the neckline of her dress, teasing the fichu free. His hot moist breath set her skin on fire.

Too many clothes, too much fabric…

He seemed to sense her need, because he rose on his knees. 'Will you allow me to unlace you?'

Dizzy with desire, she stifled a nervous giggle and half sat, turning to present her back. He made short work of the ties, drawing the bodice off her shoulders and arms. He worked the gown down her torso, and to help him she lifted her hips. How very bold she was in this dim room, with the crackle of the fire and the stars shining down. How exotic it seemed, among the cushions and throws. Like another world, some Far Eastern country where the delights of the body were paramount.

He was her mysterious pasha and she was his willing concubine.

The thought made her shudder with desire.

'Tell me,' he demanded. 'What makes you tremble?'

Heat devoured her face. 'An image.' She gave an embarrassed laugh, glad he could not see her blushes. 'I pictured us in a seraglio. A harem.'

'Interesting.' His voice deepened. 'Do you like your master?'

Her inner muscles tightened. 'He's kind and gentle,' she whispered, feeling a little ashamed of her wanton thoughts. 'But strong and demanding.'

His fingers traced a path down her upper arm. 'And does he please you?'

'Yes.' A whisper.

'Tell me what you see,' he murmured in her ear.

She closed her eyes and drifted to the fantastical place she'd often glimpsed but tried to keep veiled from her wicked longings.

'At first he is wearing a robe, and I…' she felt hot '…I am naked.'

His hands stroked up and down her arms. 'I like the sound of that.' His voice sounded rough. He untied the strings of her stays and let them fall free, then set about the ribbon at the neck of her chemise. Her breath caught, her chest rose and fell, brushing against his knuckles. 'Rise up on your knees for me, please, my sweet.'

His voice acted like chocolate on her senses, thick and rich and dark and tempting. His gentle touch made her feel delicate, cared for. The desire to melt against him weakened her limbs, and yet she found the strength to do as he bade, to kneel facing him, breasts close to his broad chest.

He cradled both sides of her face in his hands and tipped up her face. 'How lovely you are.'

'It is too dark to see,' she said, laughing a little, aware of her near-nakedness while he was fully clothed. The idea of it made her inner muscles quiver with anticipation.

'I don't need to see when I can smell, taste and caress,' he murmured. Gently, he drew her lower lip down with his thumb. He dipped his head and licked inside.

Her lungs emptied at the illicit shock of it. Only his strong hands kept her from collapsing as explosions fired in her veins.

'Dear God, you are responsive,' he muttered. 'Heaven help me but I need you out of this now.' He plucked at the hem of her chemise.

'Whatever you desire,' she murmured, and lifted her arms.

He whisked it over her head and ran his hands over her body, his fingers and palms shaping her curves, learning her sensitive spots, like the indentation beside her hipbone that made her wriggle. It seemed to go on for ever. Her skin tingled where his hands touched, as if he had brought it to life, and mourned when he moved on, while his tongue teased her breasts, laving her nipples, then grazing them with his teeth. Hot and wet, his mouth attacked each peak one after another, and then he suckled.

The pure pain of pleasure arrowed all the way to her core. Her insides tightened unbearably. An arm came around her and gently lowered her to the cushions.

He loomed over her, a shadow against the starry sky above. 'Now do I undress?' Laughter and need filled his roughened voice.

'No,' she said.

He growled.

'I undress you.'

'Hell,' he muttered. 'Do you do it alone? Or do I get to

help?' He stripped off his coat and waistcoat and was out of his shirt before she could get her dazed mind to form her reply.

His hand went to his waistband.

'This is my part, all-powerful master.'

He stilled. The sound of a shuddering breath filled her ears. A man trying to maintain control. She fumbled with the buttons. It wasn't easy in the dark. At least not easy for her, though it had seemed to have caused him little difficulty. Lots of practice, no doubt.

She huffed out a breath and willed her fingers to stop trembling and finish their task. With the buttons finally undone, she pushed the tight-fitting breeches down his narrow hips. His erection brushed against her breasts.

She froze.

He muttered a curse. 'Don't stop now, Star of the Heavens and Temptress of the Deep. I command you.'

A hot jolt of lust hit her stomach. The man certainly knew how to enter into her fantasy. 'Lie down, my pasha.'

He complied without a murmur, stretching out on his back. Lit by the warm glow of the fire, he was gorgeous, long limbed, with curling dark hair on his chest. What she had taken for thinness was, on his lean frame, a wiry strength, with the muscles in his arms and abdomen defined and sculpted. There was no softness about this man; he was all whip-corded power. Yet there was a softening around his mouth as her fingers trailed through the crisp curls on his chest. With his eyes half closed, his dark lashes shadowing his penetrating eyes, he looked young, vulnerable, and heartbreakingly handsome.

Would he break her heart? Probably. A horrid squeezing pain just below her ribs caught her off guard and her breath hitched.

His eyes opened. He lifted a hand and trailed his forefinger down her arm. 'Is something wrong?'

She made a sound that was half laugh, half desperate sob. How could he know? How could he possibly know how deep his effect? How could she protect herself if he knew her so well?

He raised his head from the cushion and looked down his length at where her hand hovered over the plane of his stomach. A flood of relief rushed through her. Of course he had no idea. He was merely wondering why she'd stopped the game.

'Patience,' she ordered.

He grinned. 'That's easy for you to say.'

No, it wasn't easy. She lowered her lashes and cast him a sideways glance in what she hoped looked like sultry promise. 'Arguing will delay matters.'

He lay back with a soft groan. 'Hussy.'

The need for him inside her, for fulfilment, tightened deep in her core.

Yes! Tonight she was a hussy, a wanton, completely and utterly wicked. She was here to give, but also to take.

She trailed her fingers down the line of hair on his belly, lingering for a moment at his navel. She leaned forward and kissed it, open-mouthed, tasting a faint trace of salt, inhaling his musky scent. A powerful aphrodisiac.

'Mmmm,' he said. 'Just wait until it is my turn.'

Her insides turned liquid. How she found the strength to move past his arousal and pull at the tight fabric of his breeches, she didn't quite know. Perhaps the sight of his member, proudly erect, jutting from its nest of black curls at his groin, brought renewed strength. She certainly wanted him naked.

Fast, furiously impatient, she dragged the garment lower, peeling it from muscled thighs with a light dusting of dark hair, over knees where the bones stood out in sharp relief, down powerful calves and large feet in silk stockings.

Lovely calves that swelled beneath her palms and narrowed to his ankles. She ripped the stockings off and caressed those curves again, feeling the tingle of rough hair on her palms.

Lovely, hard, male legs. Legs strong enough for any sport. It had been so long!

'Sarah,' he said, a begging note in his voice. A hand came to her breast, gently massaging, encouraging.

The cord of lust tightened unbearably. But she had saved the best until last. She slid her hands up his legs.

An indrawn breath hissed through his lips. His hips jerked upward. He ran his hand up the hard flesh of his shaft in a firm swift stroke. 'All yours, my darling.'

She nearly came undone. Nearly fell over the edge just watching him. What a waste. 'Don't touch,' she breathed.

His eyes widened. 'Sorry.' He didn't sound the least bit sorry. She punished him with a too-brief kiss on the silken head of his shaft, the musky scent of it filling her nostrils.

'Ah…' he moaned. 'More.'

'Then behave.'

She cupped him in her hands, felt his weight. His hips bucked, bringing her attention to where he wanted her hands, and probably her mouth. But this was her night, her pleasure, her fantasy.

Legs pressed tight together, she lay on top of him. Grasping his wonderfully strong shoulders, she slid her body higher, her hardened nipples rubbing against warm flesh and wiry curls, so delectable. His erection jabbed hard and hot against her belly, and as she moved higher it prodded against her mons. Thighs tight, she circled her hips. Bursts of hot sweet pleasure rushed outwards, taking her closer to the peak of fulfilment. She cradled his face in her hands and took his mouth with hers, plundering with her tongue, filling his hot mouth, feeling their spirits mingle.

She opened her thighs, kneeling astride him, and lifted her head to look down into his eyes. 'Pleasure me,' she whispered.

# CHAPTER SEVEN

BRAND stared up into her soft-with-desire face and hazy lust-filled eyes. He trembled, shook deep in his bones. The heat of her bright spirit brushing against his chilly soul made him want more than mere rutting. He wanted to meld with her, join with her as if they were one. He wanted her warmth inside him.

Awe and reverence washed over him. She was lovely in ways he had never known existed. Balm to his lacerated soul, excitement to his jaded body.

He wanted her so badly he would die if he took her. Not death in the corporal sense, or in ecstasy, but spiritually. The thought of giving up what little remained of his soul left him terrified.

Idiot! Fool! They were here for one reason only. A fire had been ignited between them since the moment he'd opened the front door. What man would turn his back on a request for delights of the flesh?

Not him, God help him.

He rolled her over on her back, let his gaze drift down the rise of her lush breasts and the hollow of her waist. Blonde curls dusted her womanly flesh. The sight had him harder than granite.

He kissed her lips, the tip of her nose and her ear in quick succession. He adored the way her eyelids fluttered closed in pure pleasure, so he kissed those too and felt the faint tickle of her lashes against his mouth, along with the fragile skin of her eyelids.

Her hands wandered down his back in a tingling blazing trail of delicious sensation. He kissed a path to one breast while his hand rested beneath the other, his thumb circling the nipple.

She squirmed.

He flicked the nipple in his mouth with his tongue.

She moaned. Her fingernails dug into his back, causing exquisite pain. His shaft jerked. Lust rode him hard.

He opened his mouth and sucked in her breast. Lovely soft, sweet flesh. He wanted to gobble her up, swallow her whole, bury himself deep.

While his mouth enjoyed the taste of her breast, the tight bud of her nipple against his tongue, his palm roamed down her ribs, over the plain of her belly, until his fingers dipped into the soft whisper of damp curls, wet with wanting, wet for him.

He eased a finger inside her, found heat and moisture and tight welcoming flesh. He found her tiny nub, the source of female arousal, with his thumb, and circled and pressed. The soft cries in her throat made him ache.

Her thighs gripped his wrist. Her inner muscles spasmed around his fingers. She cried out and fell apart. The little death came upon her fast.

A groan at his own need for release forced its way from his throat. He clenched his jaw against the primal urge. She deserved better, more. Aching with the pain of need, he kissed her mouth, licked her ear, heard the rise of new passion in her gasp.

He closed his eyes briefly in thanks, and settled between her thighs as he worshipped each breast with his mouth and tongue.

'Oh, Brandon,' she cried.

He tightened at the sound of his name spoken with pleasure and pleading. He could not wait much longer. Thankfully, it seemed, nor could she. Anticipation stretched to breaking point, he reached between them to guide himself home.

Her legs came up around his waist in generous welcome. He bathed the head of his shaft in her moisture, felt the heat and the enticing narrowness. She tipped her hips, pushed upward, but he was the pasha, the gentle but commanding master. 'Lie still,' he said softly, gently.

Her eyes flew open. He smiled at her. 'Patience,' he said.

A smile curved her lips as she sighed.

He pushed in a little more. Nerve-endings screamed at him to drive into the hilt. He swivelled his hips.

She moaned.

Achingly, painfully slowly, he filled her. Her body shuddered and trembled with delight and longing. He thrust slowly, each stroke deeper than the last. She took him and took him. Open and generous, accepting and demanding. Never had he lost himself so completely yet still been so aware. Her cries filled the small chamber and tore up into the night. Her head moved back and forth on the pillow as her nails scored his back and she drew him in deeper.

Into her whole self. Not just her body, but her spirit. Never had he felt so at home.

Blood coursed hot and heavy through his veins to his groin. He drew back in one long steady stroke and plunged deep and hard.

The soft heat of welcome.

His mind slipped away. Control gone, he pounded into her, using his body to take her to the distant stars, striving to please her as much as she pleased him, to take her where she wanted to be.

She shattered, breaking through the boundary of earth. Unbelievable pleasure held him in its grip, shook him to his very soul, and sent him spinning after her. Some shred of sense percolated through the haze. He withdrew and spilled on her belly. A deep sense of sadness pierced the warm dark of satiation. He would like to give this woman a child of his loins.

No! No more children. No rivals for Jonathon. He'd sworn it.

He collapsed with barely enough strength to roll aside and gather her safely within his arms. She snuggled against him beneath the blanket with a sigh of contentment.

For the first time in years he felt whole. For the first time in years he wanted something for himself. Her: a sharp-witted sensual governess.

She deserved much better.


Curled against Brandon, her head on his chest, one leg beneath his heavy thigh, Sarah felt lassitude grip her. How long had she slept?

Minutes? Hours? She had no sense of time. The fire still glowed in the hearth. Brandon's naked chest rose and fell beneath her cheek, his heart a steady rhythm in her ear and against her palm.

Well, she'd really done it this time—risked all for a fleeting night of bliss. She should be thoroughly ashamed.

She wasn't.

True, she felt a little bit wicked—like a child caught stealing apples from a neighbour's orchard—but she didn't regret a moment. At least not right now. Perhaps regrets would come later.

She raised her head, drinking in his sleeping form, absorbing what she might never see again. He lay on his back, one hand behind his head, the other warm beneath her back and curled around her waist.

In sleep he looked young, untroubled. His peaceful expression brought a smile to her lips, a silent chuckle to her heart. She'd put that expression there. Had he too experienced something deeper than mere satiation?

She breathed in. She felt complete, whole. Had she finally killed off the regrets of her past? Annihilated years of wishing she'd chosen to be a little more selfish?

He shifted, turning towards her. She snuggled into the hollow of his shoulder.

Was that why she didn't feel the slightest bit ashamed? Or was it because she now recognised what her heart had known the moment she saw him? She'd fallen in love.

Could he possibly feel the same way? If she thought about it sensibly, she had to say no. Noblemen didn't marry governesses, or indigent widows.

They took them as mistresses.

If he asked her to stay with him, what would she answer? Did she even have the strength to walk away?

It would mean becoming even more of a pariah in her family's eyes. It would mean moving out of this house and receiving him somewhere discreet, hiding from his son. It would mean never having children in her life—not even those belonging to others.

She stared up at the open skylight: there were no stars. Clouds must have rolled in. A robin trilled a brief liquid stanza, then a sparrow tweeted. The dawn chorus would soon start in earnest. She certainly did not want to be found missing from her bed when the maid came to light the fire.

The night was over. The day's reality had to be faced and decisions had to be made. She tipped her head back and kissed his rough bearded chin. 'Let me up.'

He jerked upright, looking startled. 'I must have fallen asleep.'

She grabbed for the blanket. Heat rose in her face. 'It is time I returned to my room.'

Staring at her, he scrubbed a hand through his hair, making it stand on end. He looked adorably rumpled. She wanted to kiss him. Instead she searched amid the cushions for her chemise and the rest of her clothes, while he encircled her waist with his strong arms and nuzzled her neck with searing kisses. Shivers raced down her spine and a trickle of desire spread out from her belly.

'Must you go?' His voice was low, a velvet seduction irresistible to her feminine core, which fluttered with renewed excitement.

'I must,' she said.

'Who says so?' he grumbled. 'I thought I was the pasha here.'

His reminder of their game aroused her more. If she didn't leave soon she would melt into his arms and they might never leave this room.

Not necessarily a bad thing, the naughty part of her mind whispered. The practical part pointed out disaster. 'I have duties to perform.'

She pulled her chemise over her head and followed it with her gown. No point in troubling with the stays. Not when she'd be undressing in her chamber in a few minutes. 'Can you tie the laces, please, oh great Pasha?'

He groaned. 'If I must.'

There was laughter in his voice, and a touch of resignation. He knew, just as she did, that they could not flaunt their affair in the eyes of the world. She cast him a grateful glance over her shoulder. 'Thank you.'

He tugged on the laces and tied the bow.

She rose to her feet, stepping through the cushions and blankets to her slippers.

'Wait,' he said. 'I'll come with you.'

When she turned, he had his back to her, his shirt on, and was pulling up his breeches. She caught a flash of lean bare flank before he tucked in the billowing fabric.

So tempting. She would never be able to look at him without seeing him as she had last night.

'It would be better if we were not seen together.'

He cast her a glance over his shoulder. 'Damn it,' he said, frustration etched in the lines around his mouth.

'Yes,' she agreed, unable to prevent a regretful smile. She opened the door.

He caught her before she could slide out. Pulled her into his arms. Branded her with his kiss, hot and wet and punishingly deep. He broke away on a shuddering breath, as if it pained him to stop. 'We'll talk later.'

Her heart gave a little twist. Sadness. Yes, they would talk later. There would be much to say.

The expected request to see his lordship arrived by way of Trenton at the conclusion of Jonathon's lessons the next afternoon. Sarah hurried down the stairs, trying to ignore the hot and cold flushes racing through her body at the thought of seeing Brandon.

She let go a small sigh. She must think of him as Ralston again, or my lord. It would not do to let his name slip in case anyone heard—particularly Jonathon.

Her stomach dipped. She could not be both Jonathon's governess and Brandon's lover. To set such an example before a child who clearly adored his father would be wrong. She would never be able to keep the love from her eyes, to stop herself from reaching out to touch Brandon's arm, his cheek, or presenting her mouth for his wonderful kiss.

After a morning of reflection she had made her decision, despite her body's urging to say yes to whatever he proposed. She'd always feel ashamed. The genuine affection in his eyes as they parted this morning however, had nourished a secret hope that he might want more than a sordid affair.

A place in her chest ached with yearning.

Holding her breath, she knocked on the study door and entered.

He was not at his desk.

A quick glance found him at the window, his back to the room, outlined by light. His spine was straight, almost too straight, his broad shoulders rigid within tight navy superfine cloth. Neatly ordered dark hair which needed cutting curled over his collar. She half smiled at the wifely thought.

He didn't move. He hadn't heard her arrival.

'You sent for me?' she murmured, and closed the door.

He jerked around to face her, the bleak anger is his gaze and the hardness of his mouth making her flinch.

He held up a sheet of paper clutched in his fist. 'You lied.'

Staring at the paper, unable to produce a word from her dry throat, she backed away a step.

A muscle in his jaw jumped. 'I wrote to Mrs Blackstone.'

He'd doubted Iris's letter.

'Why?' she asked stupidly.

His eyes flashed. 'I'm not a complete fool, Mrs Drake. There had to be a reason you didn't provide a letter from your previous employer.'

'I can explain,' she said, clasping her hands together.

'Can you?' His lip curled. 'My wife had explanations too. Reasons for her prolonged absences from ballrooms. Reasons to visit her sister. Reasons for staying in Town when I had duties here.'

'I'm not your wife.'

He grimaced. 'But you planned to be. Well, you made a mistake.'

The words were like a slap to the face. The faint hope in her heart withered and died in a painful rush of emotion, at the murderous look on his face. If she had any sense she'd open the door and run. But it wasn't just anger she saw in his eyes. It was terrible hurt.

A huge blockage formed in her throat. Her breath would go neither in nor out. She felt dizzy and nauseous, but worst of all she couldn't utter a word.

He balled the letter and fired it at the hearth. It hit the grate and bounced out, rolling to a stop on the rug. 'Damn you! You seduced a mere *boy*.'

Mouth dry, heart pounding, she swallowed. 'It was a misunderstanding.' Her voice barely reached the level of a whisper.

'Is it also a *misunderstanding* that you are really Lady Sarah Carstairs, and that you trapped your first husband the same way you tried to catch Blackstone's heir?'

Sarah gasped. 'No! I mean I *was* Lady Sarah before I married, but I didn't trap my husband.' She'd offered John a kiss of comfort for a soldier leaving for war and they'd been caught. Only afterwards had she learned he'd planned it deliberately, hoping her connections would bring him fame and fortune. Mostly fortune.

What a disappointment she'd been to his ambition.

Ralston's bitter smile grew more pronounced. 'Liar! Your own aunt calls you a viper in her bosom, while Mrs Blackstone labels you an unconscionable opportunist. I assume Iris Chivers is part of your scheme?'

Sarah felt the blood drain from her face. The current Lady Eltham had been only too pleased to force her and John into marriage. Sarah's explanations had been gleefully ignored.

It had been a perfect opportunity to be rid of the previous Earl's daughter.

Hot-cheeked, she raised her gaze. 'I did nothing wrong.'

'So John Drake was *not* forced to marry you or risk his career?'

'It is one way to look at it, yes. But—'

'Enough.' Ralston clenched his fists at his sides, his face dark with a fury hot enough to burn the carpet beneath his feet. 'And then you failed to trap the Blackstone lad into marriage, so you thought to try your wiles out on me. Well, it won't work.'

Cruel words, scornfully delivered without a proper hearing. The backs of her eyes scalded and her vision blurred. She gazed into those dark angry eyes, at the scornful twist of his lips, and anger freed the blockage in her throat. Like lava, words boiled over.

'For a man who murdered his wife, you are exceedingly righteous, my lord.' Dear God, had she really said it? Well, he'd accused *her* of something almost as bad.

His face blanched.

'There is no smoke without a fire? Isn't that what you are saying about me?'

His laugh was so bitter and black she wanted to weep.

He took one long stride towards her, then another. She backed away until her back pressed against the door.

'Did you imagine I was desperate for female company?' he whispered silkily. 'Is that why you chose me? Be assured, I have had all I want from you.'

The bitter words cut her like whips. She raised her chin. Bravado forced a smile to her lips. 'Are you sure?'

He raised his hands, fingers curled like talons inches from her throat. She felt their heat and their power, knew their strength to crush.

She stared into his eyes, refusing to cringe.

His hands closed into fists and he spun away with a curse. 'And to think I trusted you with my son.'

'You don't trust anyone. You certainly didn't trust me, or you wouldn't have written to Mrs Blackstone.' Defeat rolled over her, dark and unrelenting. How could she have been so stupid as to hope? Afraid she might collapse she grasped the door handle. 'I will leave first thing in the morning.'

He jerked his chin in assent. 'I'll order the carriage.' His voice had a biting edge. 'In the meantime, you will oblige me by staying away from Jonathon.'

She closed her eyes to absorb the blow, then fumbled with a door handle she could scarcely see. A trickle of something cold ran down her cheeks.

*Blast!* She was crying.

Damn. She had let him break her heart.

Brand drained the brandy in a single gulp. It burned down his gullet all the way to his gut. Dear God, he wished he'd never written to Mrs Blackstone. He'd been happy in his ignorance, fool that he was. He should be glad he'd found her out before he did something stupid.

He still found it hard to believe those clear crystalline eyes had lied so easily. All he could picture was her sweet smile, her generous lovemaking, her cries of passion.

Such a damned fool.

Something twisted in his chest. He inhaled a sharp breath at the pain. He really was an idiot.

If his father had found him lacking, how could he expect a woman to find him worthy of respect?

Why had she chosen him? It barely made sense. A reputed wife-murderer was hardly a catch—even for a predatory female like Mrs Drake.

Well, she'd soon be gone, and he could go back to his solitary life. He'd see to Jonathon's lessons until the male tutor arrived. No more governesses. No more untrustworthy women.

The study door swung back.

His heart leapt in his chest at the thought it might be Sarah coming to plead her case. Breath held, not sure what he'd say, he turned his head against the chair cushions.

Jonathon ran to his side. 'Papa.' There were tears in his son's bright blue eyes. He looked just like his mother, reminding Brand of his need to be strong for his son.

He put a comforting arm around his son's small shoulders. 'What is it?'

'Mrs Drake is packing.'

Damn the woman! 'She is leaving.'

Jonathon pulled away, his gaze watery, his bottom lip protruding. 'Make her stay.'

'She cannot stay.' Brand shook his head.

His son wriggled free, eyes narrowed, fists clenched, his cheeks flushed red. 'She's leaving because you shouted.'

Brand winced. 'You don't understand.' He leaned forward to catch the boy, to hold him close and offer comfort. To somehow make the pained look in his eyes go away.

Jonathon backed away more. 'You made Mama go away and Maddy. And now you are making Mrs Drake go too. I hate you.' He turned and ran.

Brand staggered to his feet and wearily followed him, arriving in time to see Jonathon slam his bedroom door and hear the key turn in the lock.

Brand crashed his fist against unyielding wood then hammered on it. He pressed his ear to the door, taking his child's sobs into his chest like the stabs of a rapier.

'Jonathon!' he yelled. 'Open this door. Now.'

'Go away.' The heavy panels muffled the tearful words. 'I hate you.'

'Damn all women to hell.'

At a prickle of awareness, he turned. Sarah was watching him gravely from along the corridor. Watching him being locked out by his son. How it must please her to see him punished.

Her eyes contained nothing but sorrow.

'Why did you have to come here?' The words tasted like acid on his tongue, burning and bitter, and his throat was scraped raw. 'We were fine before you arrived.'

Unable to bear the sight of her sadness, even if it was a lie, he turned and stormed off down the hallway. Jonathon would come round. And if not Brand would come back when he was in control of his temper and have someone take the door off its hinges.

At this moment he needed another drink.

# CHAPTER EIGHT

HE WAS wrong. Sarah stared at the untouched food on her supper tray. He hadn't been fine before she arrived, but sadly she'd made things worse.

She should not have let down her guard. In so doing she'd left herself vulnerable to Mrs Blackstone's vindictive accusations. And she'd inflicted more pain on Brand than she would have thought possible by causing a rift between him and his son. She'd never wanted to hurt anyone. She'd just wanted to help.

All she'd ever wanted was a place she could call home. She twisted her hands together. She was leaving in the morning and she had nowhere to go—because she'd become involved in lives in which she had no place.

How naïve she'd been to think he might also have been struck by this mad thing called love. He still grieved for his wife and he only loved his son.

He didn't want *her*.

He'd wanted her last night, a little voice reminded her.

But that had been a different need: lust, desire. Not a longing for completion of the heart and soul.

She closed her eyes against the pain in her chest. Drew in a deep breath. There was nothing left but to accept his offer of a ride to the coaching house and travel to London. She'd look for a new position. If not as a governess, then as a housemaid or some such.

Unless Iris could be persuaded… Her insides trembled. Iris had given her an ultimatum: succeed or don't come back. She couldn't ask Iris to risk her good reputation—not a second time, not even for friendship's sake. Indeed, it was an act of unkindness even to consider making such a request.

A knock at her door jerked her onto her feet. With a hand to her chest she tried to calm her fast-beating heart. So foolish to think it might be Brandon. It would be one of the servants for her tray.

She opened the door. Her heart stilled. He stood on the threshold, eyes wild, coatless, looking much as he had the first night she had arrived. She moved back a step. 'Yes?'

He shifted, and the light streaming from her doorway caught his expression. The anxiety in his gaze hit her like a blow. 'Is Jonathon with you?' He peered over her shoulder, as if expecting to find the boy cringing in a corner.

She stiffened. 'You forbade me to have anything to do with your son, my lord.'

'Oh, Lord.' He scrubbed a hand through his hair, looking lost. 'I hoped beyond hope I'd find him with you.'

Her heart picked up speed. 'Isn't he with Peter?'

Ralston's lips thinned. 'Peter went on a visit home. I was to stand guard tonight.' Fury darkened his face. 'Langford's taken him. There is no other explanation. If he's harmed one hair on his head…' He stumbled as he turned away.

'Wait,' she called out. 'Why would Mr Langford take Jonathon?'

He stopped, and spoke without looking back. 'Because he'd do anything to see me punished for Maria's death. He claims he's Jonathon's father.'

Her knees weakened. 'What?' She grabbed the doorjamb for support.

He turned then, striking the palm of his hand with his fist. 'He'll fill Jonathon's head with lies. Jonathon is *my* son. Langford will not take him from me too.'

'How would he enter the house unnoticed?'

'He could if someone helped him.'

'No one would do such a thing.'

He stared at her silently and she took a step back. 'Oh, no. You will *not* accuse me of stealing your son.'

Jonathon had been angry and confused. She'd heard his sobs from behind his door. 'He's probably hiding.'

A disgusted sound issued from his throat. 'I guarantee you he is nowhere in this house. This room was my last hope. Langford's got him, and by God he'll return my son if I have to put a gun to his head.'

The menace in his tone froze her to the bone, but a strange sense of certainty bloomed in her chest. Ralston was wrong. 'Have you looked out on the moors? He feels close to his mother up on the hill.'

He stared at her blankly.

'Surely you of all people can understand?' She reached out a hand. 'He is probably sitting up there in the dark, hoping you will find him. Trust me in this if you won't in anything else.'

His lip curled. 'Trust a liar?' He barked a laugh. 'Jonathon knows better than to go on the moors after dark. Is this your way of putting me off the scent? Helping Langford?'

'I'm trying to help *you*,' she shouted at his thick head, anger flaring at his scorn.

'Help by staying out of my way.' He swung round and marched off down the corridor.

She glared at his back. She'd actually asked him to trust her. Hah! The man didn't know the meaning of the word. To him everyone was an enemy.

Langford hadn't looked like a madman. He'd barely shown

any interest in the child. Every instinct told her the little boy was somewhere up on the hill behind the house.

But her instincts had been wrong before—about John Drake, about Ralston.

Jonathon was none of her concern. Ralston had said so. But the image of the child alone and scared in the dark wouldn't fade. She knew how it felt to be alone. Cold dread filled her stomach. What if a storm blew up? What if she was right and they found him too late?

Her jaw clenched. If his father wouldn't look for him, she blasted well would. She grabbed up her cloak, raced down the back stairs and out into the night.

Outside, away from the house, with clouds obliterating any light from the sky, Sarah peered ahead into the pitch-black. Stumbling over a rock, she stubbed her toe. She should have brought a lantern. She glanced back at Merrivale Hall to get her bearings. The ground was steep, and far more uneven than she remembered. She continued the climb, panting as much with fear as with exertion.

At last the rocky outcrop, jagged and full of crevasses, rose from the dark in front of her. What if they never found him? Or found him… No, she couldn't think of that.

'Jonathon!' she yelled. Oh, why had she brought him up here?

A small body barrelled into her, clutching at her skirts, making her stagger. 'Mrs Drake?'

Never had relief hit her with such force. She sank to her knees, her arms around the boy.

'Oh, Jonathon. Are you all right, child?' She ran her hands over his body, felt his face, felt the dampness of tears. She squeezed him tight.

'I was lost,' he said into her shoulder.

'Not any more, sweetheart.' She cupped his cheeks in her hands. 'You gave us all a terrible scare.'

'I wanted Papa to be sorry for making you go, so I runned and I runned. Then I got scared of the goblings. I could hear them.' He started to sob, his small body shaking. She hugged him tight and prayed Ralston had done nothing dreadful.

Brand knew every inch of the land around his home. He climbed swiftly, by instinct. His breathing rasped in his ears. He couldn't seem to get enough air. Panic. For Sarah. What was she thinking, coming up here alone? Thankfully, Trenton had seen her leave and come to the stables. A minute later and Brand would have been gone.

It was easy to get lost out here. People died on these moors at night—even those who knew them.

He looked back over his shoulder. Where was Algie with the lantern? He was supposed to follow.

He stopped to listen.

'Is Papa very angry?'

His little boy's piping tones sent him to his knees. Thank God! She'd found him. She'd found his son. He should have listened to her.

'He's worried.'

Sarah's voice was soft. He couldn't see them but sensed their direction from the sound. He got up, moving slowly, not wanting to startle them into running.

'Will he make me dead like Mama for running away?'

His stomach heaved. The ground beneath him shifted. His throat constricted so tight he couldn't breathe. He couldn't move a step. His son believed him to be a killer.

'Who told you such a wicked thing?' Sarah asked. 'Your Papa loved your mother very much.'

Brand knew he didn't deserve such loyalty.

'Maddy said he made Mama dead. She made me promise not to tell. Then he made Maddy dead. I don't want to be dead and not see anyone again.' His voice rose in a wail.

'I don't believe your father made *anyone* dead, Jonathon,' Sarah was saying in a no-nonsense voice. 'Your father would never hurt you. He loves you.'

The sweet comfort in her voice, the certainty, made something in his chest swell. She was defending him in spite of his cruelty. Her generosity made him feel humble.

Brand didn't deserve her kindness.

'He yelled at you,' Jonathon said. 'He's making you dead.'

Sarah made a sound somewhere between a laugh and a sob, and Brand wanted to hold her and beg her forgiveness. Because right at that moment he felt as if he *had* made her dead. Dead to him. He took one step closer, silently, carefully, afraid of what he would see in their faces.

'Hush, now,' she murmured. 'Your father was right to yell. I did something bad.'

'I don't want you to go.' He sniffled.

Brand finally found his voice, and some words he knew he could say without breaking down. 'I don't want her to go either.' His voice cracked in the middle.

Sarah gave a little scream. 'Ralston!'

'Daddy.' Jonathon flung himself at Brand's legs.

He knelt and hugged him tight.

Small cold hands twined around his neck. The fragile body trembled against his chest, where his own heart threatened to break loose. 'Papa, I'm sorry.'

'Me too, my boy. Me too.' Brand buried his face in hair damp from the night. He breathed in his little-boy scent and the smell of dirt and sheep dung. It was the sweetest smell he'd ever inhaled.

'I thought I'd lost you.' His voice shook. His throat rasped like a rusty saw and the back of his nose prickled and burned.

Jonathon sniffled. 'Mrs Drake found me.'

'Yes, she did. Don't ever run from me again.' He blinked the moisture from his eyes and swallowed hard. 'Promise me.'

'I promise. Papa, you are hurting me. I can't breathe.'

Brand eased his grip. He glanced around for Sarah. He couldn't see her in the dark. 'Sarah?'

No answer.

All he could see was the glow of two lanterns headed up hill.

'Over here!' he yelled. 'Sarah? Wait.'

'Will you make her stay, Papa?'

Lifting his son in his arms, Brand strode for the lanterns. 'I'm not sure I can.' Just putting the thought into words carved a hole in his gut.

Algie reached him first, then a wheezing Trenton.

'Ye found him. Thanks be,' the butler said. He wagged a finger. 'What're you about, young master? Frightening us half to death.'

Jonathon hid his face in Brand's neck, his breath hot on his skin.

'Did either of you see Mrs Drake?' Brand asked, scanning the inky black between him and the house.

'She passed us,' Algie said.

'Damn.'

The butler cocked his scraggy head on one side. He looked like a puckish goblin. 'Fine young woman, that. You best hurry if you want to catch her, my lord. Let Algie carry Lord Jonathon. When we get back Wister'll soon have him trigged up with a nice hot bath.'

'And chocolate?' Jonathon raised his head and looked shyly at his father. 'May I, please, Papa?'

'Nothing like choc'late after a walk on the moors,' Algie said, his voice more than a little thick.

Brand kissed his son's cheek, and gave him another squeeze

before handing him over. 'Go along, then. I need to talk to Mrs Drake. Give me your lantern, Trenton. Algie will guide you down.' He took off at a run.

'Make her stay Papa,' Jonathon called after him.

Heart banging against his ribs, he caught her up in the rose garden.

'Sarah, wait.'

She stopped in a patch of light shining from the library windows and turned to face him. 'If you'll excuse me, my lord, I have an early start in the morning.'

She sounded heartbreakingly calm.

He lifted the lantern to see her face and saw she'd been crying. 'Give me a few moments, please.'

She closed her eyes briefly, as if his words caused her pain. 'I think we have said all we need to say.'

His chest ached at the sadness in her face. His stomach cramped. He could feel the dampness of sweat on his palms. He'd found his son, but lost the woman he…he loved. His mouth dried. 'Sarah, I don't want you to go.' His voice sounded dry and parched.

But, God, it was true. He needed her to stay as he needed blood in his veins. But he'd hurt her badly.

She made that awful little half-laugh half-sob that sliced right through his heart and turned away. 'Please, my lord, there is nothing to be served by continuing this conversation.'

She wasn't going to talk to him. And why would she? He'd been unforgivably cruel. His father turning away from him and Maria's disloyalty had changed him. He'd become suspicious and hard. Sarah was right. He had forgotten how to trust.

Yet she deserved the truth. 'You were wrong when you told Jonathon I loved Maria.'

He felt her little gasp of dismay like a whiplash.

He didn't let it stop him. 'Ours was a marriage of duty.'

Guilt rose in his throat like bile. 'But I should have done more to make her happy.'

She didn't speak. A barrier had risen between them. He felt it—a tangible, impenetrable thing wrought of her stiff shoulders and her hidden face. But she hadn't walked away. He took a deep breath and stumbled on.

'It went well enough until after Jonathon's birth. Once she'd done her duty she started seeing other men.' He spoke carelessly, but even now the pain of that discovery bit deep. It wasn't that he'd loved his wife, but he had expected her loyalty.

'I let anger cloud my judgement. I brought her here. Away from temptation.' He gave a hard laugh. 'Temptation lived on the neighbouring property.' Old bitterness crept into his voice. 'Langdon, my best friend, of all men. She used to sit up on the hill, staring at his house. For all I know they met up there too—though I barely let her out of my sight. After she died I wished to hell I'd let her go. I had my heir. My pride was hurt, yes, but I'd made her unhappy. She loved parties and adoring men. She hated it here. The more miserable she became, the more I hemmed her in—until in the end we were both sick of the sight of each other.'

Sarah sank slowly onto a stone bench. He hung his lantern on a bush, where it illuminated her face, and sat beside her. Her expression was sad. Sad for Maria, no doubt, because *he* certainly didn't deserve any sympathy.

'Maddy helped her arrange a flight with Langford. By then I was tired of the whole thing. If she hadn't taken Jonathon I might have let her go.' He tipped his head back and looked up at the sky. No stars. No answers. 'I like to think I would. I don't know any more.'

'How did she die?' Her whispered words cut to the heart of his guilt. His hands balled into fists. He forced himself to continue.

'I returned from a visit to London earlier than expected, and discovered she'd taken the boy and left in a hired chaise. I went after them. The idiot post-boy took a corner too fast.' Visions of the carriage tumbling into a ditch seared across his vision. 'I almost went crazy, trying to get them out of the vehicle. I was too late. Maria's neck was broken. By some miracle Maddy and Jonathon were untouched, and the post-boy had a broken arm. If I had just let her go… The rumours are right. I as good as killed her.'

She placed a hand on his arm, her touch light, gentle and searing. 'The post-boy made a mistake.'

Too kind. He cracked a rough-sounding laugh. 'No, I chased him. He said he thought I was a highwayman. It didn't end there. When the coroner declared it an accident, Langford lost his head. He demanded satisfaction. I refused, and people started gossiping about Jonathon's parentage. So we hid away here, where the vileness couldn't reach him. Only Maddy wouldn't let it rest. When Jonathon asked me who his father was, I knew she had to go home to Ireland.'

She gasped. 'How could she…?'

'Maddy had served my wife all her life. She'd loved her. And I had killed her.' There. He was done. But the black abyss of the future remained. 'One day I'll have to tell Jonathon. But not yet. Not while he's so young.'

'Oh, Brandon,' she said softly, hesitantly. 'I understand your desire to protect Jonathon, but he's already heard things. He's all mixed up. You need to explain.'

'What if he never forgives me?'

'He loves you. Don't speak badly of his mother. Just explain that the post-boy caused an accident. Give him the facts.'

In the light cast by the window, with her eyes hidden in shadow, she looked other-worldly, and her voice was full of kindness and understanding he didn't deserve. He sighed. 'It sounds simple, but it doesn't alter the guilt I feel every time I pass that corner. I thought by marrying a woman for whom I didn't have strong feelings I wouldn't end up like my father. He was an empty shell after Mother died. He and I rarely spoke a word, because he couldn't bear to look at me and see her.'

'Oh, Brand.' Her voice was full of tears.

His tears. Tears he'd never shed. 'All I did was make her miserable.'

'Don't blame yourself. You did what seemed right at the time.' She put a hand over his on his thigh. 'Jonathon is your son. He trusts you. He will believe you.'

He rubbed a hand across his chest. It didn't ease the pain. 'If you hadn't known where to look for him tonight I might have lost him too.'

'But you didn't.' She pulled her cloak closer around her and rose. 'It is long past time you went to your son. He needs you.'

He touched her arm. 'He needs you too.'

She shook her head. 'I can't stay.'

He swallowed a lump in his throat. It seemed he'd left it too late. 'Sarah, I'm sorry I didn't listen before. To your explanation. I should like to hear it.'

She swung round. 'I don't know…'

He longed to hold her in his arms, to tell her that whatever had happened it didn't matter, but he knew in his gut that would be the wrong thing to say.

'Tell me. Please.'

'All right.' She took a breath. 'I too made a marriage of convenience,' she began softly. 'My cousin Perry met John at a cockfight and invited him home. At the time I thought he was a friend, not a mere acquaintance. He was dashing in his cavalry uniform, and he saw me as an opportunity for advancement.' She clasped her hands together and looked at the ground. 'He played on my sympathies and like a fool I let him kiss me.' She huffed out a breath. 'To cut a sad tale short, we were discovered in an embrace. There was no option but marriage. My cousin insisted. I was ruined. John demanded a commission to save my honour. Unfortunately John's lineage was not of the best, and my family refused to have anything to do with me after the wedding.' She gave a sad little laugh. 'The irony is that my father was the Earl of Eltham, but the title passed from him to what he would have called a bunch of cits, who decided John and I were beneath their notice. What little money I had John used up, and when he died I had to find some means of support.'

It was hard to imagine a woman being forced from her family. Anger boiled in his veins. 'And the Blackstone debacle?' His voice sounded harder than he'd intended. He reached out and took her hand. 'If I sound angry it is on your behalf.'

Her fingers twitched inside his palm. He firmed his grip. He wasn't about to let her go. Not willingly.

'Simon Blackstone was sent down from university. His father was furious. Simon came to the schoolroom dreadfully upset, talking of making an end to his life.' She laughed wryly. 'So dramatic. I talked him out of his megrims and he hugged me. It was nothing,' she said defensively. 'A brief squeeze. But one of the children mentioned it to Mrs Blackstone, and she accused me of seducing her son. I was dismissed.' She shrugged. 'Iris suggested working for you for a month or two would give me the reference I needed for a permanent position. I was wrong to hide the truth, but I didn't lie.'

'I can see why you might not have wanted to tell me,' he said carefully. The ground beneath his feet had a swampy feel. One wrong step and he'd drown. 'It sounds as if you were in the devil of a fix.'

'Thank you.' She took a quick breath that caught in her

throat. He had the feeling she was very close to tears. He felt close to tears himself.

'Will you stay?' he asked.

She shook her head. 'Things are too…complicated.' She glanced up at him, her smile rueful. 'I've given it careful thought. I find I am too strict in my notation to be a mistress. It is not who I am. What I am.'

He stared at her blankly.

'It would bring more scandal to my family's name.'

A glimmer of hope fired in his chest. 'Sarah, I'm offering marriage. I would never insult you with anything less.'

She hesitated.

His heart thumped.

'Thank you,' she said, with a shake of her head. 'It is very kind, but no.'

He felt as if she'd plunged a dagger between his ribs and the blood was draining into the ground at his feet. He wanted to argue, to put his case—but wasn't that what he'd done to Maria? Forced her to stay against her will?

'My leaving is the best thing for all concerned,' she said firmly.

Not the best thing for him. But he couldn't blame her for wanting someone better than him. Hell, she deserved whatever her heart desired. And if he wasn't it, then he had to accept her decison.

But he couldn't just let her go into an unknown future, never knowing if she was safe. Never knowing if she was well. There had to be something he could do for her.

'You like children,' he said. 'Would you like to open your own school? I'd give you the money.'

'What?' This time she looked him full in the face, her eyes wide and…and angry. 'I'm not looking for payment.'

He recoiled. 'No. *No.* I didn't mean that. I'll give you

glowing references, of course, if that's all you want. Though I doubt a reference from me would do you much good.'

He drew in a breath. Like plunging into freezing water, every nerve protested at the thought, yet it had to be done. 'I can't force you to stay.' He rubbed his hands on his thighs, because this was not what he wanted to say. 'I thought if you'd like your own school I could endow it. You wouldn't have to feel ashamed. No one ever need know I am the benefactor.'

'Ashamed?' Her voice broke. 'I wouldn't be ashamed. Oh, Brandon, it is very kind of you, but it wouldn't be right.'

'So you won't accept my help?'

She gazed up at him. Tears glittered like jewels on her lashes. Tears he'd caused—tears that gave him leave to hope.

Something around his heart cracked open. It hurt worse than any pain he'd ever known. It was as if all pride had been ripped from his chest. 'Don't leave, Sarah. I need you.'

God, were those tears he heard in his voice?

He shook his head as she opened her mouth to speak. He dropped to one knee. 'I want you to be my wife. Marry me, Sarah. Please.' He took her hands in his and kissed each one in turn. 'I need you, Sarah. I never thought I'd say this to any woman, but...I love you.'

For a moment Sarah didn't quite believe she'd heard correctly. It seemed like a figment of her imagination. Or a wishful dream. Yet there he was on one knee, with hope carved on his face.

The joyful lift of her heart told her she should believe. A *yes* hovered on her tongue, but other thoughts tumbled into her head. 'How can I? The gossips will say I trapped you.'

He let go a hard sigh, his eyes closing briefly. 'I don't care if people call me a fool—not when I know that you are the best thing that has ever happened in my life. But if you are refusing me because you don't love me, then tell me. I swear…' His voice cracked. 'I swear I will never trouble you again.' He took a deep breath. 'I love you, Sarah. I didn't know it until I knew I would lose you. You see, I never loved anyone before.'

The ache in his voice pulled at her heart. Emotion too large to contain surrounded them in a light and warmth no bonfire could match. He'd said he loved her.

She sank to her knees in front of him, gazed into his dark eyes. 'I fell in love the first time you kissed me, but I never dared hope you'd love me in return.'

He shook his head in wonder, then flashed a grin. 'So if I kiss you now, will you love me now? And agree to be my wife?'

She felt as if she'd come home after a very long absence. 'Oh, Brandon.'

'I want to hear you say it, Sarah. Please say yes.'

Her heart swelled until she felt it might burst from her chest and take wing. 'Yes, Brandon. *Yes.*'

'Thank God.' He drew her to her feet and embraced her. The warmth of his body enfolded her. His kiss scorched all the way down to her toes.

Finally he released her. 'Come, let us share our good news with Jonathon. He loves you nearly as much as I do.'

He put his arm around her shoulders, enfolding her in a strength and warmth she'd never hoped to know.

Slowly, with short stops for kisses, they walked to the front door. It stood wide open, welcoming them home. Through the blur of happy tears she could have sworn she saw the house smiling.

Brand stopped at the steps, his mouth against her lips. 'I love you, Sarah,' he murmured. It was as if he couldn't stop saying the words.

'I love you, Brandon,' she whispered.

He swept her up in his arms. 'Welcome home, my darling.' The sound of a galloping horse had him turning. 'Damn.'

She peered around his shoulder. The rider pulled up and walked his horse into the light cast by the lanterns beside the door. Langford.

Brandon stiffened. He set Sarah on her feet and turned to face his old rival. 'What are you doing here, Langford?'

Langford dismounted. 'I heard from one of the grooms that the boy is missing.'

'He's found.'

'Thank God.' The man sagged against the horse's withers.

'Why would *you* care?' Brandon said, his voice like ice. 'He's my son.'

'Yes. He's your son. I never thought otherwise, but the word was you thought I'd had something to do with his disappearance.' He hesitated, staring at Brand, his lips white. 'Maria and I—we couldn't help what happened between us. When she died I blamed you. I wanted to hurt you. But Maria never betrayed you in that way. Never. I'm sorry.'

Brandon stood as still as a statue, staring at Langford, his expression carved from granite.

Sarah held her breath, praying he would let the past go. For his own sake.

He glanced down at her, and then back at his old friend. He put out his hand. 'I'm sorry too.'

Langford took his hand and clapped him on the shoulder. 'Thank you.' He glanced at Sarah. 'And congratulations.'

'Goddamned gossips,' Brandon said.

Langford grinned.

Brandon grinned back.

Sarah's heart felt too full for her chest. She squeezed his hand.

'I hope you will excuse us,' Brandon said, looking down

at her. 'My fiancée is chilled to the bone, and I think it is time I warmed her up. We will send you an invitation to the wedding.'

'I'd like that,' Langford said.

Brandon swept Sarah off her feet and headed back up the stairs.

She twined her arms around his neck, and whispered in his ear. 'Warm me up?'

'Mmm. After we tell Jonathon the good news.'

'I like the sound of that.'

'So do I, Sarah. More than I can say.'

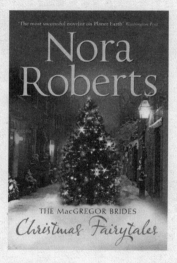

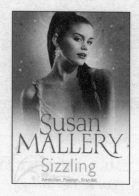

# THE *Balfour* LEGACY

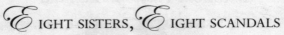

## EIGHT SISTERS, EIGHT SCANDALS

### VOLUME 1 – JUNE 2010
*Mia's Scandal*
by Michelle Reid

### VOLUME 2 – JULY 2010
*Kat's Pride*
by Sharon Kendrick

### VOLUME 3 – AUGUST 2010
*Emily's Innocence*
by India Grey

### VOLUME 4 – SEPTEMBER 2010
*Sophie's Seduction*
by Kim Lawrence

8 VOLUMES IN ALL TO COLLECT!

# THE

### *Balfour*
## LEGACY

## EIGHT SISTERS, EIGHT SCANDALS

### VOLUME 5 – OCTOBER 2010
*Zoe's Lesson*
by Kate Hewitt

### VOLUME 6 – NOVEMBER 2010
*Annie's Secret*
by Carole Mortimer

### VOLUME 7 – DECEMBER 2010
*Bella's Disgrace*
by Sarah Morgan

### VOLUME 8 – JANUARY 2011
*Olivia's Awakening*
by Margaret Way

8 VOLUMES IN ALL TO COLLECT!

*www.millsandboon.co.uk*